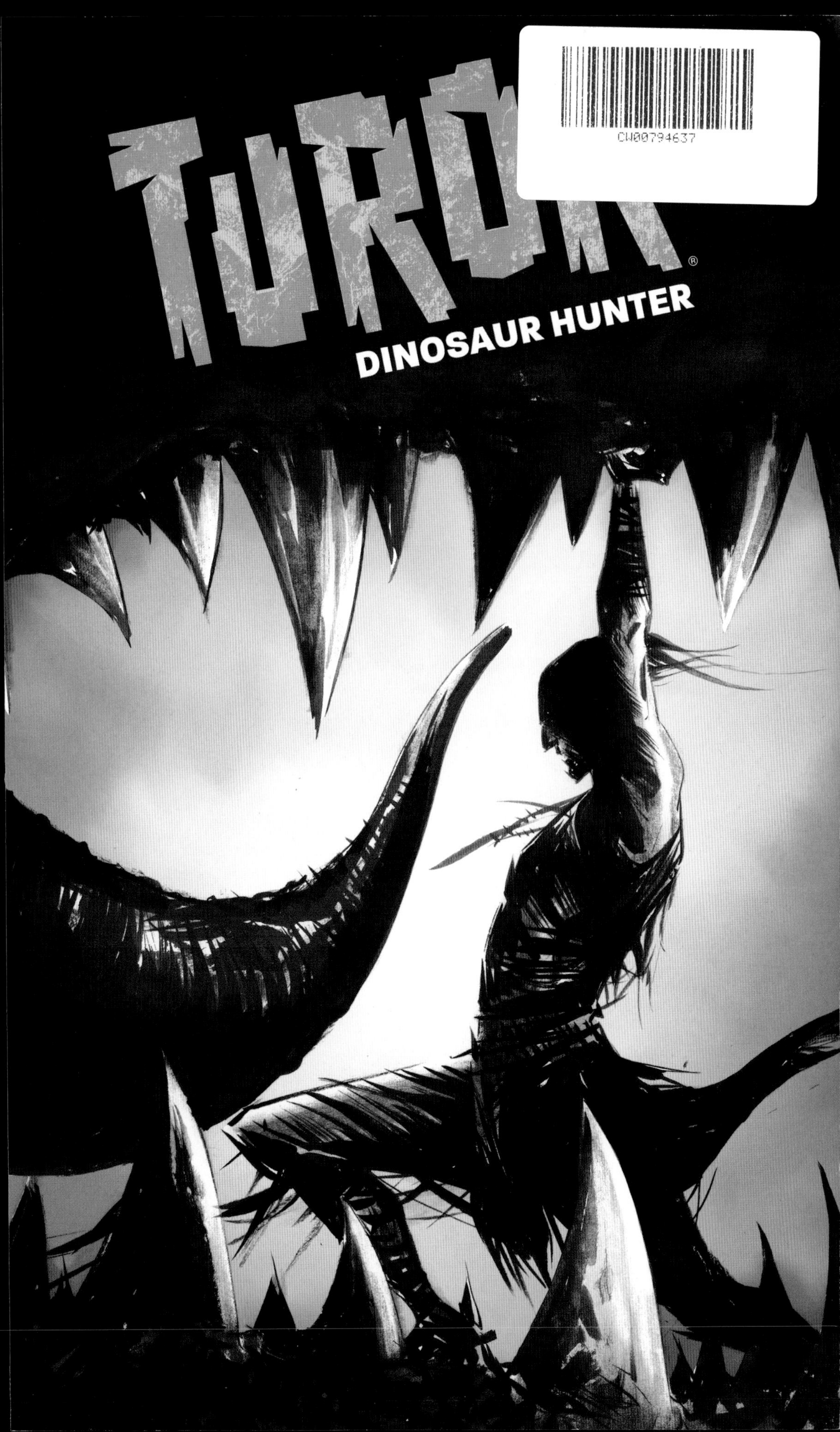
TUROK®
DINOSAUR HUNTER

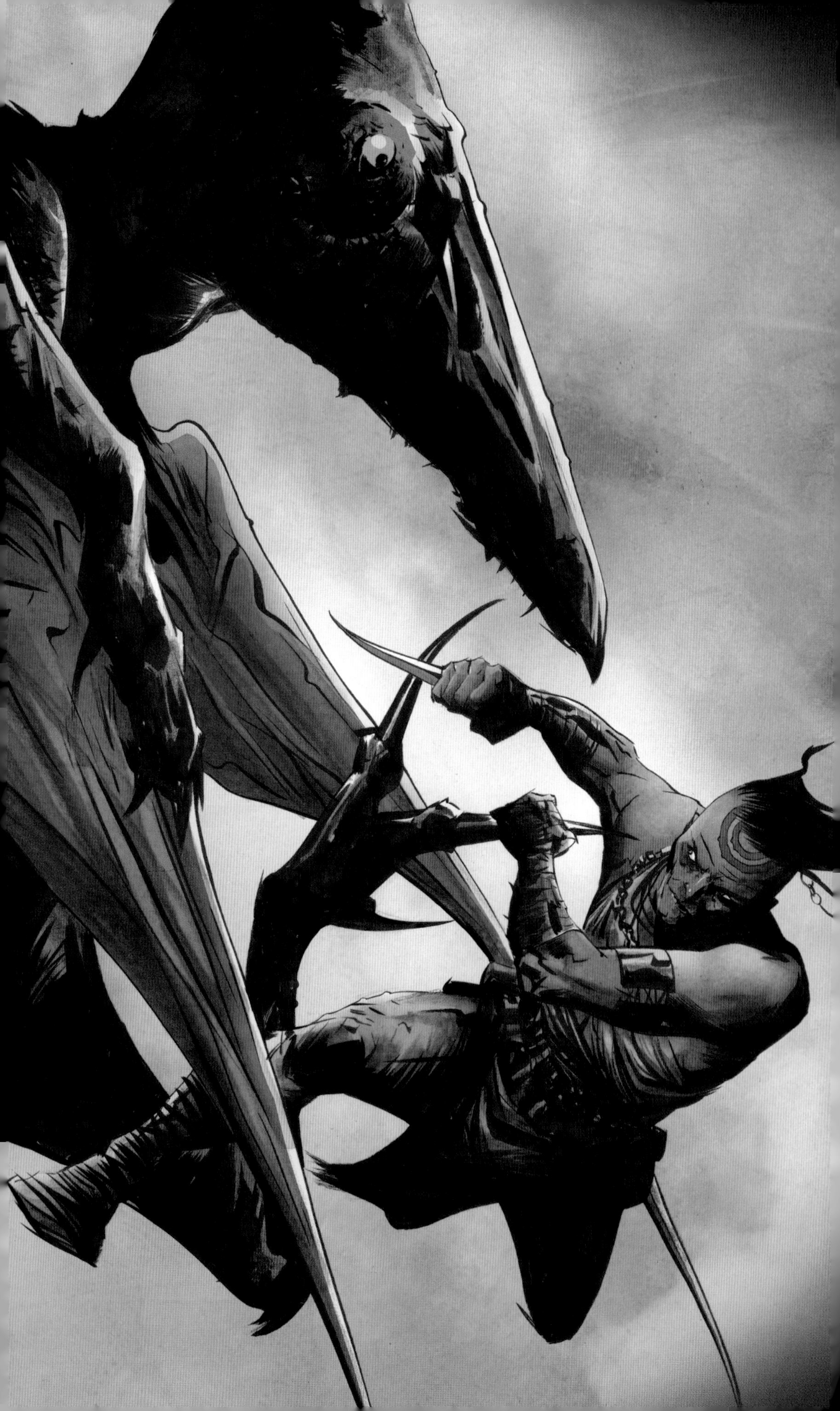

TUROK ®

DINOSAUR HUNTER

WEST

WRITTEN BY
GREG PAK

ART BY
TAKESHI MIYAZAWA

COLORS BY
MAURÎCIO WALLACE
MARK DALE
LUIGI ANDERSON
MICHAEL SPICER

LETTERS BY
MARSHALL DILLON
DERON BENNETT

COLLECTION COVER BY
BART SEARS

COLLECTION COVER COLORS BY
NEERAJ MENON

COLLECTION DESIGN BY
KATIE HIDALGO

TUROK LOGO DESIGN BY
RIAN HUGHES

SPECIAL THANKS TO **TOM ENGLEMAN, BEN CAWOOD,
NICOLE BLAKE, COLIN MCLAUGHLIN** AND **SIMON BOWLAND**

PACKAGED AND EDITED BY **NATE COSBY**
OF COSBY AND SONS PRODUCTIONS

THIS VOLUME COLLECTS ISSUES 5-8 OF TUROK:
DINOSAUR HUNTER BY DYNAMITE ENTERTAINMENT.

DYNAMITE ®

k Barrucci, CEO / Publisher
n Collado, President / COO
n Young, Director Business Development
th Davidsen, Marketing Manager

Rybandt, Senior Editor
nah Elder, Associate Editor
ly Mahan, Associate Editor

on Ullmeyer, Design Director
ie Hidalgo, Graphic Designer
is Caniano, Digital Associate
hel Kilbury, Digital Assistant

Visit us online at **www.DYNAMITE.com**
Follow us on Twitter **@dynamitecomics**
Like us on Facebook **/Dynamitecomics**
Watch us on YouTube **/Dynamitecomics**

ISBN-10: 1-60690-598-8   ISBN-13: 978-1-60690-598-2   First Printing   10 9 8 7 6 5 4 3 2 1

TUROK: DINOSAUR HUNTER®, VOL. 2: WEST. This volume collects material originally published in Turok: Dinosaur
Hunter #5-8. Published by Dynamite Entertainment. 113 Gaither Dr., STE 205, Mt. Laurel, NJ 08054. TUROK: DINOSAUR
HUNTER is ® and Copyright © 2015 by Random House, Inc. Under license to Classic Media, LLC. All rights reserved.
DYNAMITE, DYNAMITE ENTERTAINMENT and its logo are © & ® 2015 Dynamite. All rights reserved. All names, characters,
events, and locales in this publication are entirely fictional. Any resemblance to actual persons (living or dead), events or
places, without satiric intent, is coincidental. No portion of this book may be reproduced by any means (digital or print) without the written permission of Dynamite Entertainment except for review purposes. The scanning, uploading and distribu-
tion of this book via the Internet or via any other means without the permission of the publisher is illegal and punishable
by law. Please purchase only authorized electronic editions, and do not participate in or encourage electronic piracy of
copyrighted materials. **Printed in China**

For information regarding press, media rights, foreign rights, licensing, and advertising e-mail:
marketing@dynamite.com

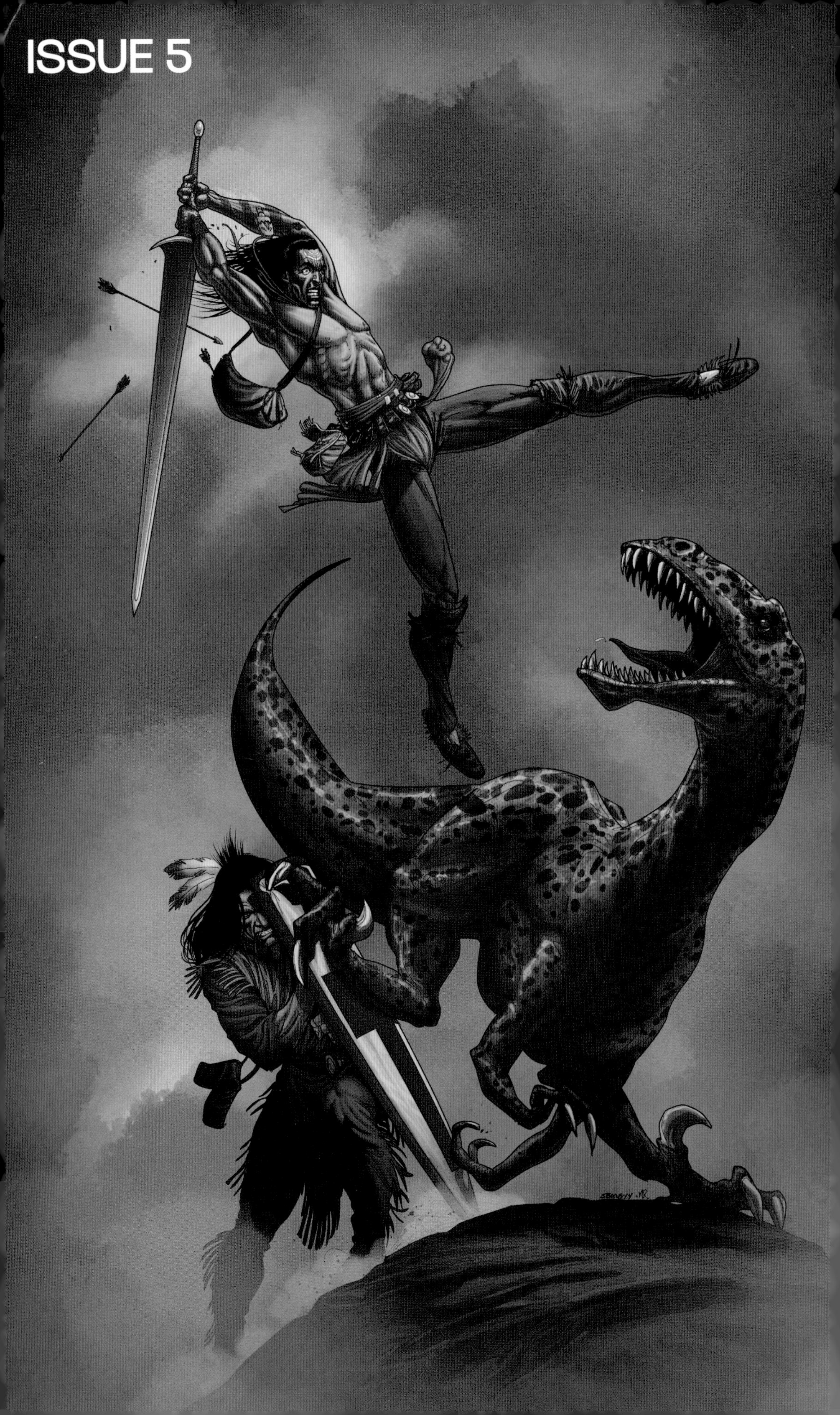
ISSUE 5

IT'S BEEN *TWO MOONS* SINCE I LEFT THE TRIBE.

NNNNGH!

TWO MOONS SINCE I SAW ANOTHER HUMAN BEING.

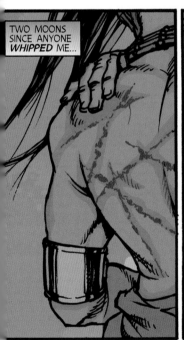

TWO MOONS SINCE ANYONE *WHIPPED* ME...

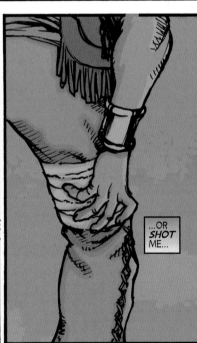

...OR *SHOT* ME...

...OR TRIED TO *CUT ME* TO *PIECES*.

RRR

RUMMMBLE

THIS COULD BE A *GOOD LIFE*...

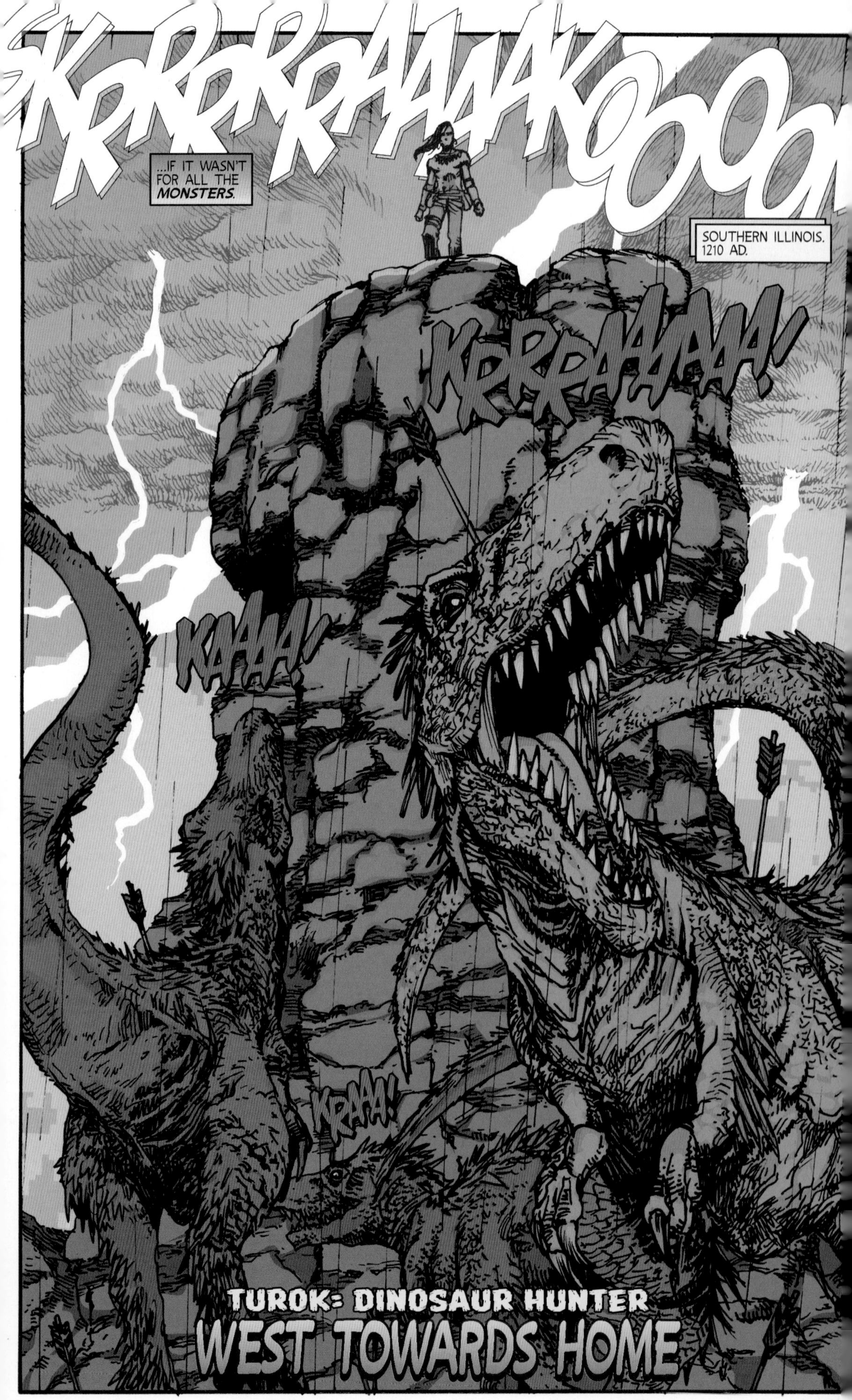

SKRRRAAAAKOOOO
...IF IT WASN'T FOR ALL THE MONSTERS.
SOUTHERN ILLINOIS. 1210 AD.
KRRRAAAAAA!
KAAAA!
KRAAA!
TUROK: DINOSAUR HUNTER
WEST TOWARDS HOME

SKRRAAK

KAAAAA!

THE *CRAB MEN* FROM ACROSS THE *OCEAN* BROUGHT THE *RUNNING* AND *SWIMMING* MONSTERS...

KAAAAAAA!

BUT NOW THEY'RE *FLYING?*

KAAAAAAAAAA!

HYAAAA!

AND *RIDING?*

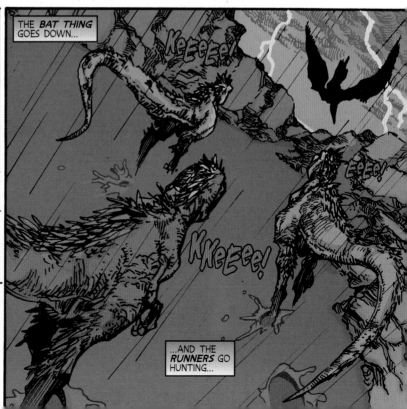

THE *BAT THING* GOES DOWN...

KEEEEE!

KEEEEE!

EEEE!

...AND THE *RUNNERS* GO HUNTING...

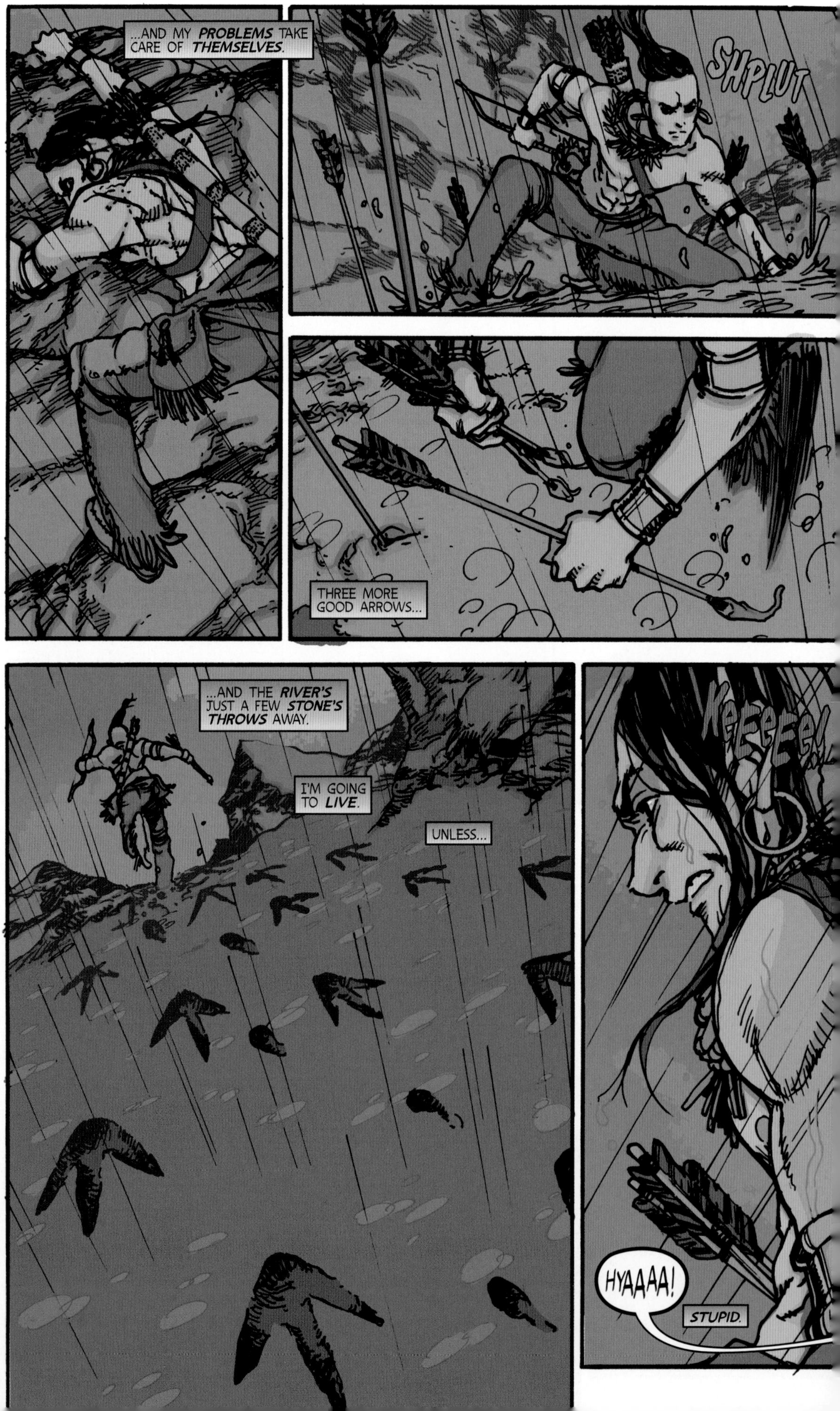
...AND MY PROBLEMS TAKE CARE OF THEMSELVES.
SHPLUT
THREE MORE GOOD ARROWS...
...AND THE RIVER'S JUST A FEW STONE'S THROWS AWAY.
I'M GOING TO LIVE.
UNLESS...
KEEEEE!
HYAAAA!
STUPID.

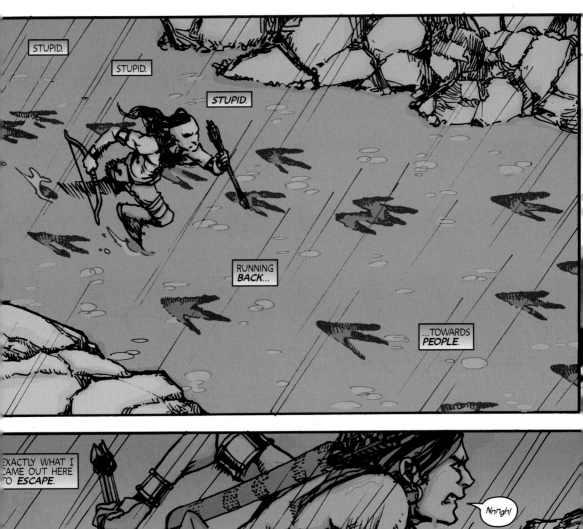

STUPID.

STUPID.

STUPID.

RUNNING BACK...

...TOWARDS PEOPLE.

EXACTLY WHAT I CAME OUT HERE TO ESCAPE.

Nnngh!

THE ARROW WOUND ANDAR GAVE ME THROBS.

THE SCARS IN MY BACK CATCH FIRE.

I'VE ONLY GOT SIX ARROWS.

AND WHOEVER WAS SCREAMING IS PROBABLY ALREADY DEAD--

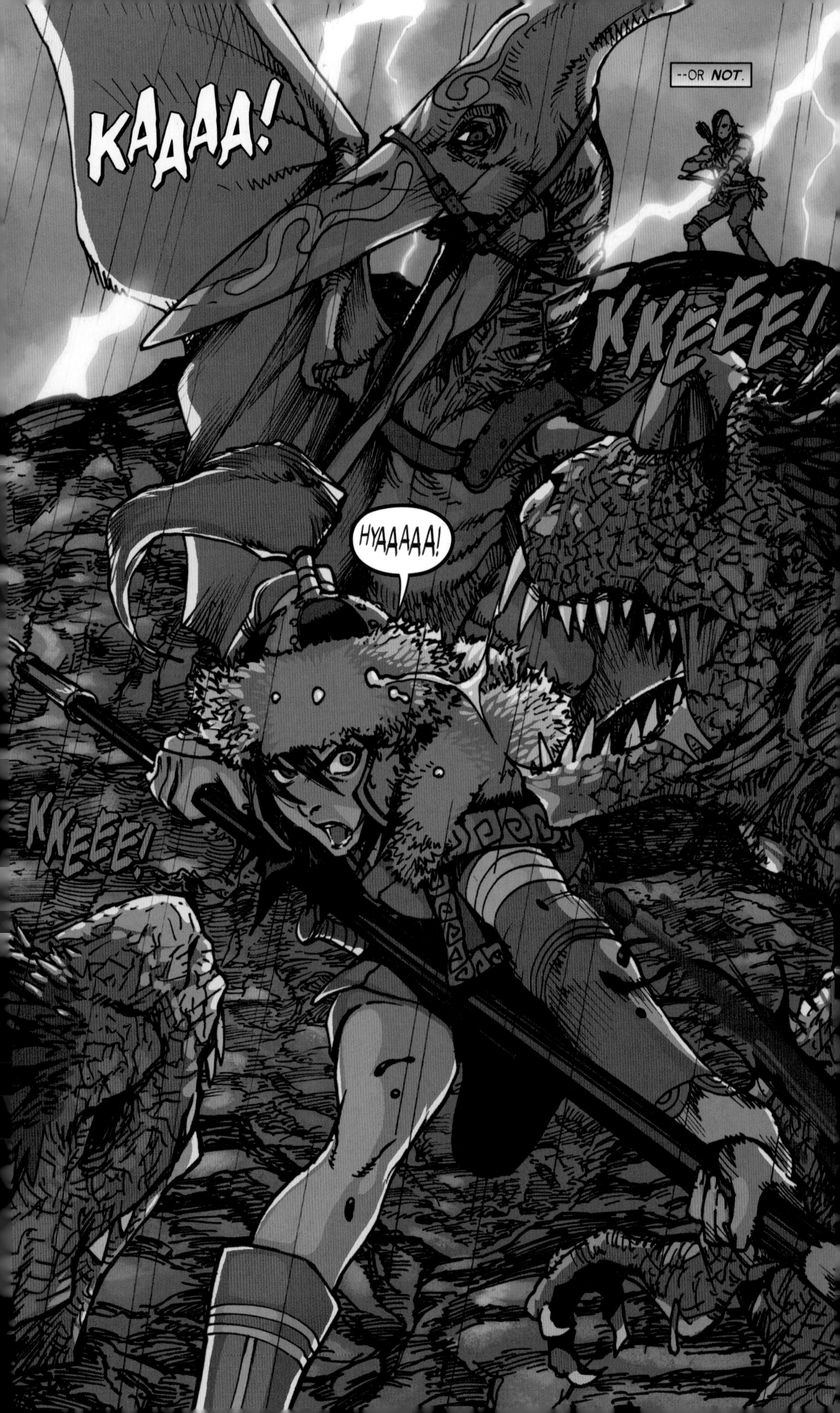
--OR NOT.
KAAAA!
KKEEE!
HYAAAAA!
KKEEE!

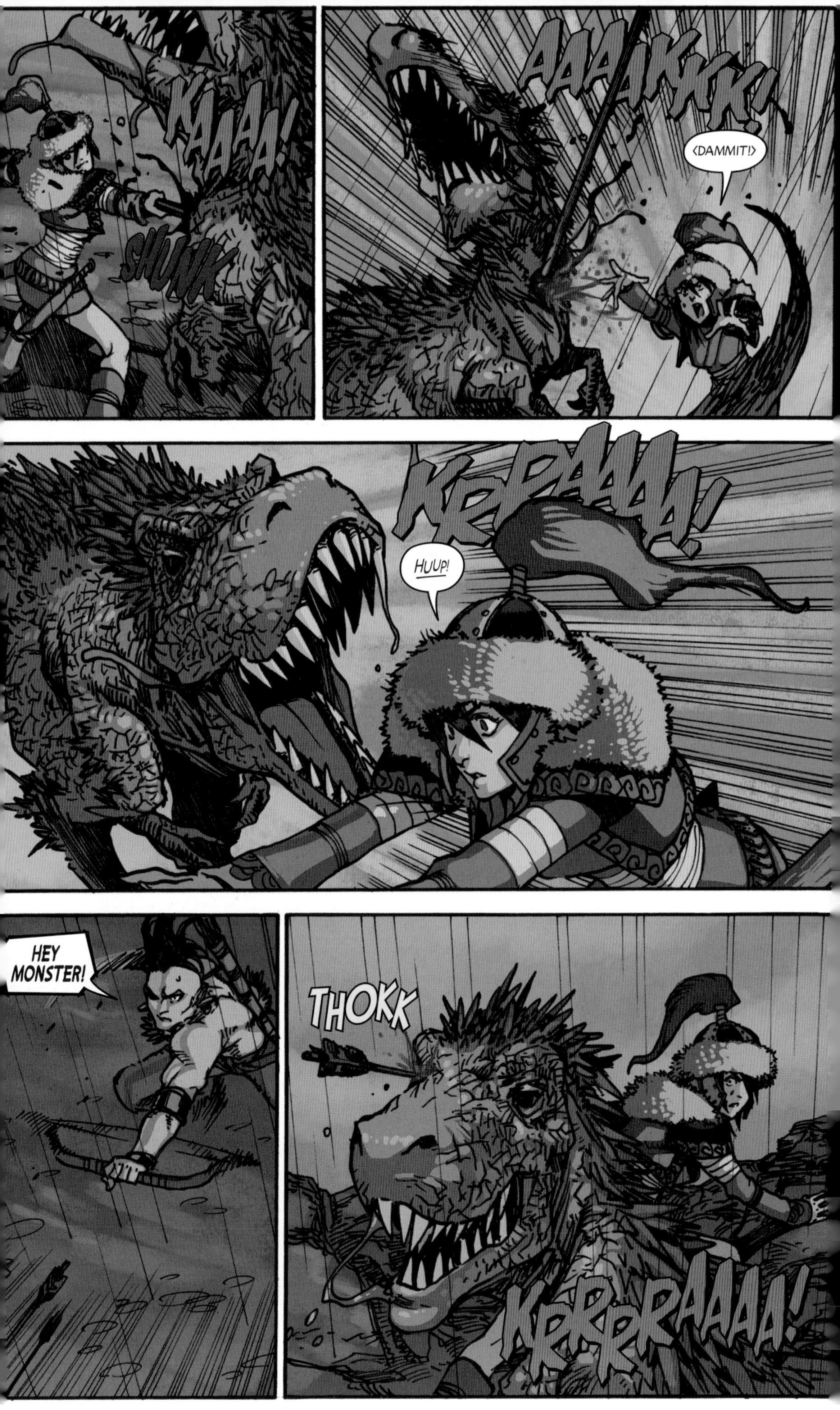
KAAA!
SHUNK
AAAIKKK!
‹DAMMIT!›
KRRAAAAA!
HUUP!
HEY MONSTER!
THOKK
KRRRRAAAA!

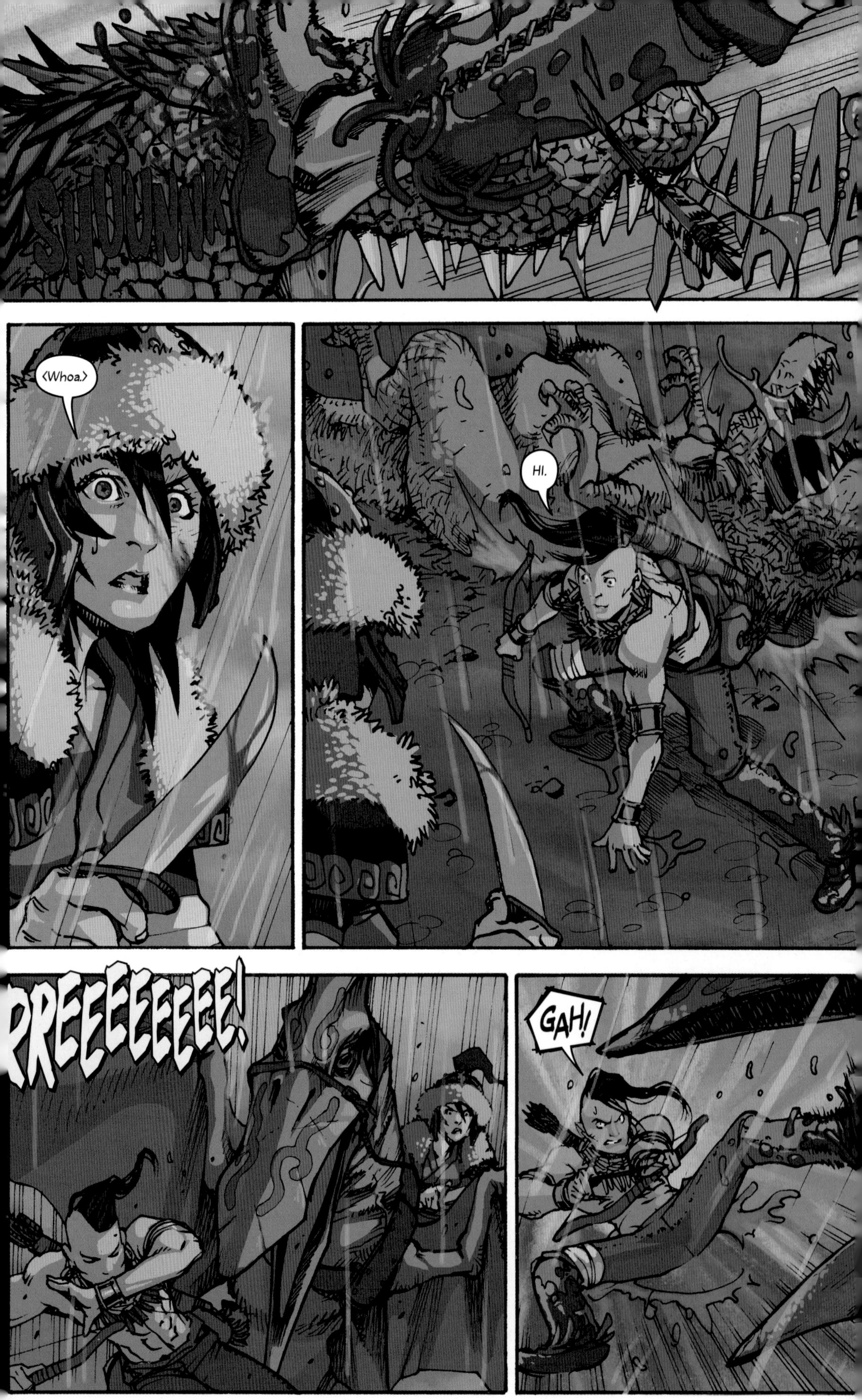
SHUUNNK!
⟨Whoa.⟩
HI.
PREEEEEEEE!
GAH!

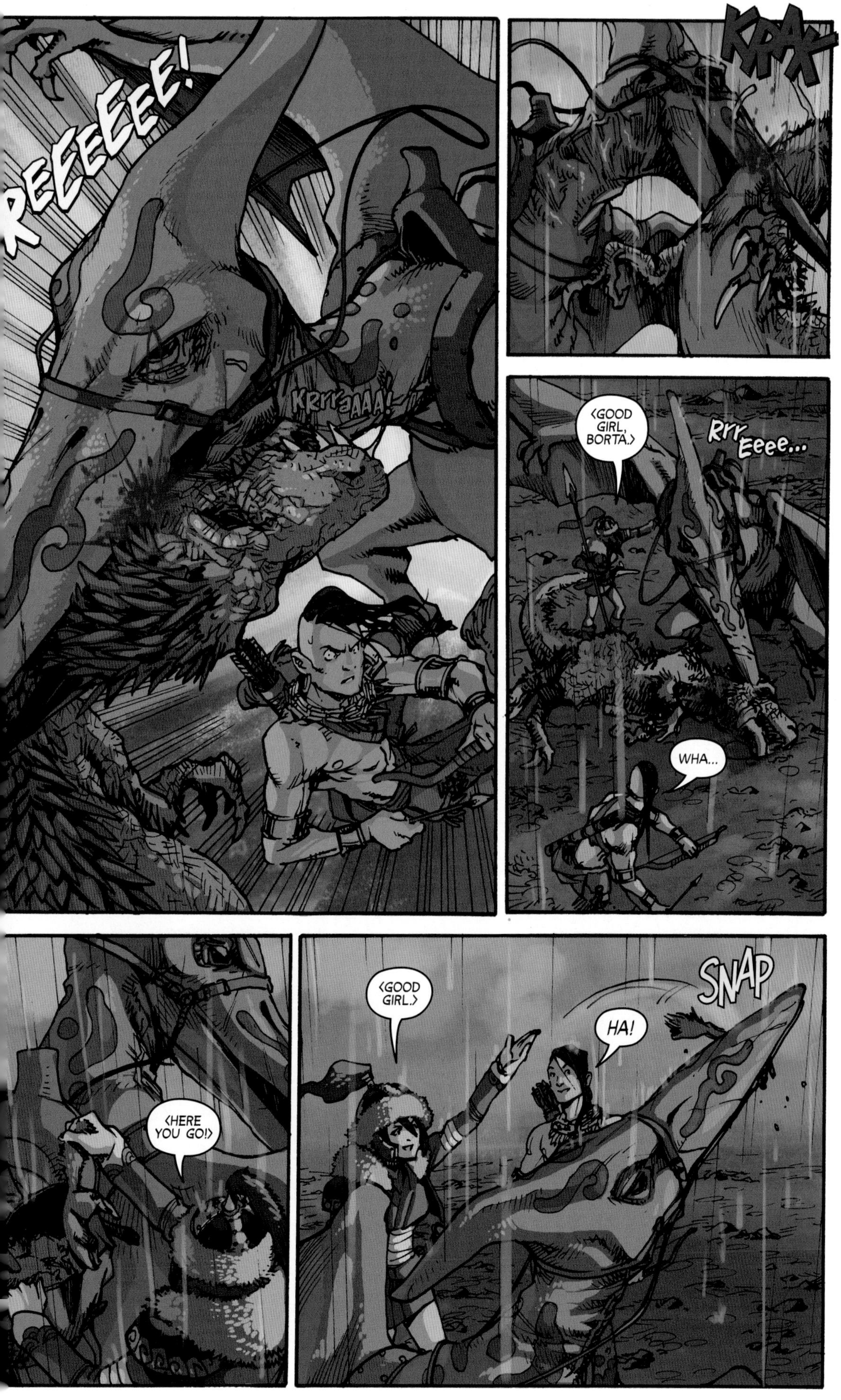
REEEEEEE!
KRRRAAAA!
KRAK
‹GOOD GIRL, BORTA.›
Rrr Eeee...
WHA...
‹HERE YOU GO!›
‹GOOD GIRL.›
HA!
SNAP

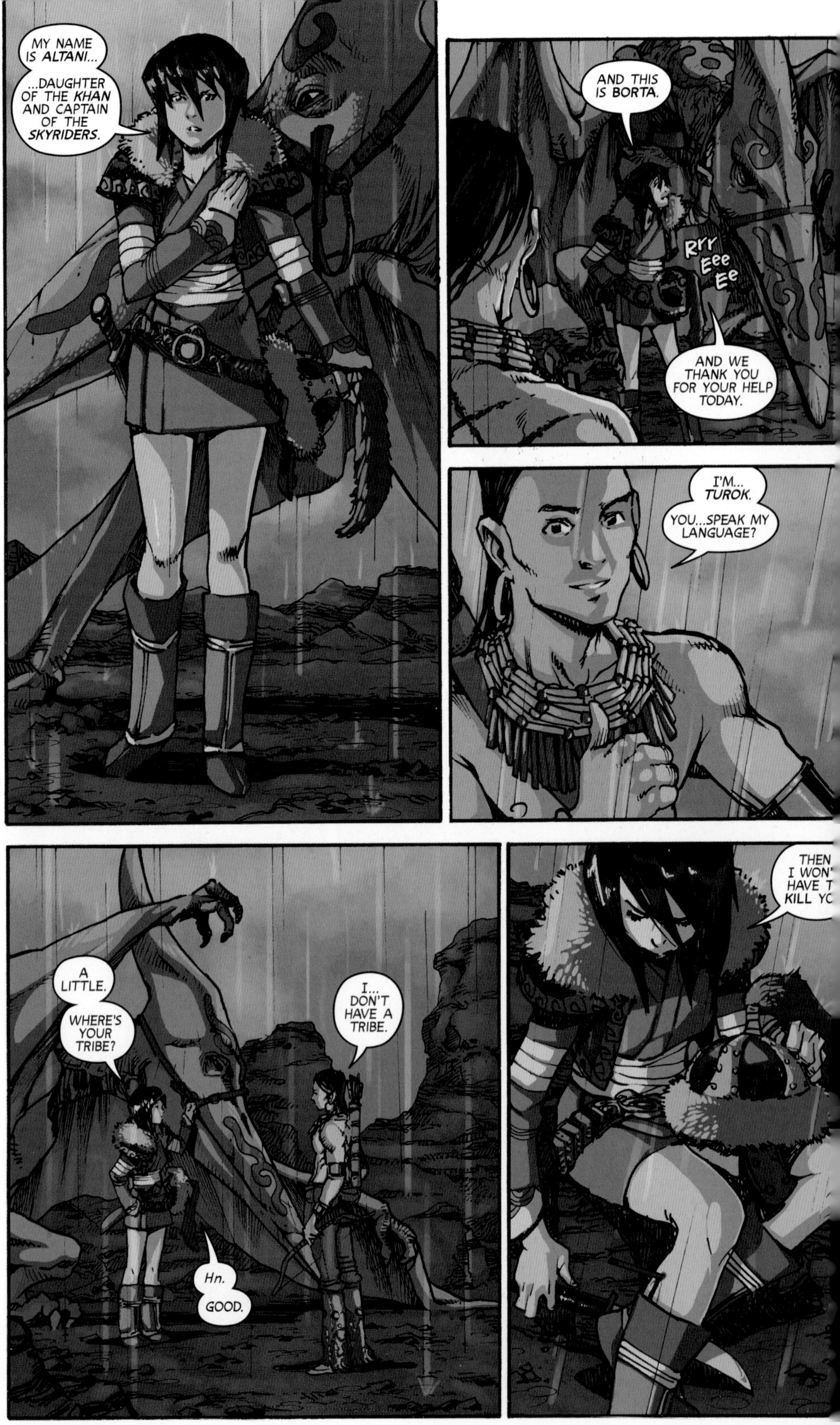
MY NAME IS ALTANI...
...DAUGHTER OF THE KHAN AND CAPTAIN OF THE SKYRIDERS.
AND THIS IS BORTA.
Rrr Eee Ee
AND WE THANK YOU FOR YOUR HELP TODAY.
I'M... TUROK.
YOU...SPEAK MY LANGUAGE?
A LITTLE.
WHERE'S YOUR TRIBE?
I... DON'T HAVE A TRIBE.
Hn.
GOOD.
THEN I WON' HAVE T KILL YO

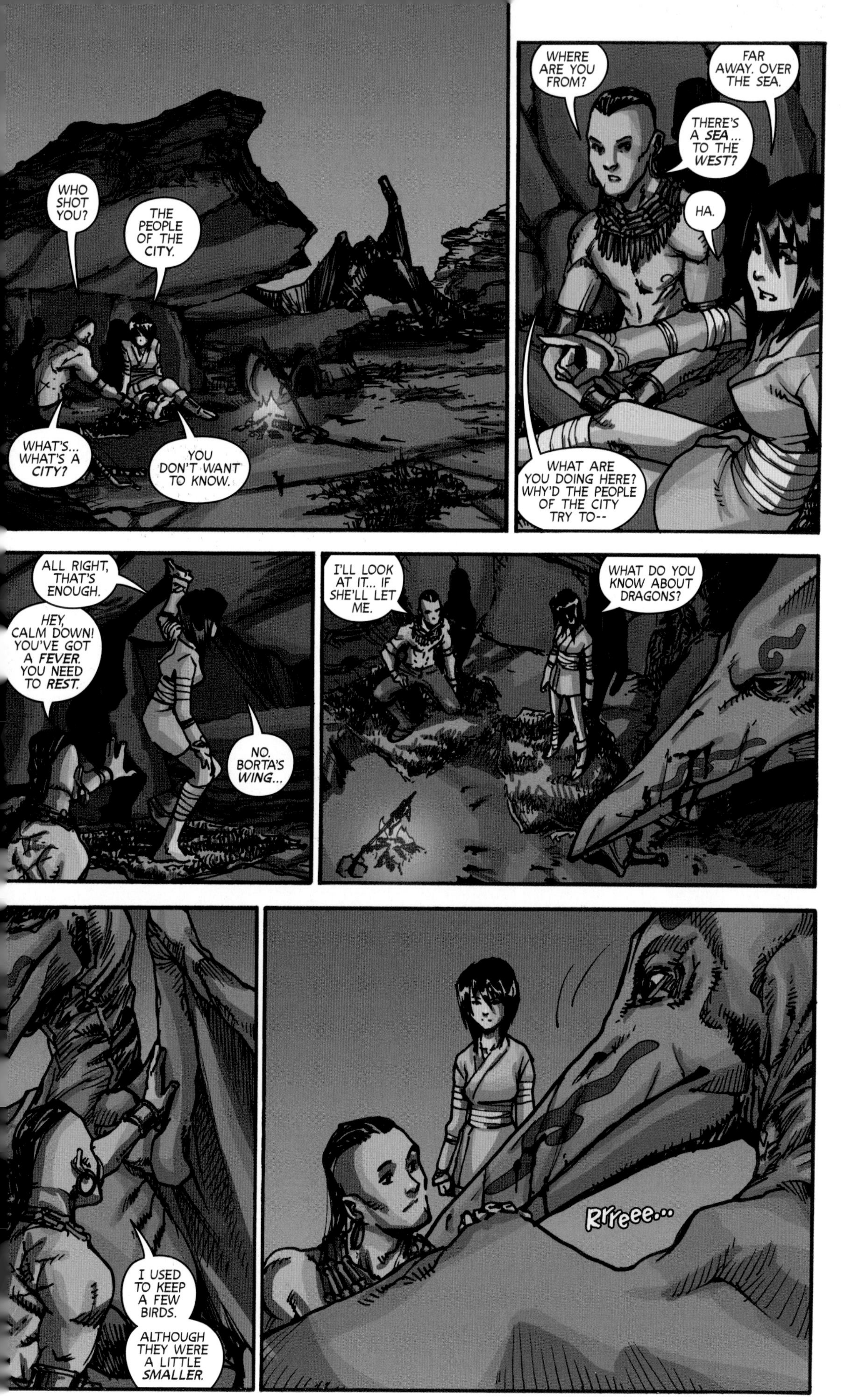
WHO SHOT YOU?
THE PEOPLE OF THE CITY.
WHAT'S... WHAT'S A *CITY*?
YOU DON'T WANT TO KNOW.
WHERE ARE YOU FROM?
FAR AWAY. OVER THE SEA.
THERE'S A *SEA*... TO THE *WEST*?
HA.
WHAT ARE YOU DOING HERE? WHY'D THE PEOPLE OF THE CITY TRY TO--
ALL RIGHT, THAT'S ENOUGH.
HEY, CALM DOWN! YOU'VE GOT A *FEVER*. YOU NEED TO *REST*.
NO. BORTA'S *WING*...
I'LL LOOK AT IT... IF SHE'LL LET ME.
WHAT DO YOU KNOW ABOUT DRAGONS?
I USED TO KEEP A FEW BIRDS.
ALTHOUGH THEY WERE A LITTLE *SMALLER*.
Rrreee...

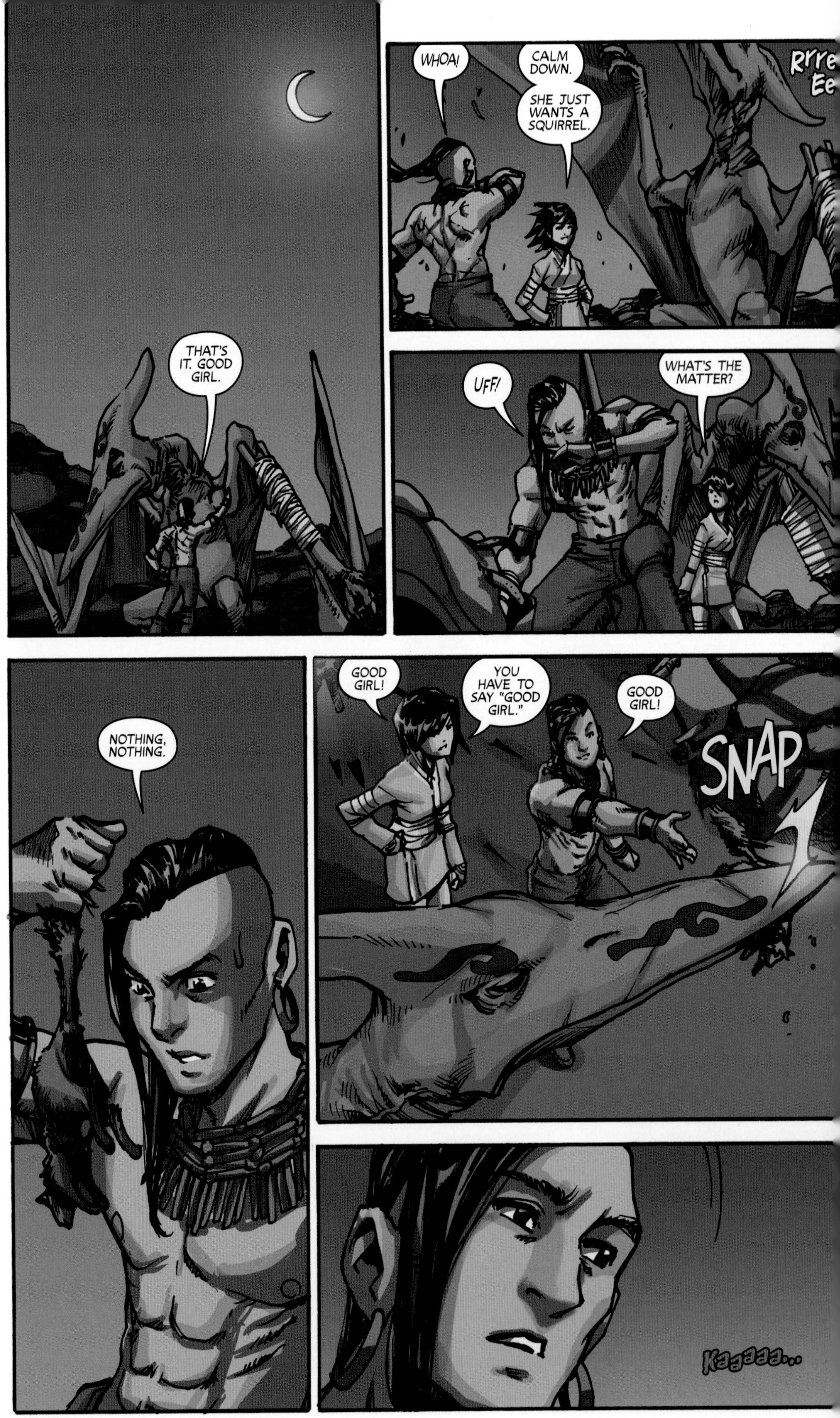
THAT'S IT. GOOD GIRL.
WHOA!
CALM DOWN.
SHE JUST WANTS A SQUIRREL.
UFF!
WHAT'S THE MATTER?
NOTHING, NOTHING.
GOOD GIRL!
YOU HAVE TO SAY "GOOD GIRL."
GOOD GIRL!
SNAP
Kaaaaa...

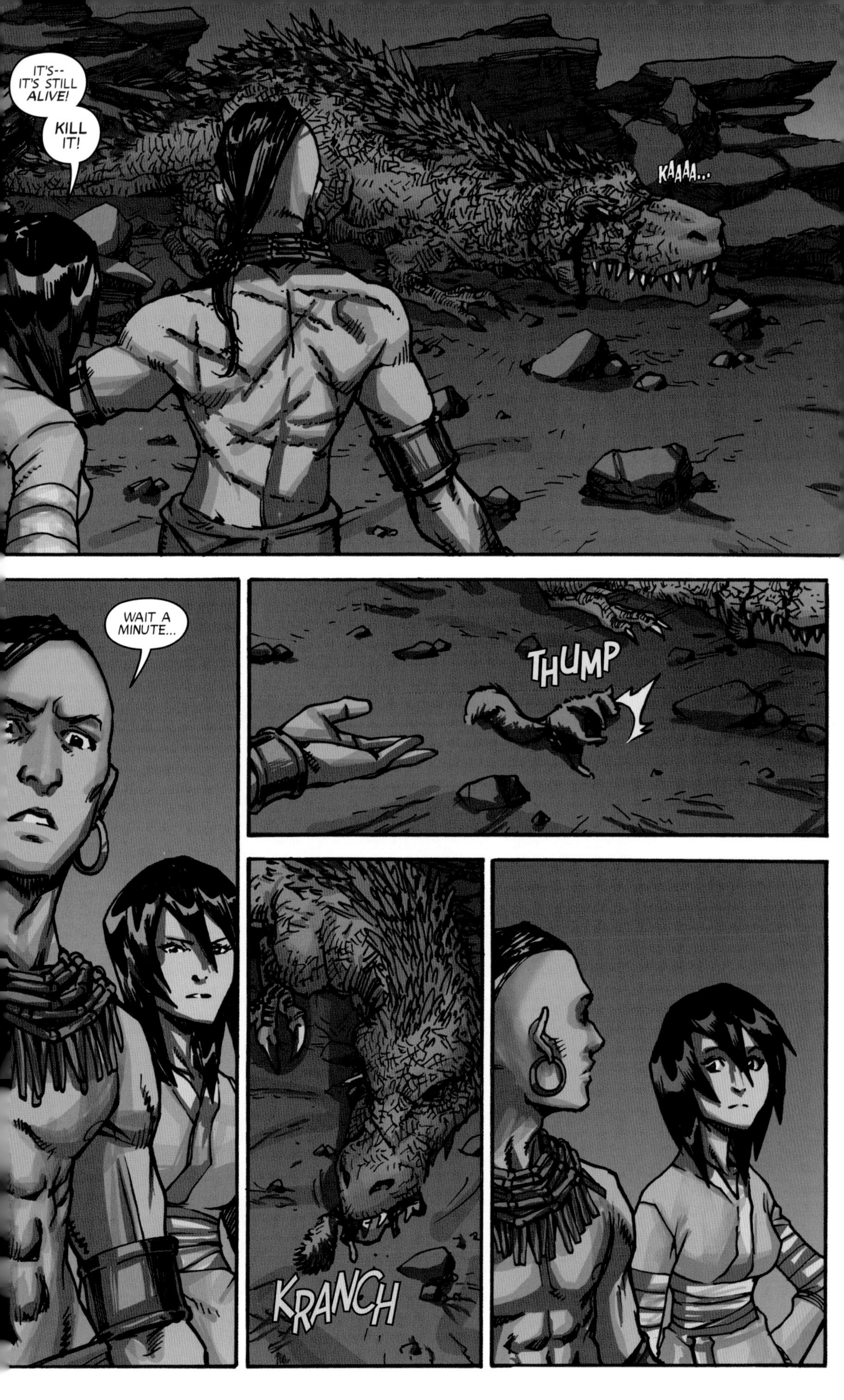
IT'S-- IT'S STILL ALIVE!
KILL IT!
KAAAA...
WAIT A MINUTE...
THUMP
KRANCH

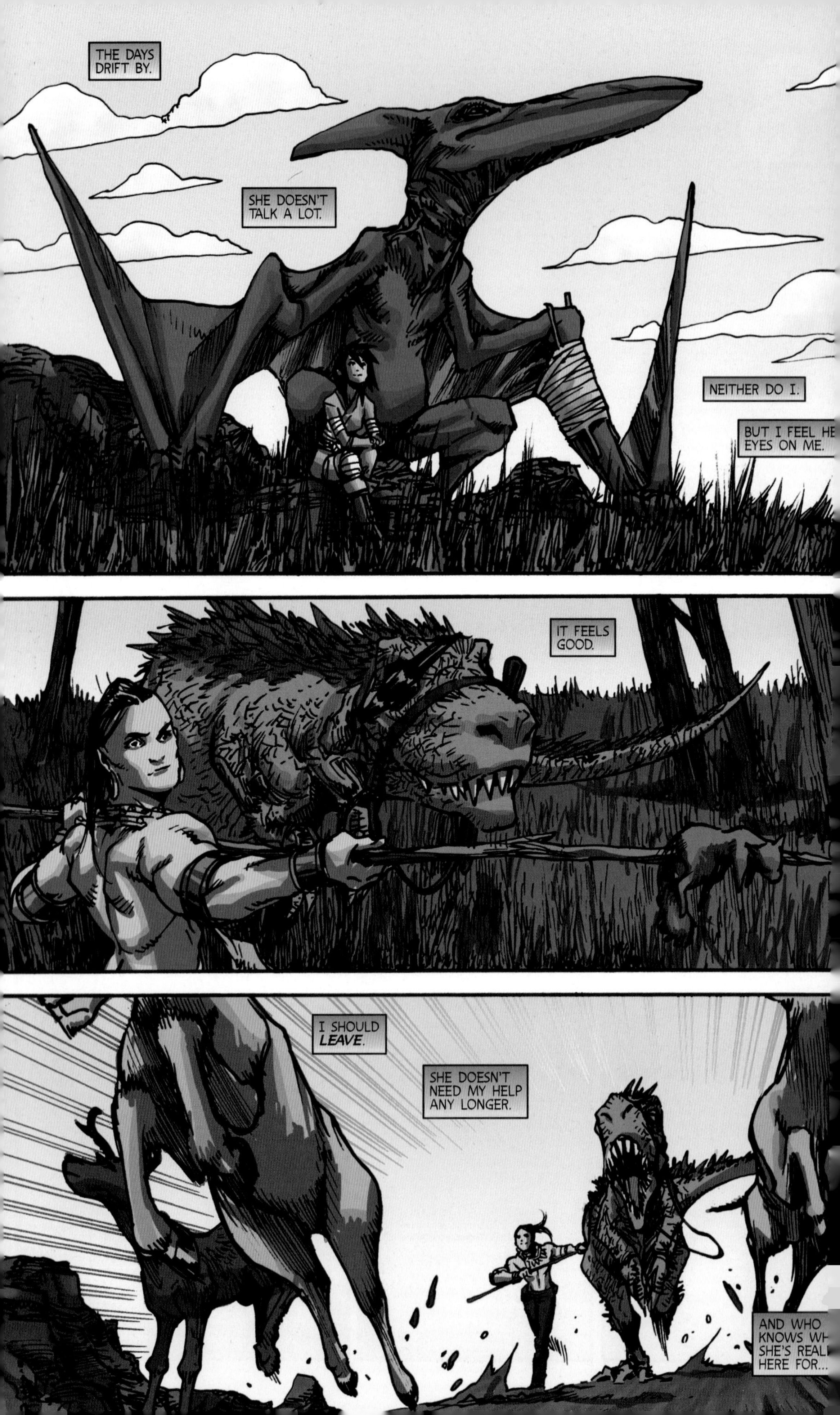

THE DAYS DRIFT BY.
SHE DOESN'T TALK A LOT.
NEITHER DO I.
BUT I FEEL HE EYES ON ME.
IT FEELS GOOD.
I SHOULD *LEAVE*.
SHE DOESN'T NEED MY HELP ANY LONGER.
AND WHO KNOWS WH SHE'S REAL HERE FOR...

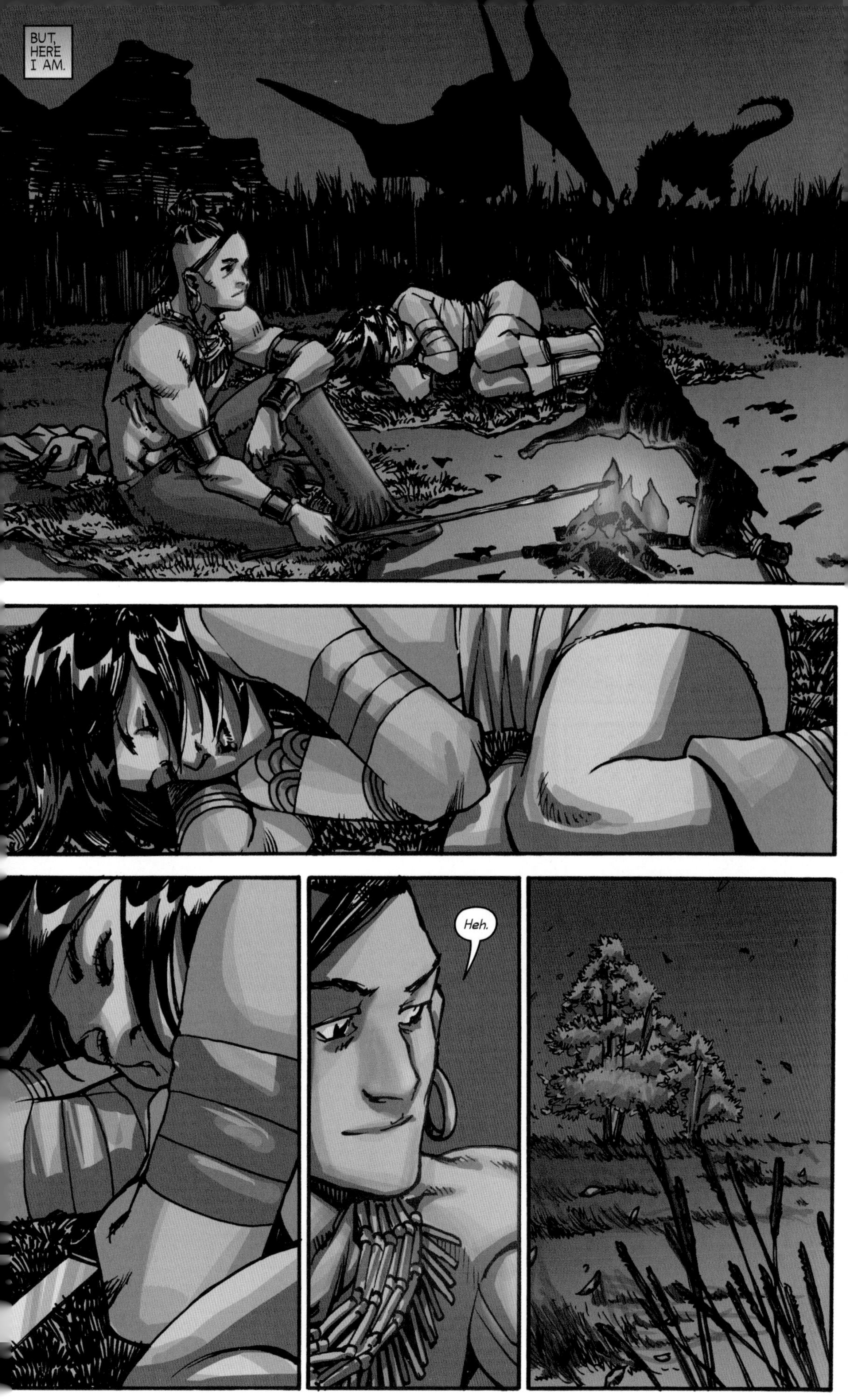
BUT, HERE I AM.
Heh.

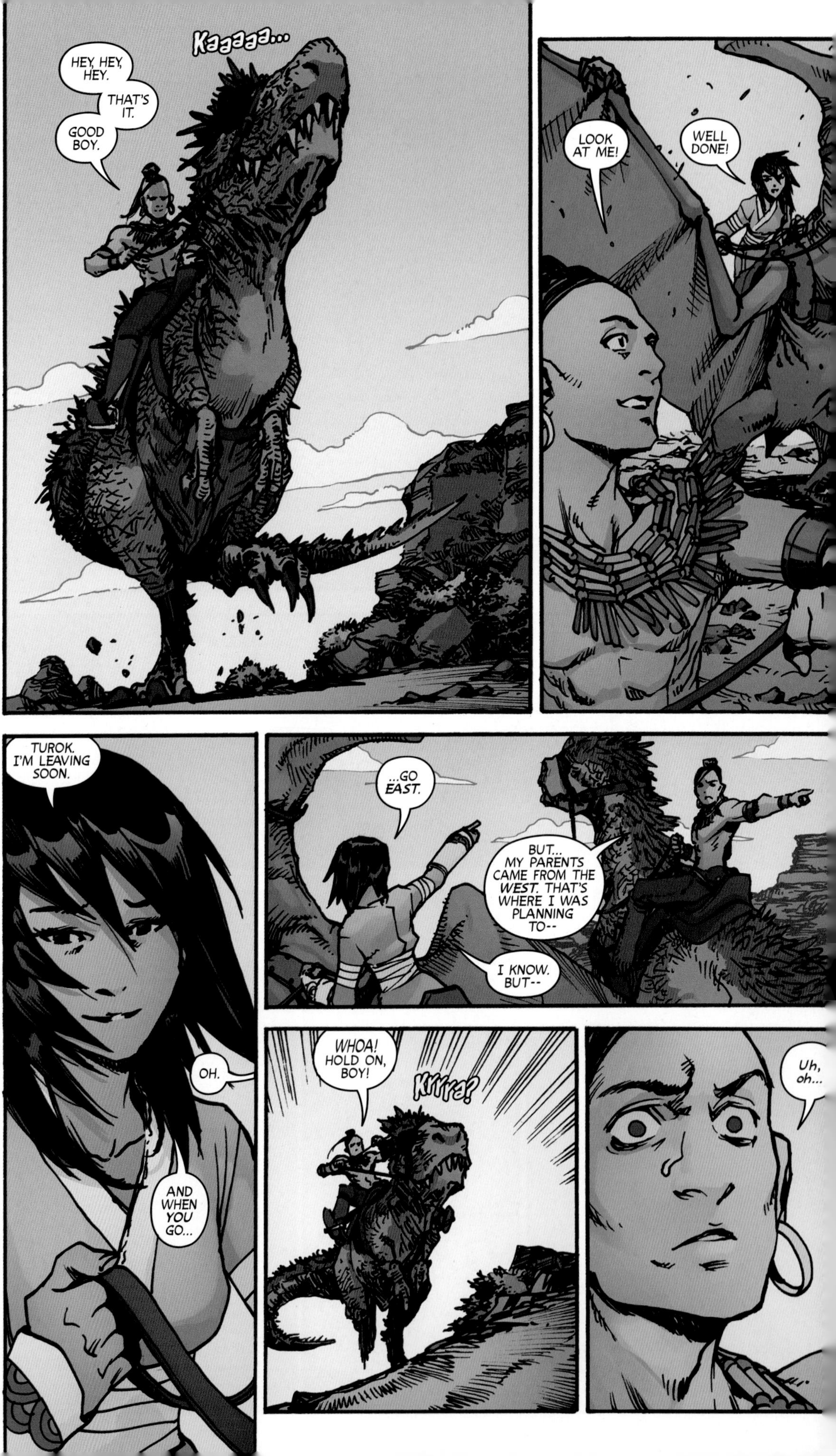
Kaaaaa...
HEY, HEY, HEY.
THAT'S IT.
GOOD BOY.
LOOK AT ME!
WELL DONE!
TUROK. I'M LEAVING SOON.
OH.
AND WHEN YOU GO...
...GO EAST.
BUT... MY PARENTS CAME FROM THE WEST. THAT'S WHERE I WAS PLANNING TO--
I KNOW. BUT--
WHOA! HOLD ON, BOY!
Kryya?
Uh, oh...

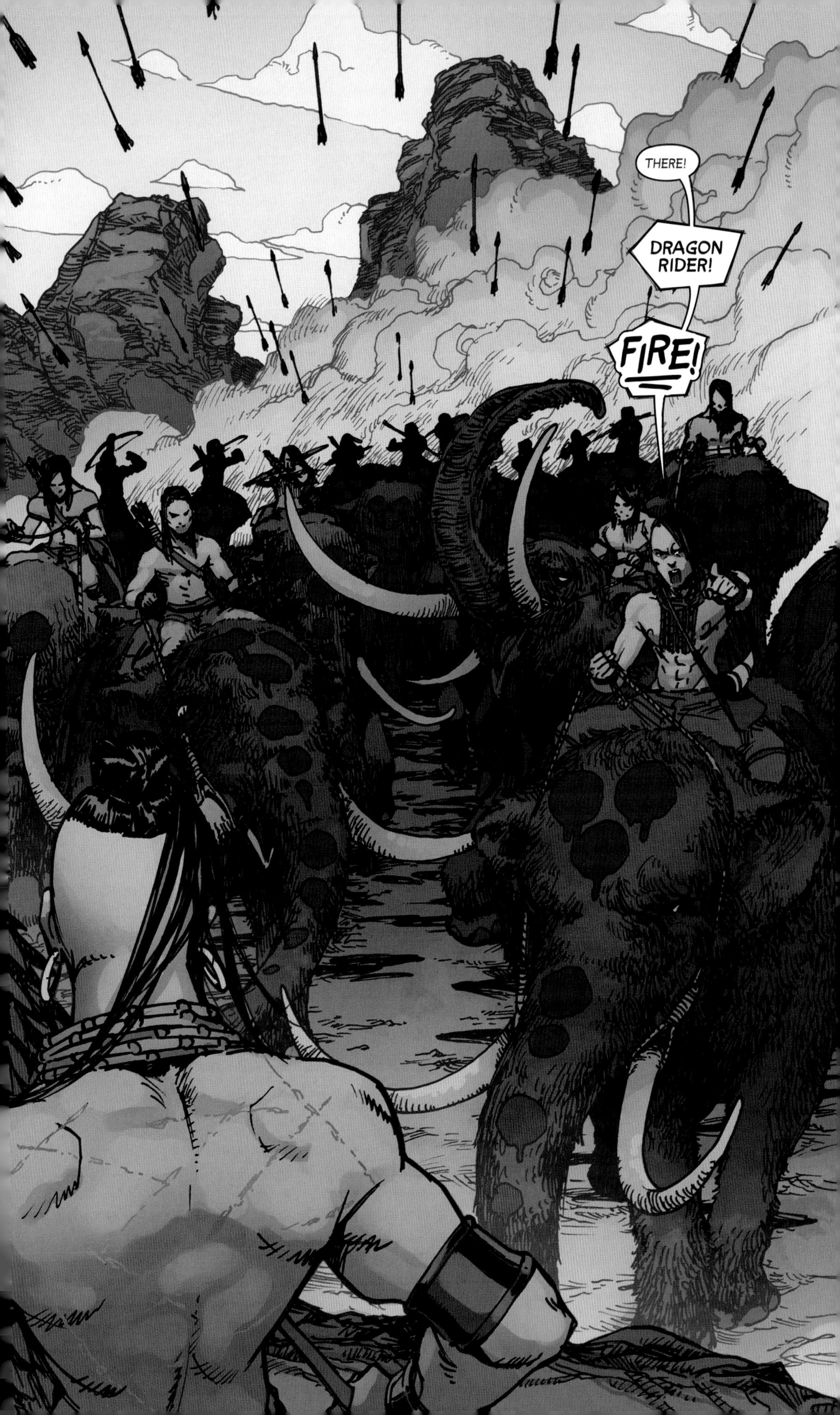
THERE!
DRAGON RIDER!
FIRE!

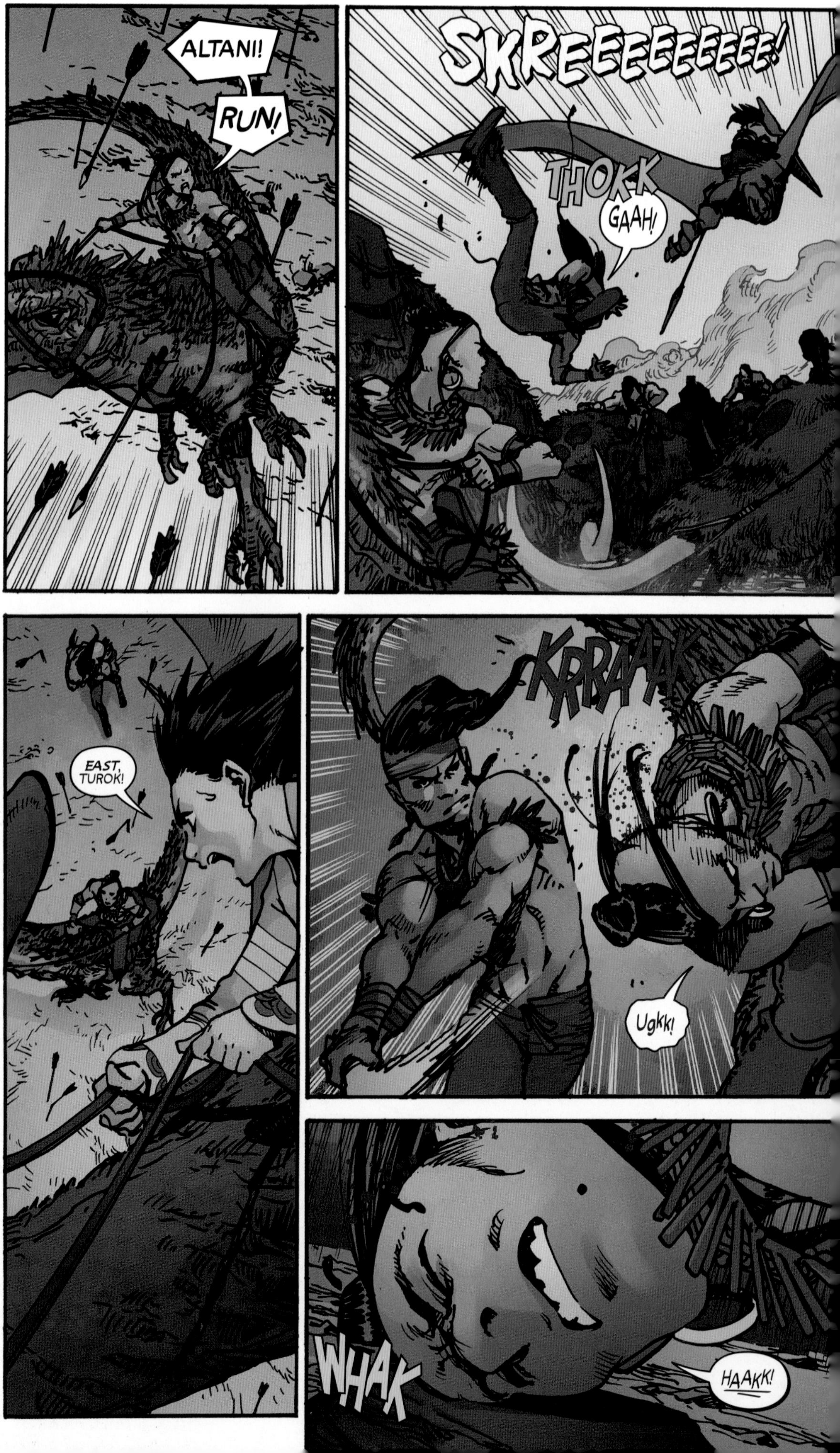
ALTANI!
RUN!
SKREEEEEEEEEE!
THOKK
GAAH!
EAST, TUROK!
KRRAAAK
Ugkk!
WHAK
HAAKK!

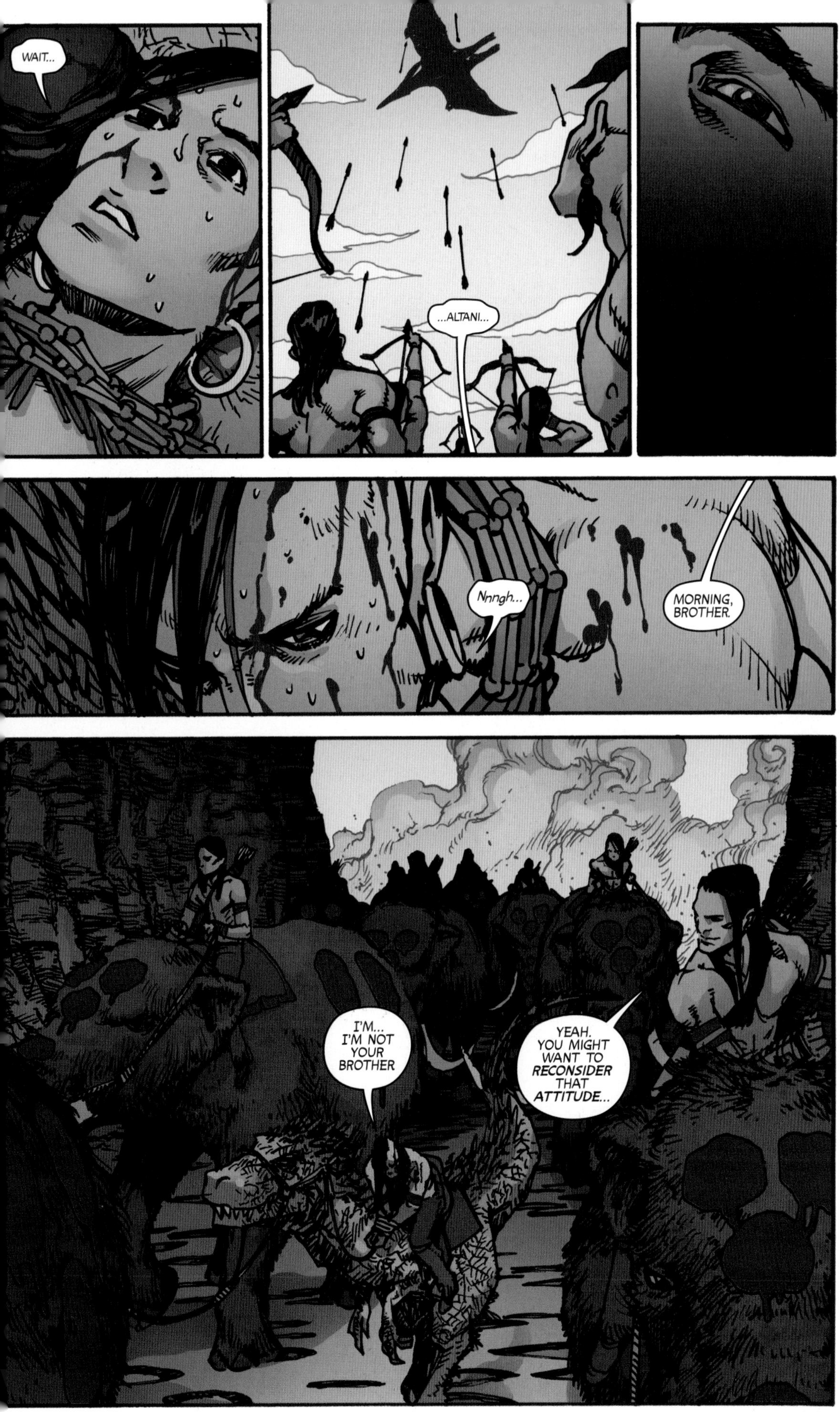
WAIT...
...ALTANI...
Nnngh...
MORNING, BROTHER.
I'M... I'M NOT YOUR BROTHER
YEAH. YOU MIGHT WANT TO *RECONSIDER* THAT *ATTITUDE*...

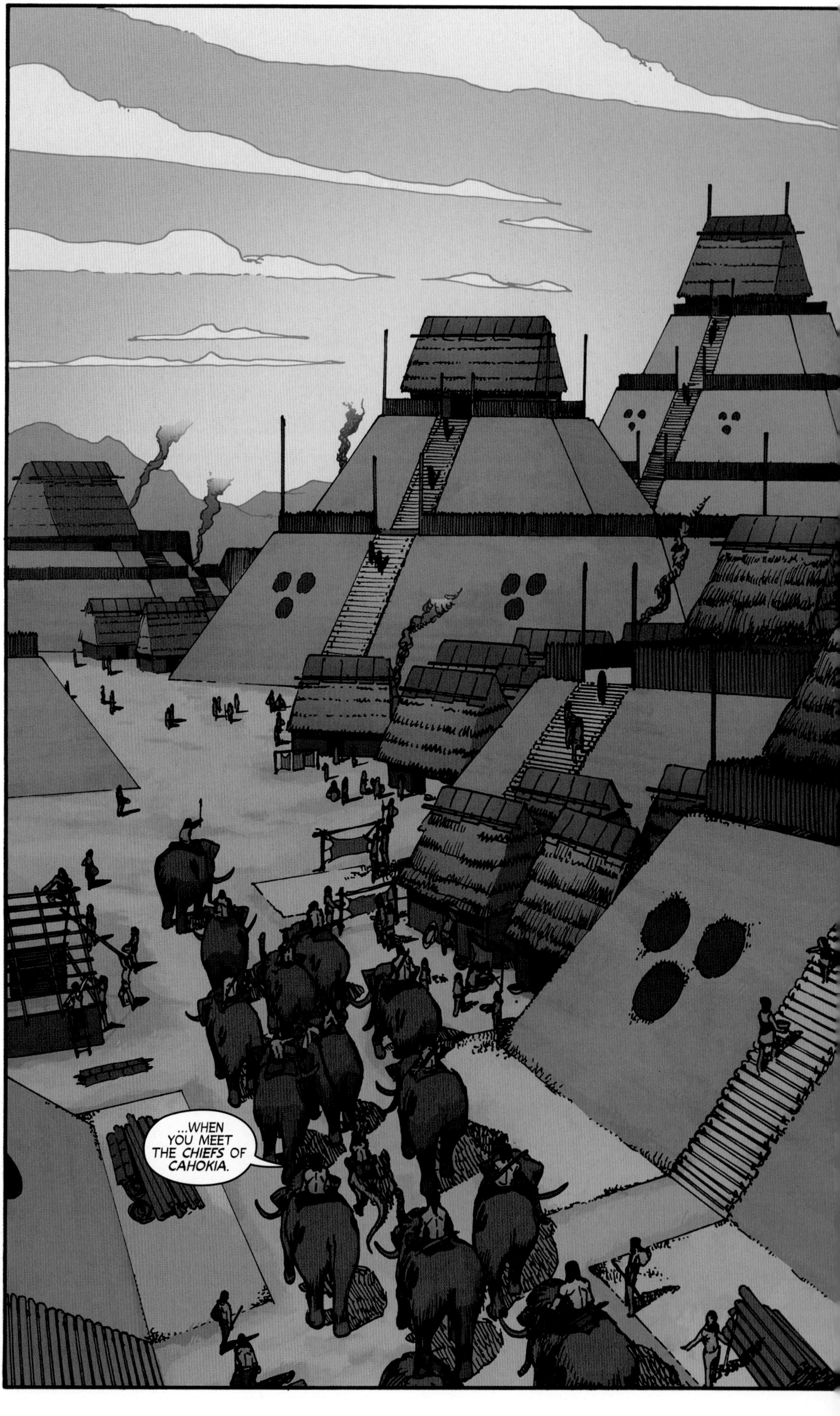
...WHEN YOU MEET THE *CHIEFS* OF *CAHOKIA*.

ISSUE 6

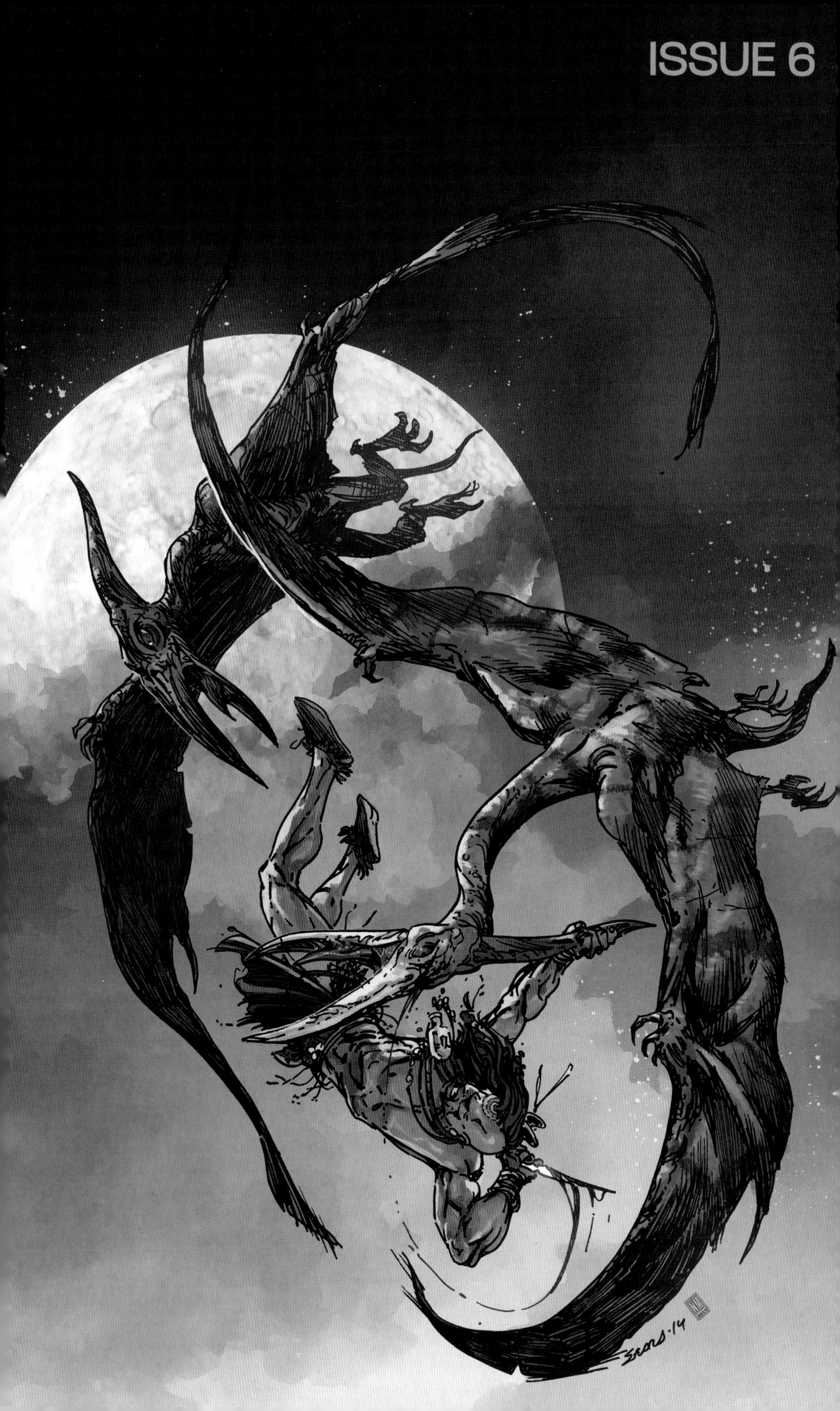

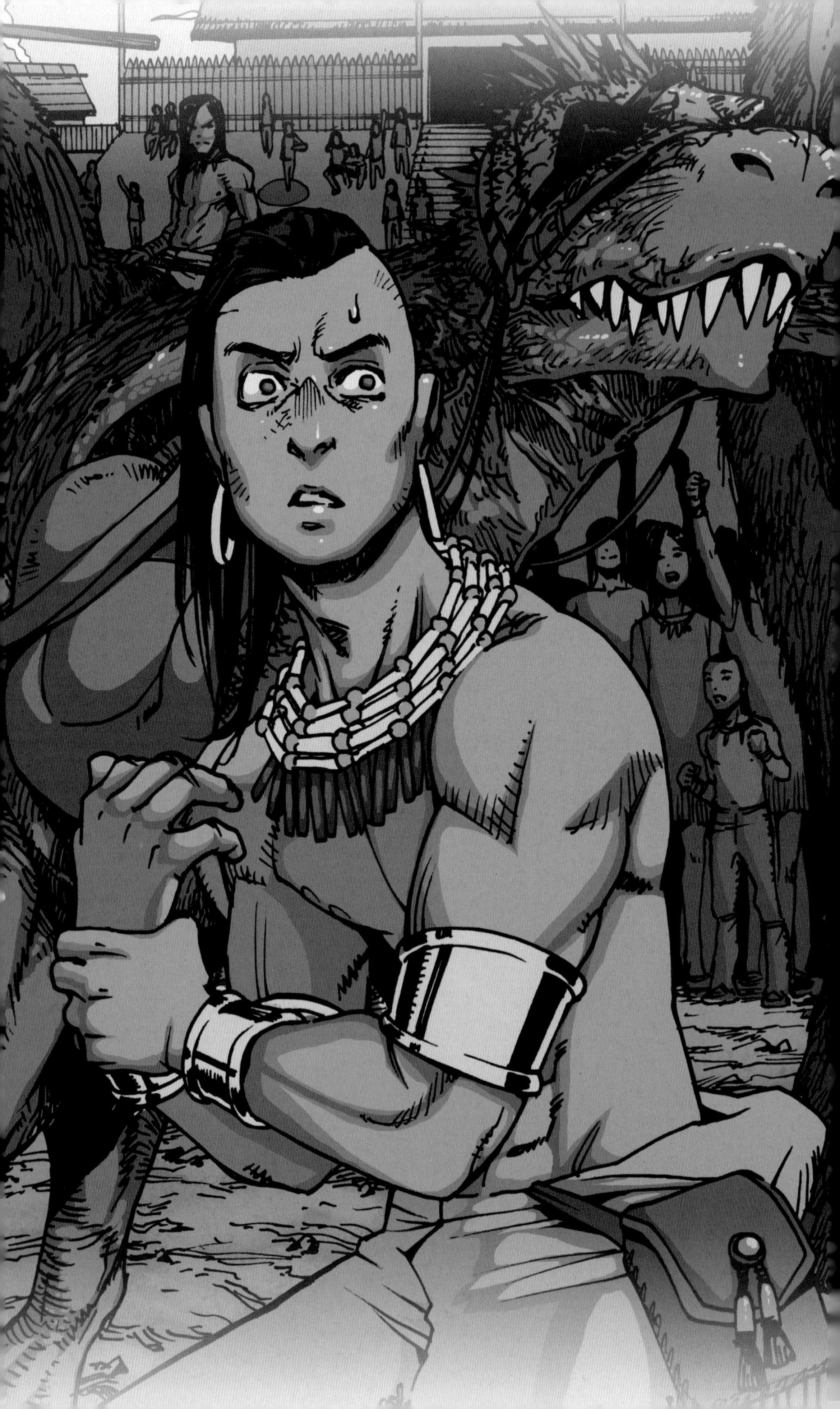

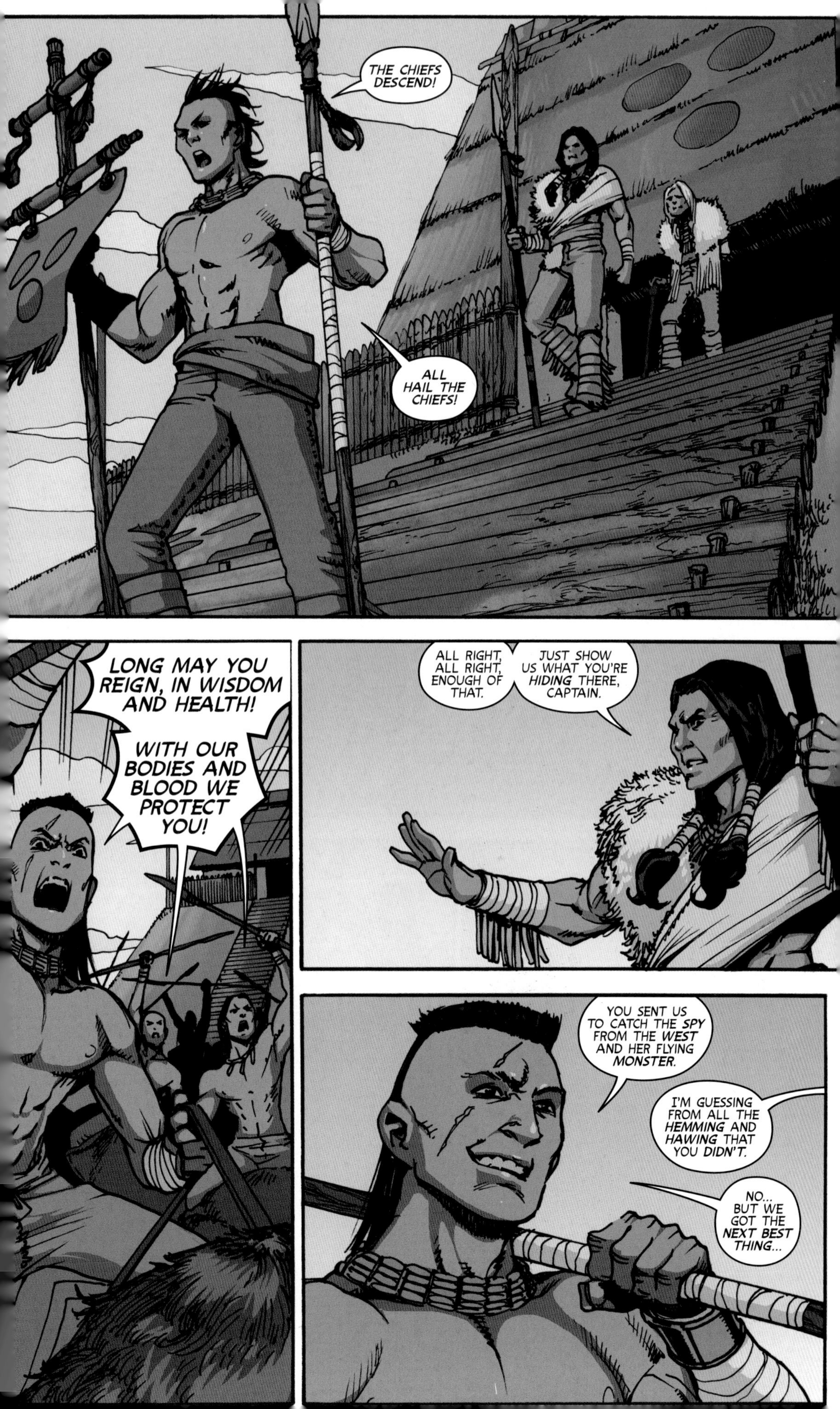

THE CHIEFS DESCEND!
ALL HAIL THE CHIEFS!
LONG MAY YOU REIGN, IN WISDOM AND HEALTH!
WITH OUR BODIES AND BLOOD WE PROTECT YOU!
ALL RIGHT, ALL RIGHT, ENOUGH OF THAT.
JUST SHOW US WHAT YOU'RE HIDING THERE, CAPTAIN.
YOU SENT US TO CATCH THE SPY FROM THE WEST AND HER FLYING MONSTER.
I'M GUESSING FROM ALL THE HEMMING AND HAWING THAT YOU DIDN'T.
NO... BUT WE GOT THE NEXT BEST THING...

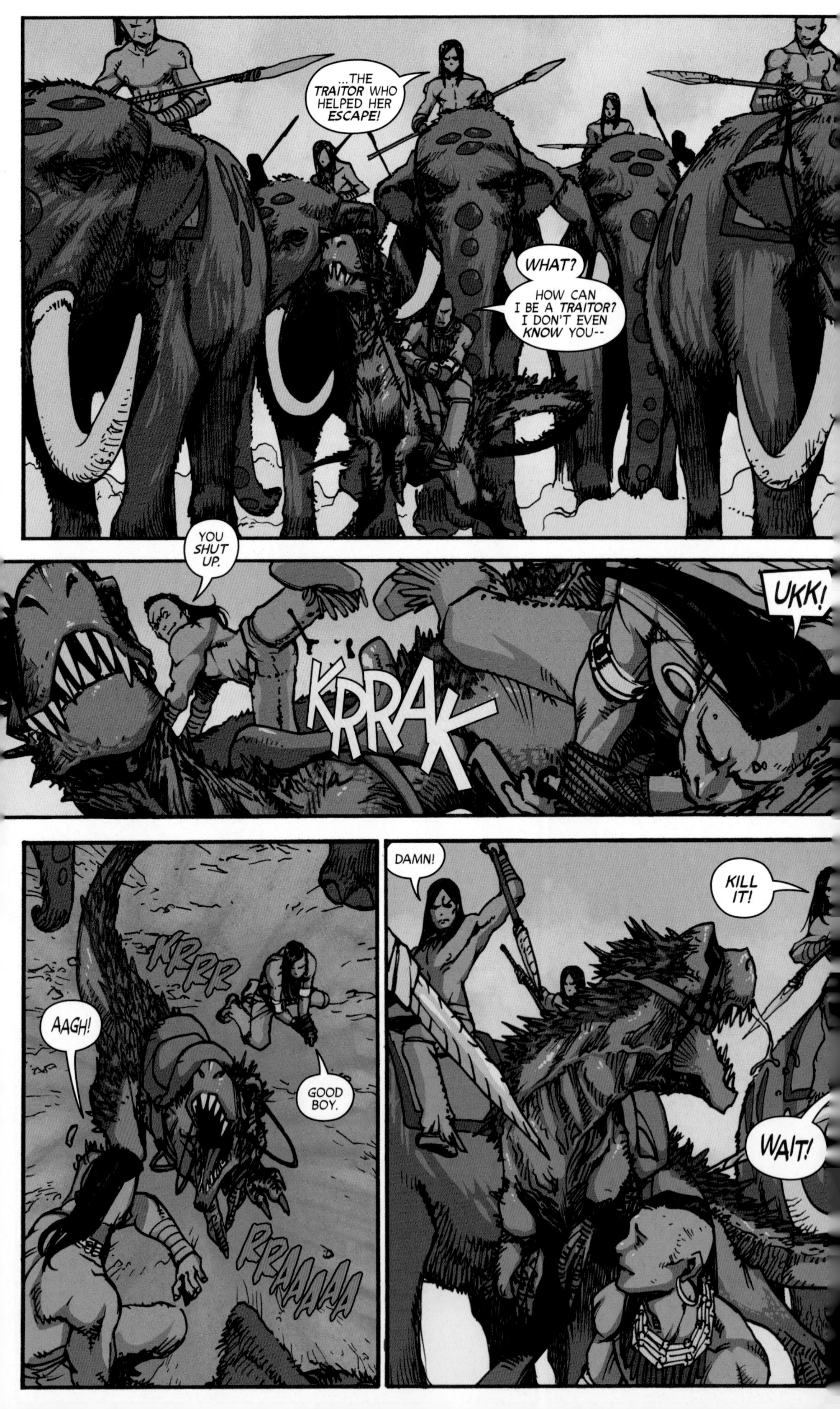
...THE TRAITOR WHO HELPED HER ESCAPE!
WHAT?
HOW CAN I BE A TRAITOR? I DON'T EVEN KNOW YOU--
YOU SHUT UP.
KRRAK
UKK!
KRRR
AAGH!
GOOD BOY.
RRAAAAA
DAMN!
KILL IT!
WAIT!

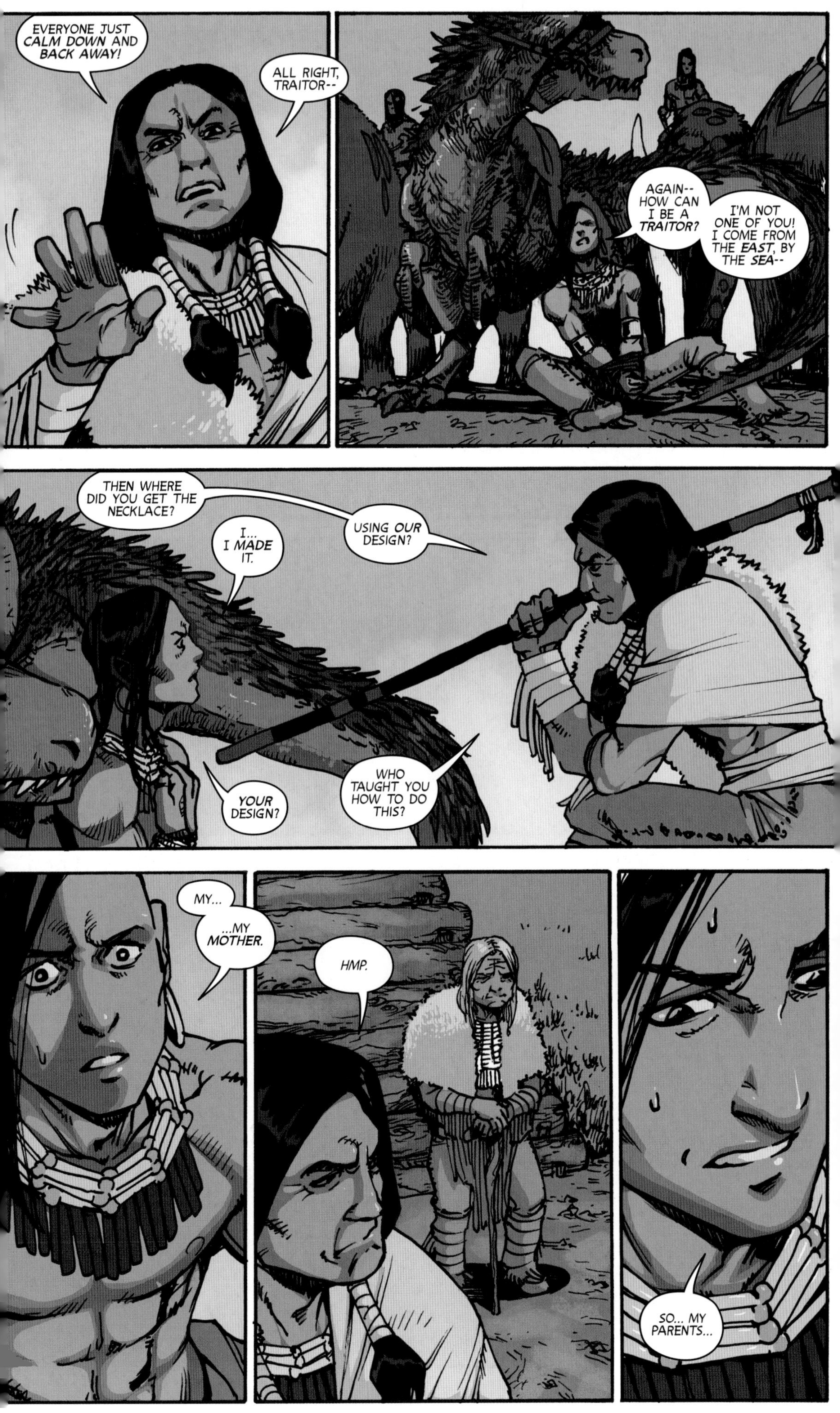
EVERYONE JUST CALM DOWN AND BACK AWAY!
ALL RIGHT, TRAITOR--
AGAIN-- HOW CAN I BE A TRAITOR?
I'M NOT ONE OF YOU! I COME FROM THE EAST, BY THE SEA--
THEN WHERE DID YOU GET THE NECKLACE?
I... I MADE IT.
USING OUR DESIGN?
YOUR DESIGN?
WHO TAUGHT YOU HOW TO DO THIS?
MY...
...MY MOTHER.
HMP.
SO... MY PARENTS...

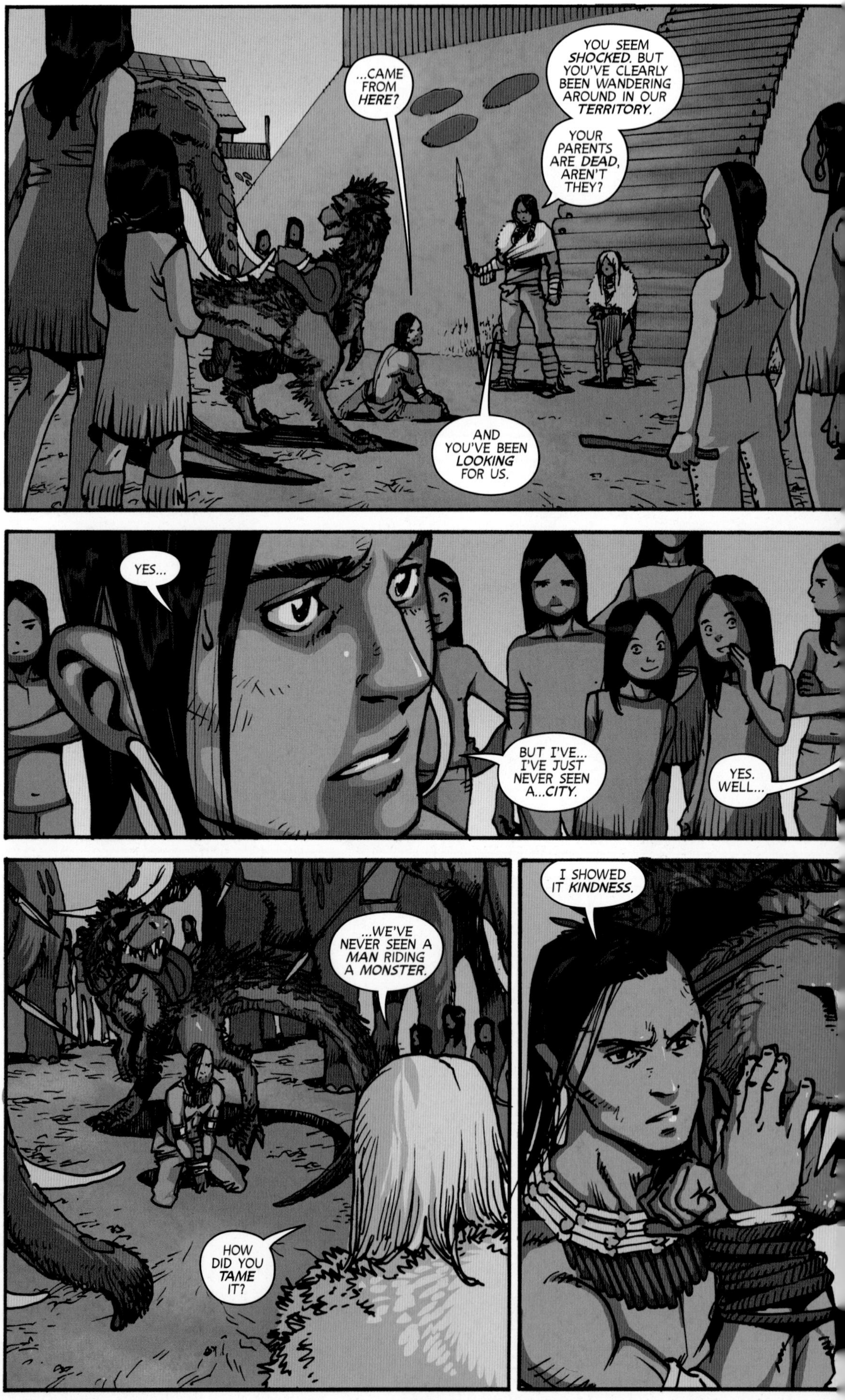
...CAME FROM *HERE?*
YOU SEEM *SHOCKED*. BUT YOU'VE CLEARLY BEEN WANDERING AROUND IN OUR *TERRITORY*.
YOUR PARENTS ARE *DEAD*, AREN'T THEY?
AND YOU'VE BEEN *LOOKING* FOR US.
YES...
BUT I'VE... I'VE JUST NEVER SEEN A...*CITY*.
YES. WELL...
...WE'VE NEVER SEEN A *MAN* RIDING A *MONSTER*.
HOW DID YOU *TAME* IT?
I SHOWED IT *KINDNESS*.

HNH.

ALL RIGHT, THEN.

WHAT'S YOUR NAME, BOY?

TUROK.

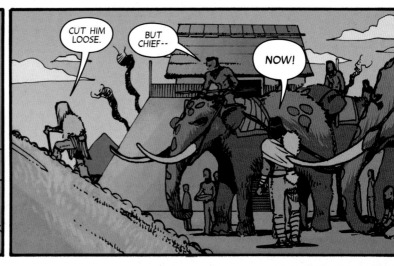

CUT HIM LOOSE.

BUT CHIEF--

NOW!

CHILDREN OF CAHOKIA!

YOUR CHIEFS COMMAND YOU--

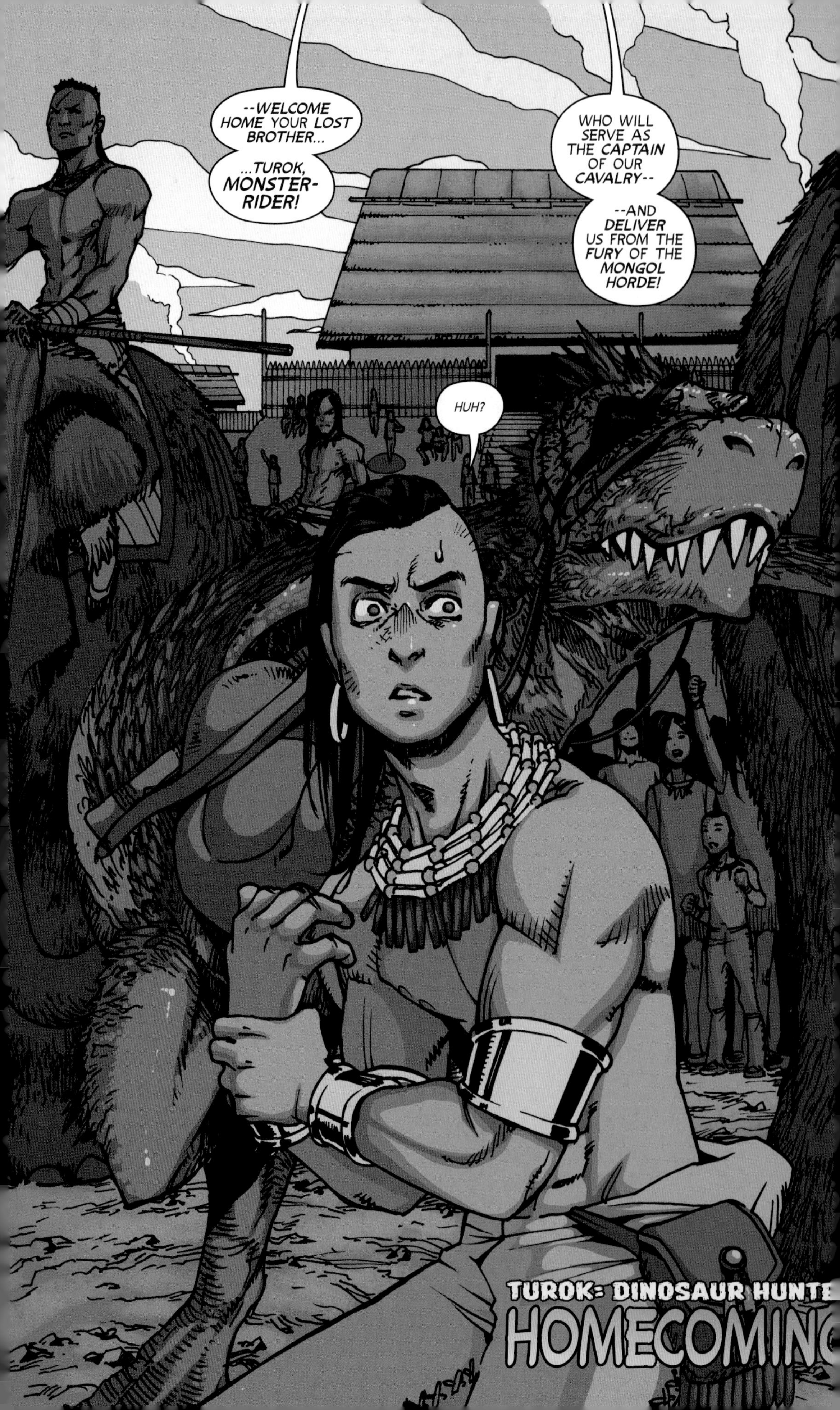
--WELCOME HOME YOUR LOST BROTHER...
...TUROK, MONSTER-RIDER!
WHO WILL SERVE AS THE CAPTAIN OF OUR CAVALRY--
--AND DELIVER US FROM THE FURY OF THE MONGOL HORDE!
HUH?
TUROK: DINOSAUR HUNTE
HOMECOMIN

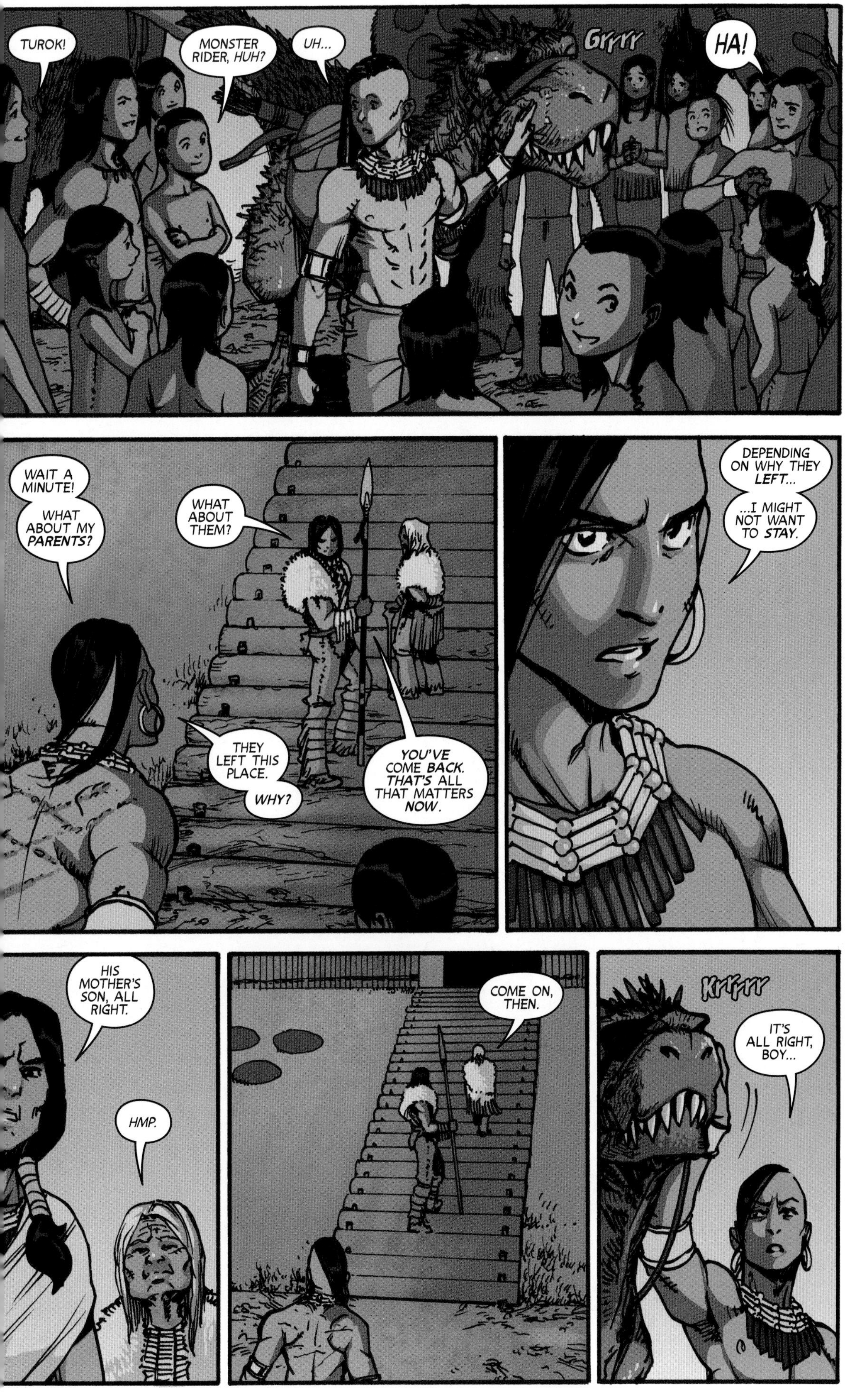
TUROK!
MONSTER RIDER, *HUH?*
UH...
Grrrr
HA!
WAIT A MINUTE!
WHAT ABOUT MY *PARENTS?*
WHAT ABOUT THEM?
THEY LEFT THIS PLACE.
WHY?
YOU'VE COME BACK. THAT'S ALL THAT MATTERS NOW.
DEPENDING ON WHY THEY *LEFT*...
...I MIGHT NOT WANT TO *STAY*.
HIS MOTHER'S SON, ALL RIGHT.
HMP.
COME ON, THEN.
Krrrrr
IT'S ALL RIGHT, BOY...

...I'LL BE BACK.

REMEMBER, YOU WANTED TO SEE THIS.

SEE WHAT?

WHAT YOUR PARENTS RAN AWAY TO AVOID.

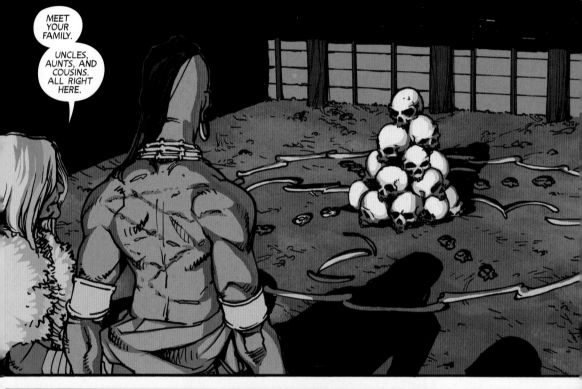

MEET YOUR FAMILY.

UNCLES, AUNTS, AND COUSINS. ALL RIGHT HERE.

WHAT... HAPPENED?

WHEN A CHIEF DIES, HE'S *BURIED* WITH HIS GREATEST *ENEMIES.*

AND ALL THEIR *FAMILIES.*

YOU--YOU MEAN YOU *KILL* THEM?

...

THAT'S... *CRAZY.*

IT CUTS DOWN ON *ASSASSINATION* ATTEMPTS.

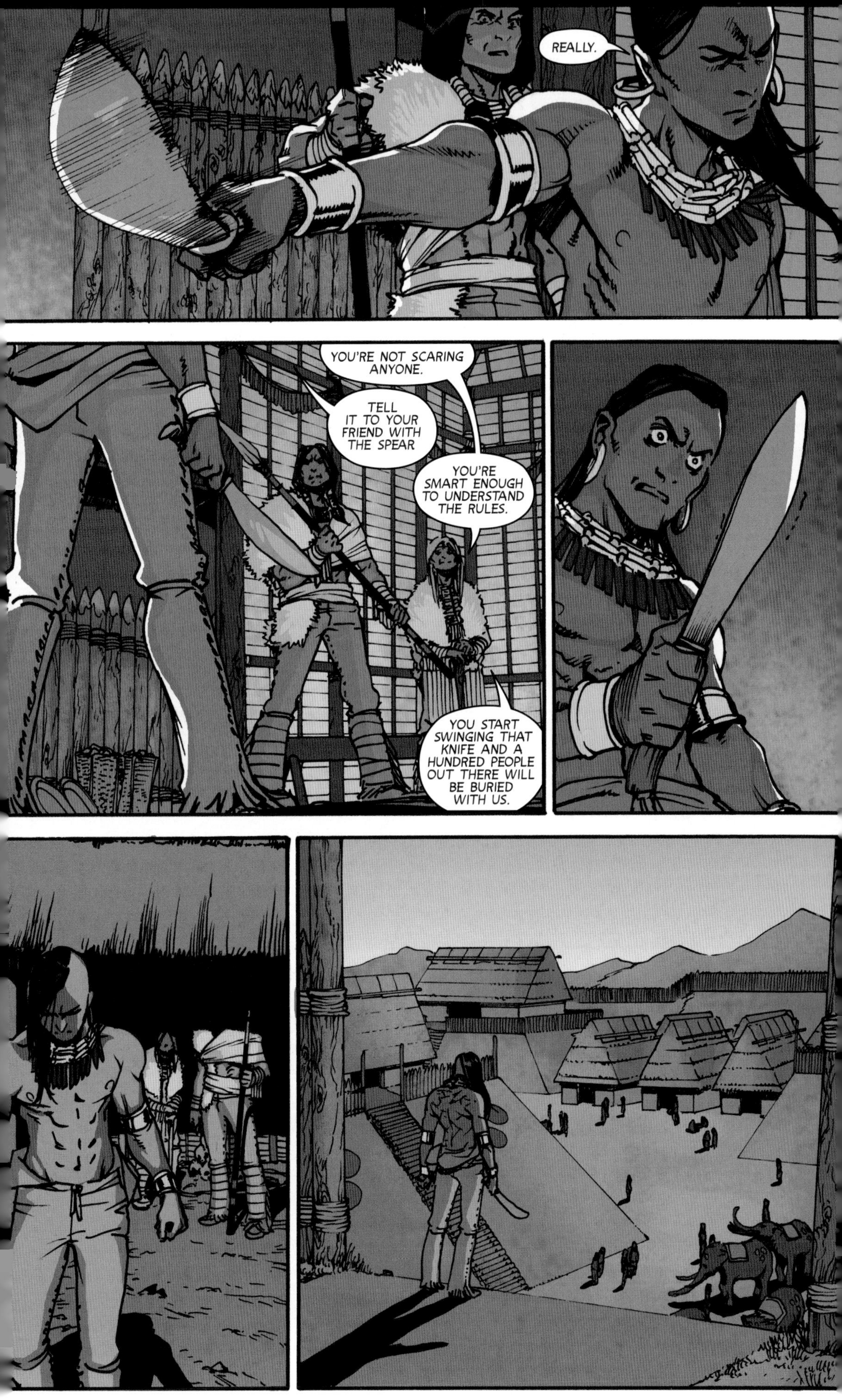
REALLY.
YOU'RE NOT SCARING ANYONE.
TELL IT TO YOUR FRIEND WITH THE SPEAR
YOU'RE SMART ENOUGH TO UNDERSTAND THE RULES.
YOU START SWINGING THAT KNIFE AND A HUNDRED PEOPLE OUT THERE WILL BE BURIED WITH US.

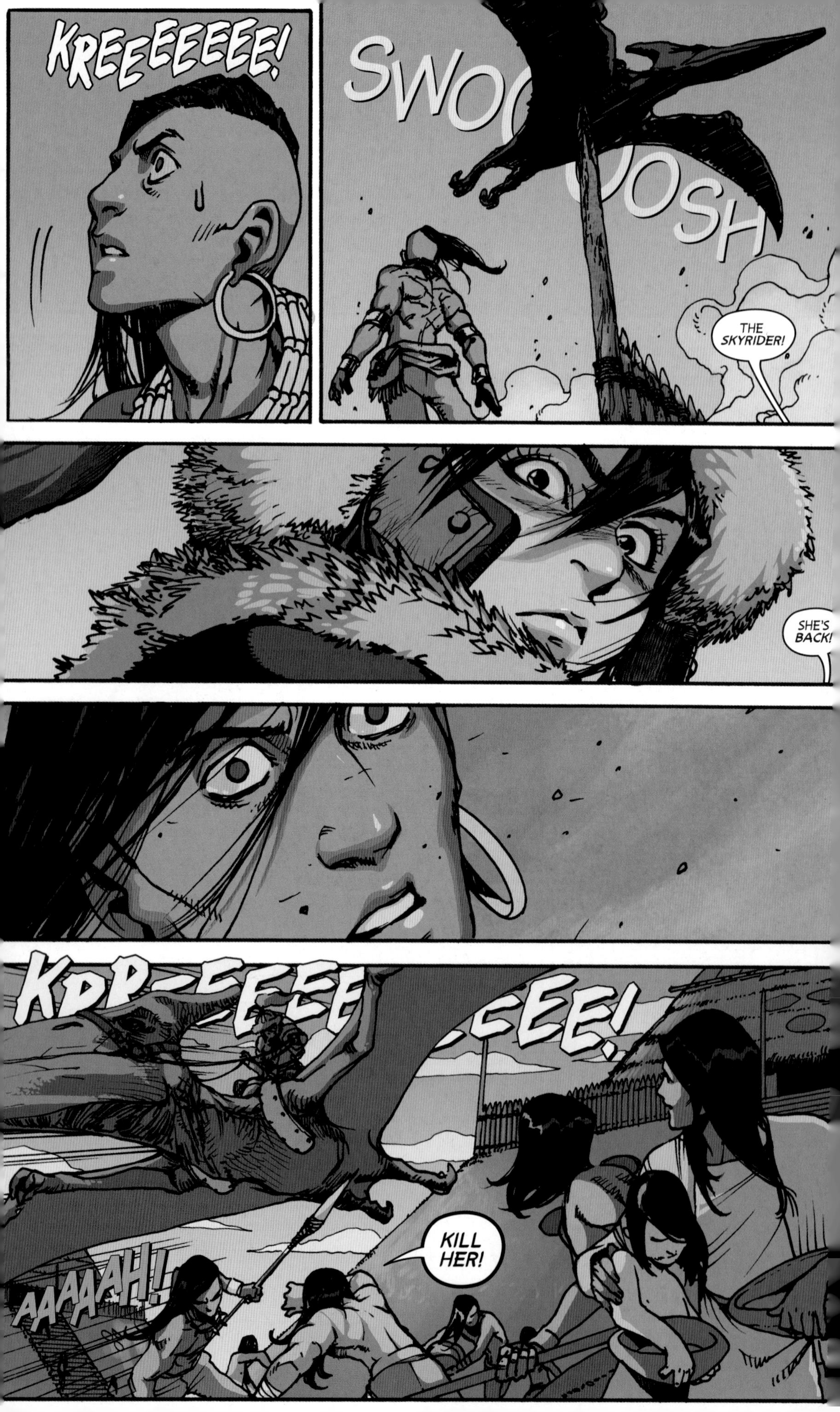
KREEEEEEEE!
SWOOOOSH
THE SKYRIDER!
SHE'S BACK!
KRR-EEEE-EEE!
KILL HER!
AAAAAH!!

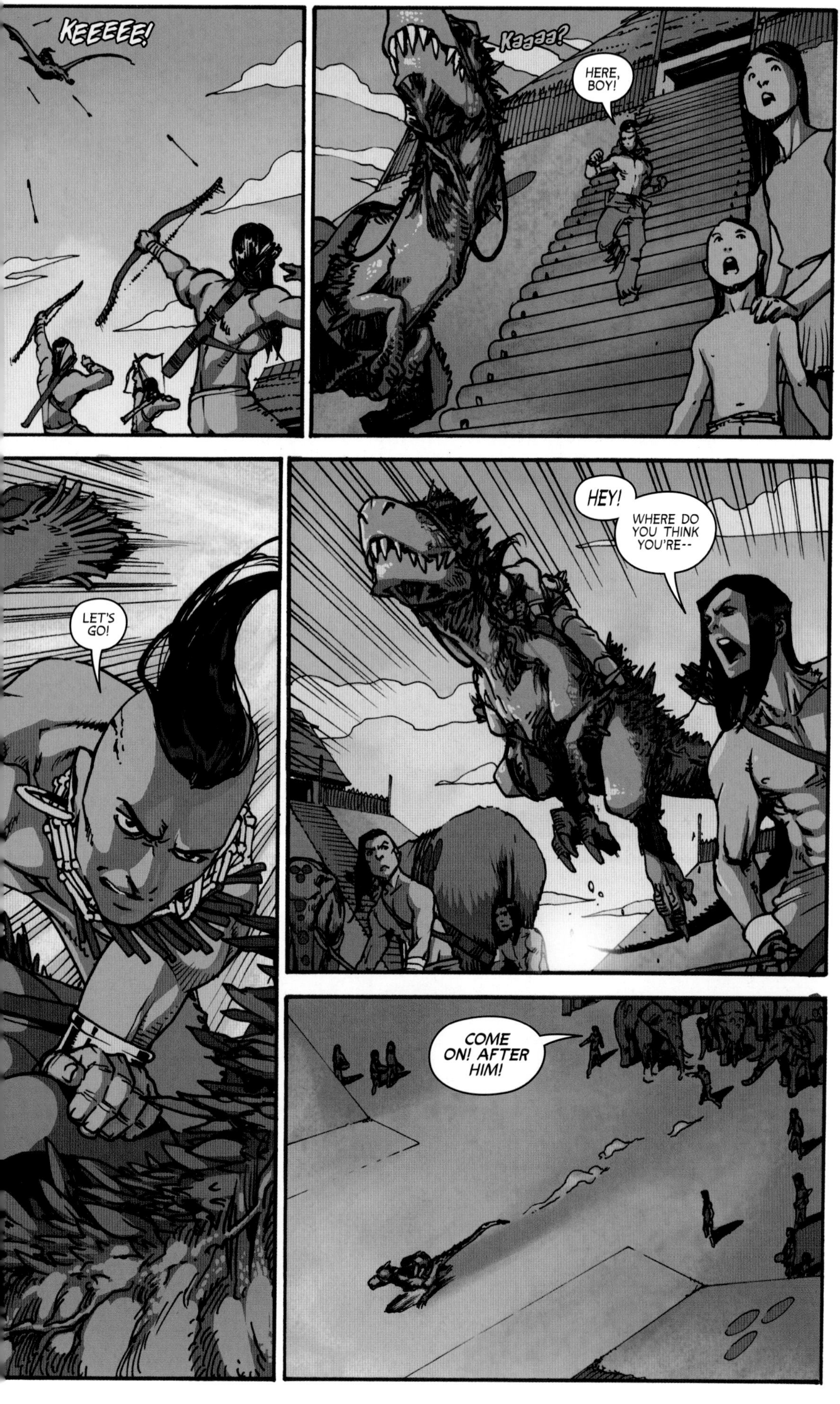
KEEEEE!
Kaaaa?
HERE, BOY!
LET'S GO!
HEY!
WHERE DO YOU THINK YOU'RE--
COME ON! AFTER HIM!

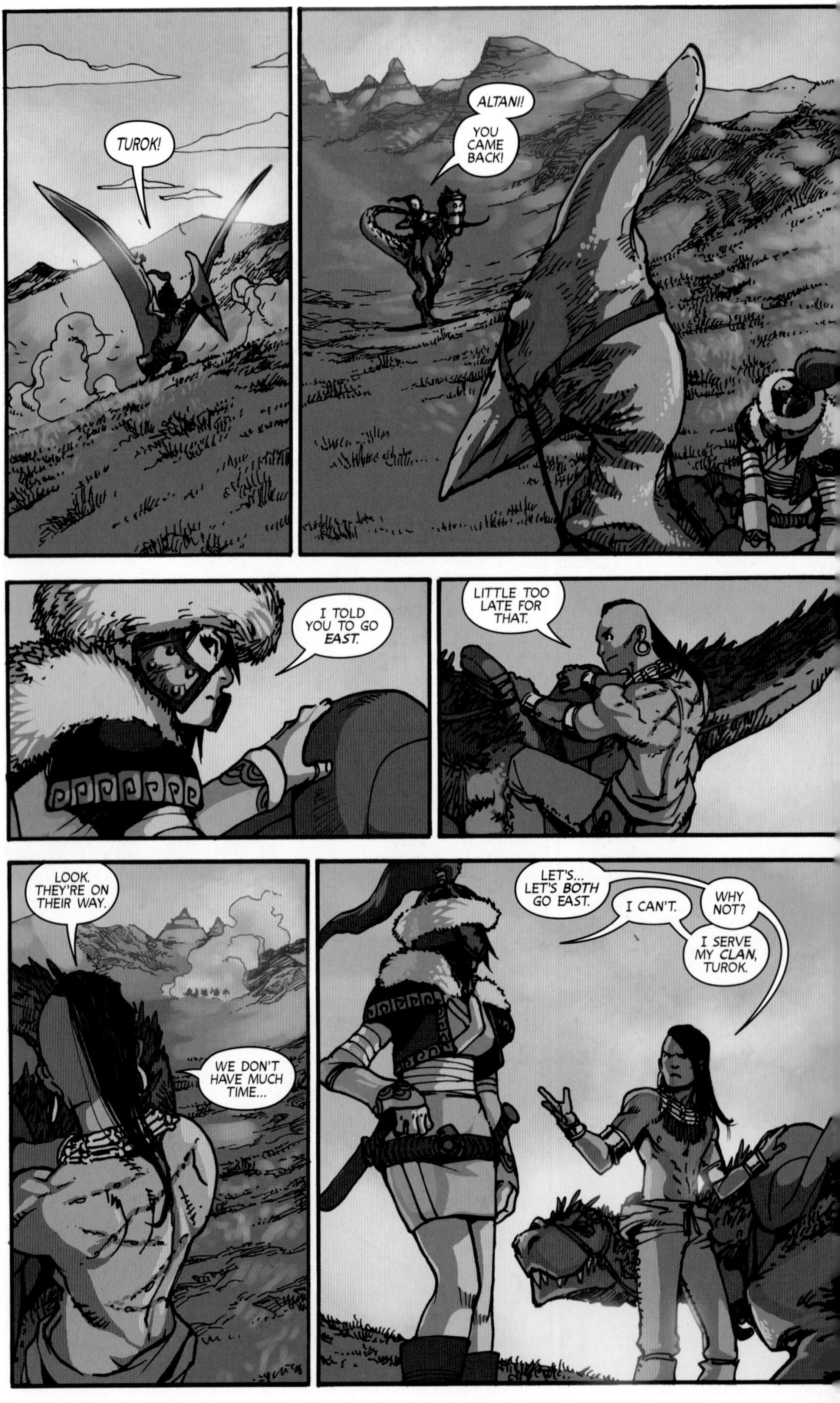
TUROK!
ALTANI!
YOU CAME BACK!
I TOLD YOU TO GO EAST.
LITTLE TOO LATE FOR THAT.
LOOK. THEY'RE ON THEIR WAY.
WE DON'T HAVE MUCH TIME...
LET'S... LET'S BOTH GO EAST.
WHY NOT?
I CAN'T.
I SERVE MY CLAN, TUROK.

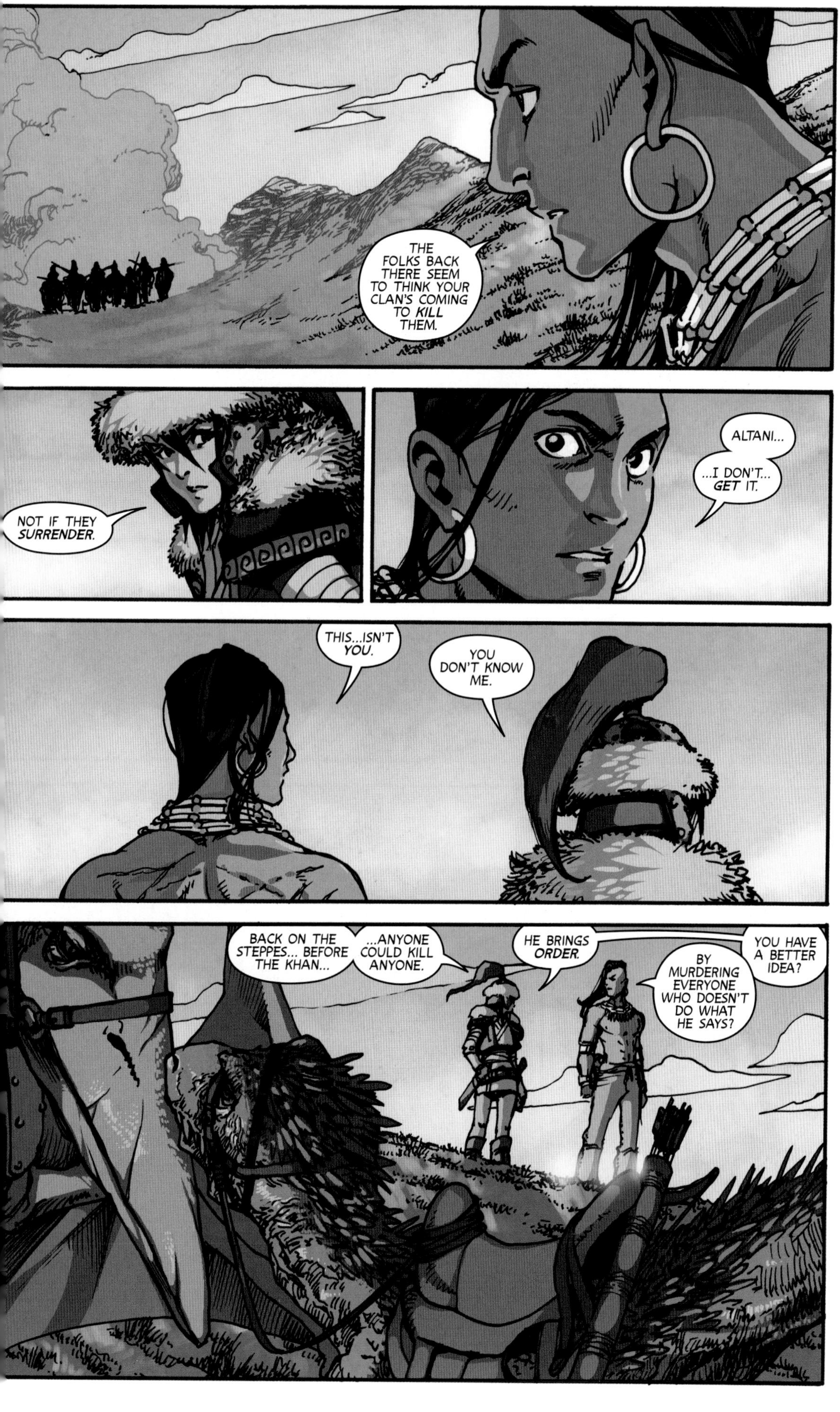
THE FOLKS BACK THERE SEEM TO THINK YOUR CLAN'S COMING TO *KILL* THEM.
NOT IF THEY *SURRENDER*.
ALTANI...
...I DON'T... *GET* IT.
THIS...ISN'T *YOU*.
YOU DON'T KNOW ME.
BACK ON THE STEPPES... BEFORE THE KHAN...
...ANYONE COULD KILL ANYONE.
HE BRINGS *ORDER*.
BY MURDERING EVERYONE WHO DOESN'T DO WHAT HE SAYS?
YOU HAVE A BETTER IDEA?

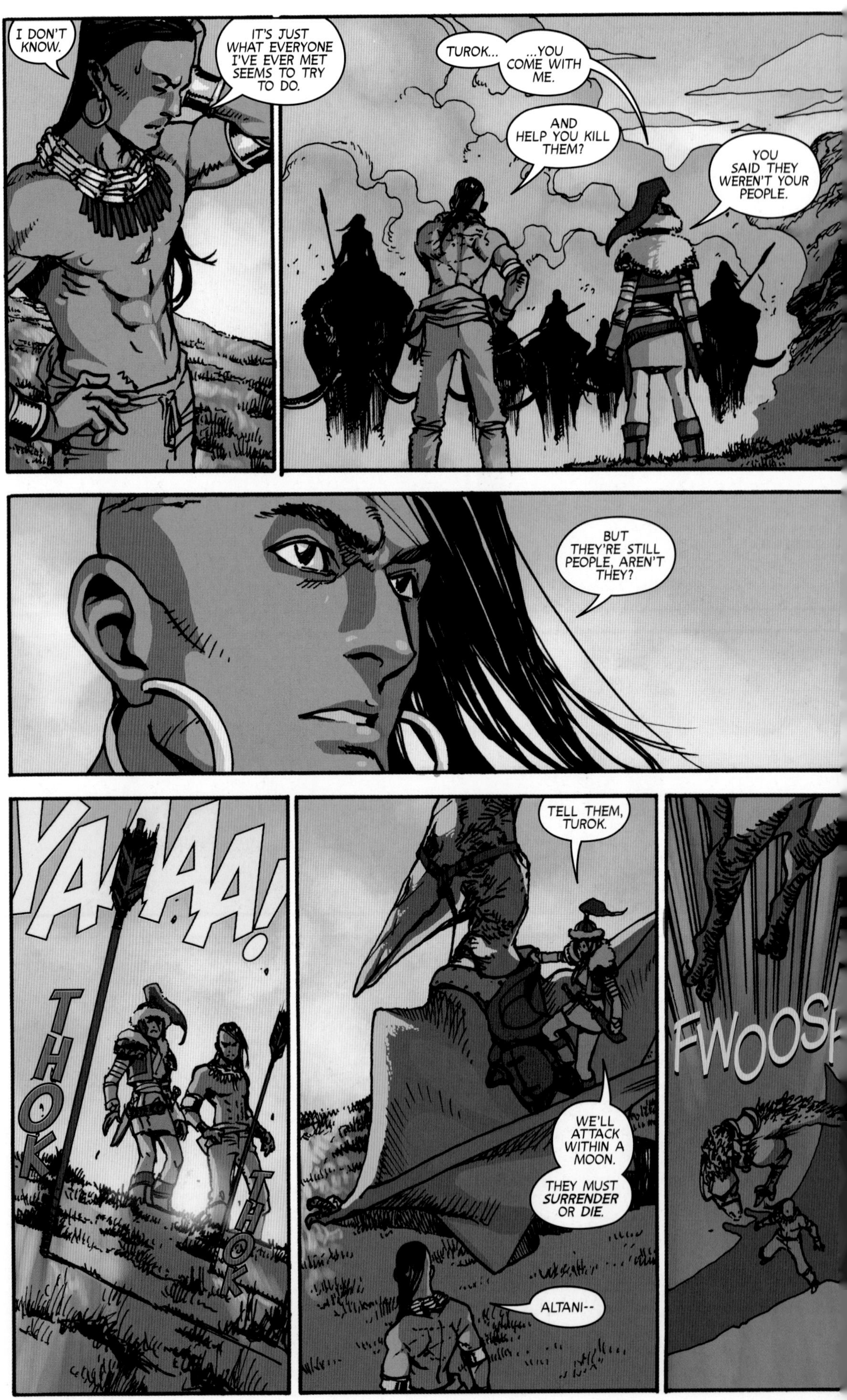
I DON'T KNOW.
IT'S JUST WHAT EVERYONE I'VE EVER MET SEEMS TO TRY TO DO.
TUROK...
...YOU COME WITH ME.
AND HELP YOU KILL THEM?
YOU SAID THEY WEREN'T YOUR PEOPLE.
BUT THEY'RE STILL PEOPLE, AREN'T THEY?
YAAAA!
THOK
THOK
TELL THEM, TUROK.
WE'LL ATTACK WITHIN A MOON.
THEY MUST SURRENDER OR DIE.
ALTANI--
FWOOS

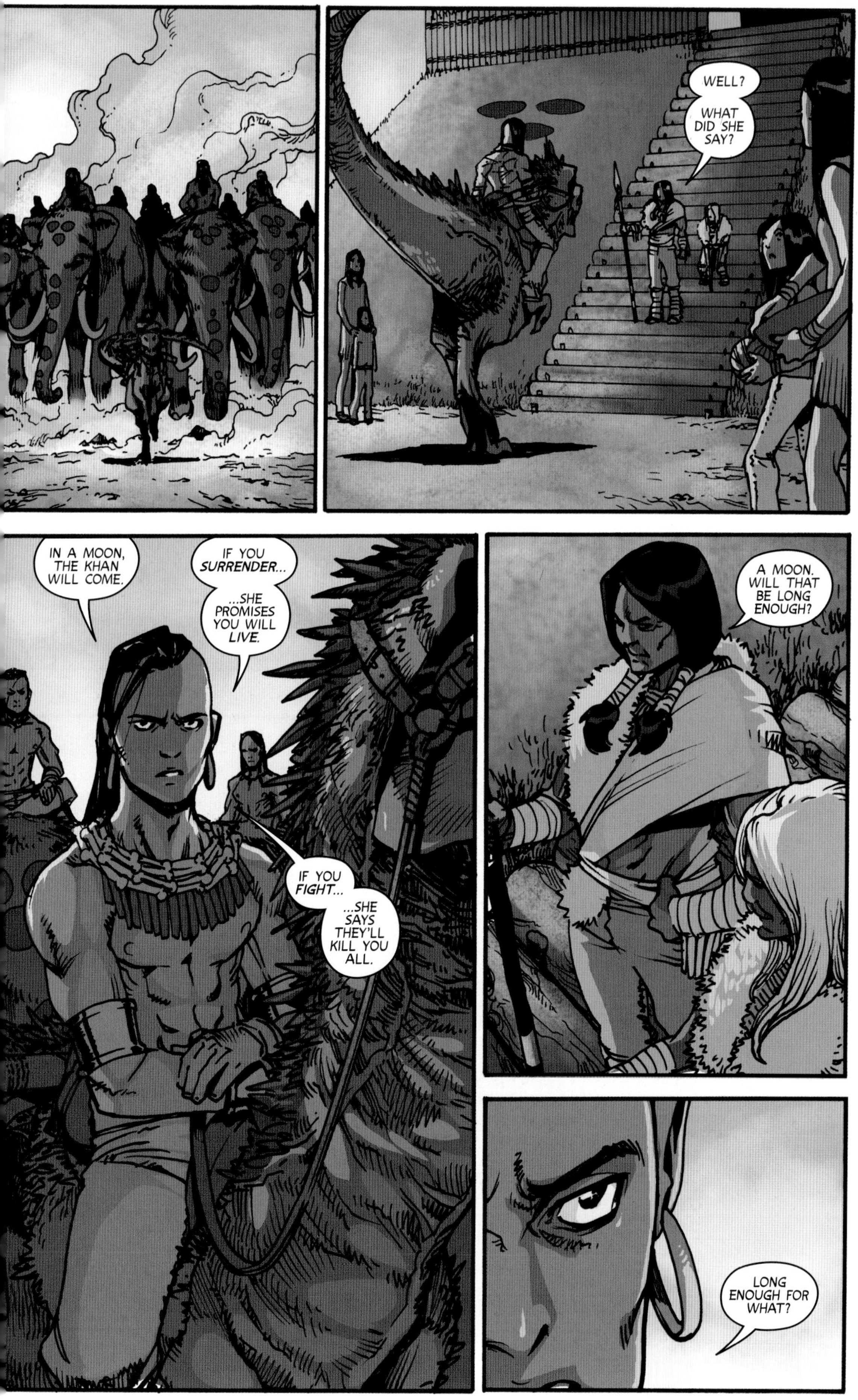
WELL?
WHAT DID SHE SAY?
IN A MOON, THE KHAN WILL COME.
IF YOU *SURRENDER*...
...SHE PROMISES YOU WILL *LIVE*.
IF YOU *FIGHT*...
...SHE SAYS THEY'LL KILL YOU ALL.
A MOON. WILL THAT BE LONG ENOUGH?
LONG ENOUGH FOR WHAT?

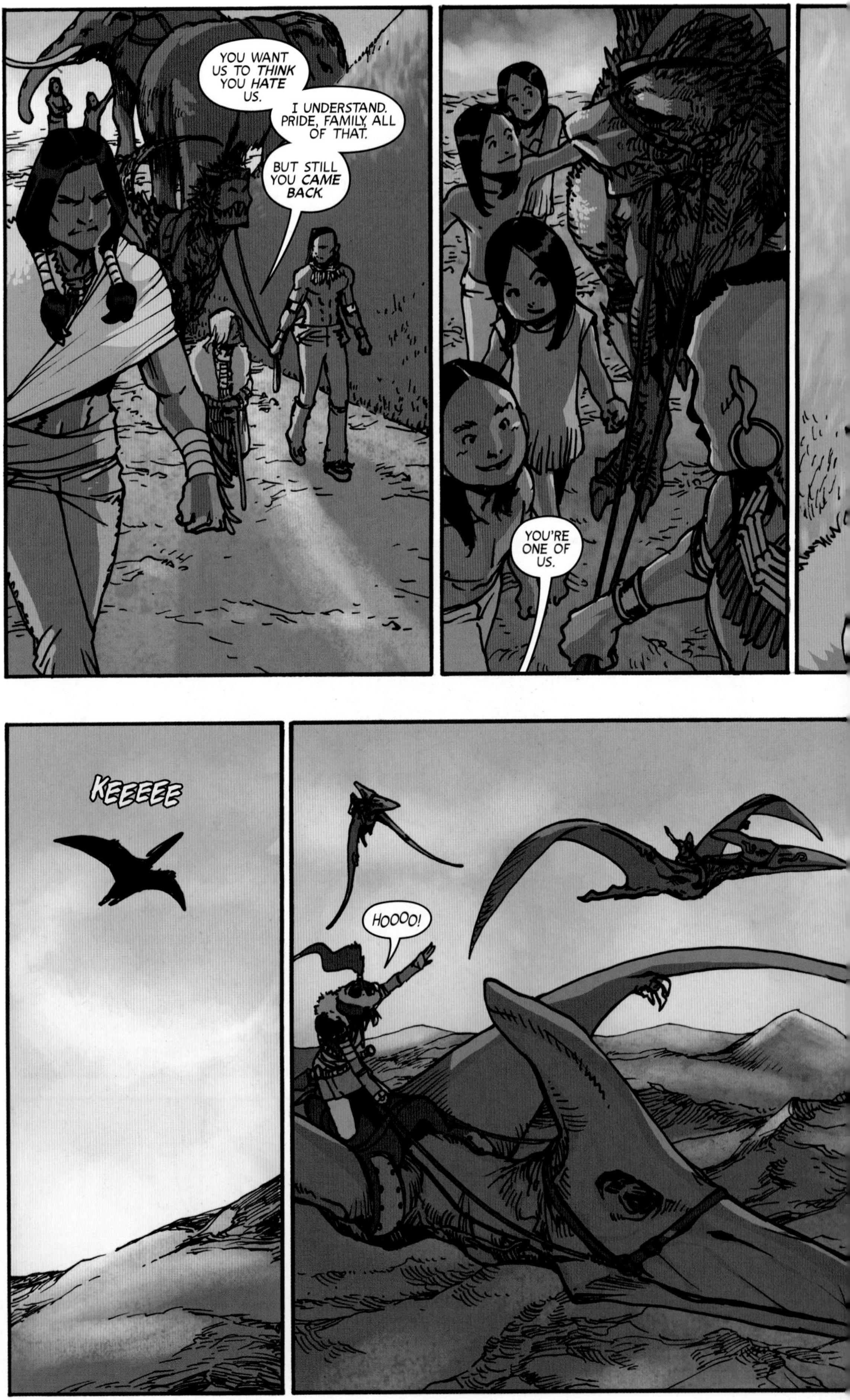
YOU WANT US TO THINK YOU HATE US.
I UNDERSTAND. PRIDE, FAMILY, ALL OF THAT.
BUT STILL YOU CAME BACK.
YOU'RE ONE OF US.
KEEEEE
HOOOO!

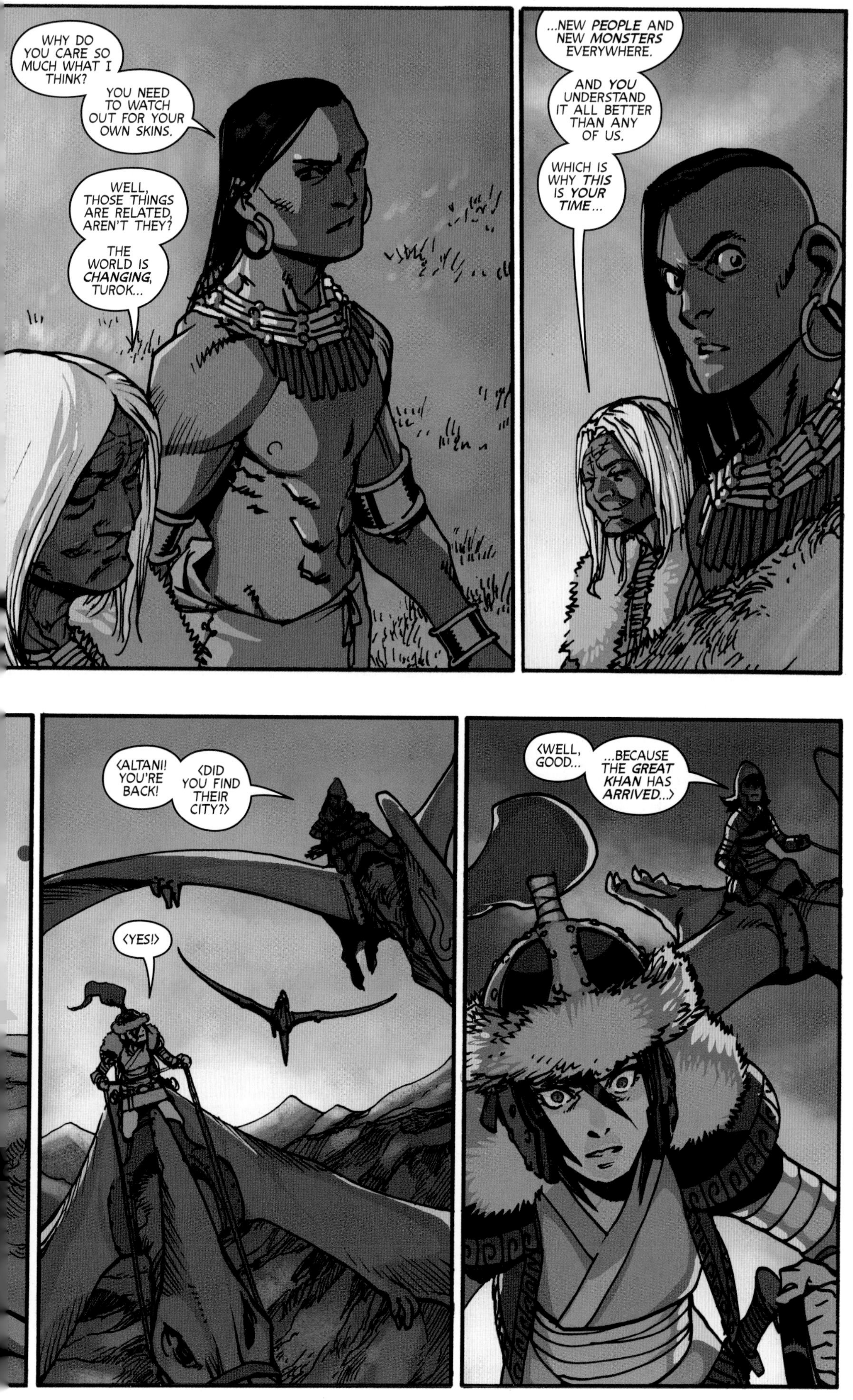
WHY DO YOU CARE SO MUCH WHAT I THINK?
YOU NEED TO WATCH OUT FOR YOUR OWN SKINS.
WELL, THOSE THINGS ARE RELATED, AREN'T THEY?
THE WORLD IS *CHANGING*, TUROK...
...NEW *PEOPLE* AND NEW *MONSTERS* EVERYWHERE.
AND *YOU* UNDERSTAND IT ALL BETTER THAN ANY OF US.
WHICH IS WHY *THIS* IS *YOUR TIME*...
‹ALTANI! YOU'RE BACK!
‹DID YOU FIND THEIR CITY?›
‹YES!›
‹WELL, GOOD...
...BECAUSE THE *GREAT KHAN* HAS *ARRIVED*...›

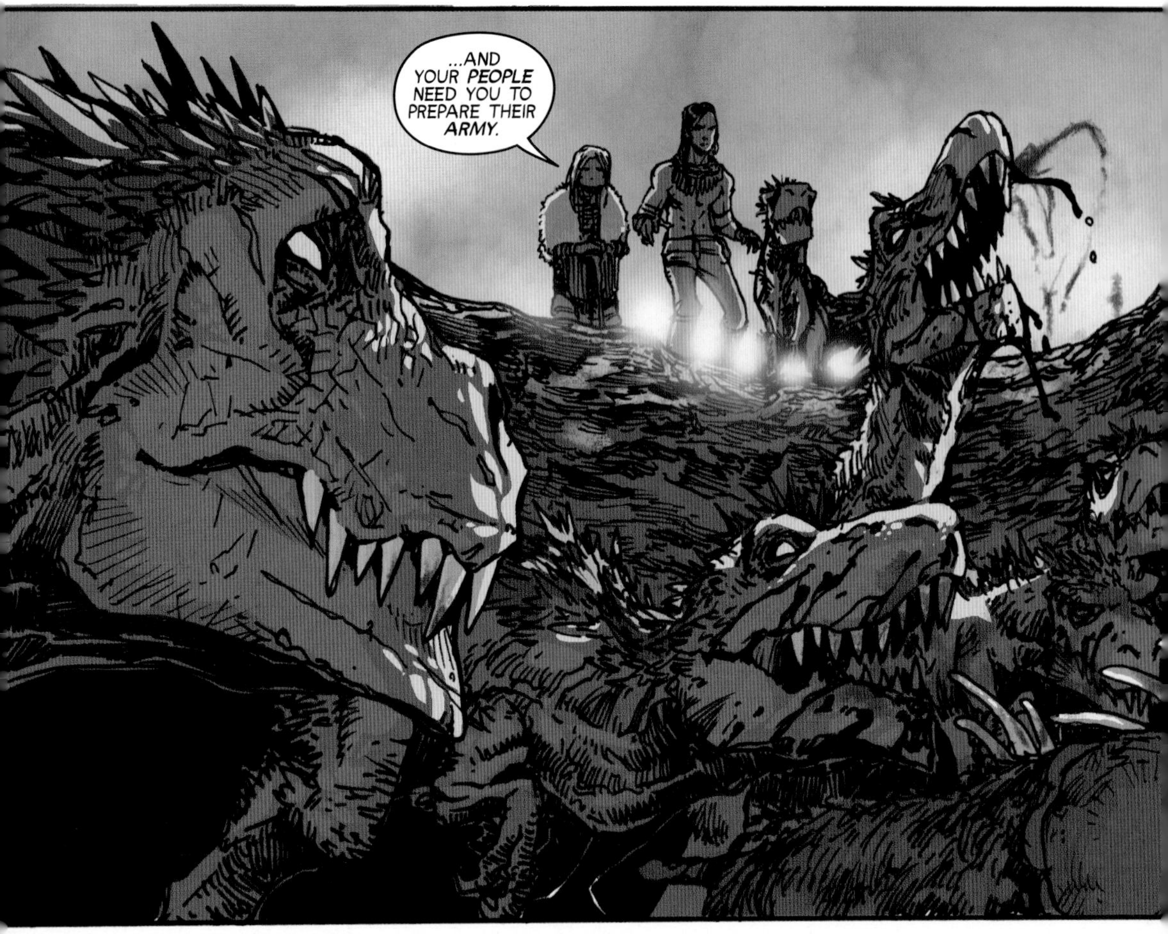
...AND YOUR *PEOPLE* NEED YOU TO PREPARE THEIR *ARMY*.

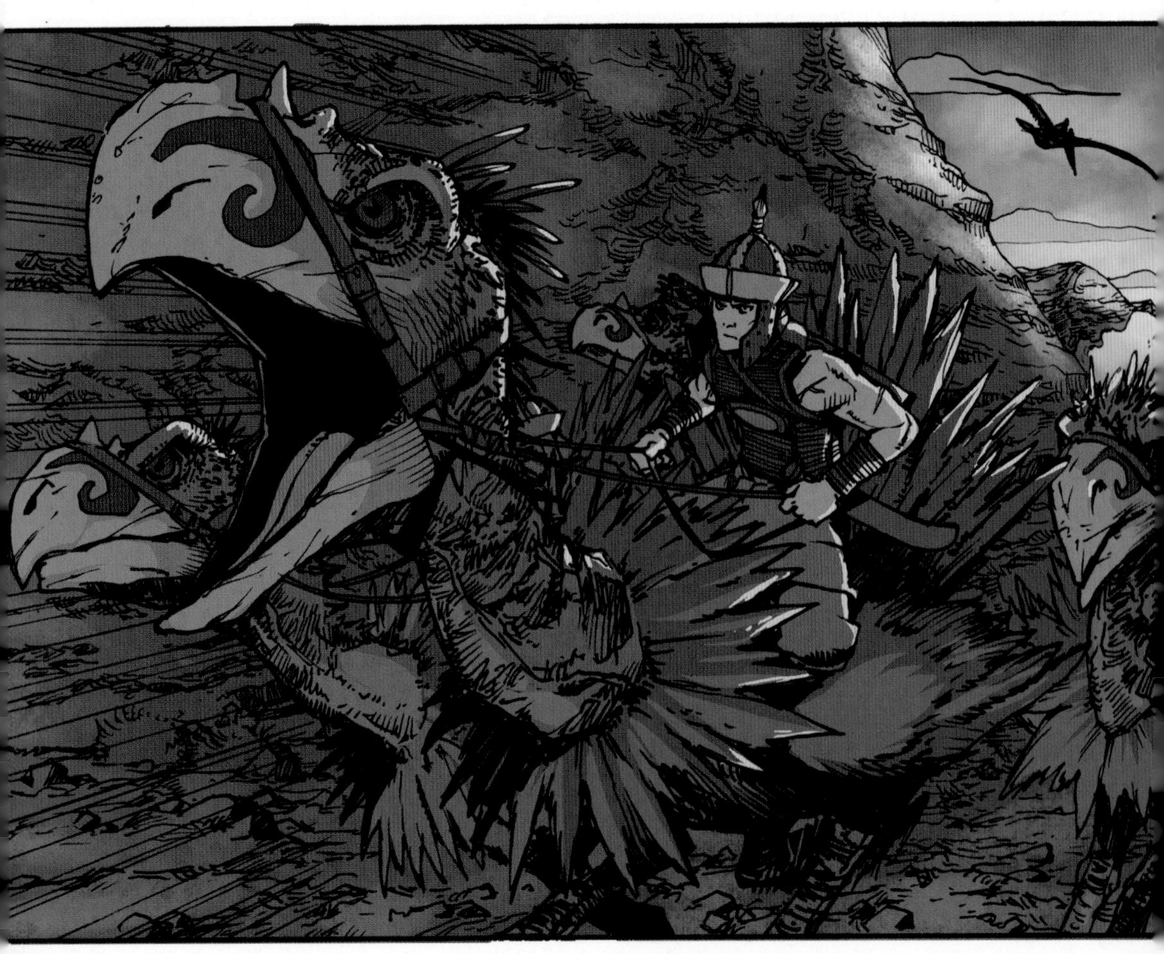

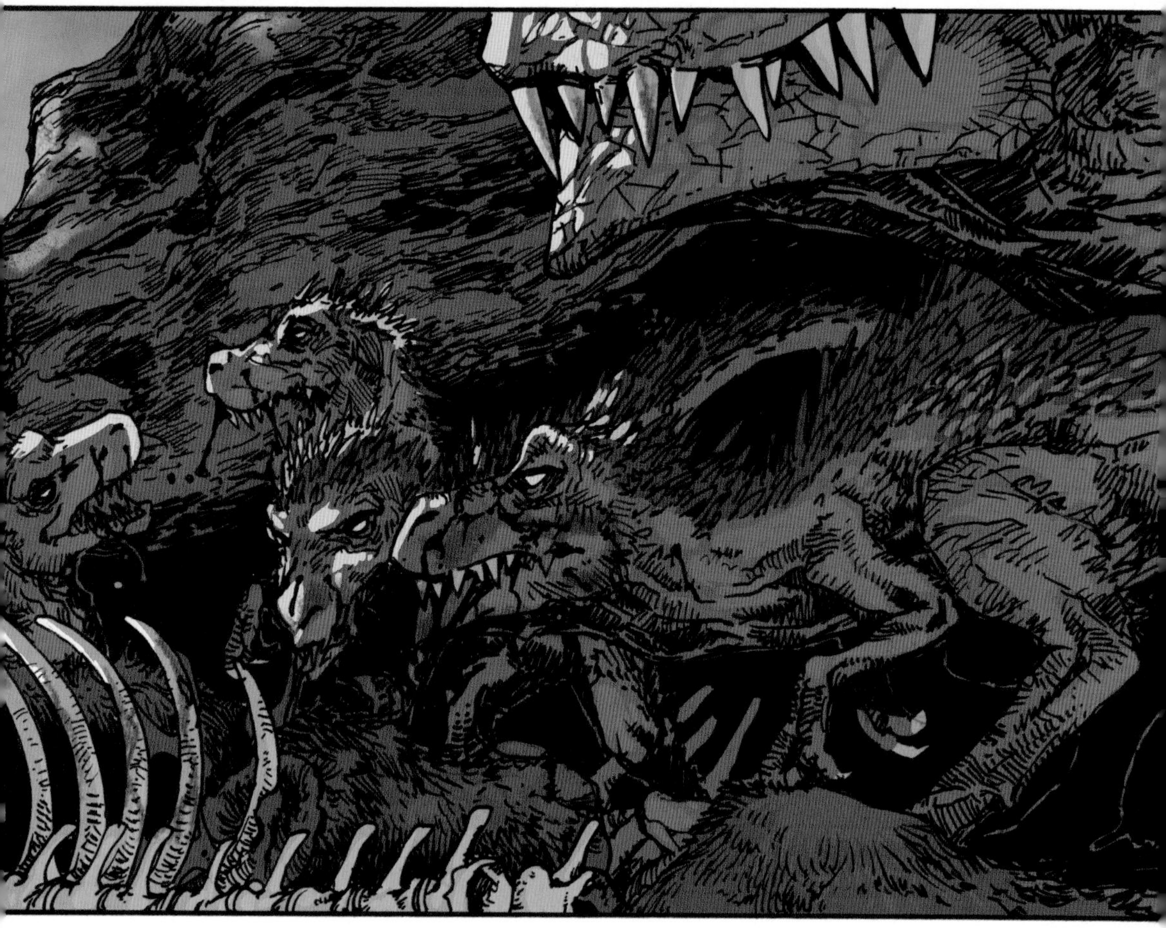

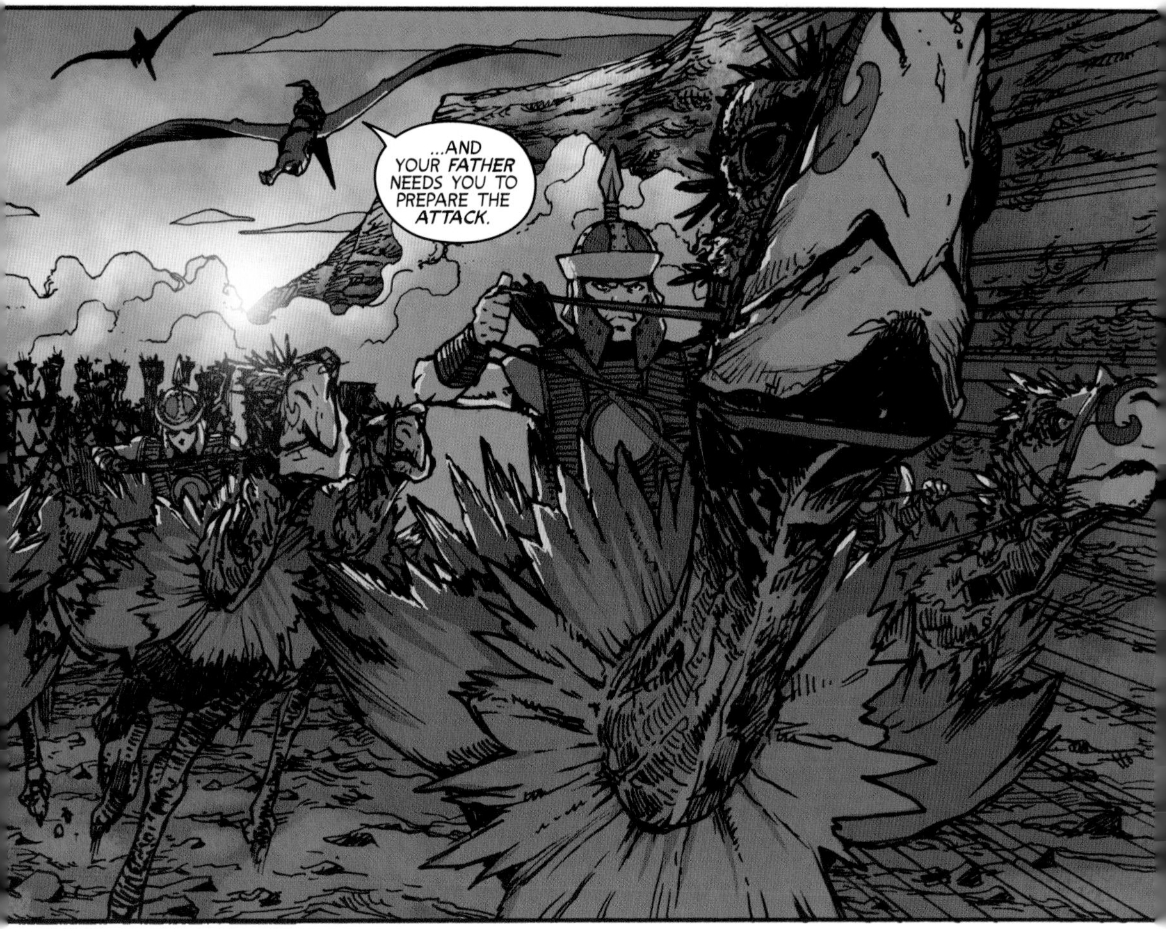
...AND YOUR FATHER NEEDS YOU TO PREPARE THE ATTACK.

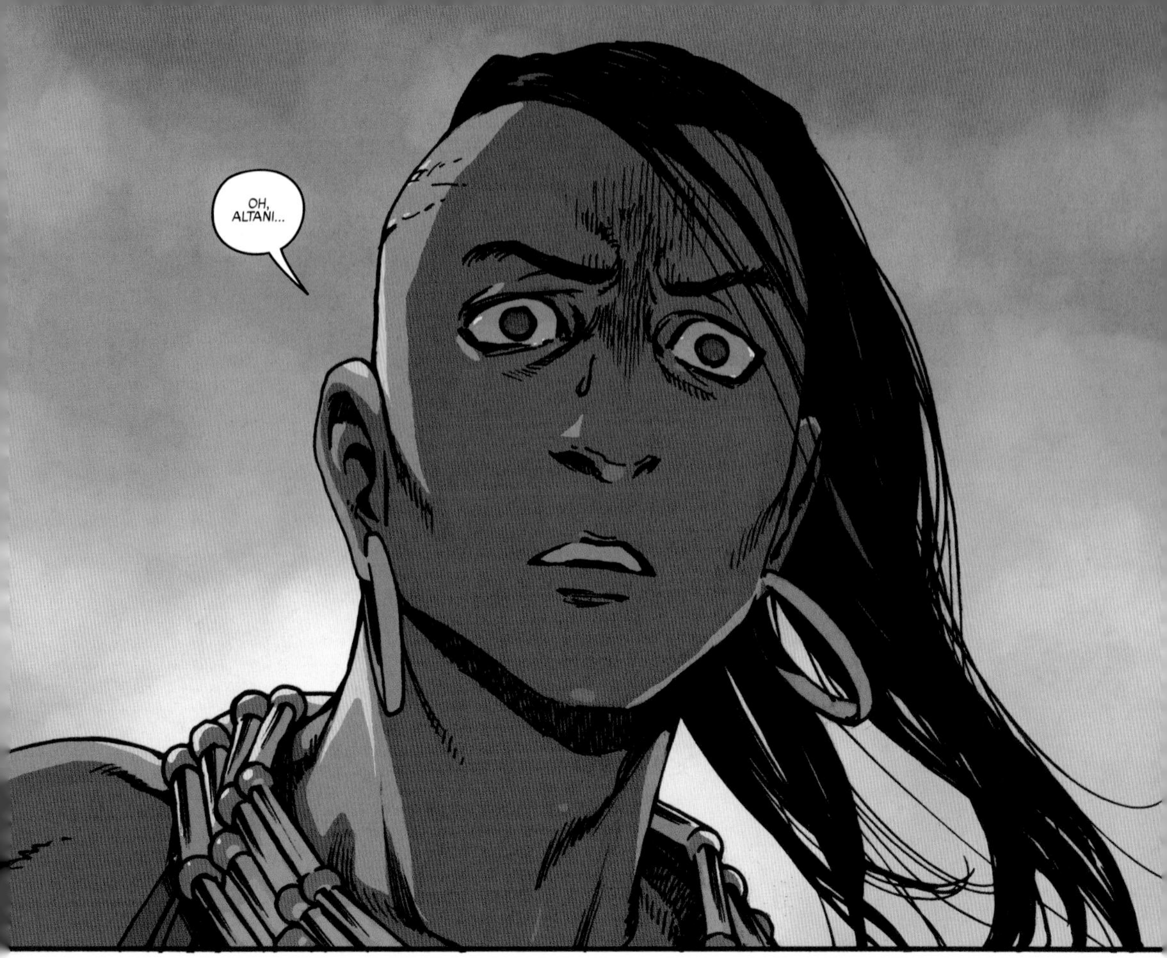
OH, ALTANI...
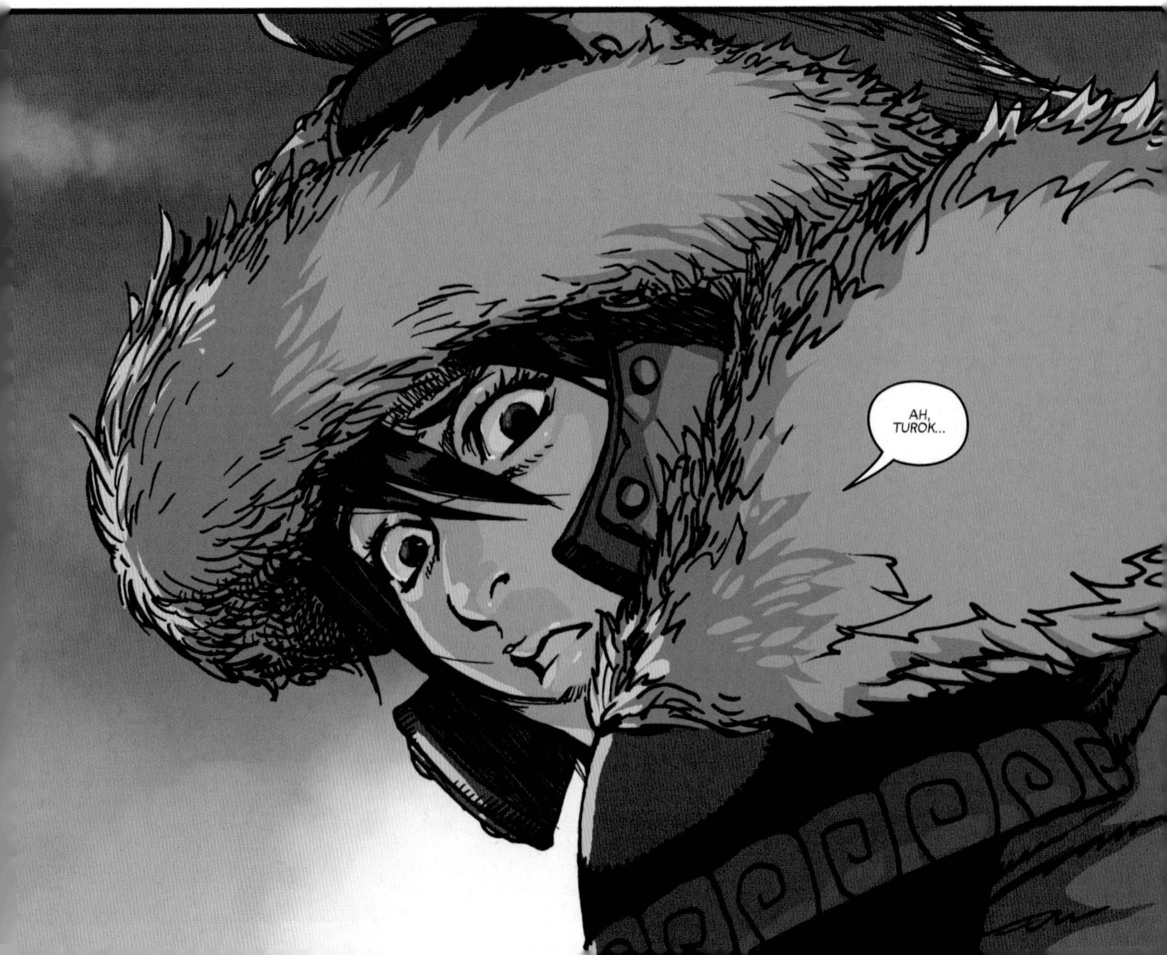
AH, TUROK...

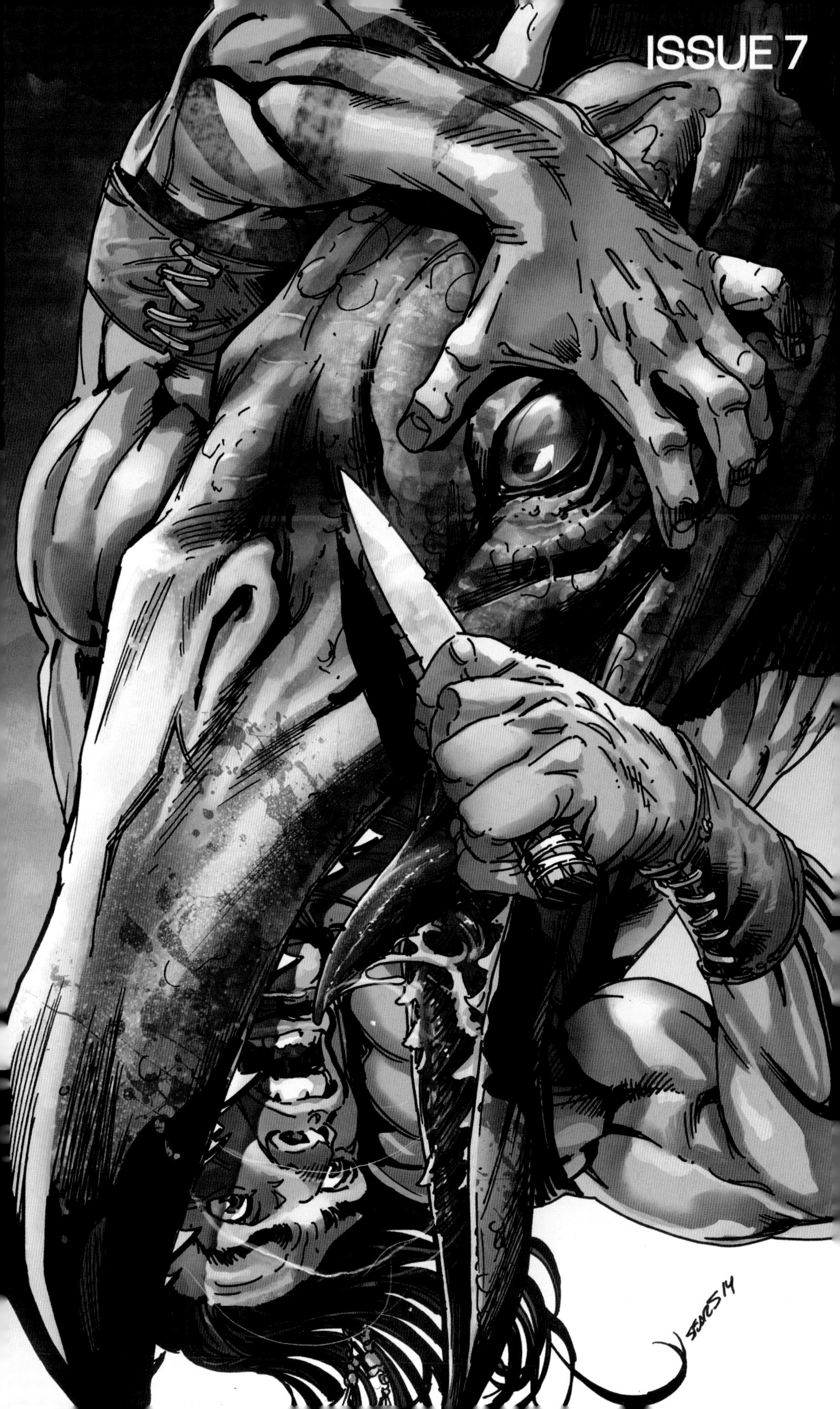
ISSUE 7

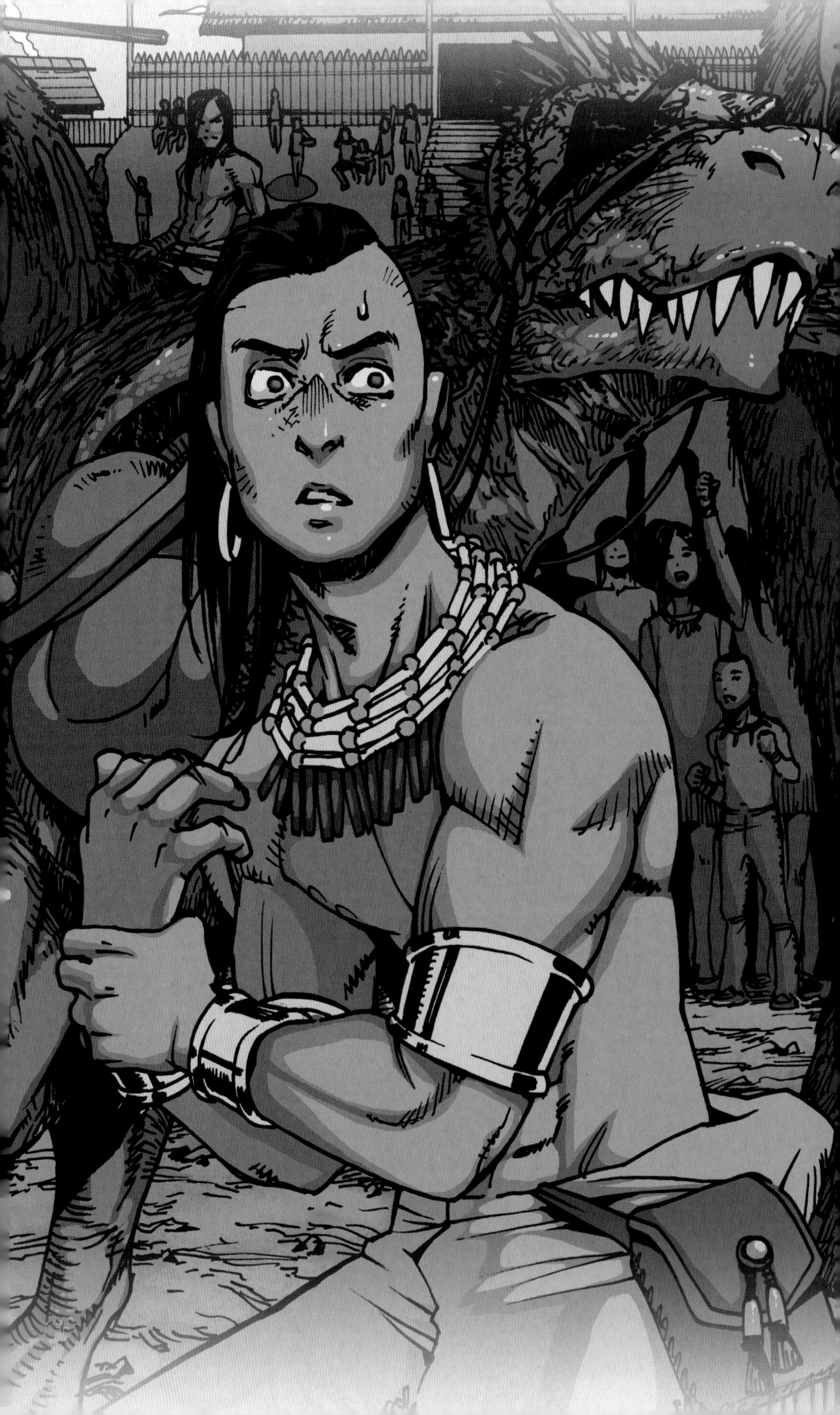

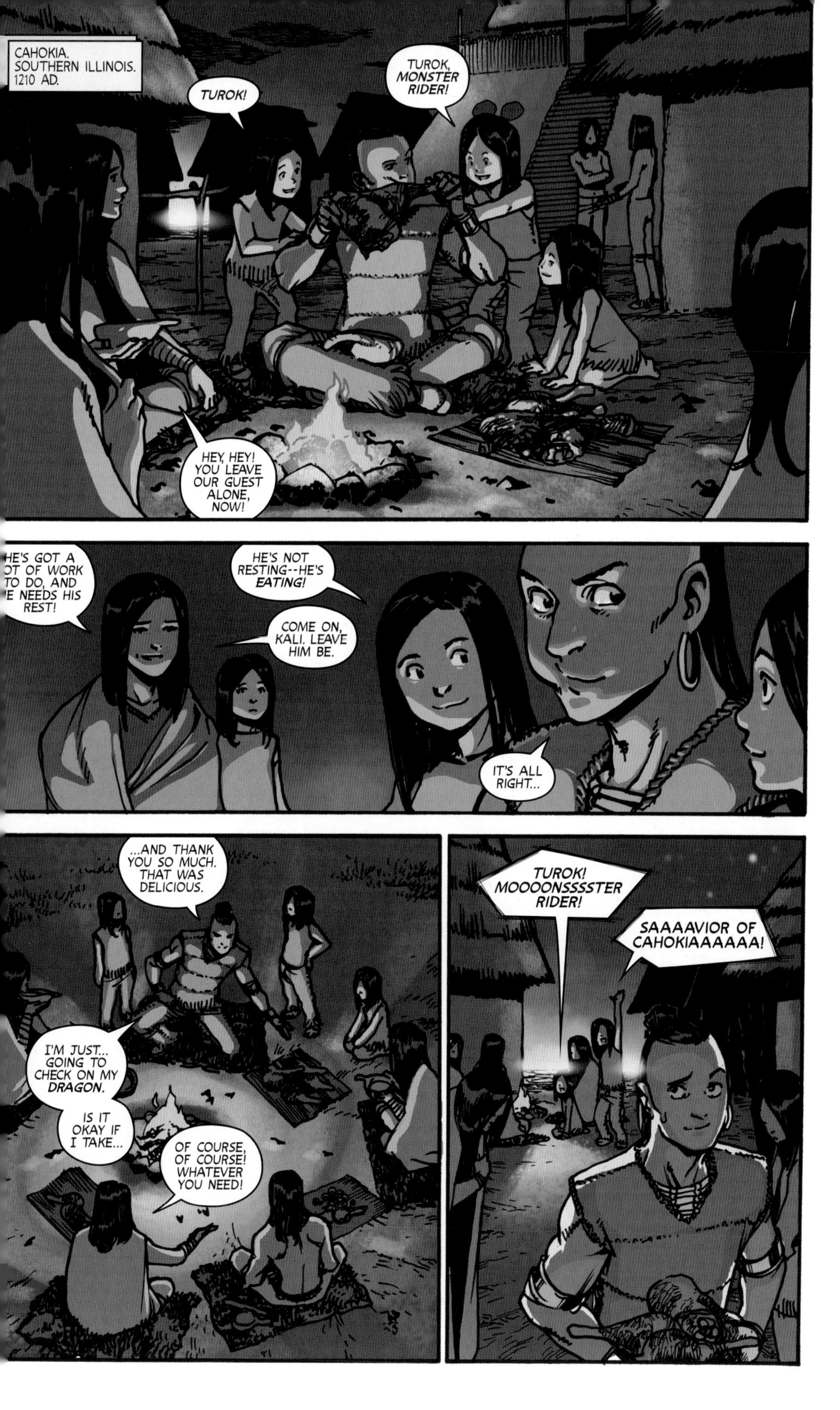
CAHOKIA.
SOUTHERN ILLINOIS.
1210 AD.
TUROK!
TUROK, MONSTER RIDER!
HEY, HEY! YOU LEAVE OUR GUEST ALONE, NOW!
HE'S GOT A OT OF WORK TO DO, AND E NEEDS HIS REST!
HE'S NOT RESTING--HE'S EATING!
COME ON, KALI. LEAVE HIM BE.
IT'S ALL RIGHT...
...AND THANK YOU SO MUCH. THAT WAS DELICIOUS.
I'M JUST... GOING TO CHECK ON MY DRAGON.
IS IT OKAY IF I TAKE...
OF COURSE, OF COURSE! WHATEVER YOU NEED!
TUROK! MOOOONSSSSTER RIDER!
SAAAAVIOR OF CAHOKIAAAAAA!

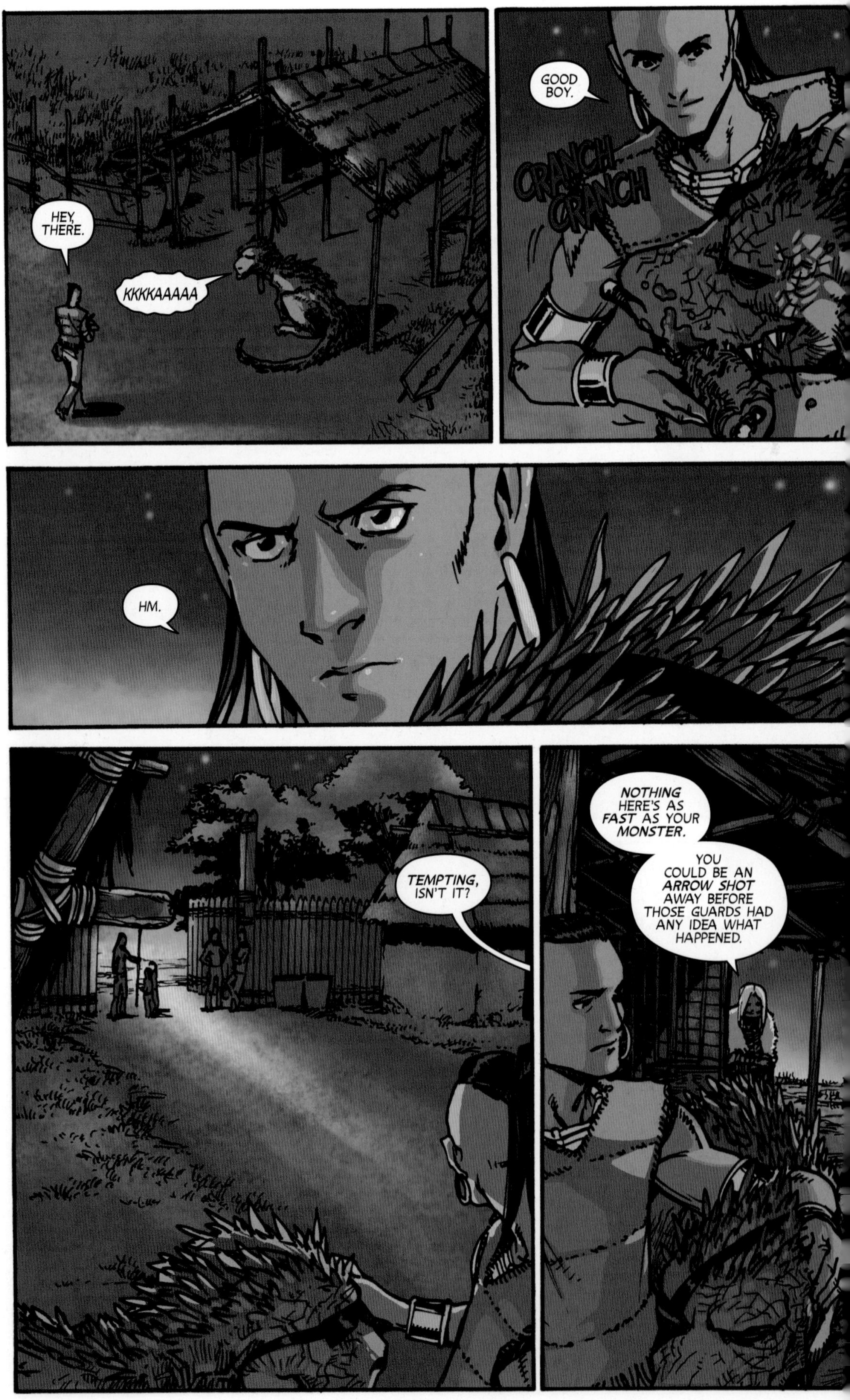
HEY, THERE.
KKKKAAAAA
GOOD BOY.
CRANCH CRANCH
HM.
TEMPTING, ISN'T IT?
NOTHING HERE'S AS FAST AS YOUR MONSTER.
YOU COULD BE AN ARROW SHOT AWAY BEFORE THOSE GUARDS HAD ANY IDEA WHAT HAPPENED.

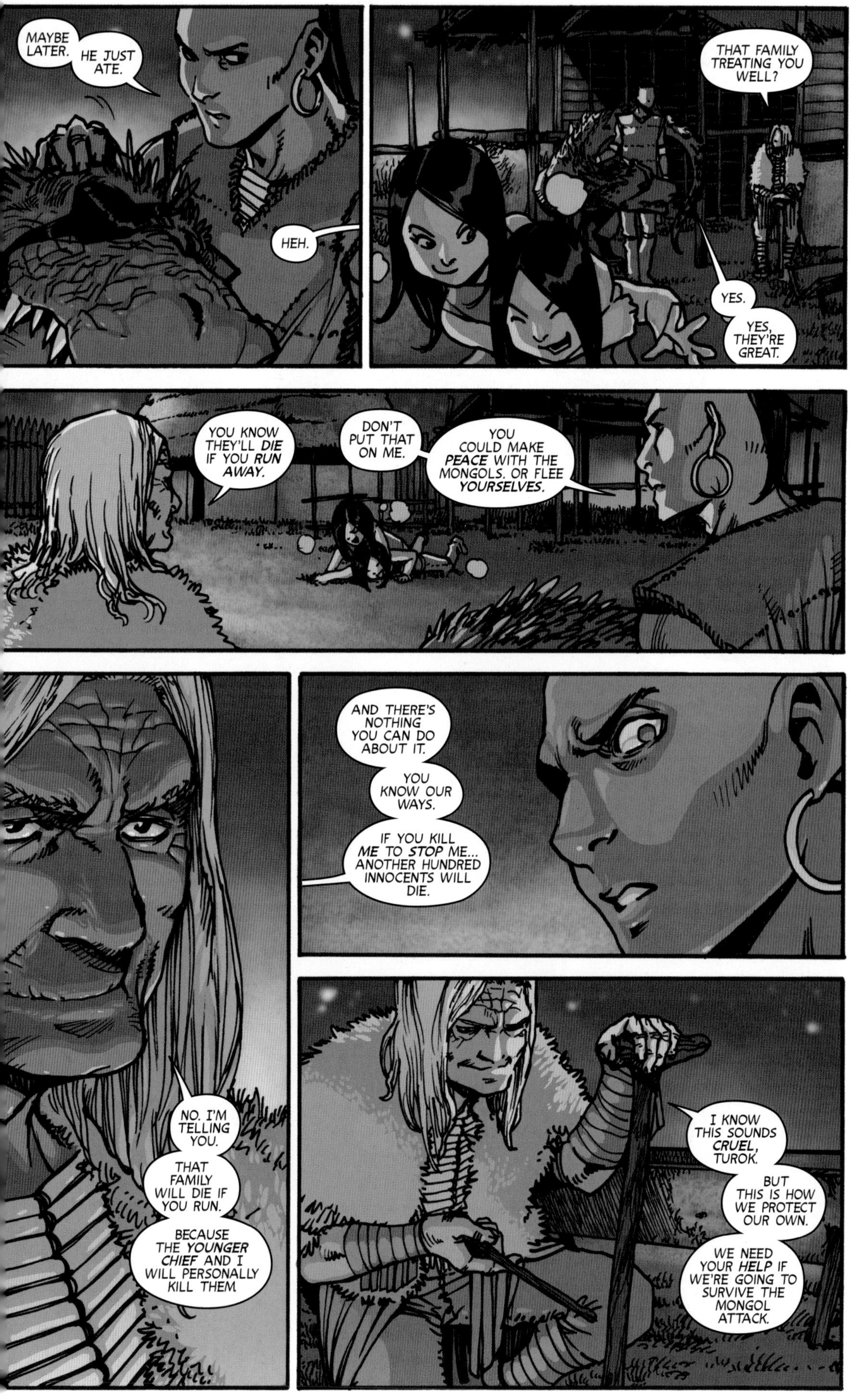
MAYBE LATER.
HE JUST ATE.
HEH.
THAT FAMILY TREATING YOU WELL?
YES.
YES, THEY'RE GREAT.
YOU KNOW THEY'LL DIE IF YOU RUN AWAY.
DON'T PUT THAT ON ME.
YOU COULD MAKE PEACE WITH THE MONGOLS. OR FLEE YOURSELVES.
NO. I'M TELLING YOU.
THAT FAMILY WILL DIE IF YOU RUN.
BECAUSE THE YOUNGER CHIEF AND I WILL PERSONALLY KILL THEM
AND THERE'S NOTHING YOU CAN DO ABOUT IT.
YOU KNOW OUR WAYS.
IF YOU KILL ME TO STOP ME... ANOTHER HUNDRED INNOCENTS WILL DIE.
I KNOW THIS SOUNDS CRUEL, TUROK.
BUT THIS IS HOW WE PROTECT OUR OWN.
WE NEED YOUR HELP IF WE'RE GOING TO SURVIVE THE MONGOL ATTACK.

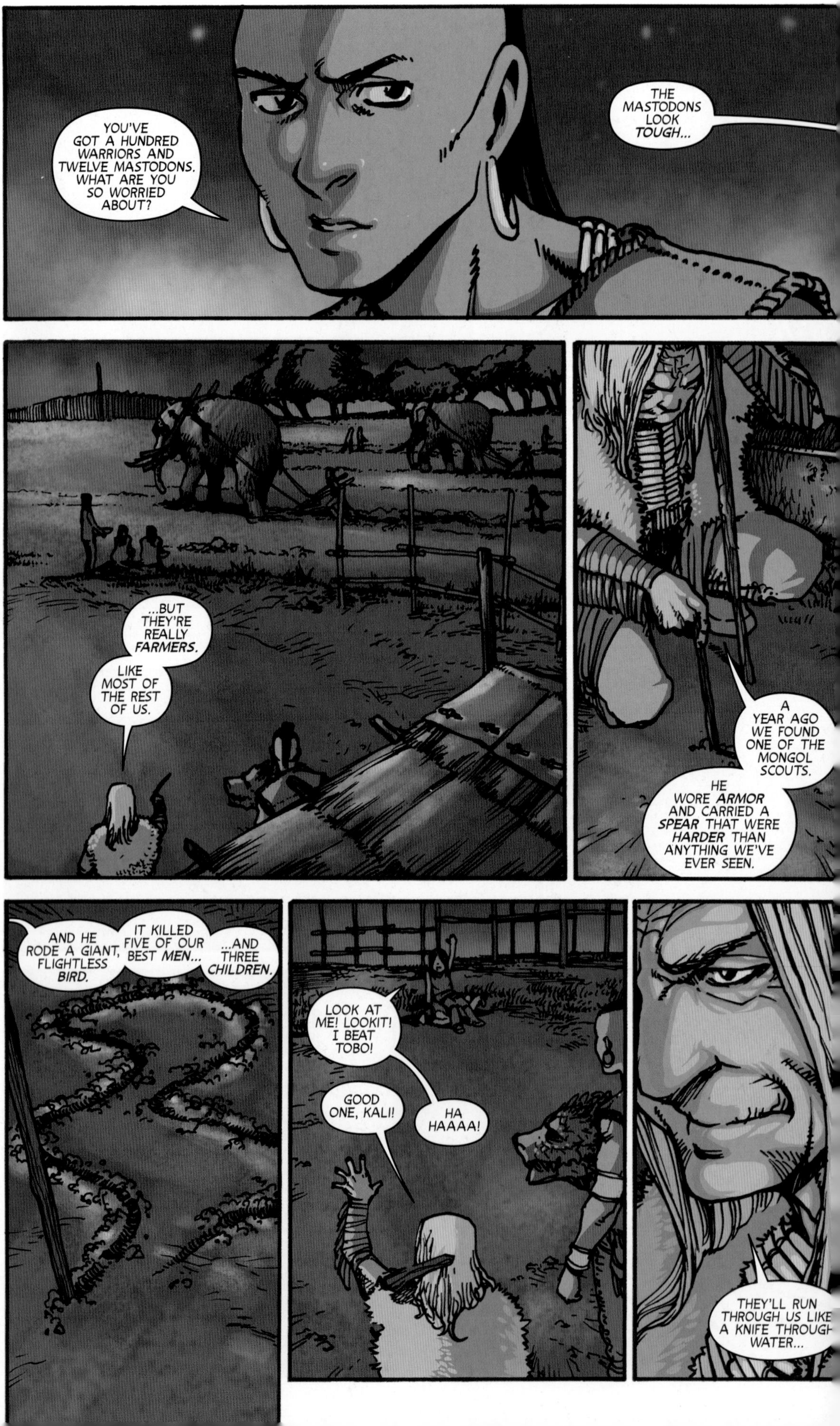
YOU'VE GOT A HUNDRED WARRIORS AND TWELVE MASTODONS. WHAT ARE YOU SO WORRIED ABOUT?
THE MASTODONS LOOK TOUGH...
...BUT THEY'RE REALLY FARMERS.
LIKE MOST OF THE REST OF US.
A YEAR AGO WE FOUND ONE OF THE MONGOL SCOUTS.
HE WORE ARMOR AND CARRIED A SPEAR THAT WERE HARDER THAN ANYTHING WE'VE EVER SEEN.
AND HE RODE A GIANT, FLIGHTLESS BIRD.
IT KILLED FIVE OF OUR BEST MEN...
...AND THREE CHILDREN.
LOOK AT ME! LOOKIT! I BEAT TOBO!
HA HAAAA!
GOOD ONE, KALI!
THEY'LL RUN THROUGH US LIKE A KNIFE THROUGH WATER...

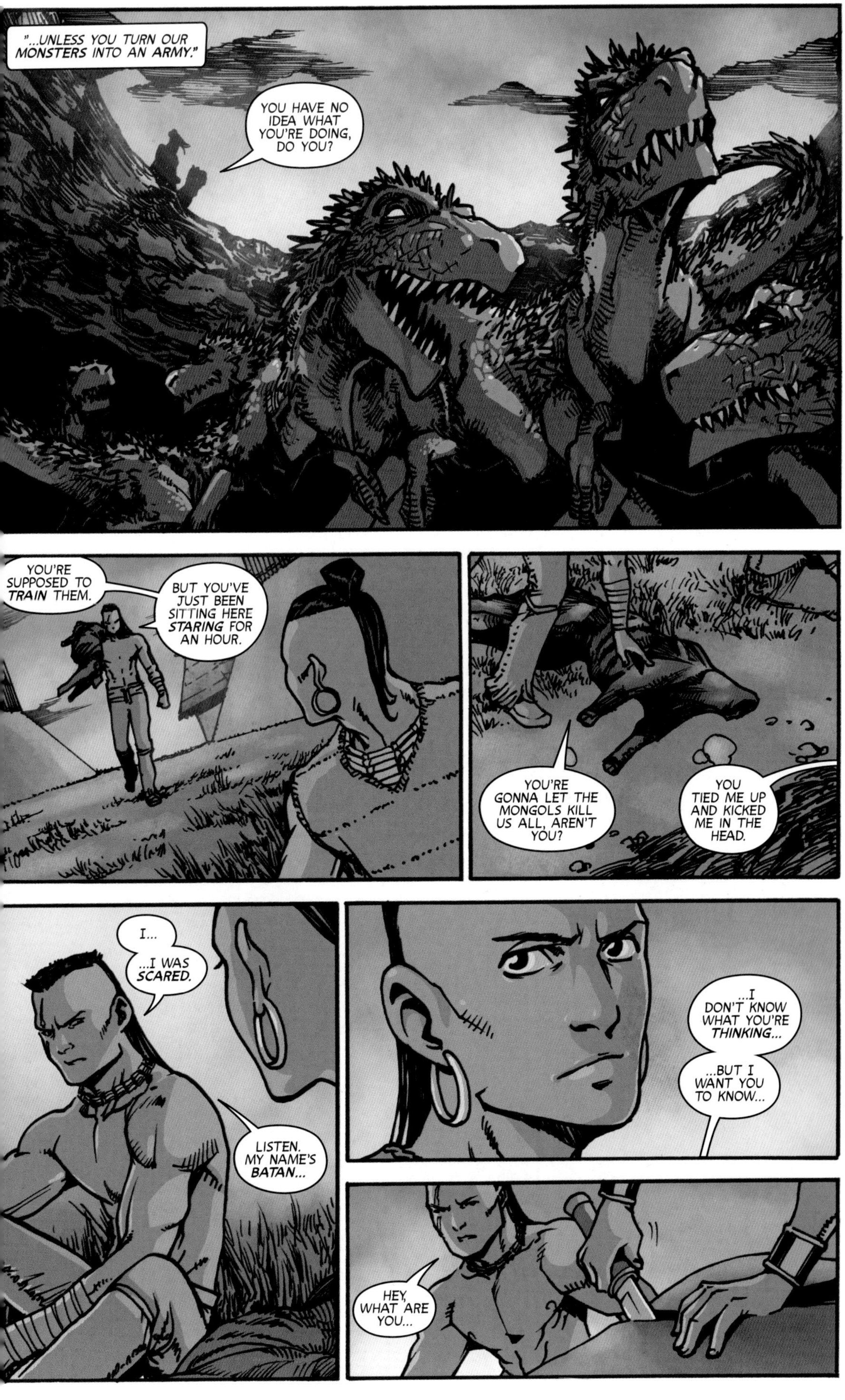

"...UNLESS YOU TURN OUR MONSTERS INTO AN ARMY."
YOU HAVE NO IDEA WHAT YOU'RE DOING, DO YOU?
YOU'RE SUPPOSED TO TRAIN THEM.
BUT YOU'VE JUST BEEN SITTING HERE STARING FOR AN HOUR.
YOU'RE GONNA LET THE MONGOLS KILL US ALL, AREN'T YOU?
YOU TIED ME UP AND KICKED ME IN THE HEAD.
I...
...I WAS SCARED.
LISTEN. MY NAME'S BATAN...
...I DON'T KNOW WHAT YOU'RE THINKING...
...BUT I WANT YOU TO KNOW...
HEY, WHAT ARE YOU...

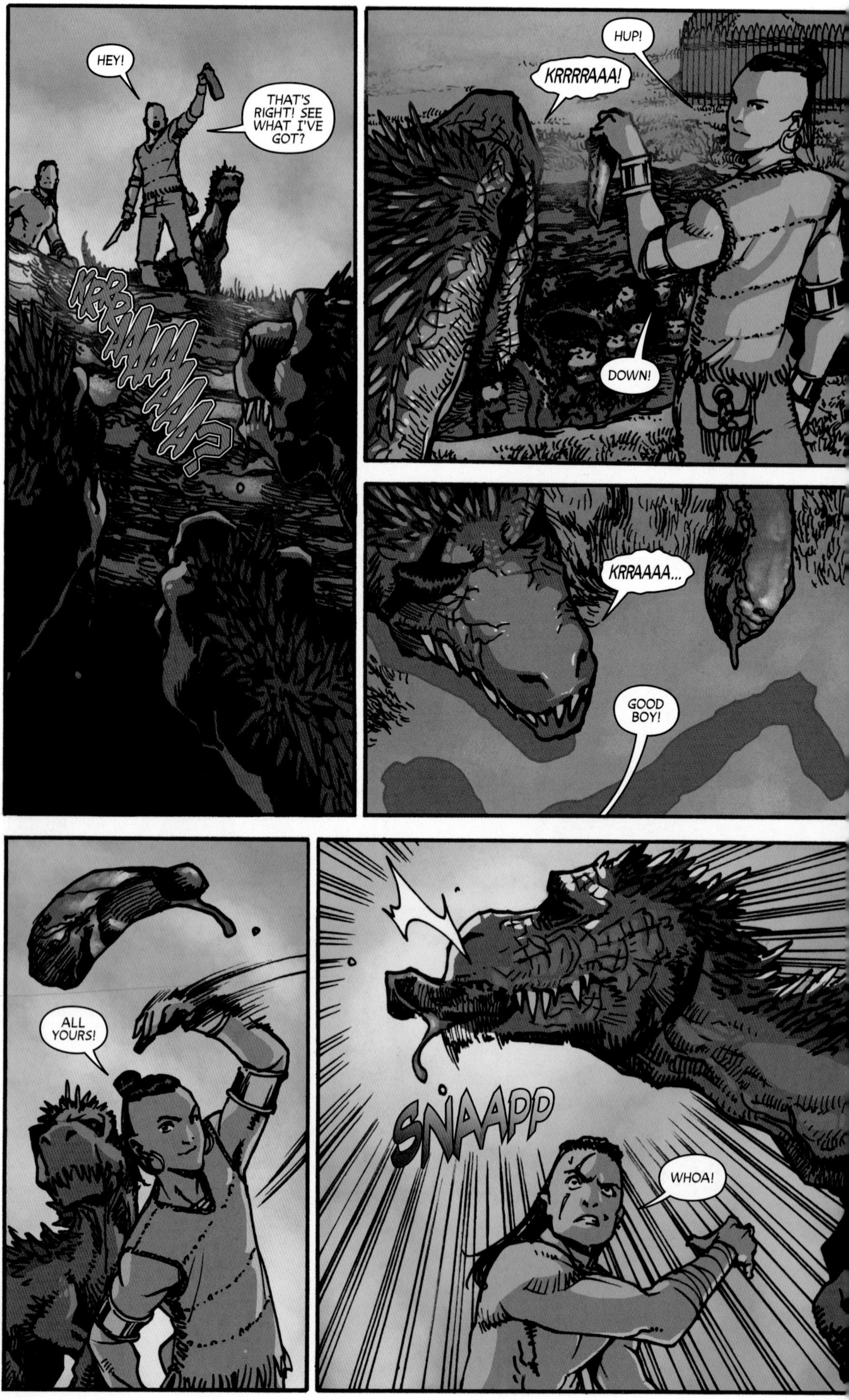
HEY!
THAT'S RIGHT! SEE WHAT I'VE GOT?
KRRAAAAAA?
HUP!
KRRRRAAA!
DOWN!
KRRAAAA...
GOOD BOY!
ALL YOURS!
SNAAPP
WHOA!

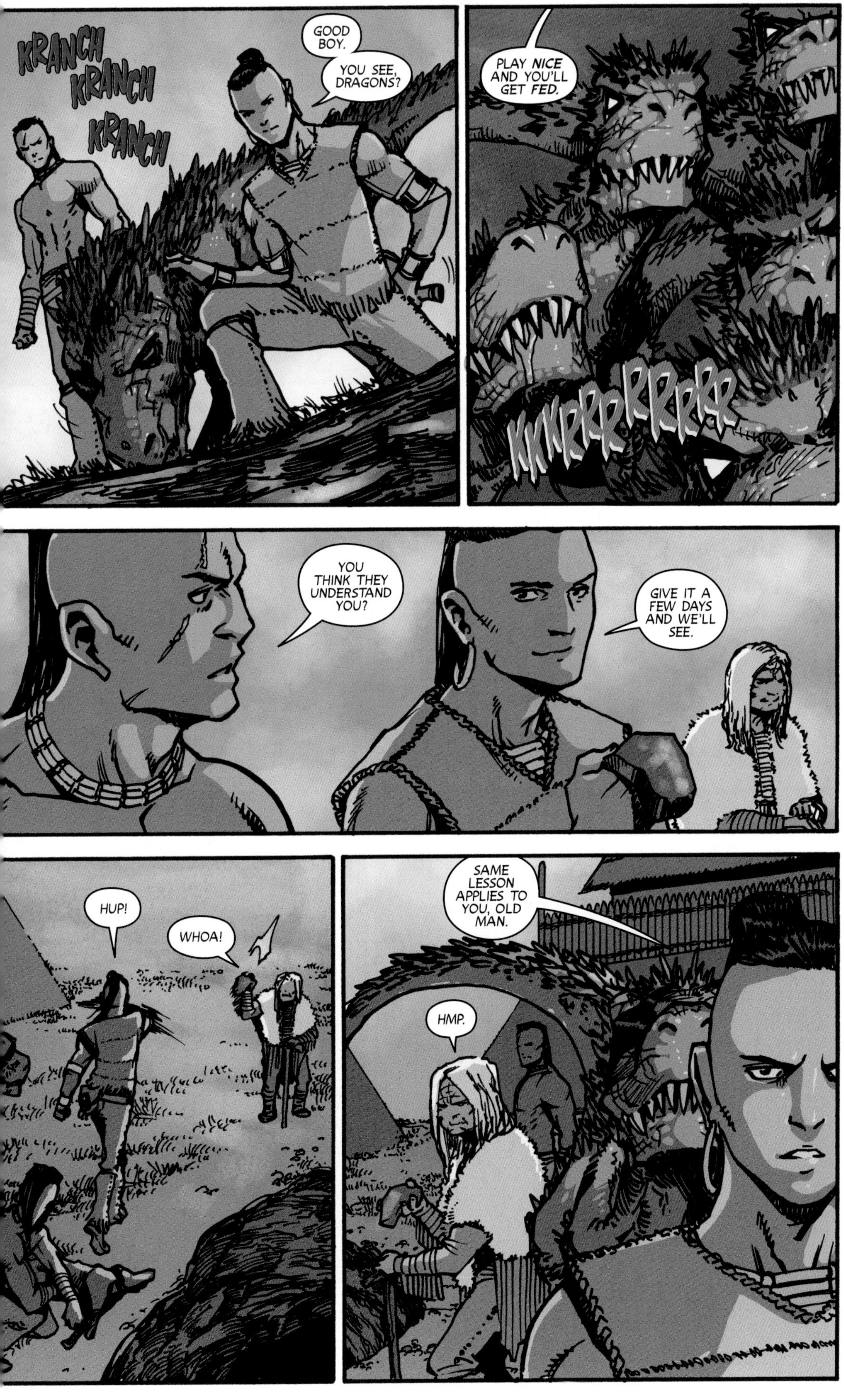
KRANCH
KRANCH
KRANCH
GOOD BOY.
YOU SEE, DRAGONS?
PLAY NICE AND YOU'LL GET FED.
KKKRRRRRRRRR
YOU THINK THEY UNDERSTAND YOU?
GIVE IT A FEW DAYS AND WE'LL SEE.
HUP!
WHOA!
SAME LESSON APPLIES TO YOU, OLD MAN.
HMP.

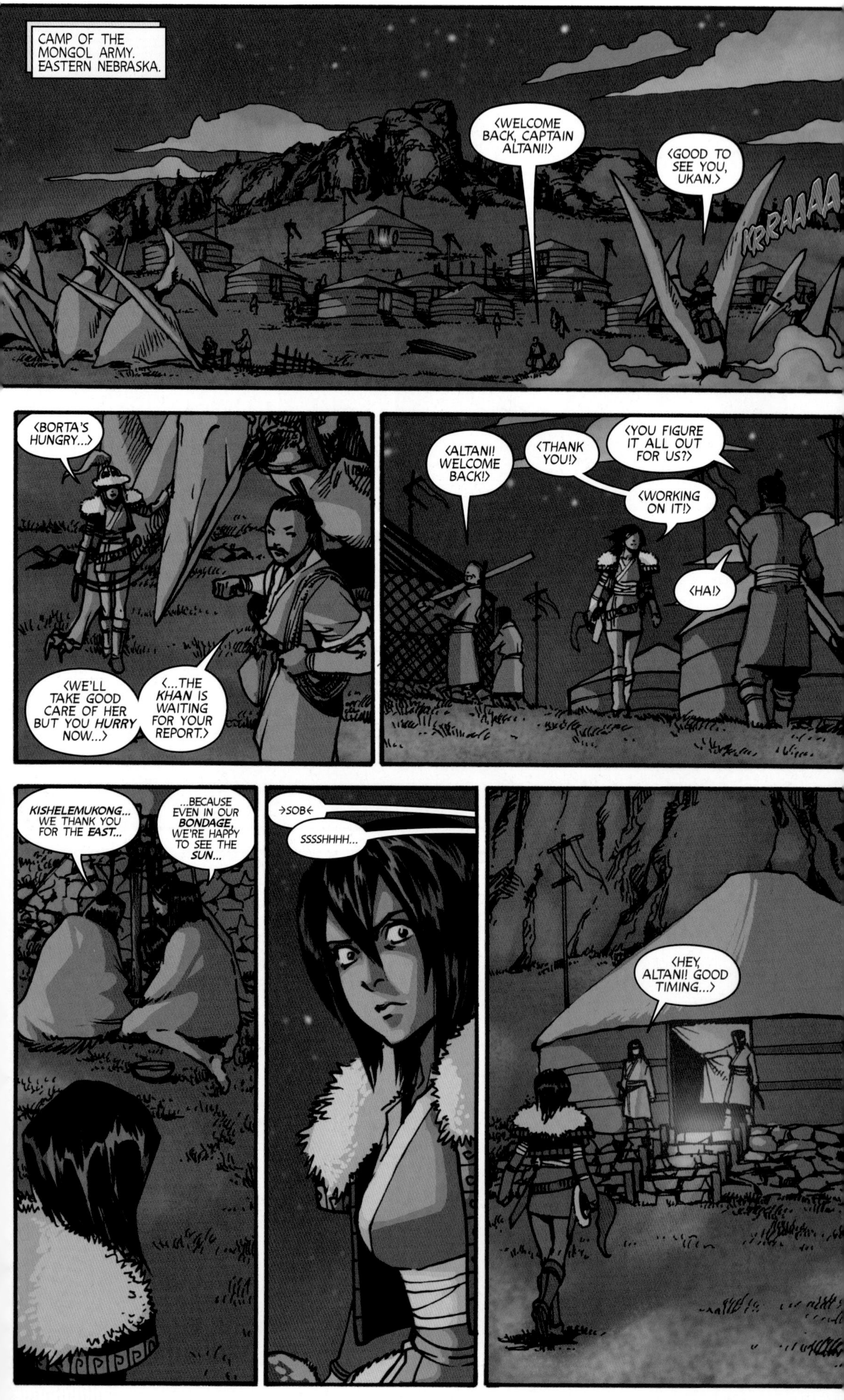
CAMP OF THE MONGOL ARMY. EASTERN NEBRASKA.
<WELCOME BACK, CAPTAIN ALTANI!>
<GOOD TO SEE YOU, UKAN.>
KRRAAAA
<BORTA'S HUNGRY...>
<WE'LL TAKE GOOD CARE OF HER BUT YOU *HURRY* NOW...>
<...THE *KHAN* IS WAITING FOR YOUR REPORT.>
<ALTANI! WELCOME BACK!>
<THANK YOU!>
<YOU FIGURE IT ALL OUT FOR US?>
<WORKING ON IT!>
<HA!>
KISHELEMUKONG... WE THANK YOU FOR THE ***EAST...***
...BECAUSE EVEN IN OUR ***BONDAGE,*** WE'RE HAPPY TO SEE THE ***SUN...***
→SOB←
SSSSHHHH...
<HEY, ALTANI! GOOD TIMING...>

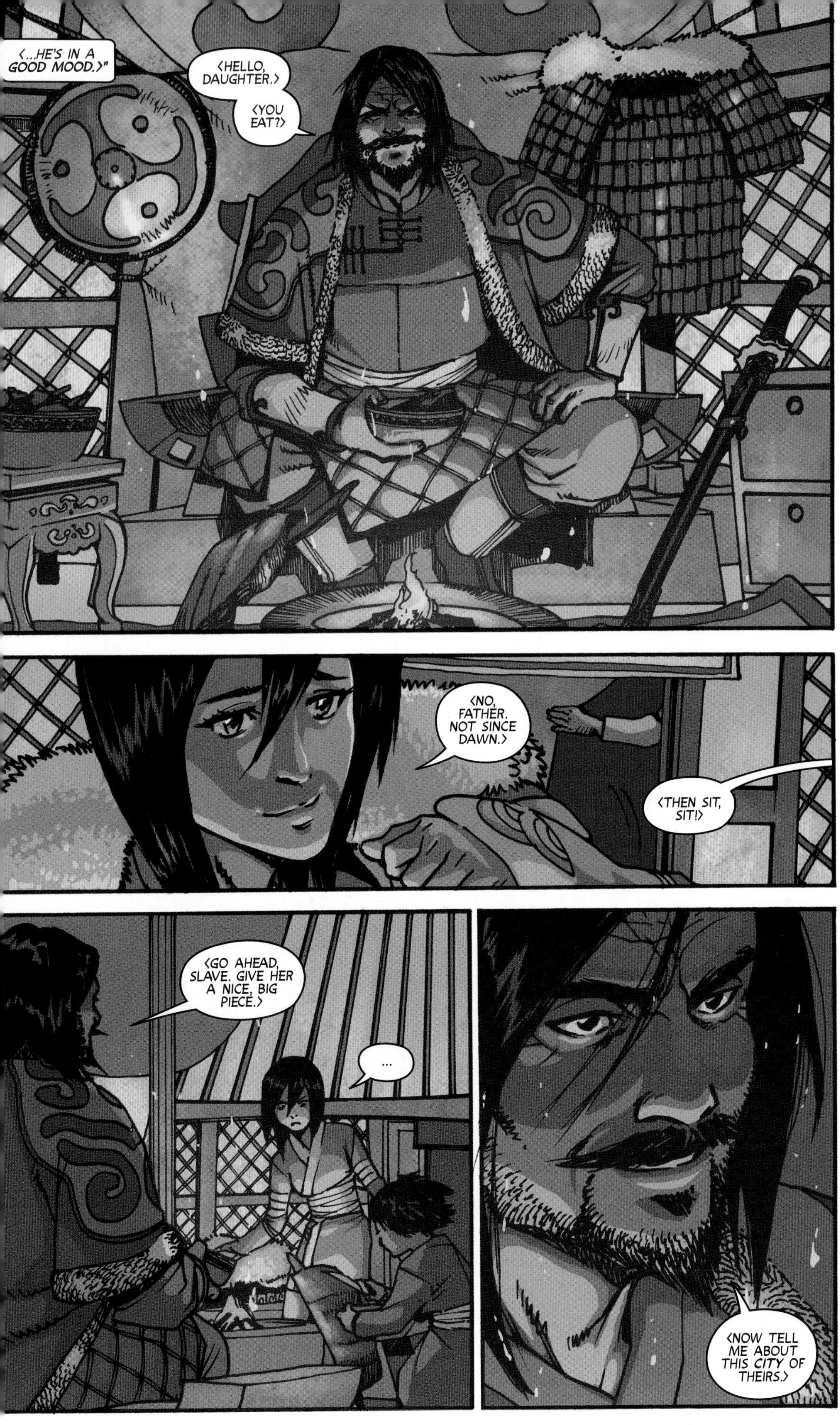
‹...HE'S IN A GOOD MOOD.›"
‹HELLO, DAUGHTER.›
‹YOU EAT?›
‹NO, FATHER. NOT SINCE DAWN.›
‹THEN SIT, SIT!›
‹GO AHEAD, SLAVE. GIVE HER A NICE, BIG PIECE.›
...
‹NOW TELL ME ABOUT THIS *CITY* OF THEIRS.›

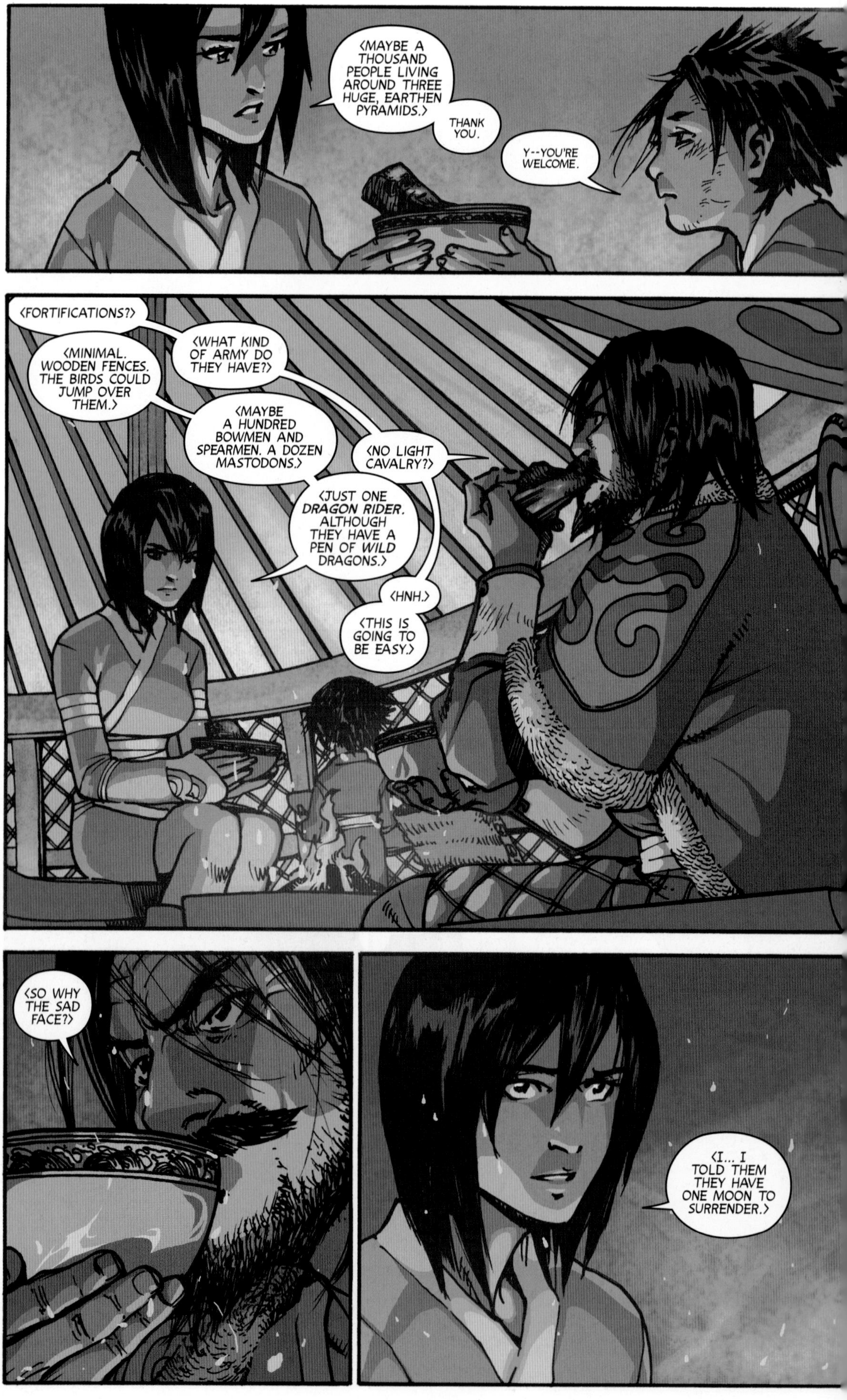

<MAYBE A THOUSAND PEOPLE LIVING AROUND THREE HUGE, EARTHEN PYRAMIDS.>
THANK YOU.
Y--YOU'RE WELCOME.
<FORTIFICATIONS?>
<MINIMAL. WOODEN FENCES. THE BIRDS COULD JUMP OVER THEM.>
<WHAT KIND OF ARMY DO THEY HAVE?>
<MAYBE A HUNDRED BOWMEN AND SPEARMEN. A DOZEN MASTODONS.>
<NO LIGHT CAVALRY?>
<JUST ONE *DRAGON RIDER*. ALTHOUGH THEY HAVE A PEN OF *WILD* DRAGONS.>
<HNH.>
<THIS IS GOING TO BE EASY.>
<SO WHY THE SAD FACE?>
<I... I TOLD THEM THEY HAVE ONE MOON TO SURRENDER.>

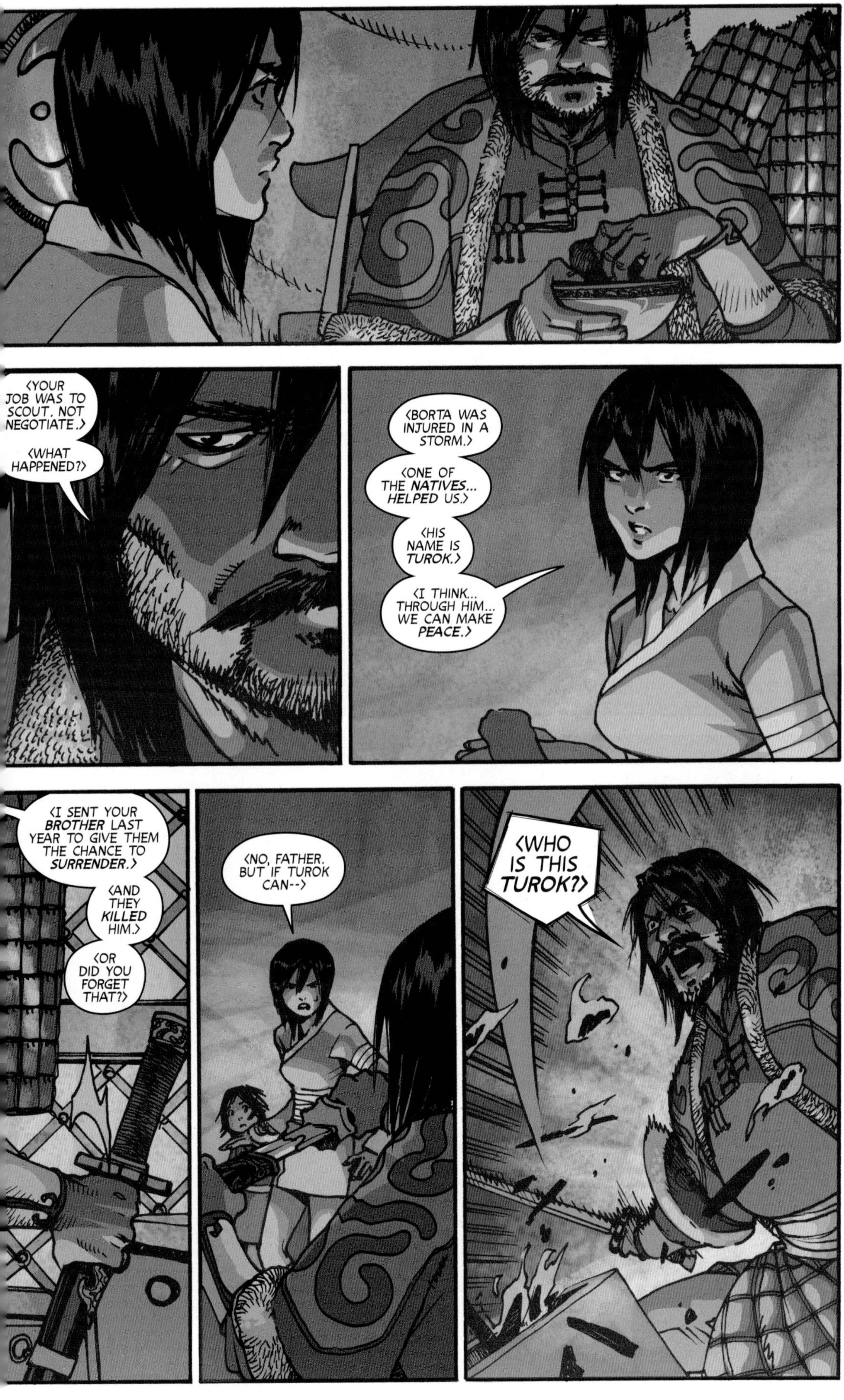
<YOUR JOB WAS TO SCOUT, NOT NEGOTIATE.>
<WHAT HAPPENED?>
<BORTA WAS INJURED IN A STORM.>
<ONE OF THE *NATIVES*... *HELPED* US.>
<HIS NAME IS *TUROK.*>
<I THINK... THROUGH HIM... WE CAN MAKE *PEACE.*>
<I SENT YOUR *BROTHER* LAST YEAR TO GIVE THEM THE CHANCE TO *SURRENDER.*>
<AND THEY *KILLED* HIM.>
<OR DID YOU FORGET THAT?>
<NO, FATHER. BUT IF TUROK CAN-->
<WHO IS THIS *TUROK?*>

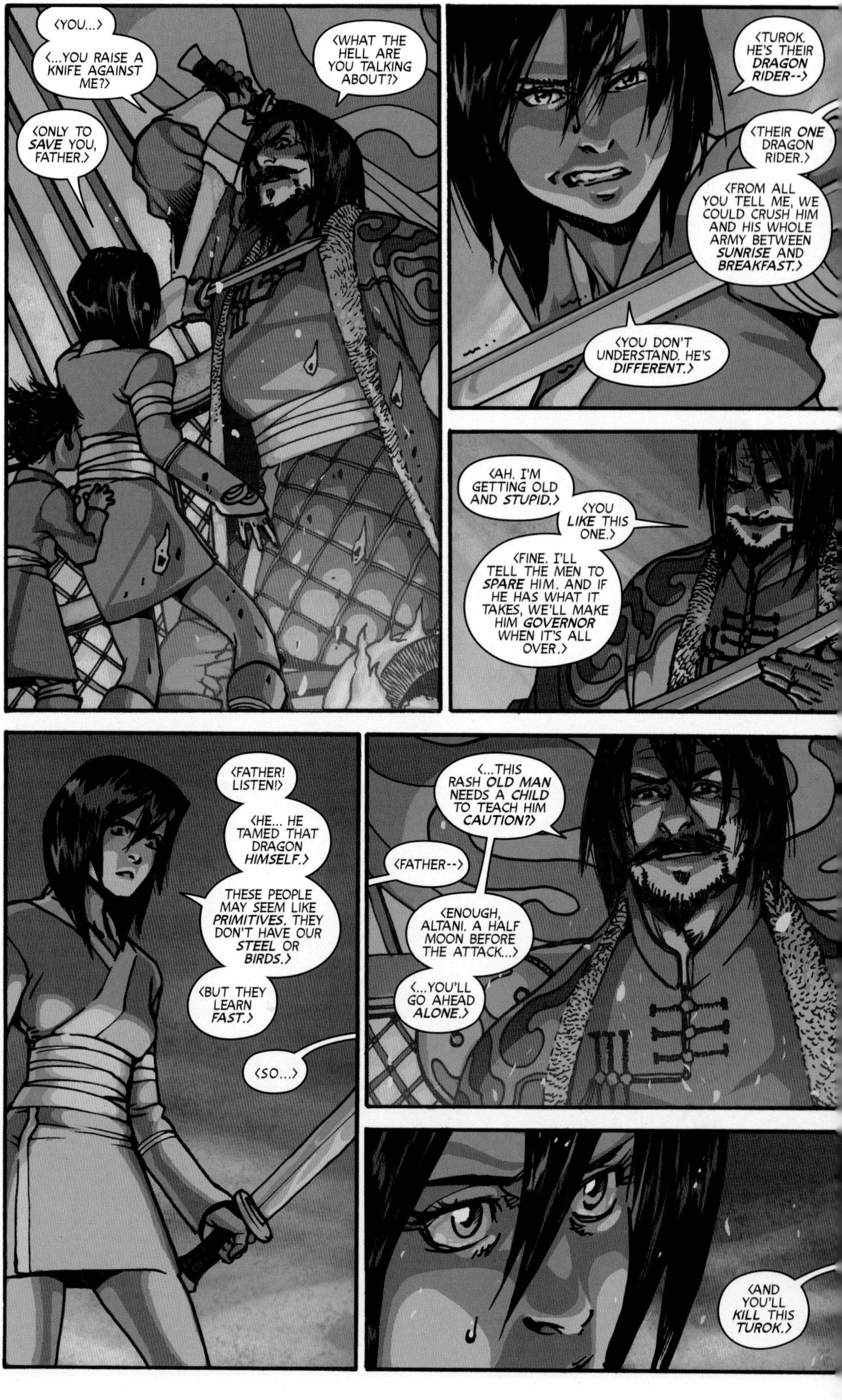

‹YOU...›
‹...YOU RAISE A KNIFE AGAINST ME?›
‹WHAT THE HELL ARE YOU TALKING ABOUT?›
‹ONLY TO SAVE YOU, FATHER.›
‹TUROK. HE'S THEIR DRAGON RIDER--›
‹THEIR ONE DRAGON RIDER.›
‹FROM ALL YOU TELL ME, WE COULD CRUSH HIM AND HIS WHOLE ARMY BETWEEN SUNRISE AND BREAKFAST.›
‹YOU DON'T UNDERSTAND. HE'S DIFFERENT.›
‹AH. I'M GETTING OLD AND STUPID.›
‹YOU LIKE THIS ONE.›
‹FINE. I'LL TELL THE MEN TO SPARE HIM. AND IF HE HAS WHAT IT TAKES, WE'LL MAKE HIM GOVERNOR WHEN IT'S ALL OVER.›
‹FATHER! LISTEN!›
‹HE... HE TAMED THAT DRAGON HIMSELF.›
THESE PEOPLE MAY SEEM LIKE PRIMITIVES. THEY DON'T HAVE OUR STEEL OR BIRDS.›
‹BUT THEY LEARN FAST.›
‹SO...›
‹...THIS RASH OLD MAN NEEDS A CHILD TO TEACH HIM CAUTION?›
‹FATHER--›
‹ENOUGH, ALTANI. A HALF MOON BEFORE THE ATTACK...›
‹...YOU'LL GO AHEAD ALONE.›
‹AND YOU'LL KILL THIS TUROK.›

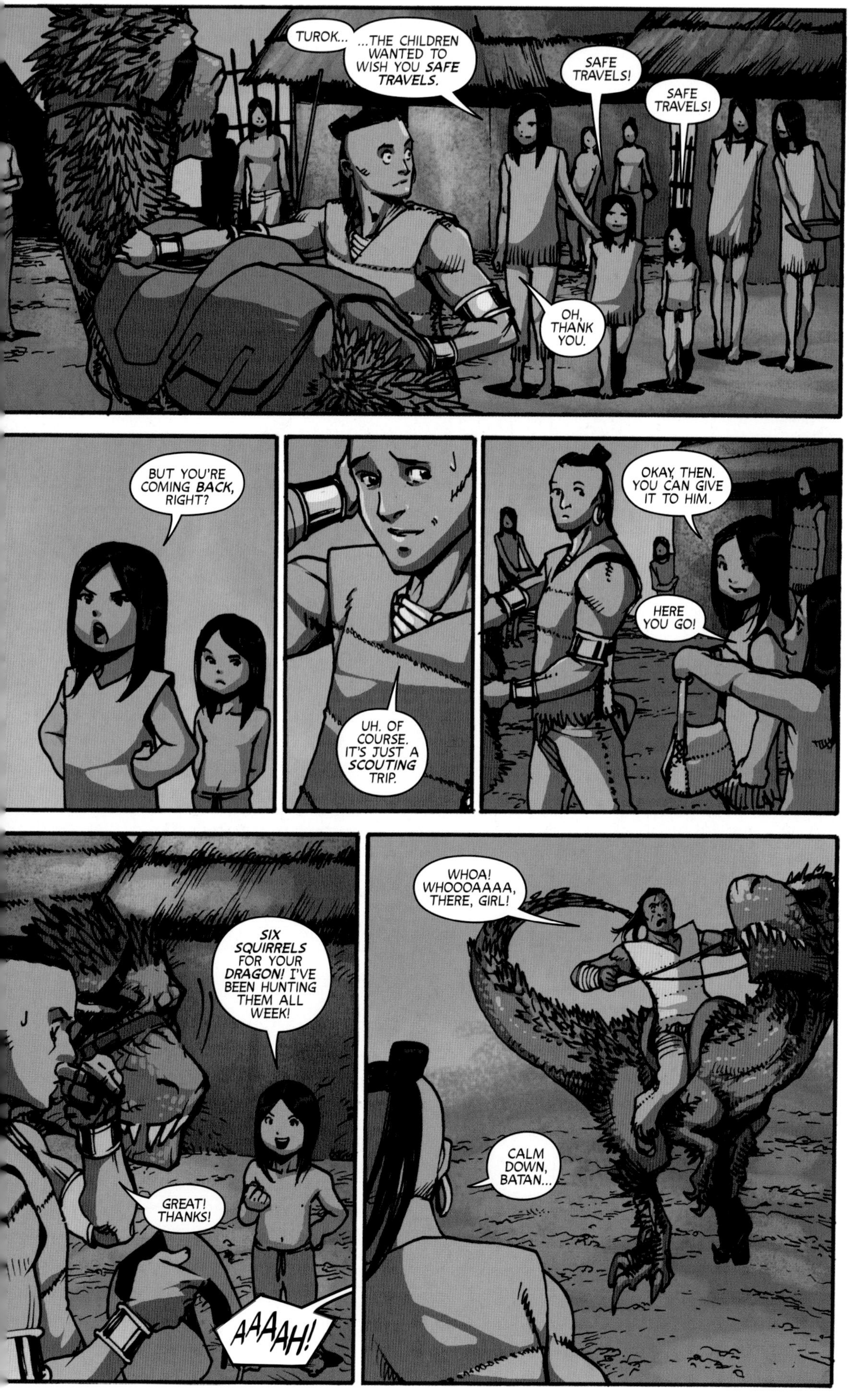
TUROK...
...THE CHILDREN WANTED TO WISH YOU SAFE TRAVELS.
SAFE TRAVELS!
SAFE TRAVELS!
OH, THANK YOU.
BUT YOU'RE COMING BACK, RIGHT?
UH. OF COURSE. IT'S JUST A SCOUTING TRIP.
OKAY, THEN. YOU CAN GIVE IT TO HIM.
HERE YOU GO!
SIX SQUIRRELS FOR YOUR DRAGON! I'VE BEEN HUNTING THEM ALL WEEK!
GREAT! THANKS!
AAAAH!
WHOA! WHOOOAAAA, THERE, GIRL!
CALM DOWN, BATAN...

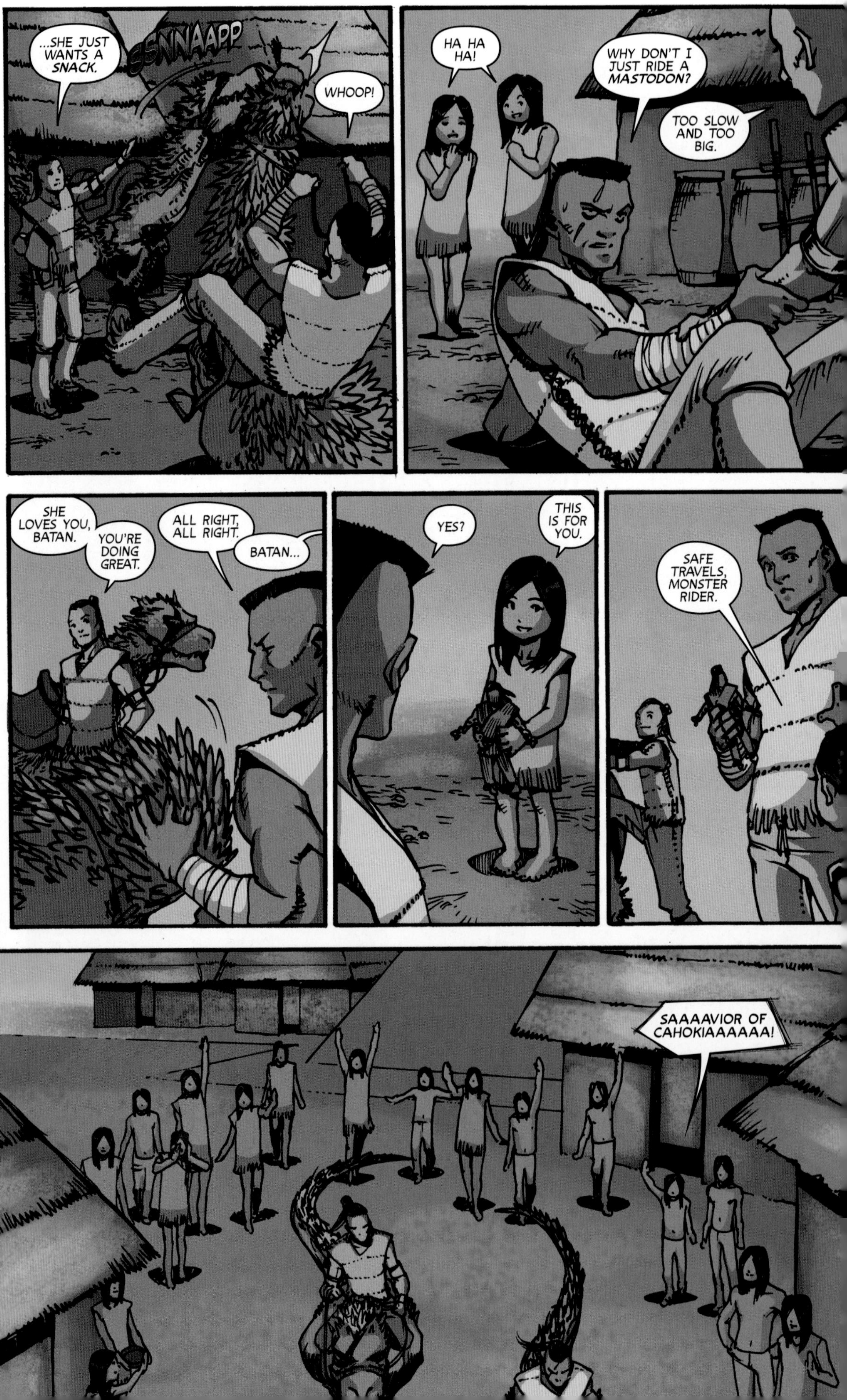
...SHE JUST WANTS A SNACK.
SSNNAAPP
WHOOP!
HA HA HA!
WHY DON'T I JUST RIDE A MASTODON?
TOO SLOW AND TOO BIG.
SHE LOVES YOU, BATAN.
YOU'RE DOING GREAT.
ALL RIGHT, ALL RIGHT.
BATAN...
YES?
THIS IS FOR YOU.
SAFE TRAVELS, MONSTER RIDER.
SAAAAVIOR OF CAHOKIAAAAAA!

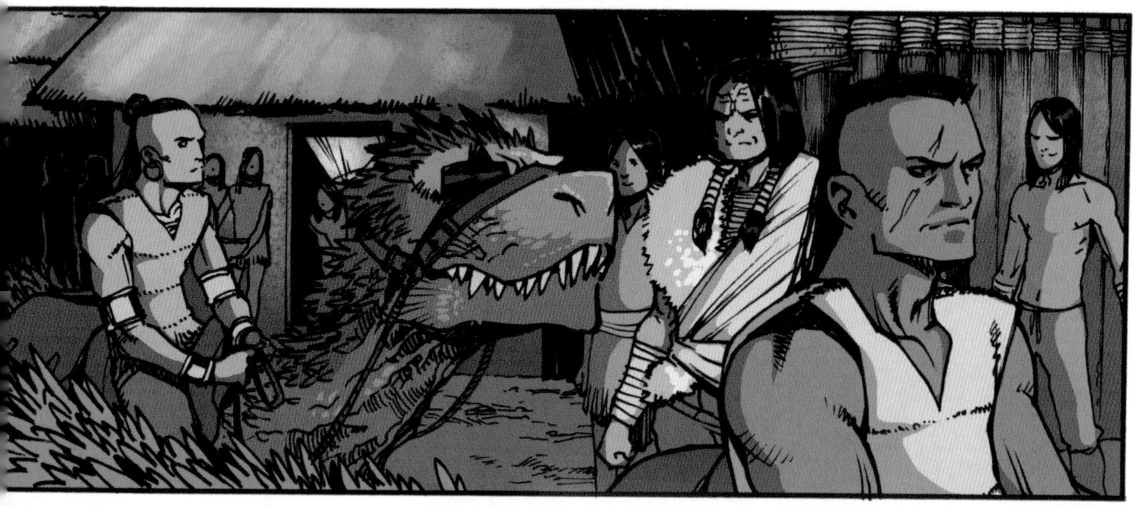

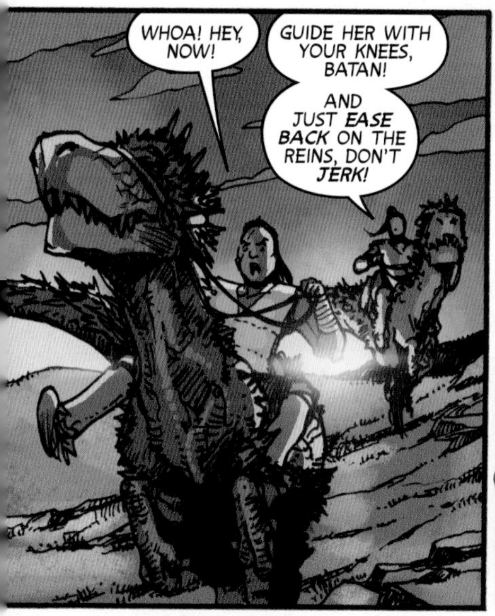

WHOA! HEY, NOW!
GUIDE HER WITH YOUR KNEES, BATAN!
AND JUST EASE BACK ON THE REINS, DON'T JERK!

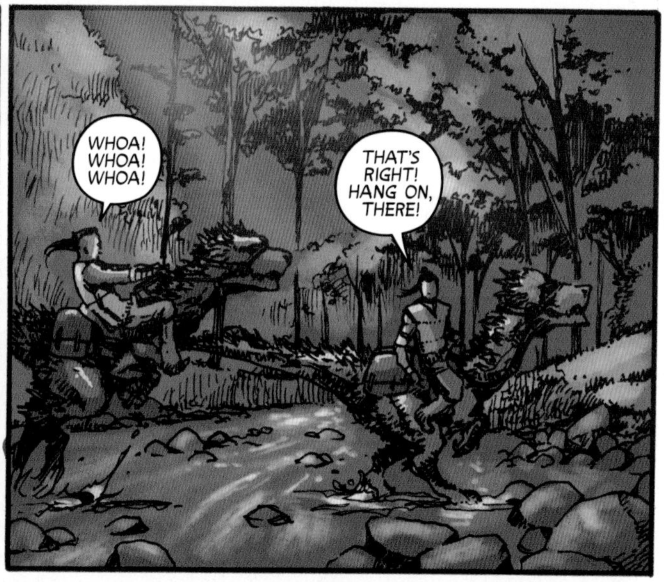

WHOA! WHOA! WHOA!
THAT'S RIGHT! HANG ON, THERE!

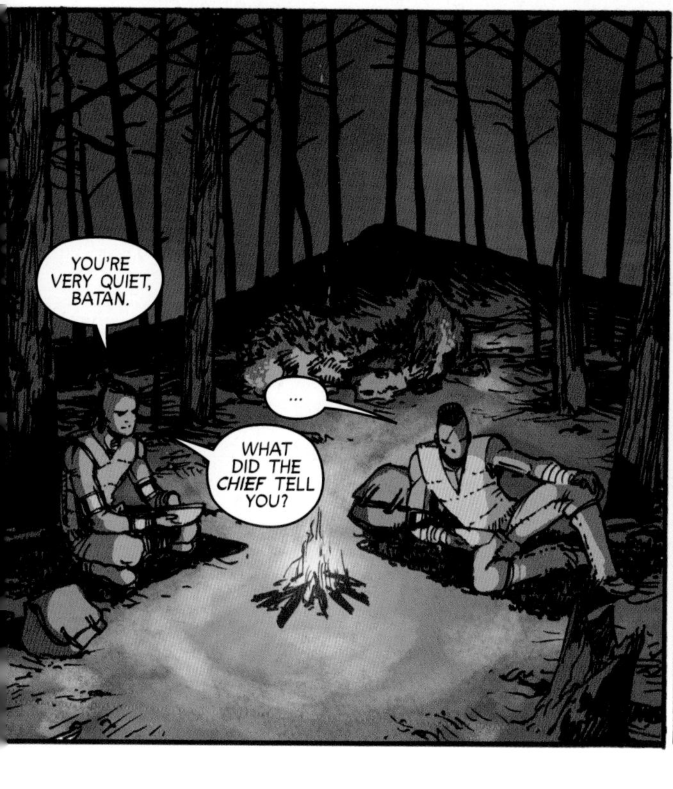

YOU'RE VERY QUIET, BATAN.
...
WHAT DID THE CHIEF TELL YOU?

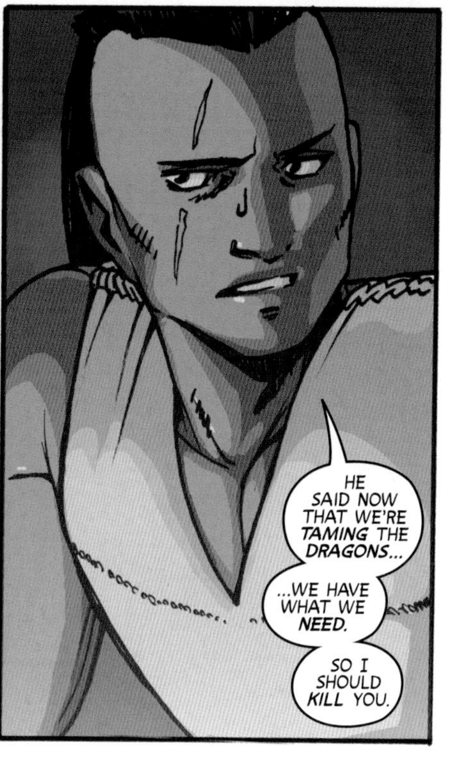

HE SAID NOW THAT WE'RE TAMING THE DRAGONS...
...WE HAVE WHAT WE NEED.
SO I SHOULD KILL YOU.

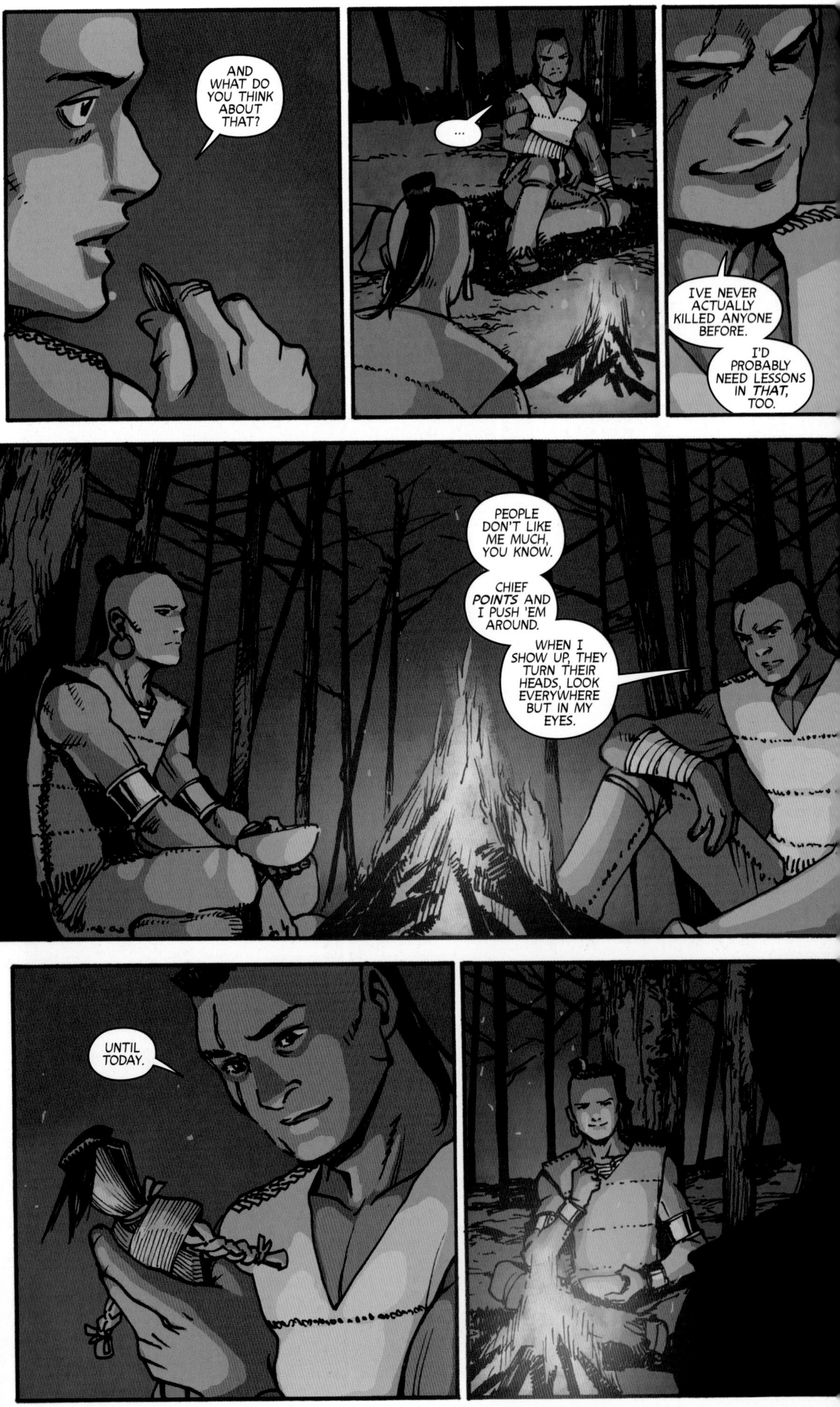
AND WHAT DO YOU THINK ABOUT THAT?
...
IVE NEVER ACTUALLY KILLED ANYONE BEFORE.
I'D PROBABLY NEED LESSONS IN *THAT,* TOO.
PEOPLE DON'T LIKE ME MUCH, YOU KNOW.
CHIEF *POINTS* AND I PUSH 'EM AROUND.
WHEN I SHOW UP, THEY TURN THEIR HEADS, LOOK EVERYWHERE BUT IN MY EYES.
UNTIL TODAY.

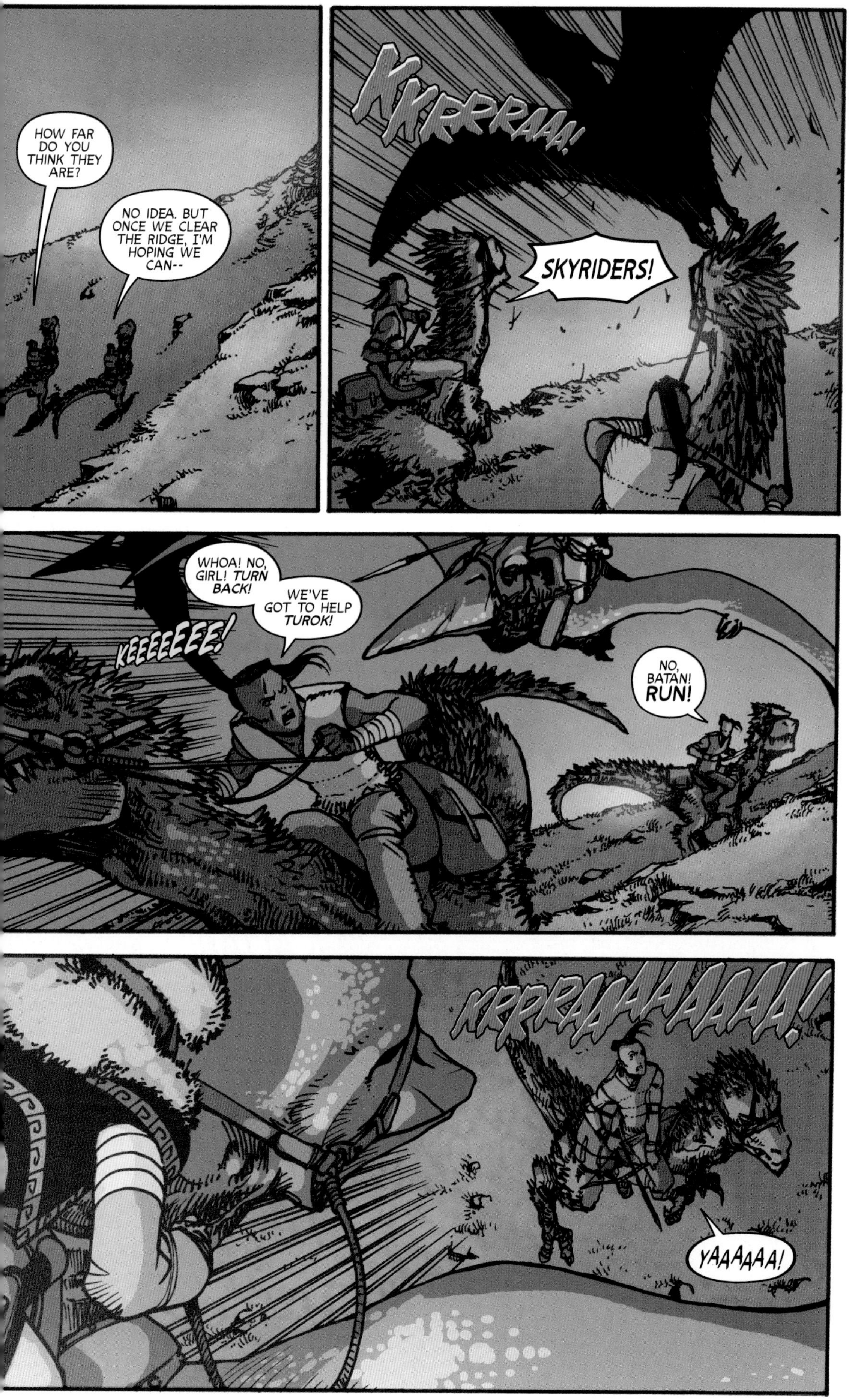
HOW FAR DO YOU THINK THEY ARE?
NO IDEA. BUT ONCE WE CLEAR THE RIDGE, I'M HOPING WE CAN--
KKRRRAAA!
SKYRIDERS!
WHOA! NO, GIRL! TURN BACK!
WE'VE GOT TO HELP TUROK!
KEEEEEEE!
NO, BATAN! RUN!
KRRRAAAAAAA!
YAAAAAA!

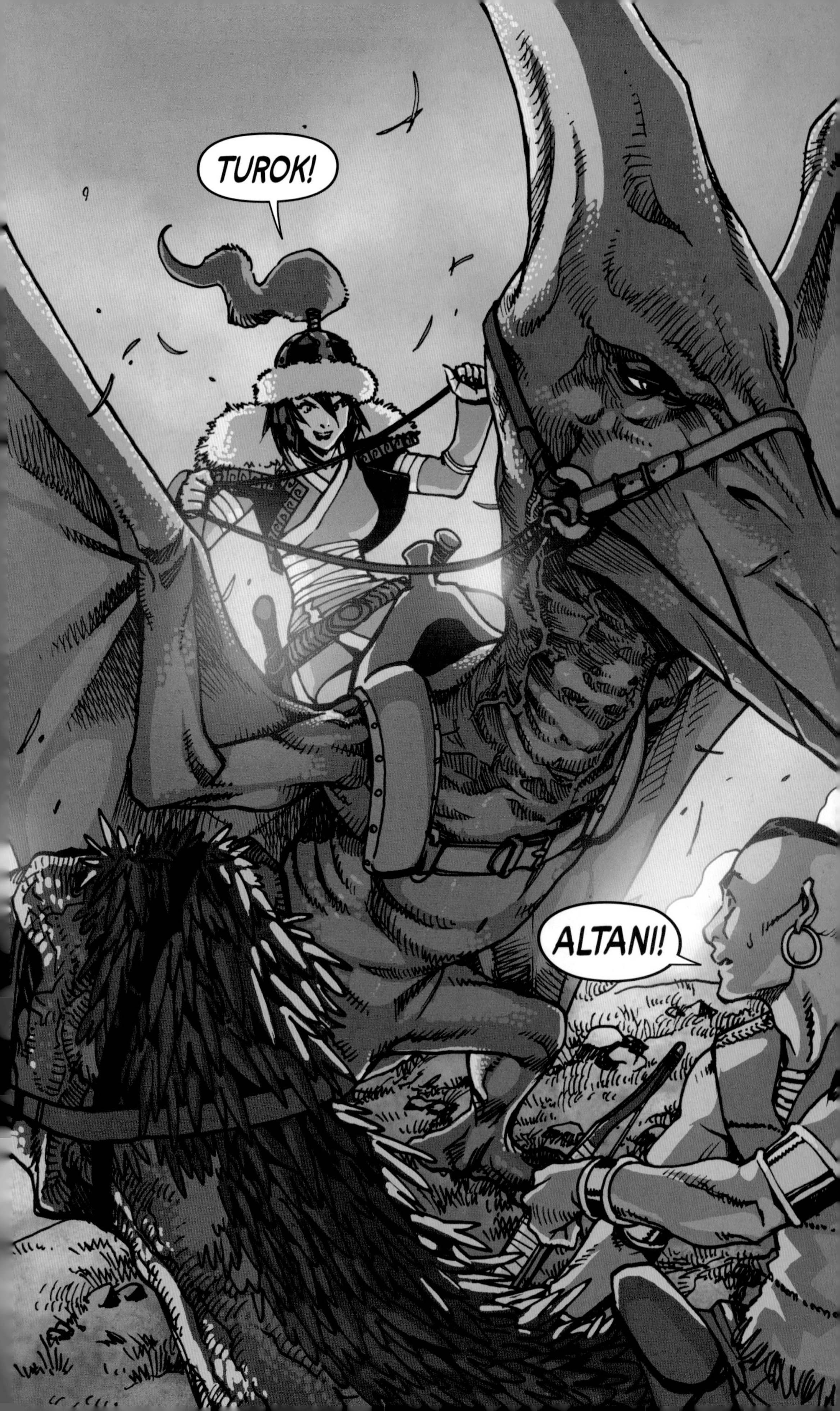
TUROK!
ALTANI!

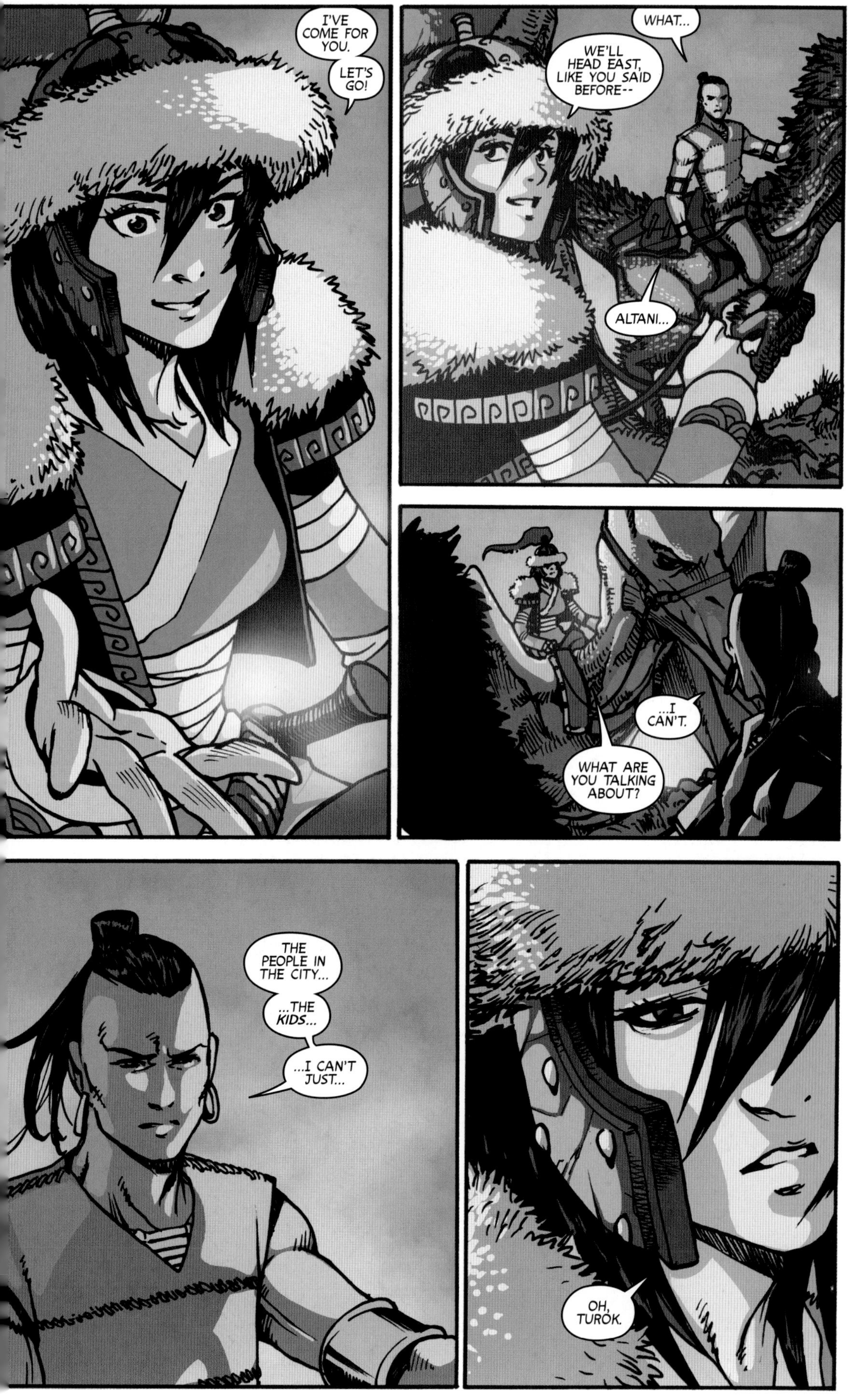

I'VE COME FOR YOU.
LET'S GO!
WHAT...
WE'LL HEAD EAST, LIKE YOU SAID BEFORE--
ALTANI...
...I CAN'T.
WHAT ARE YOU TALKING ABOUT?
THE PEOPLE IN THE CITY...
...THE *KIDS*...
...I CAN'T JUST...
OH, TUROK.

RRRAAAAA!
HYAAA!
NO--!
UKKK!
BATAN!

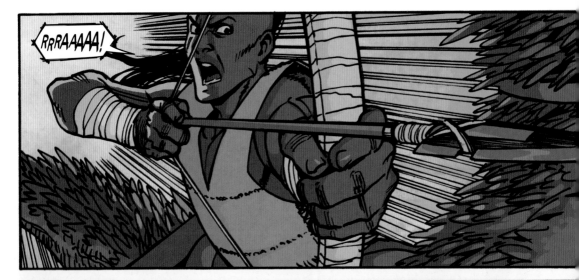

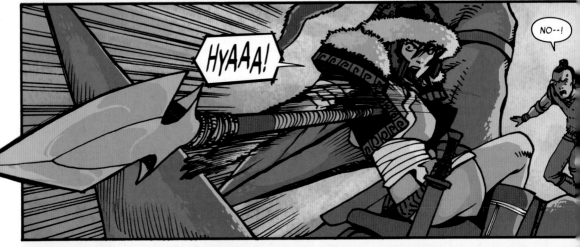

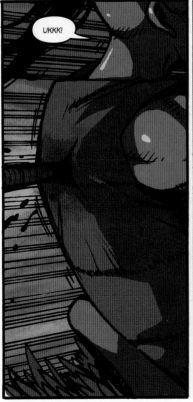

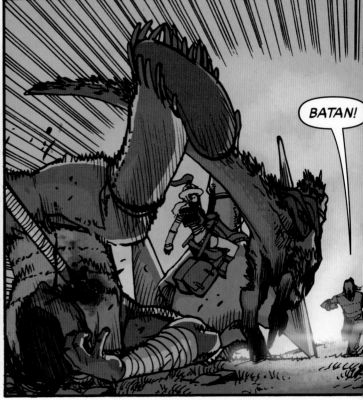

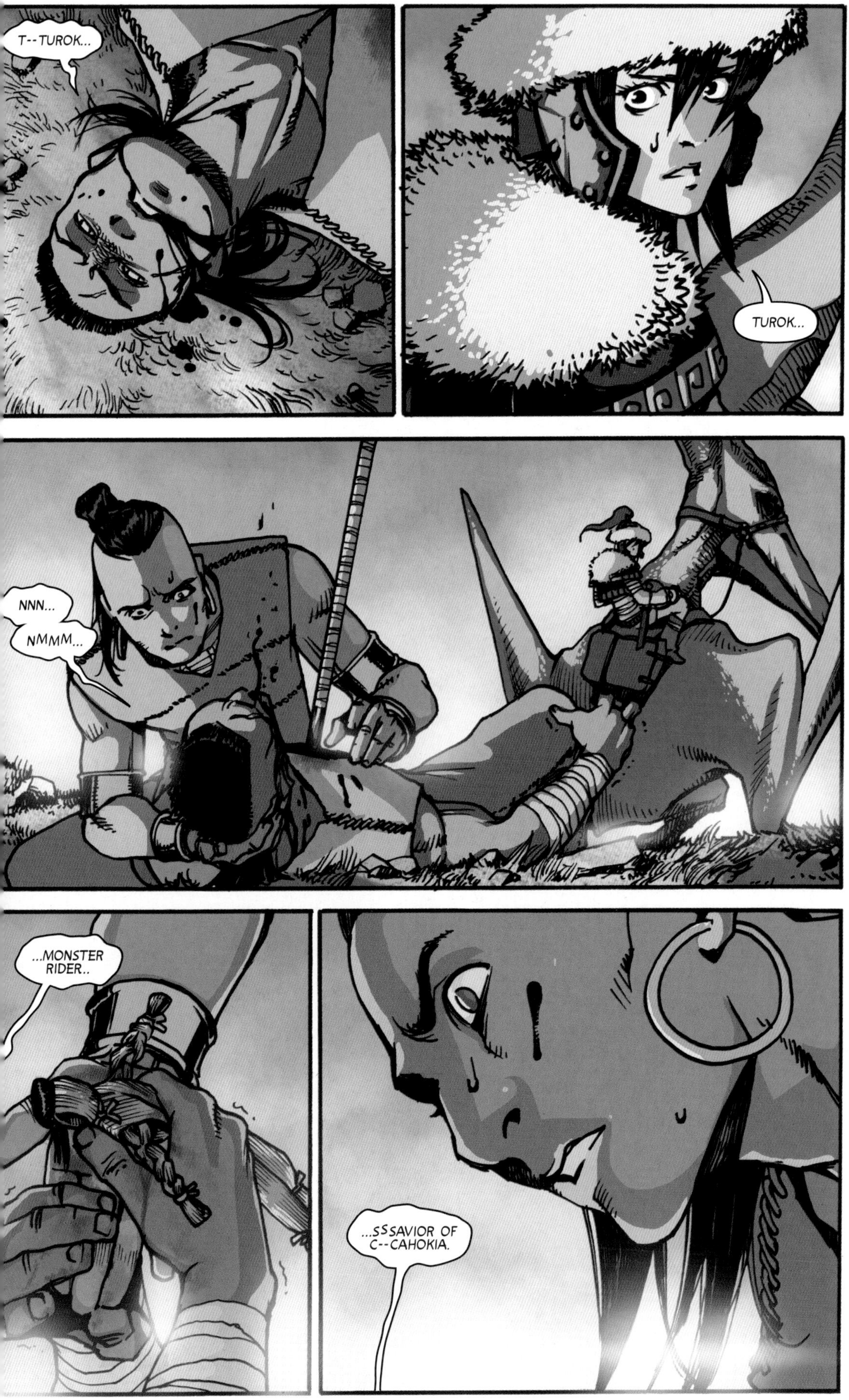
T--TUROK...
TUROK...
NNN...
NMMM...
...MONSTER RIDER..
...SSSAVIOR OF C--CAHOKIA.

ISSUE 8

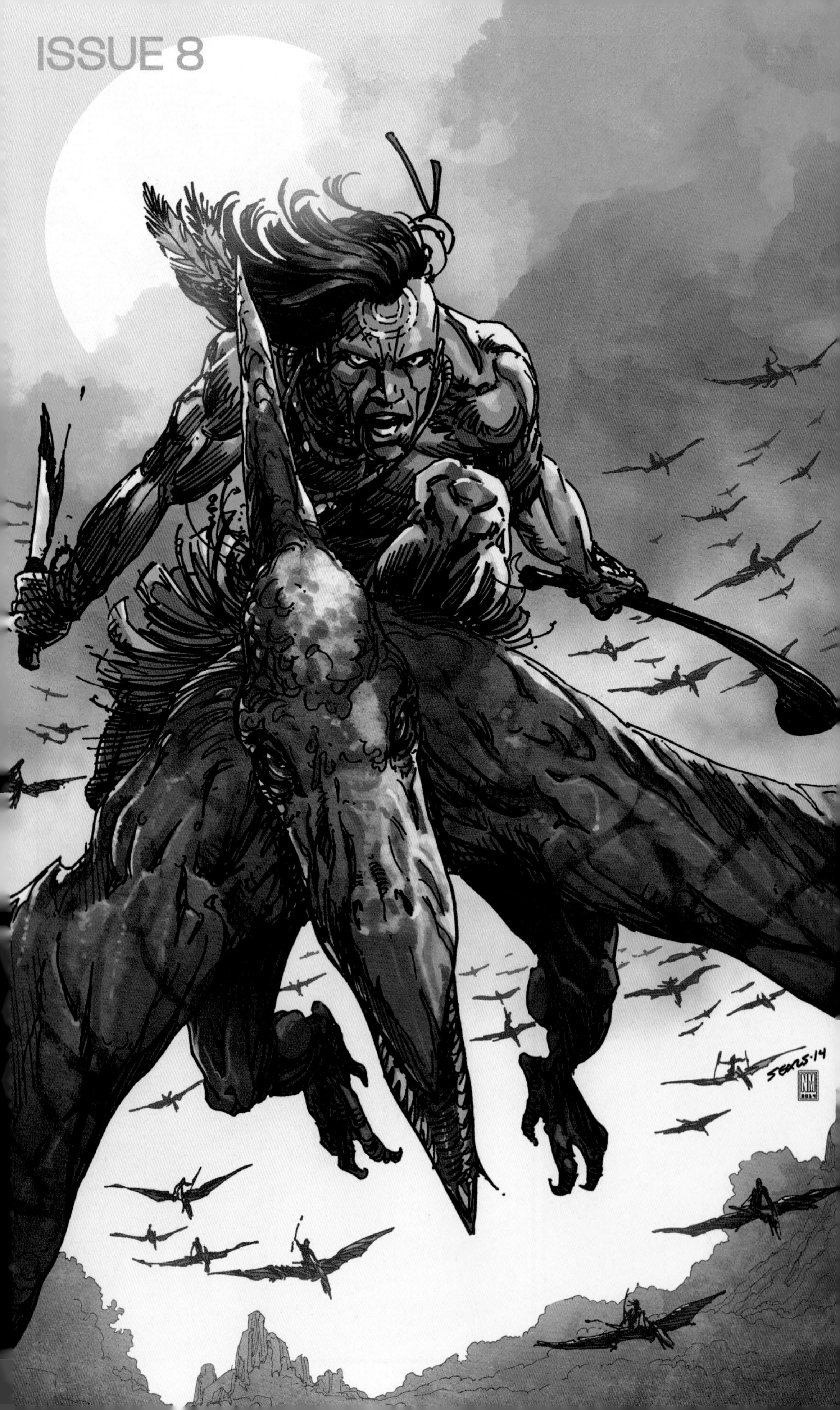

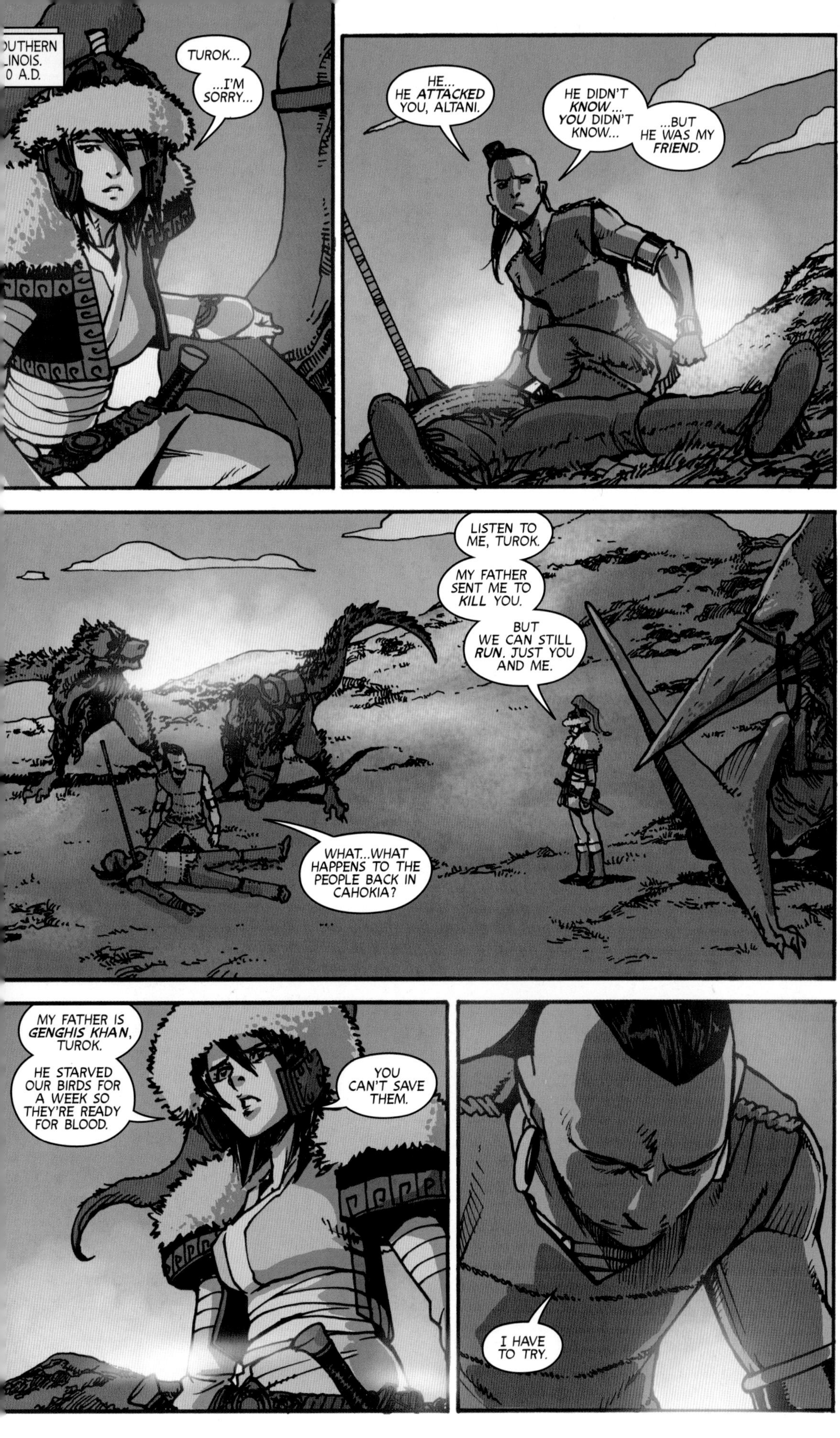

OUTHERN
LINOIS.
0 A.D.
TUROK...
...I'M SORRY...
HE... HE ATTACKED YOU, ALTANI.
HE DIDN'T KNOW... YOU DIDN'T KNOW...
...BUT HE WAS MY FRIEND.
LISTEN TO ME, TUROK.
MY FATHER SENT ME TO KILL YOU.
BUT WE CAN STILL RUN. JUST YOU AND ME.
WHAT...WHAT HAPPENS TO THE PEOPLE BACK IN CAHOKIA?
MY FATHER IS GENGHIS KHAN, TUROK.
HE STARVED OUR BIRDS FOR A WEEK SO THEY'RE READY FOR BLOOD.
YOU CAN'T SAVE THEM.
I HAVE TO TRY.

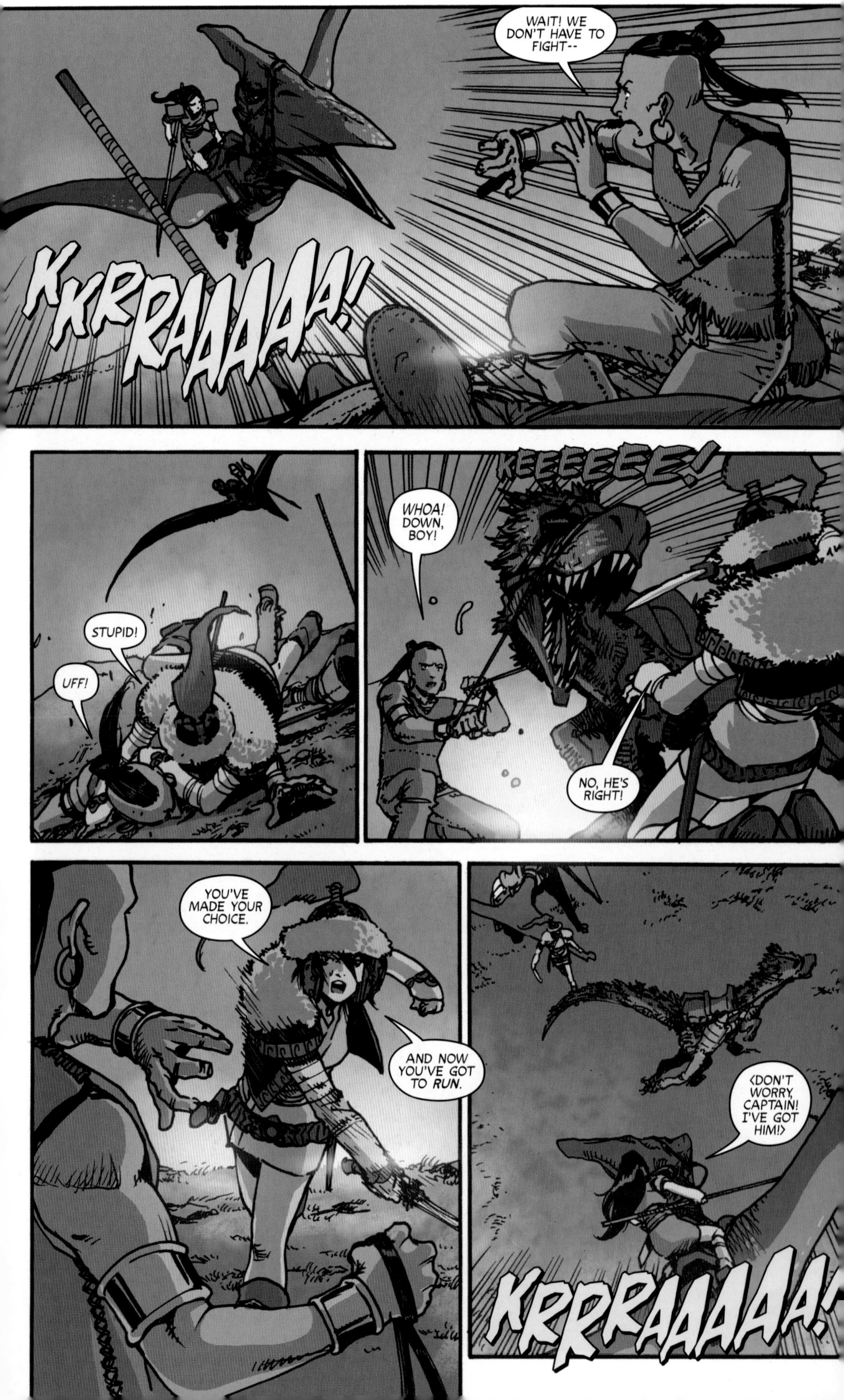
WAIT! WE DON'T HAVE TO FIGHT--
KKRRAAAAAA!
STUPID!
UFF!
KEEEEEEE!
WHOA! DOWN, BOY!
NO, HE'S RIGHT!
YOU'VE MADE YOUR CHOICE.
AND NOW YOU'VE GOT TO *RUN*.
<DON'T WORRY, CAPTAIN! I'VE GOT HIM!>
KRRRAAAAAA!

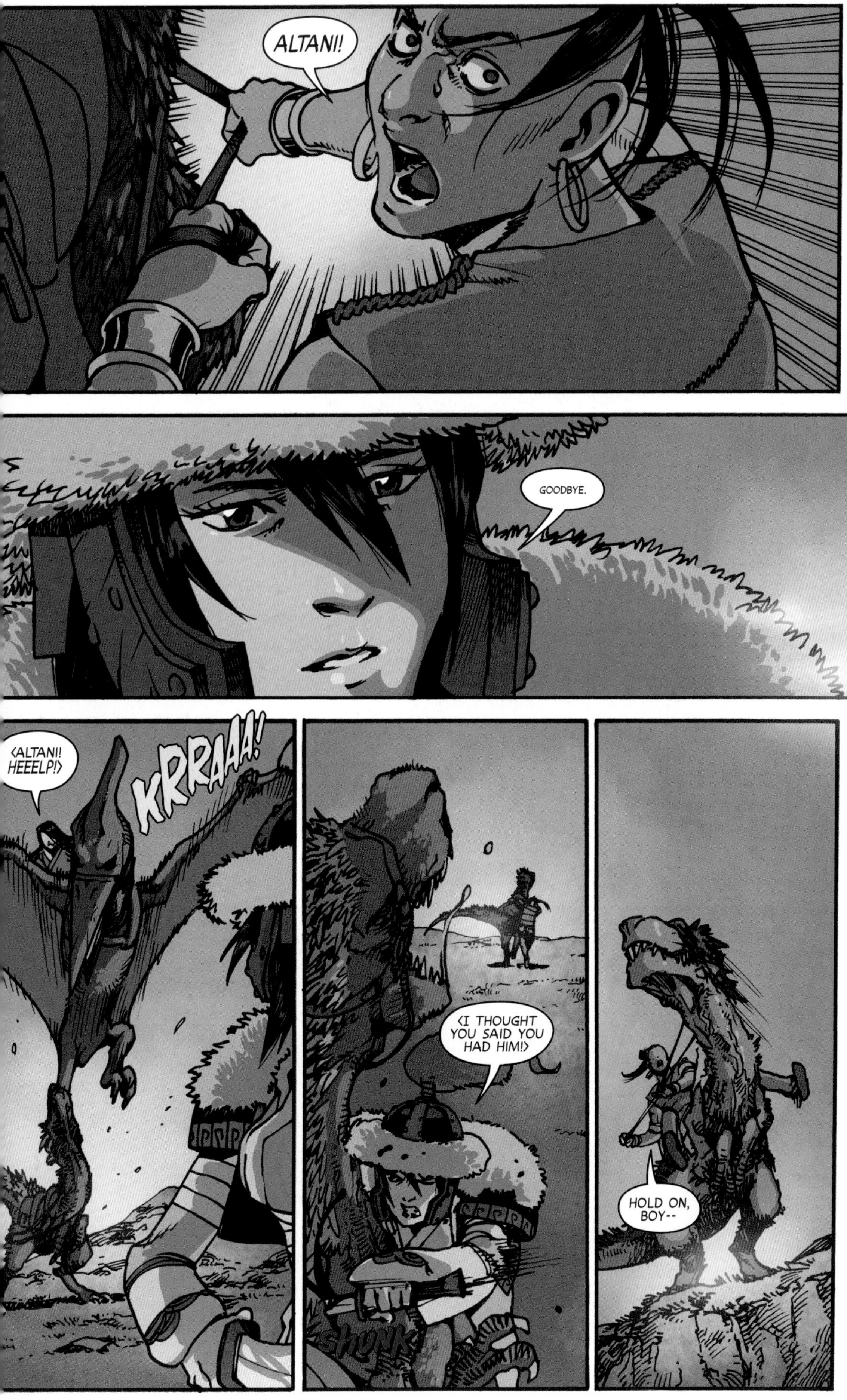
ALTANI!
GOODBYE.
<ALTANI! HEEELP!>
KRRAAA!
<I THOUGHT YOU SAID YOU HAD HIM!>
SHUNK
HOLD ON, BOY--

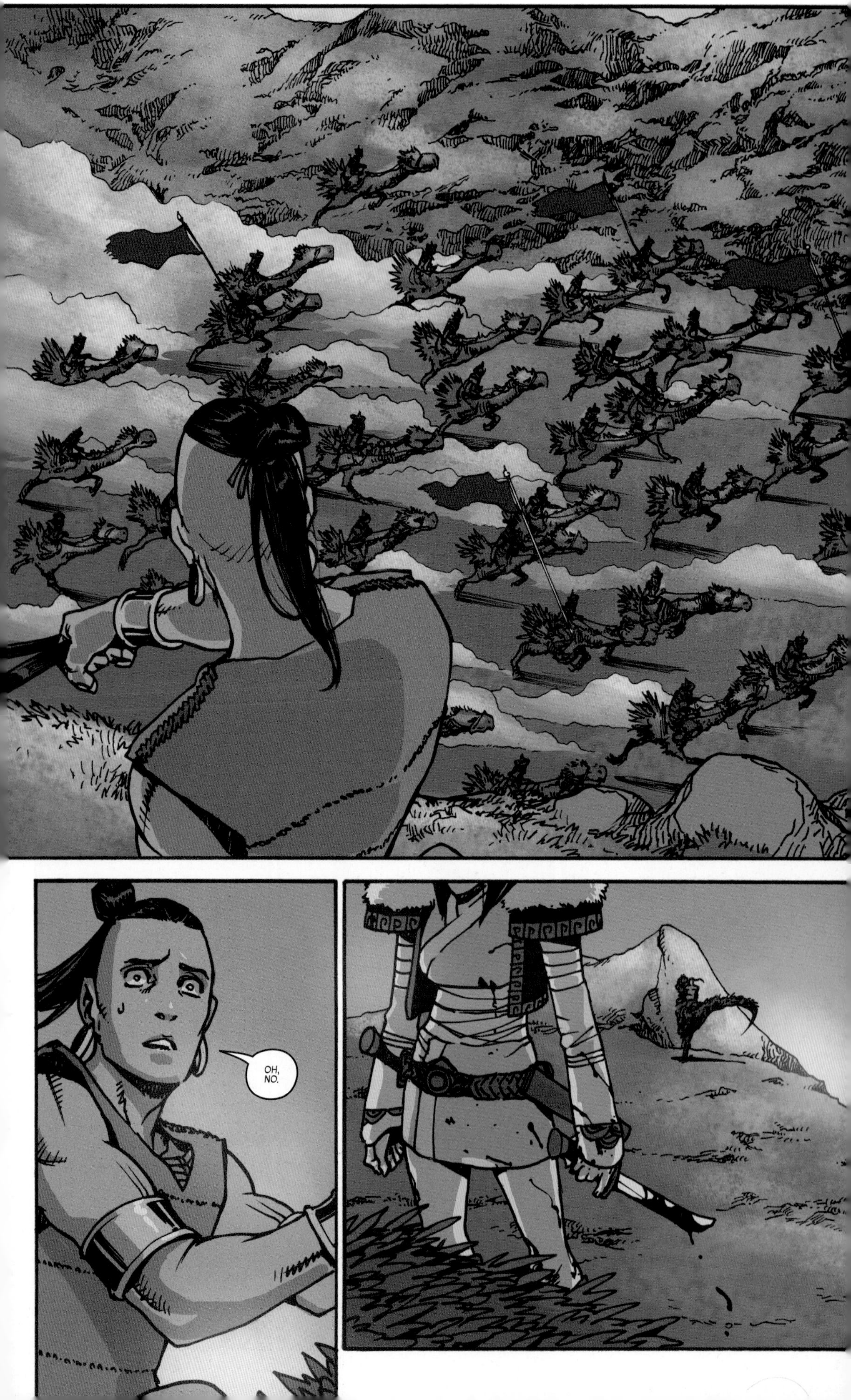
OH, NO.

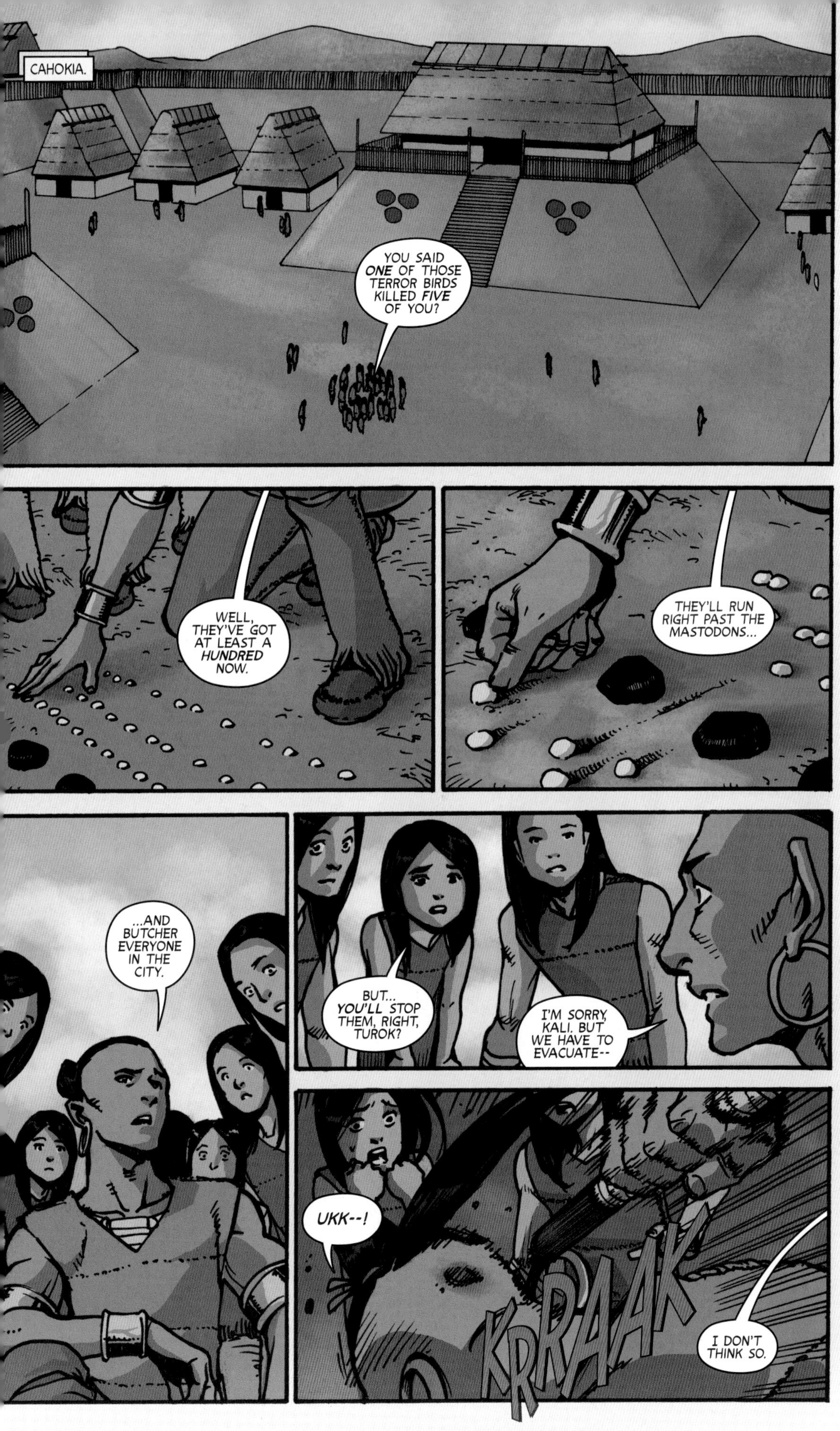
CAHOKIA.
YOU SAID ONE OF THOSE TERROR BIRDS KILLED FIVE OF YOU?
WELL, THEY'VE GOT AT LEAST A HUNDRED NOW.
THEY'LL RUN RIGHT PAST THE MASTODONS...
...AND BUTCHER EVERYONE IN THE CITY.
BUT... YOU'LL STOP THEM, RIGHT, TUROK?
I'M SORRY, KALI. BUT WE HAVE TO EVACUATE--
UKK--!
KRRAAK
I DON'T THINK SO.

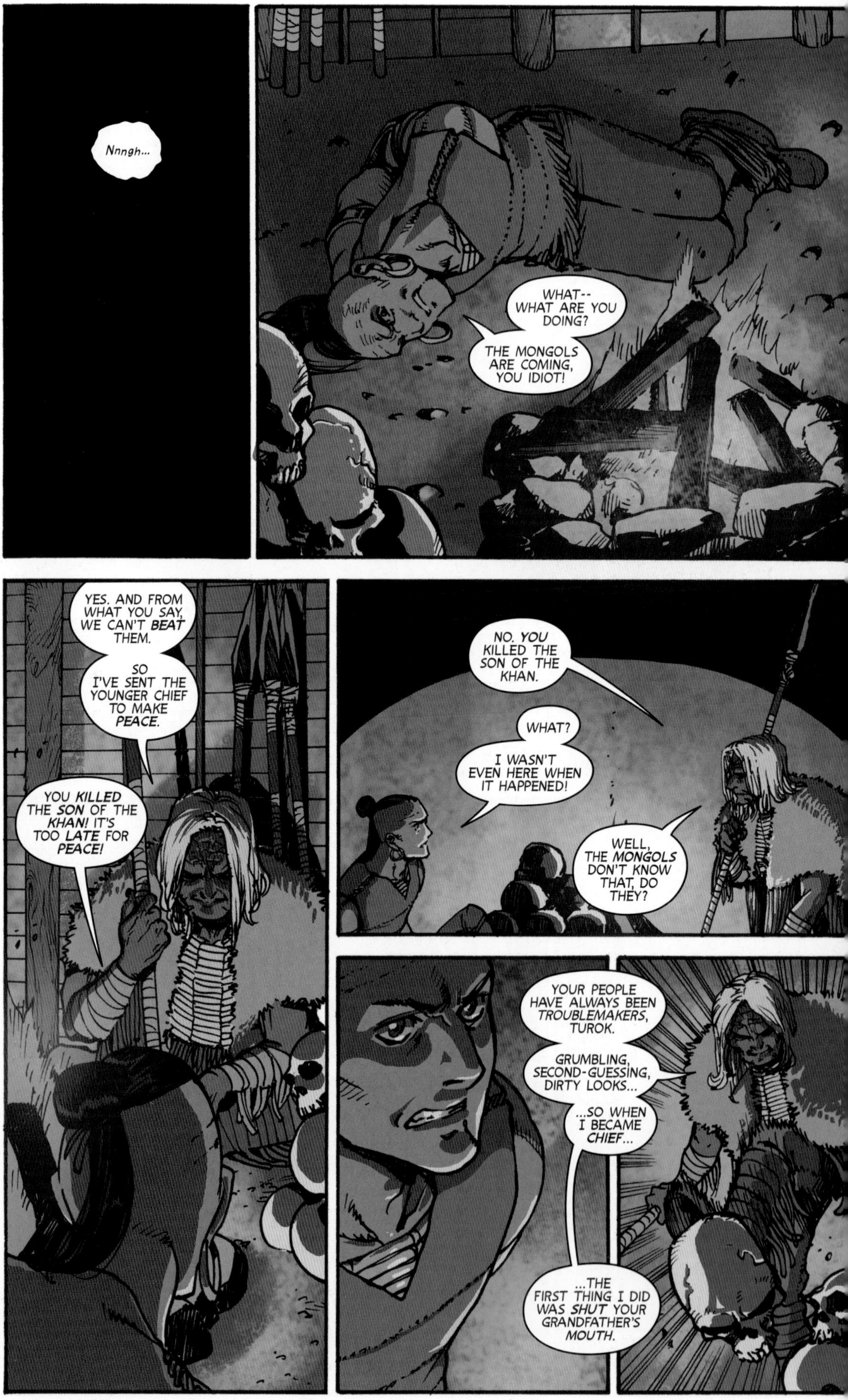
Nnngh...
WHAT-- WHAT ARE YOU DOING?
THE MONGOLS ARE COMING, YOU IDIOT!
YES. AND FROM WHAT YOU SAY, WE CAN'T *BEAT* THEM.
SO I'VE SENT THE YOUNGER CHIEF TO MAKE *PEACE*.
YOU *KILLED* THE *SON* OF THE *KHAN!* IT'S TOO *LATE* FOR *PEACE!*
NO. *YOU* KILLED THE SON OF THE KHAN.
WHAT?
I WASN'T EVEN HERE WHEN IT HAPPENED!
WELL, THE *MONGOLS* DON'T KNOW THAT, DO THEY?
YOUR PEOPLE HAVE ALWAYS BEEN *TROUBLEMAKERS*, TUROK.
GRUMBLING, SECOND-GUESSING, DIRTY LOOKS...
...SO WHEN I BECAME *CHIEF*...
...THE FIRST THING I DID WAS *SHUT* YOUR GRANDFATHER'S *MOUTH*.

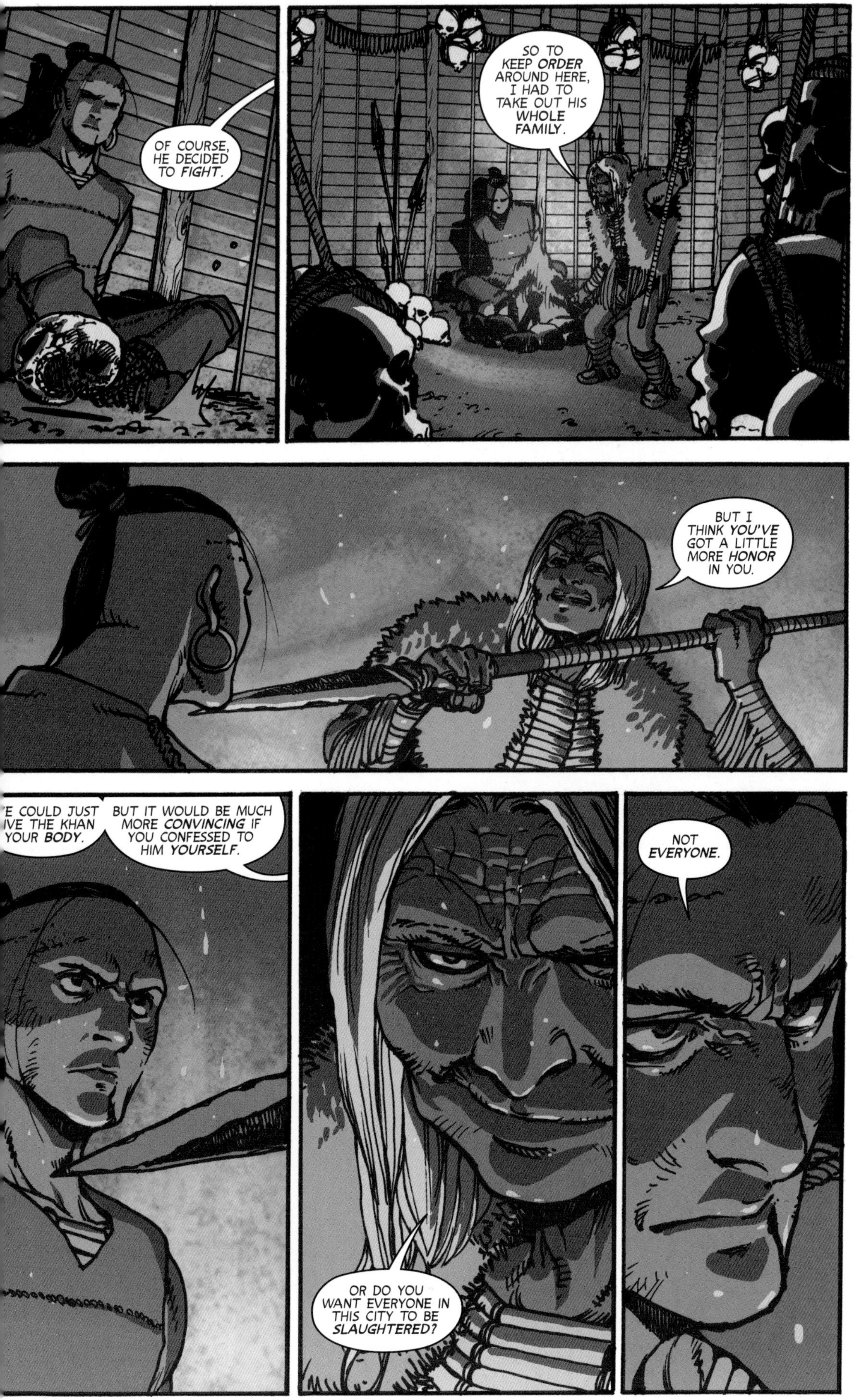
OF COURSE, HE DECIDED TO FIGHT.
SO TO KEEP ORDER AROUND HERE, I HAD TO TAKE OUT HIS WHOLE FAMILY.
BUT I THINK YOU'VE GOT A LITTLE MORE HONOR IN YOU.
'E COULD JUST IVE THE KHAN YOUR BODY.
BUT IT WOULD BE MUCH MORE CONVINCING IF YOU CONFESSED TO HIM YOURSELF.
OR DO YOU WANT EVERYONE IN THIS CITY TO BE SLAUGHTERED?
NOT EVERYONE.

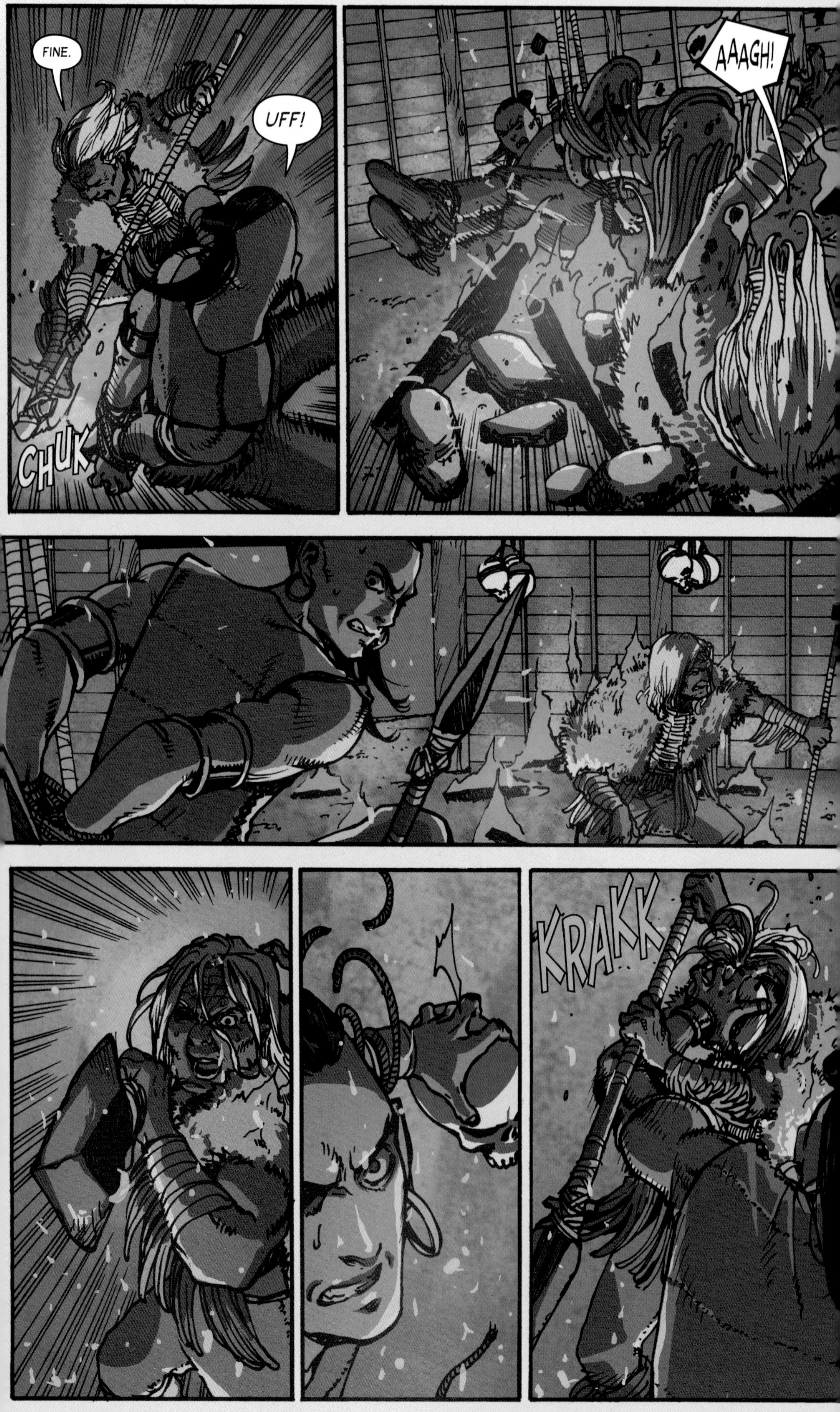
FINE.
UFF!
CHUK
AAAGH!
KRAKK

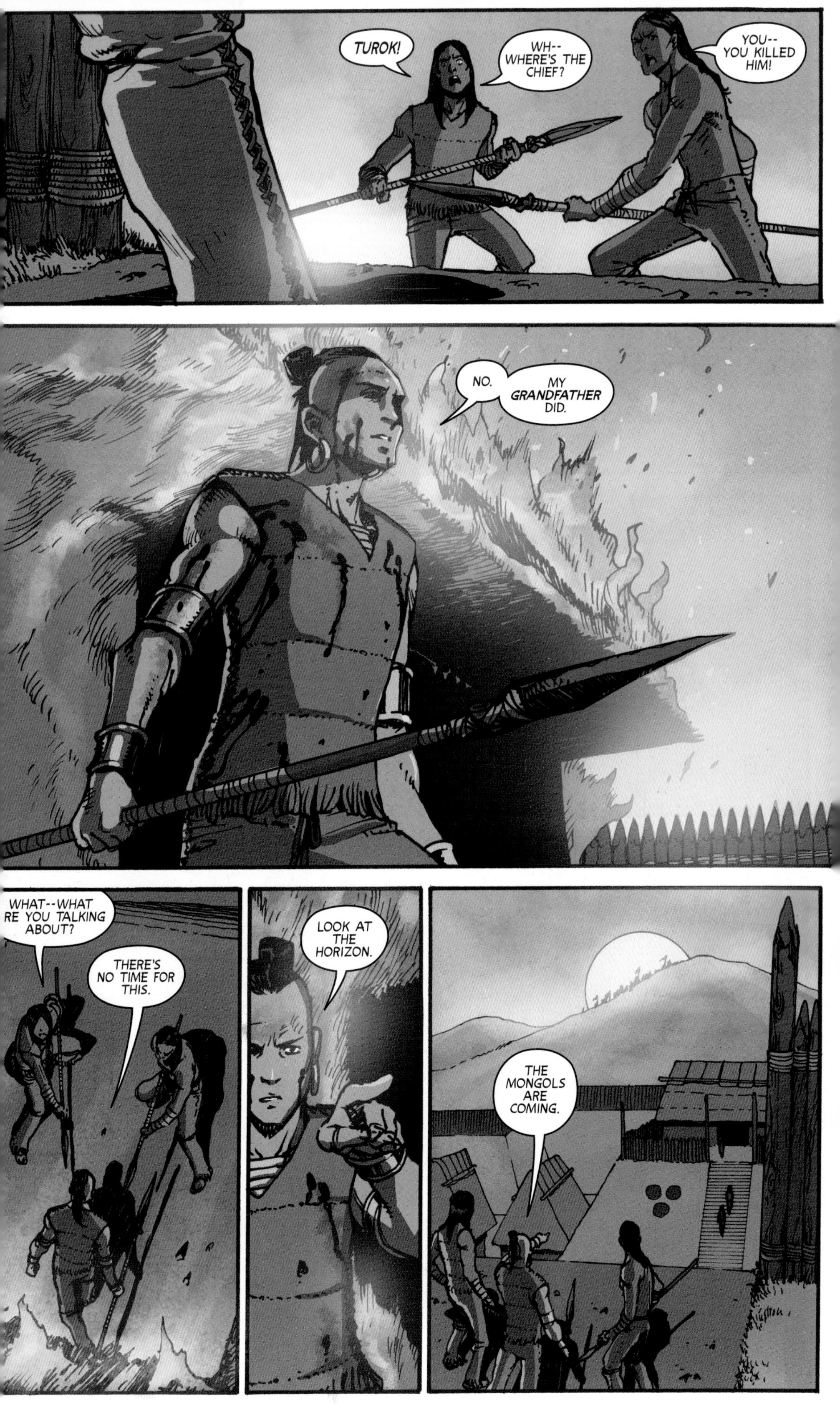
TUROK!
WH--
WHERE'S THE
CHIEF?
YOU--
YOU KILLED
HIM!
NO.
MY
GRANDFATHER
DID.
WHAT--WHAT
RE YOU TALKING
ABOUT?
THERE'S
NO TIME FOR
THIS.
LOOK AT
THE
HORIZON.
THE
MONGOLS
ARE
COMING.

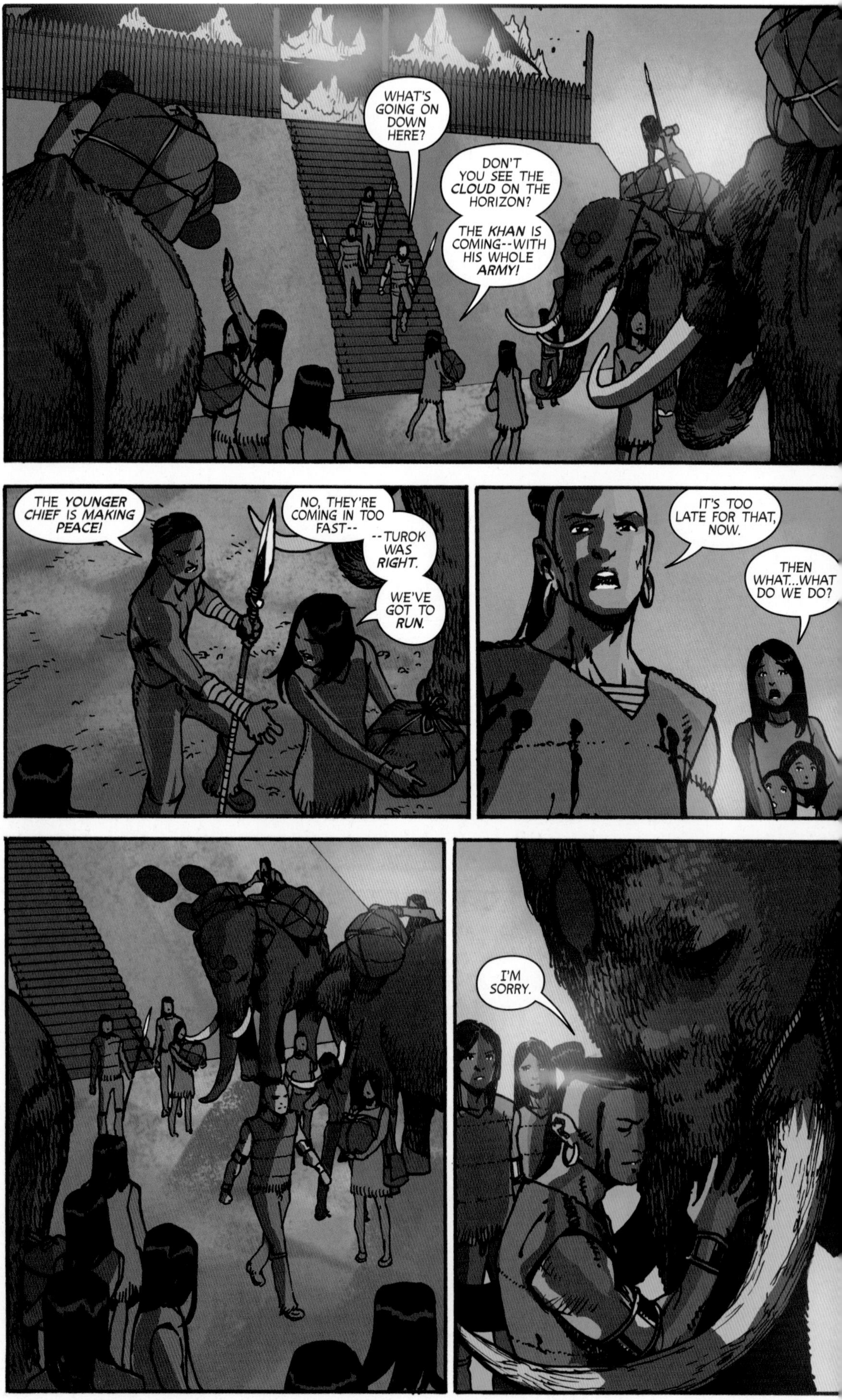
WHAT'S GOING ON DOWN HERE?
DON'T YOU SEE THE CLOUD ON THE HORIZON?
THE KHAN IS COMING--WITH HIS WHOLE ARMY!
THE YOUNGER CHIEF IS MAKING PEACE!
NO, THEY'RE COMING IN TOO FAST--
--TUROK WAS RIGHT.
WE'VE GOT TO RUN.
IT'S TOO LATE FOR THAT, NOW.
THEN WHAT...WHAT DO WE DO?
I'M SORRY.

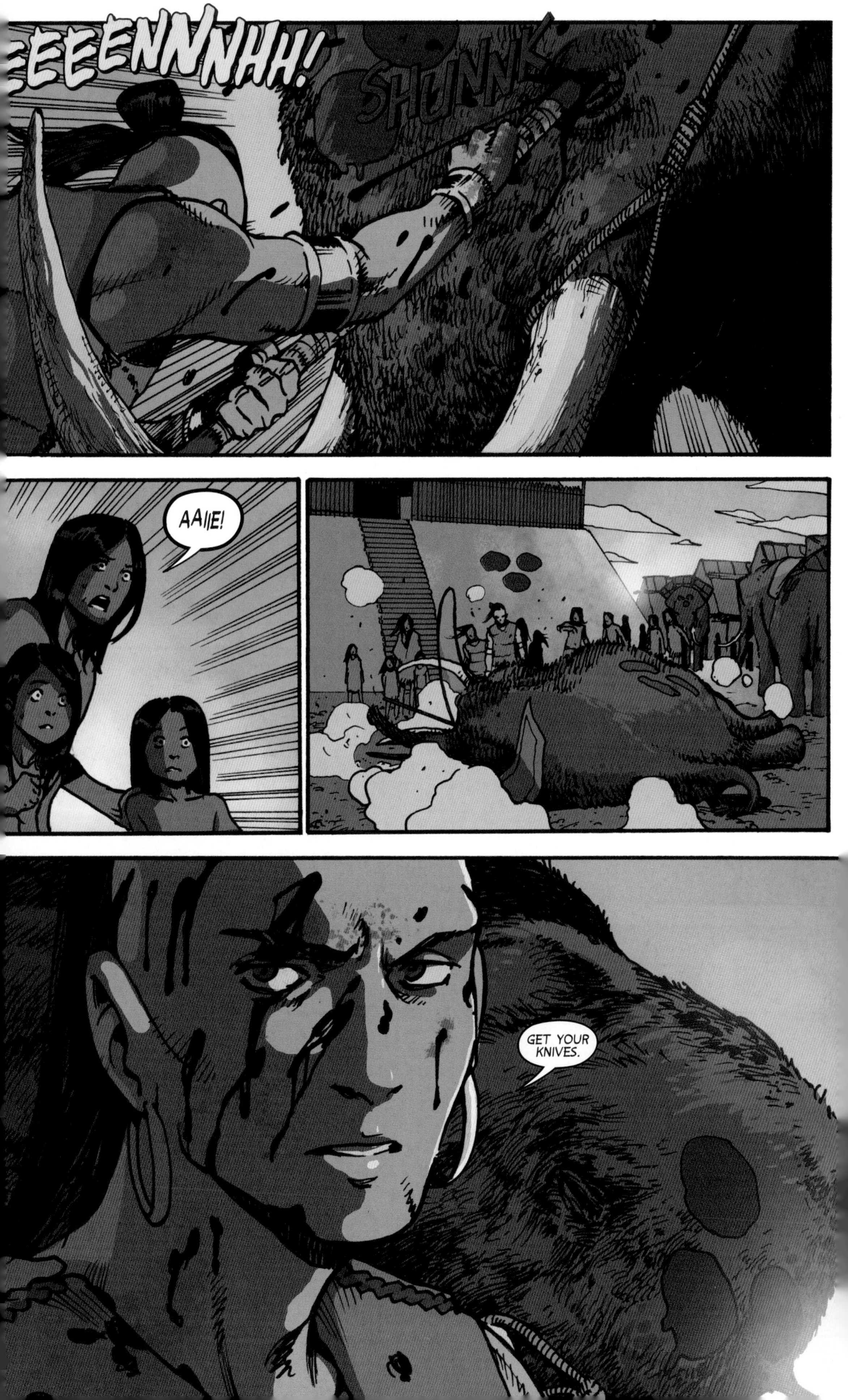
EEEENNNHH!
SHUNNK
AAIIE!
GET YOUR KNIVES.

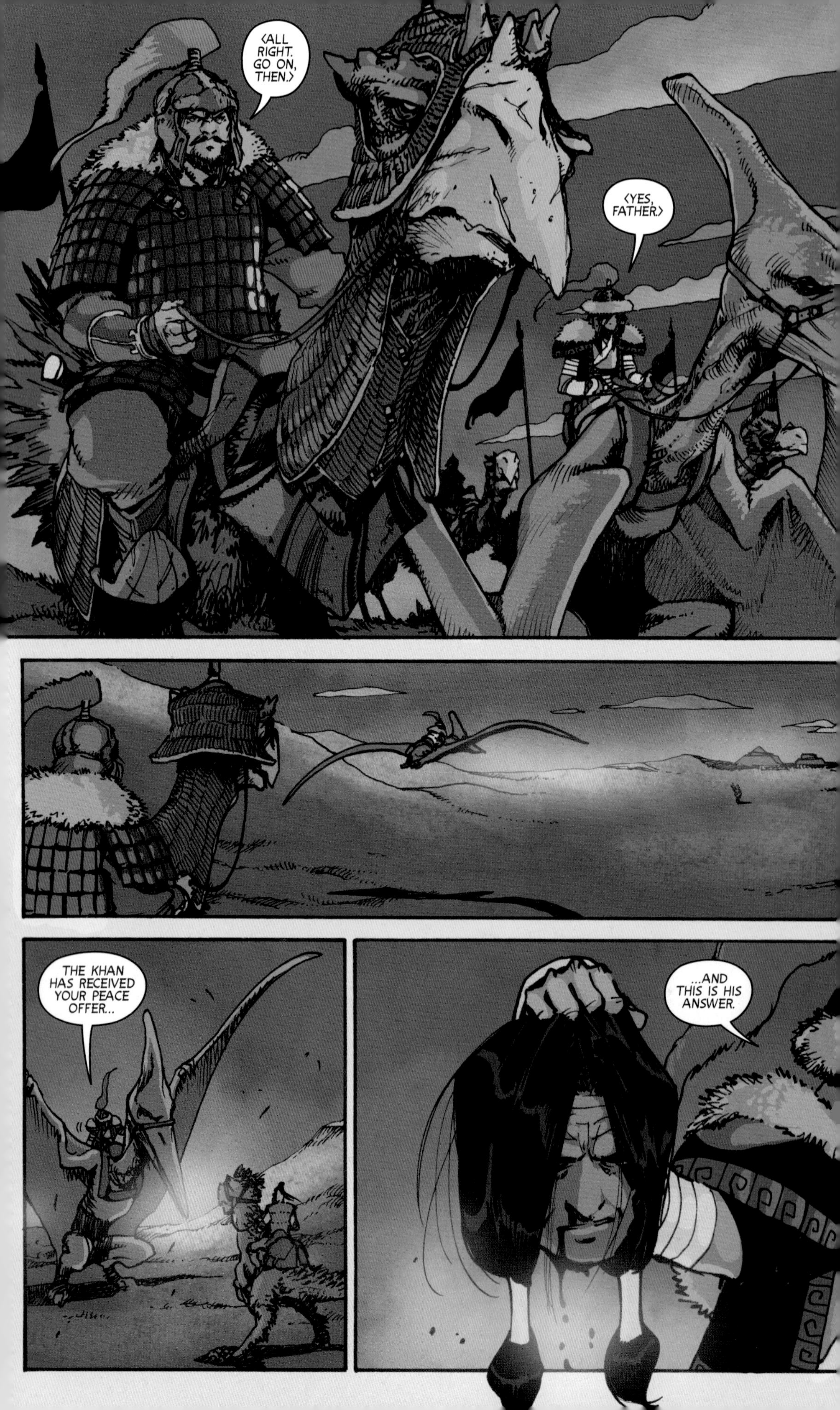

<ALL RIGHT. GO ON, THEN.>
<YES, FATHER.>
THE KHAN HAS RECEIVED YOUR PEACE OFFER...
...AND THIS IS HIS ANSWER.

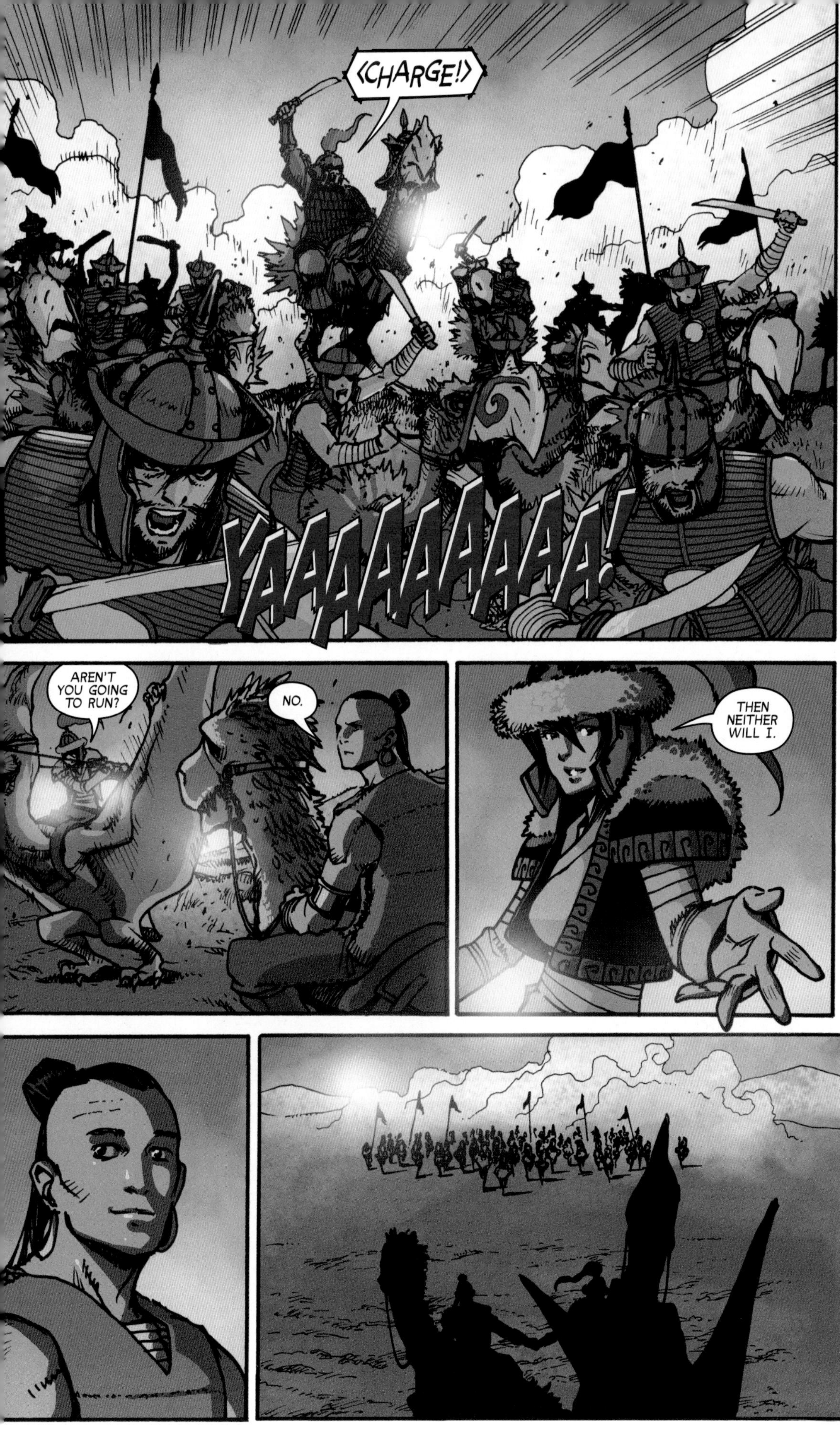
‹CHARGE!›
YAAAAAAAAA!
AREN'T YOU GOING TO RUN?
NO.
THEN NEITHER WILL I.

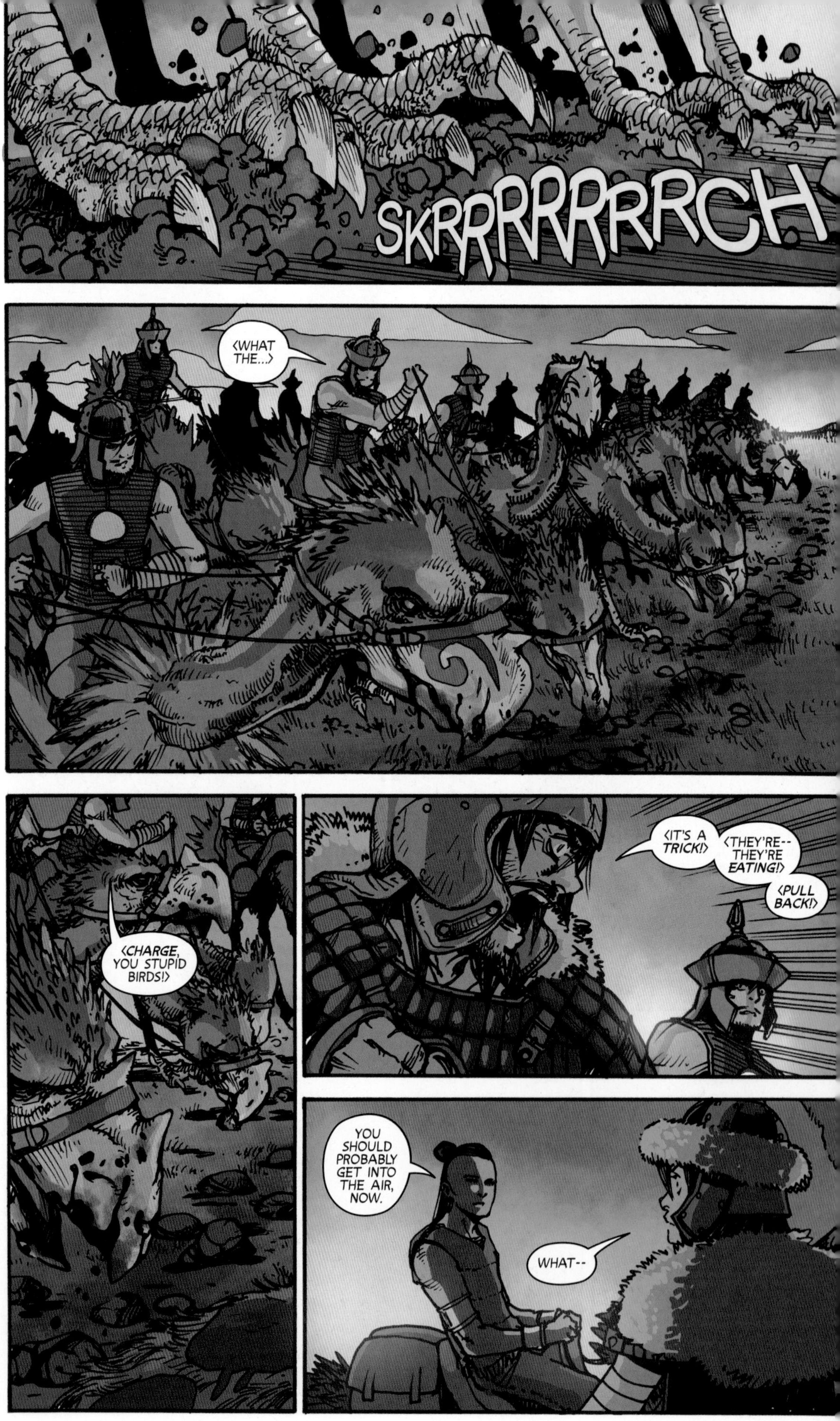
SKRRRRRRRCH
‹WHAT THE...›
‹CHARGE, YOU STUPID BIRDS!›
‹IT'S A TRICK!›
‹THEY'RE-- THEY'RE EATING!›
‹PULL BACK!›
YOU SHOULD PROBABLY GET INTO THE AIR, NOW.
WHAT--

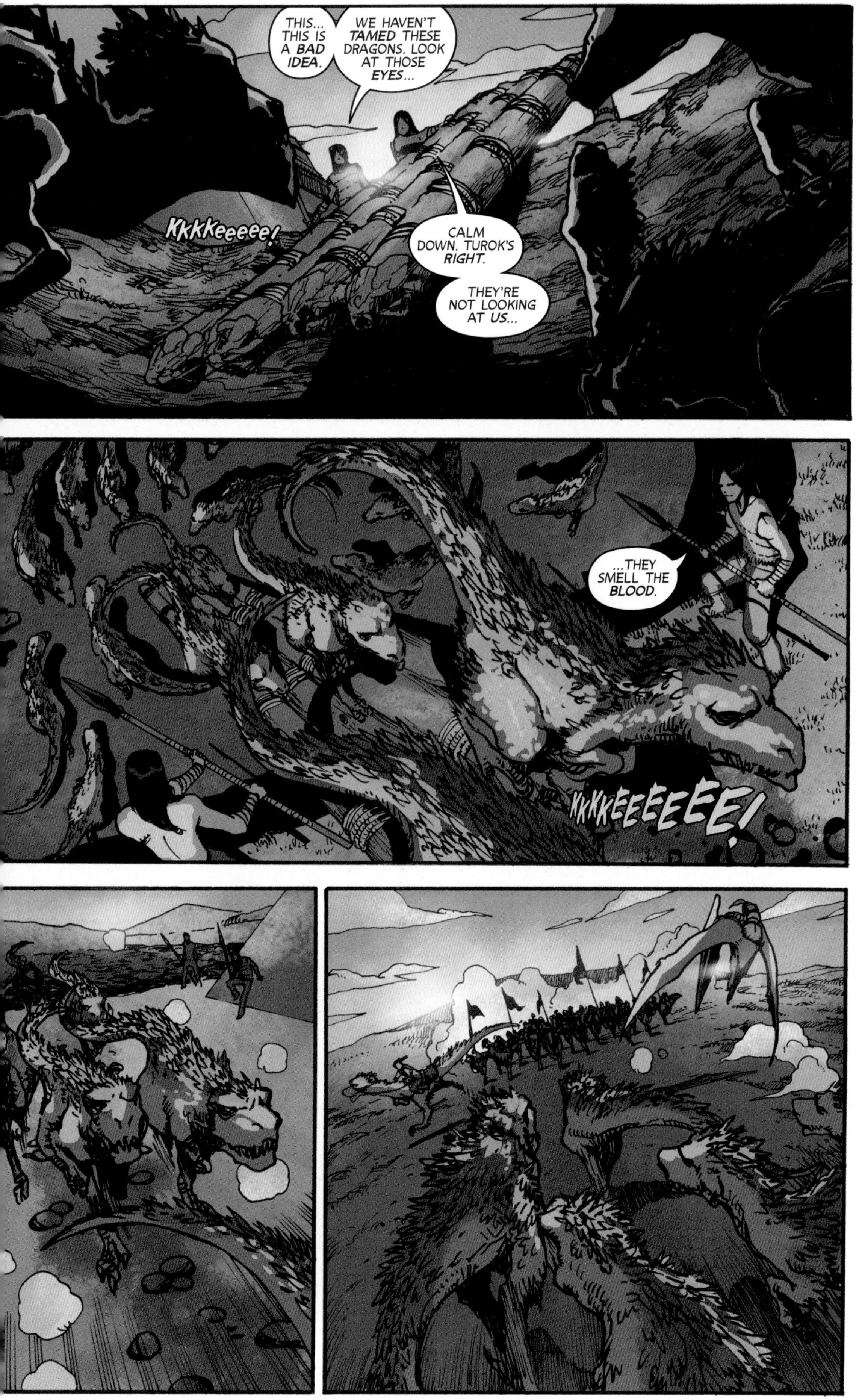
THIS... THIS IS A BAD IDEA.
WE HAVEN'T TAMED THESE DRAGONS. LOOK AT THOSE EYES...
KKKKeeeee!
CALM DOWN. TUROK'S RIGHT.
THEY'RE NOT LOOKING AT US...
...THEY SMELL THE BLOOD.
KKKKEEEEEEE!

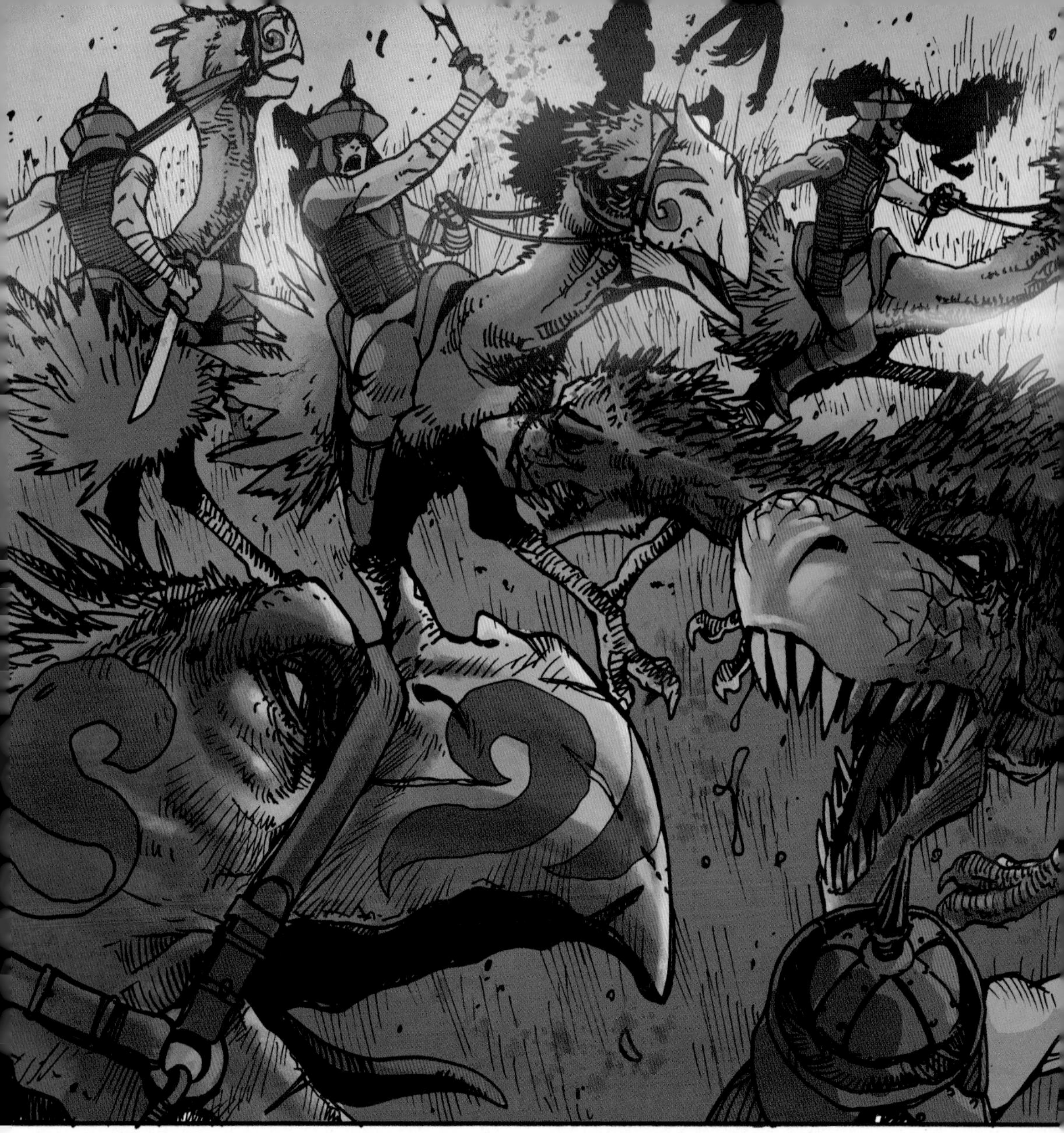

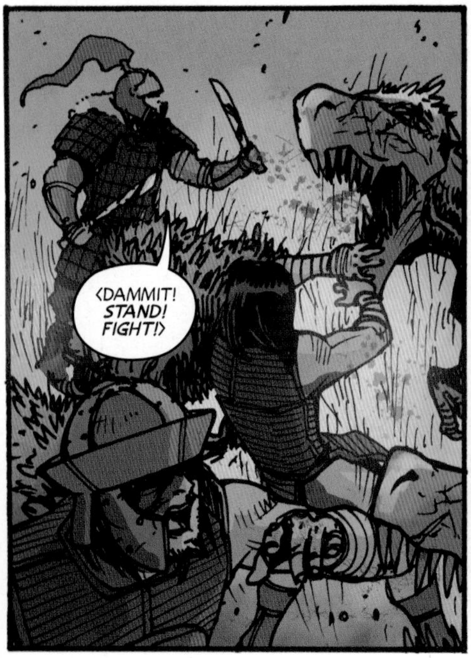

<DAMMIT! STAND! FIGHT!>

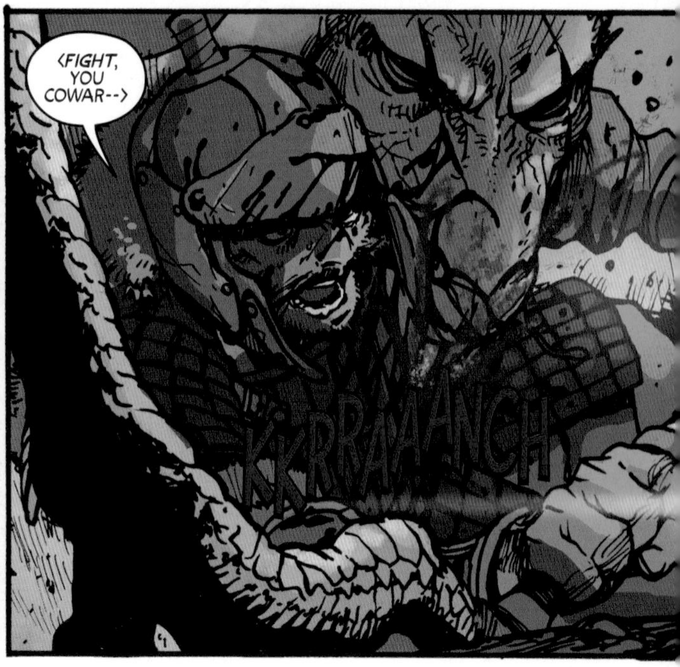

<FIGHT, YOU COWAR-->
KKRRAAANCH

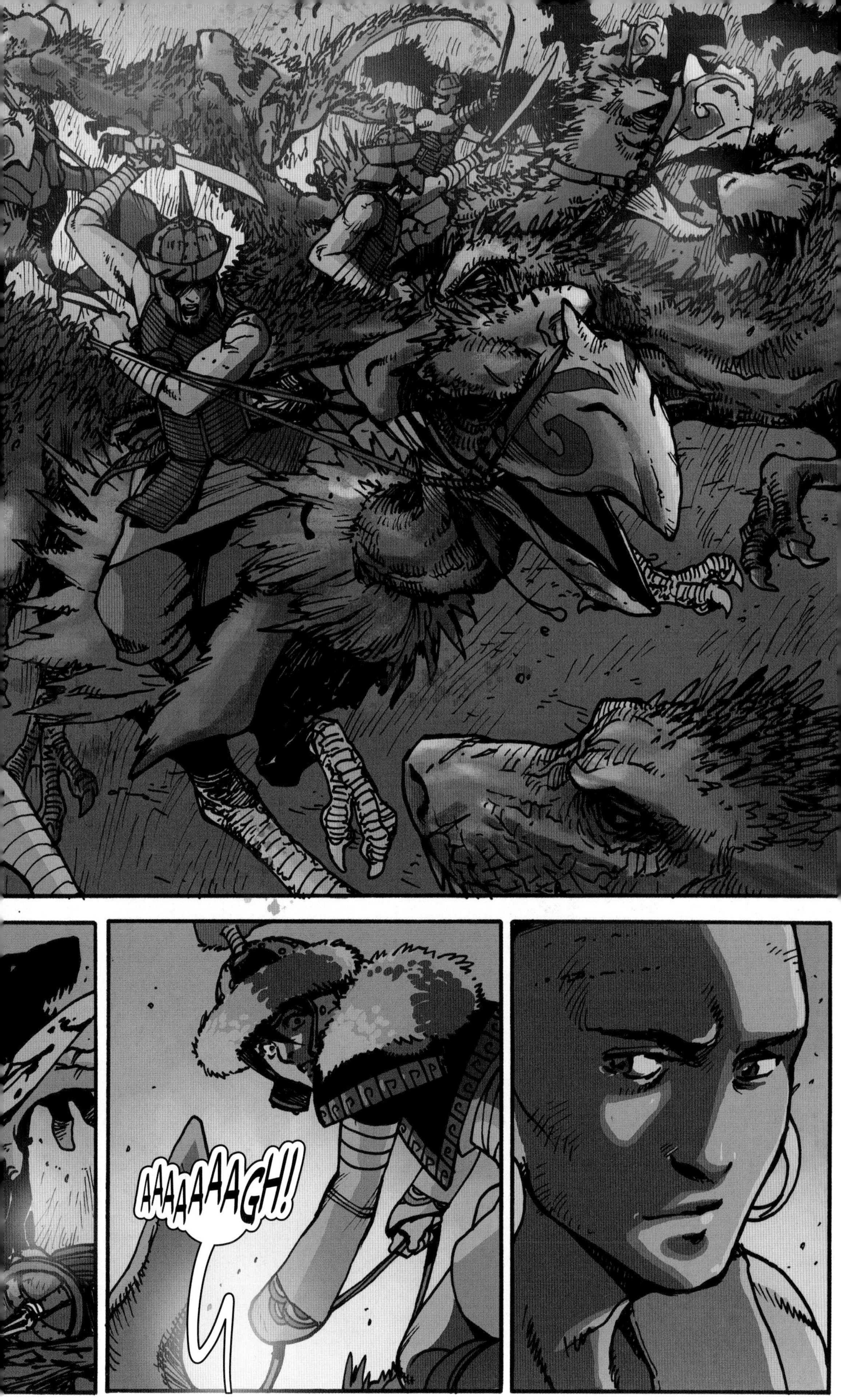
AAAAAAAGH!

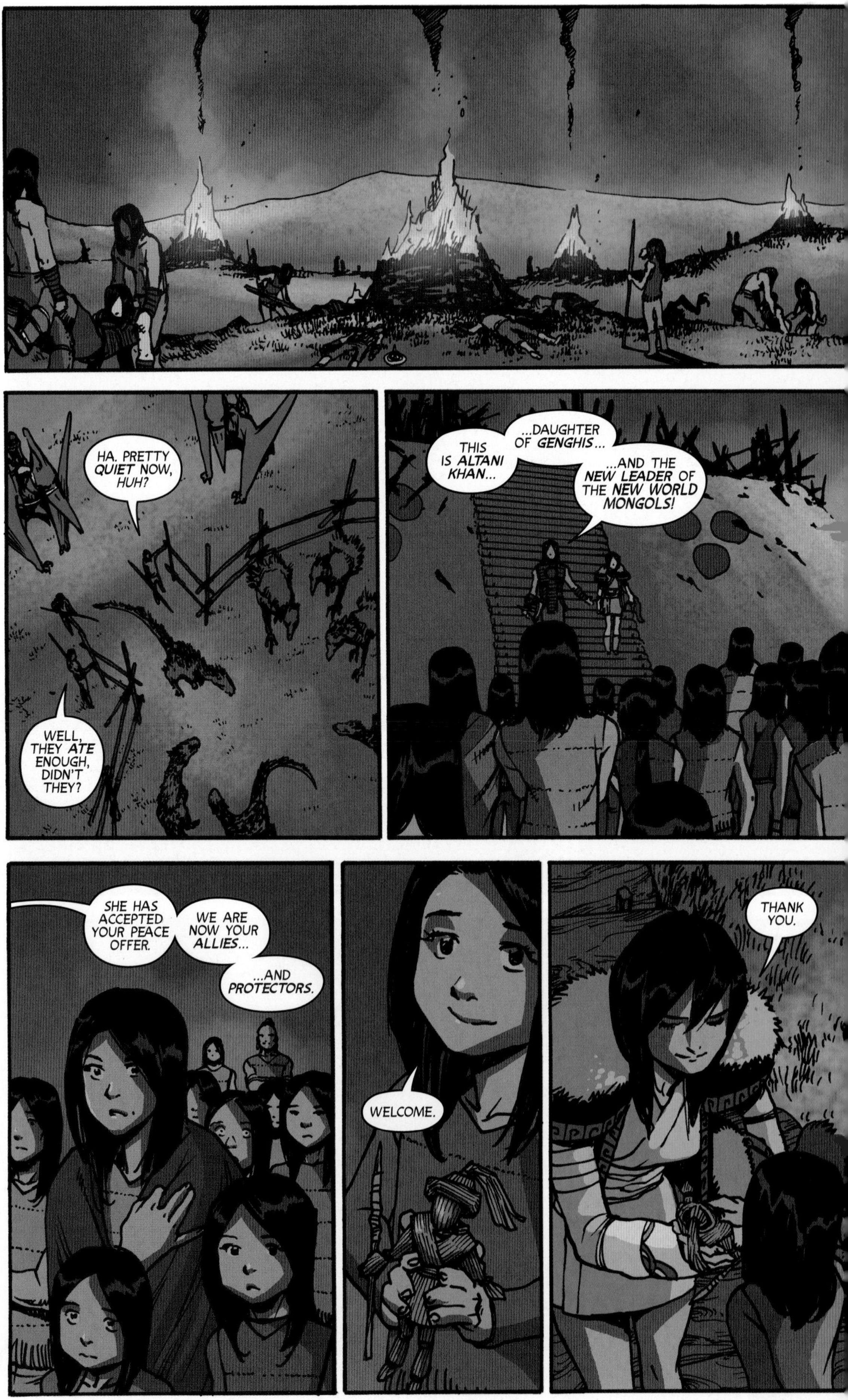
HA. PRETTY QUIET NOW, HUH?
WELL, THEY ATE ENOUGH, DIDN'T THEY?
THIS IS ALTANI KHAN...
...DAUGHTER OF GENGHIS...
...AND THE NEW LEADER OF THE NEW WORLD MONGOLS!
SHE HAS ACCEPTED YOUR PEACE OFFER.
WE ARE NOW YOUR ALLIES...
...AND PROTECTORS.
WELCOME.
THANK YOU.

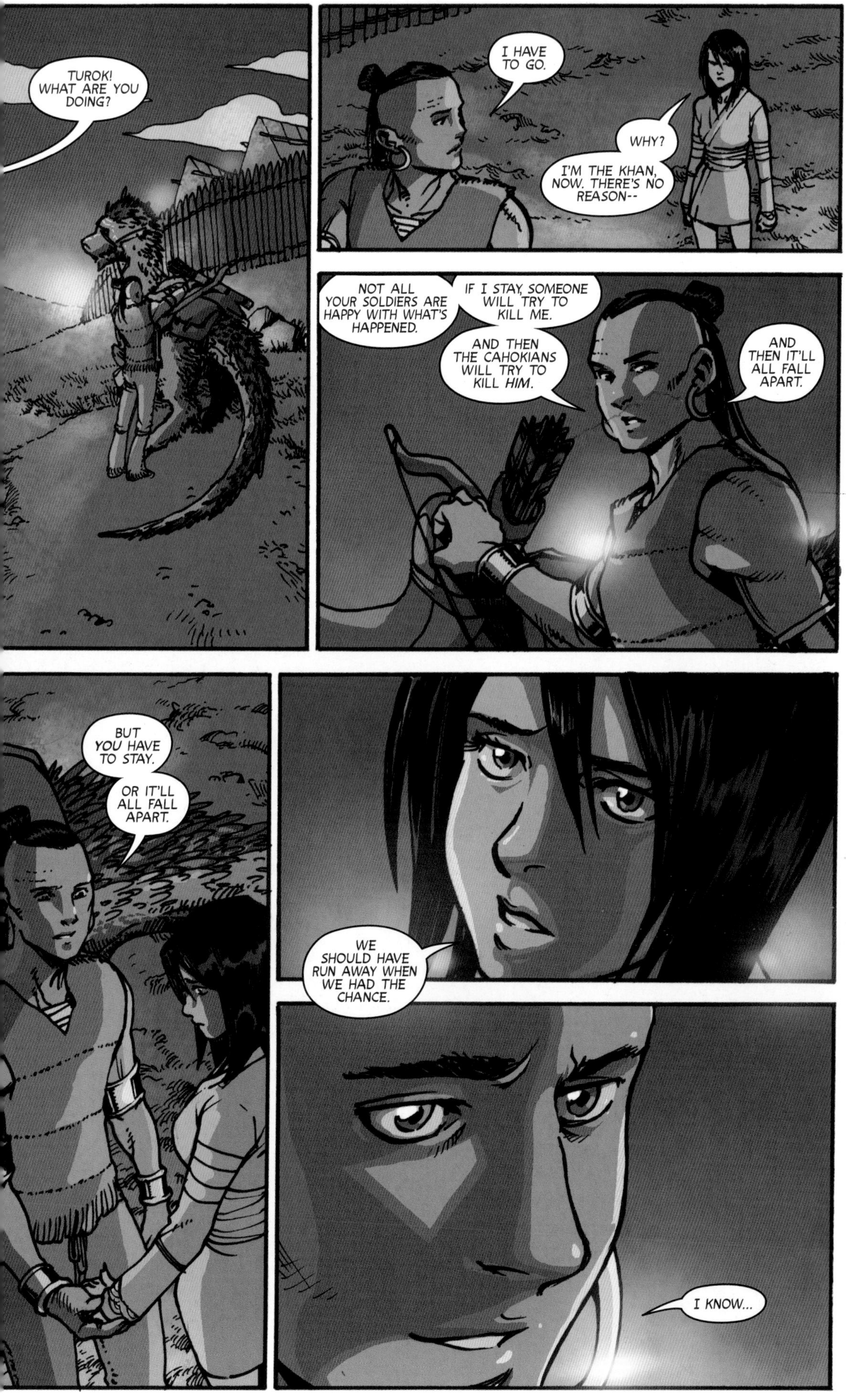
TUROK! WHAT ARE YOU DOING?
I HAVE TO GO.
WHY?
I'M THE KHAN, NOW. THERE'S NO REASON--
NOT ALL YOUR SOLDIERS ARE HAPPY WITH WHAT'S HAPPENED.
IF I STAY, SOMEONE WILL TRY TO KILL ME.
AND THEN THE CAHOKIANS WILL TRY TO KILL *HIM*.
AND THEN IT'LL ALL FALL APART.
BUT *YOU* HAVE TO STAY.
OR IT'LL ALL FALL APART.
WE SHOULD HAVE RUN AWAY WHEN WE HAD THE CHANCE.
I KNOW...

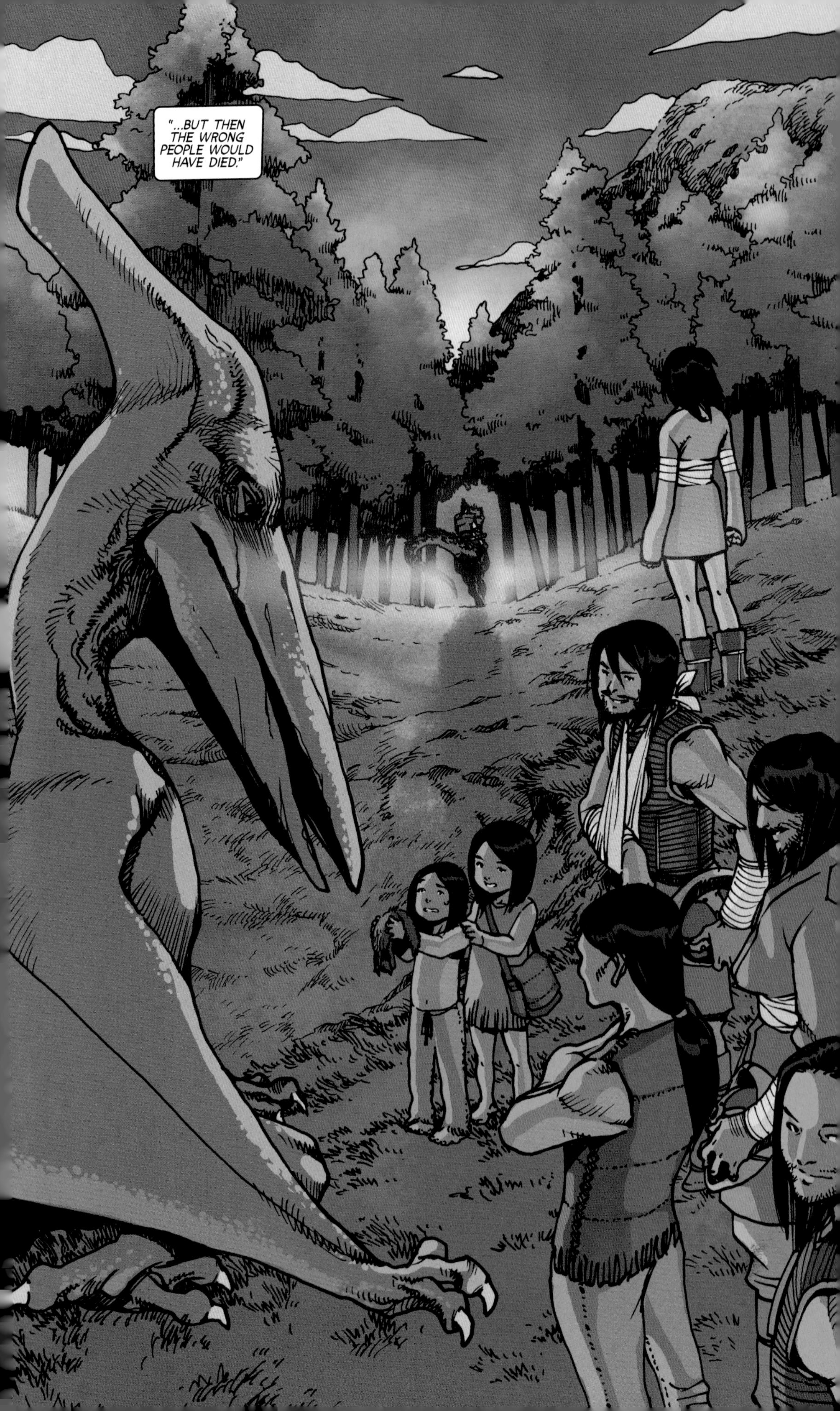
"...BUT THEN THE WRONG PEOPLE WOULD HAVE DIED."

BONUS MATERIAL

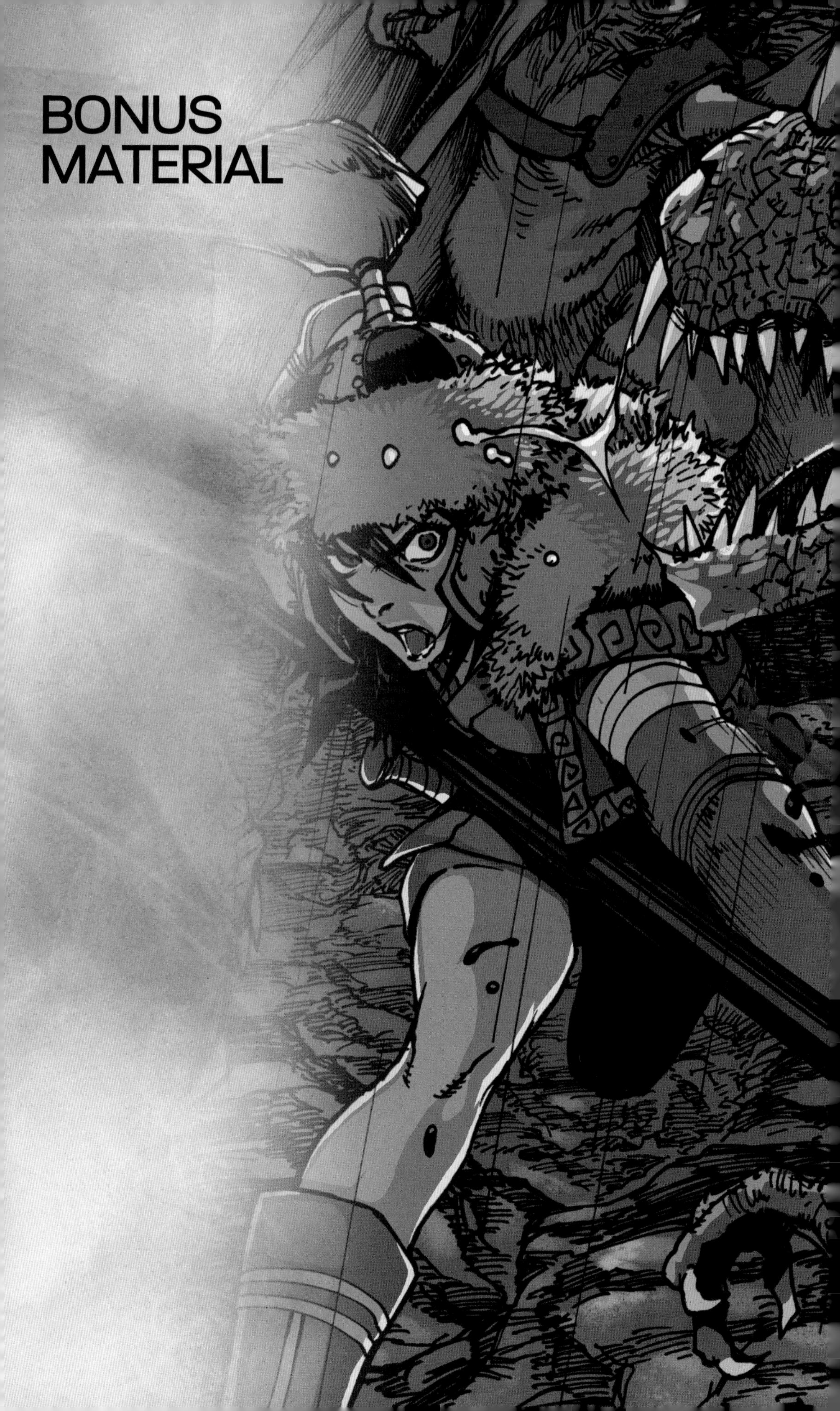

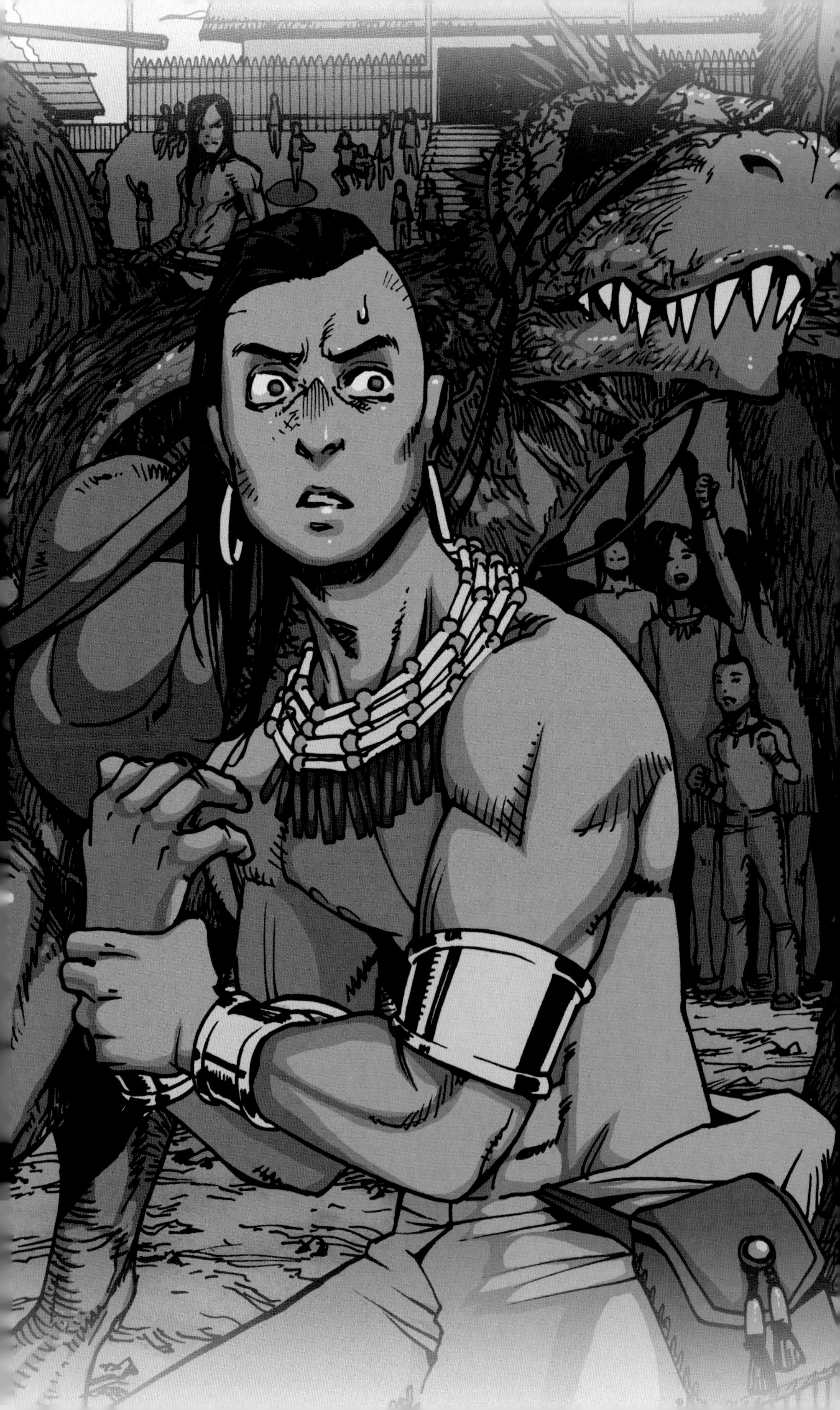

TUROK: DINOSAUR HUNTER #5

Written by Greg Pak

Edited by Nate Cosby

Note: Script is presented as originally submitted.

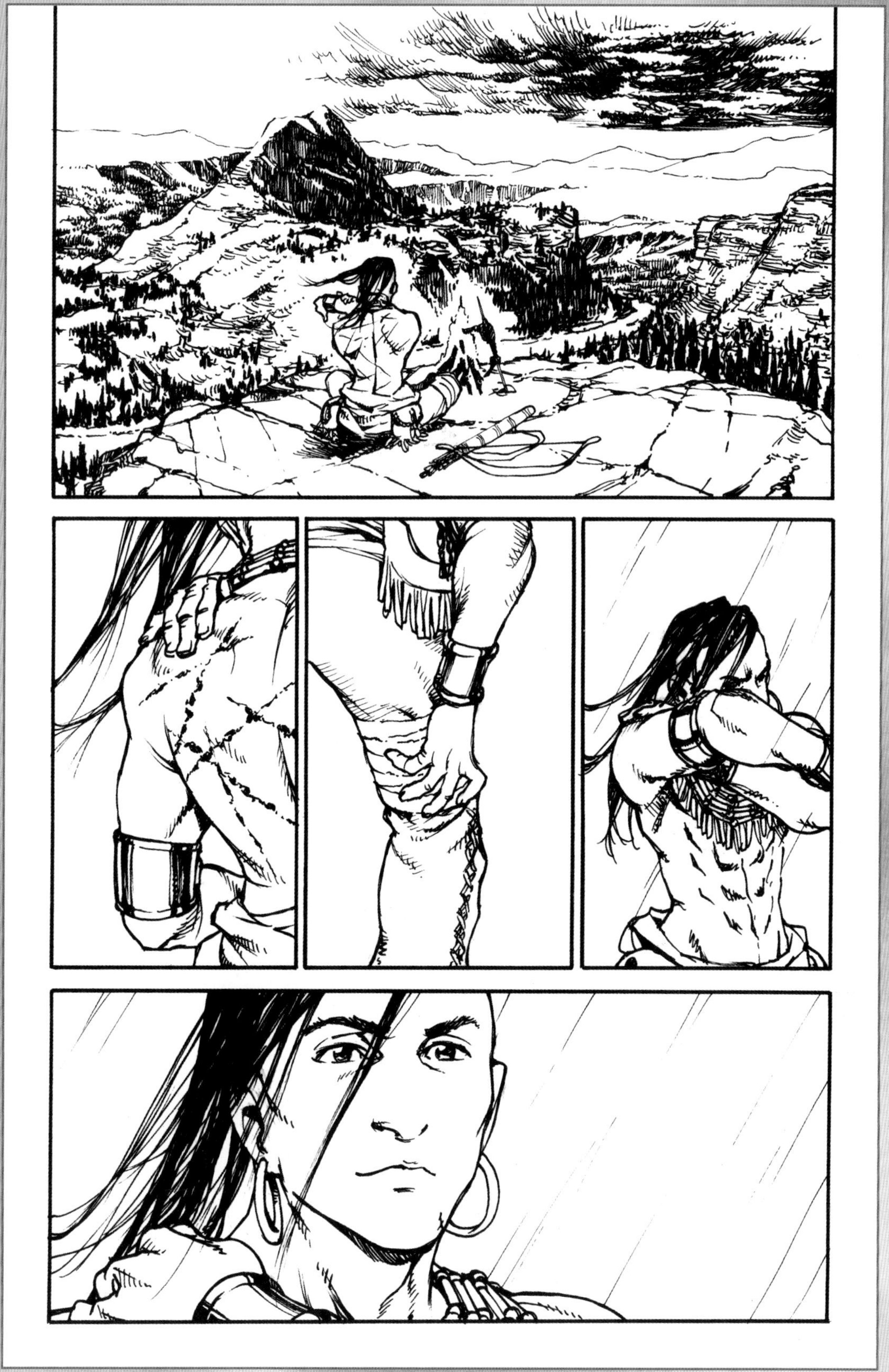

Panel 1: Turok sits by a campfire atop a rocky formation. Dark clouds starting to roil in the background over the hills and cliffs around a broad twisty river. Turok's back is to us -- we don't see his face yet. A mostly eaten rabbit's smoldering on a spit over the flame. Turok's stretching, yawning.

[Important -- we only see the top couple of feet or so of the formation, so it looks like it's just a low, wide rock -- there's a big reveal coming on the next page that we don't want to spoil.]

1. TUROK'S VOICE: It's been *two moons* since I left the tribe.

2. TUROK: yaaaaaaawn

3. TUROK'S VOICE: Two moons since I saw another human being.

Panel 2: Closer angle on Turok's back. He's stretching, reaching back, feeling the scars from the lashing he got from the Chief in issue #1.

4. TUROK'S VOICE: Two moons since anyone *whipped* me...

Panel 3: He stands, rubbing his leg. Angle on his leg, so we see the mostly healed arrow wound that Andar gave him back in issue #1.

5. TUROK'S VOICE: ...or *shot* me...

Panel 4: He rubs his shoulder. Maybe working his arm in circles, as if trying limber up stiff, strained shoulder muscles. Raindrops are starting to fall around him

6. TUROK'S VOICE: ...or tried to *cut me* to pieces.

Panel 5: Close on Turok as he gazes out over the landscape. Dark clouds rolling in behind him. Rain starting to patter down around him and wind picking up. He looks tired. But there's a small smile on his face. He's relaxed, more at peace than we've seen him.

7. SFX: rrrrruuuuummmmble

8. TUROK'S VOICE: This could be a *good life*...

Panel 1: Pull back and we see that Turok is calmly standing atop a thirty foot tall rocky formation. Big bolt of lighting in the sky overhead. Rain falling down hard now. But the biggest reveal: A trio of fifteen foot long dryptosauri (the velociraptor type dinosaurs that we saw throughout the last arc) prowl around at the base of the formation. A few arrows sticking out of them -- and scattered in the mud at eir feet. Clearly they've been tangling with Turok. They can't climb up. But they ave him trapped.

TUROK'S VOICE: ...if it wasn't for all the *monsters*.

SFX: SKRRRRRAAAAKOOOOM

DINOSAUR: KRRRAAAAAA!

CAPTION: Southern Illinois. 1210 AD.

TITLE CARD: TUROK: DINOSAUR HUNTER

TITLE CARD (big):   WEST TOWARDS HOME

TITLE CARD: [Credits, indicia, etc.]

AGE THREE

anel 1: Lightning flashes again. Turok turns to look up, eyebrow raised -- range noise coming from the sky. The wind's picking up.

SFX: SKRRRAAK

THING (off, up): KAAAAA!

anel 2: We look up over Turok's shoulder. Something huge, high in the sky, is owing past. It's silhouetted against the lightning. We can only see part of it -- the st is obscured in clouds and darkness. But what we see looks like one giant atwing.

THING: KRRRAAAAAAAA!

Panel 3: Closer on the thing as it pivots. And we catch a glimpse of a silhouetted human body hanging onto the thing! Holding onto a harness, legs flying! Let's surround this in wind and rain so we can't make it all out that clearly.

3. FIGURE: Hyaaaa!

4. THING: KAAAAAAAA!

Panel 4: Close on Turok's face. Looking shocked.

Panel 5: Wide shot. The dinosaurs at the base of Turok's rocky formation bound away, heading after the thing as it spins, crashing down over the hills in the distance.

5. DINOSAUR: KEEEEEE!

PAGE FOUR

Panel 1: As the dinosaurs head off into the rain, Turok climbs down the sheer side of the rocky formation.

[Note: I'll probably add some Turok V.O. to this later.]

Panel 2: Turok drops to the ground.

Panel 3: Detail of Turok's hand picking up a few arrows from the mud.

Panel 4: Turok runs off in the opposite direction, away from the direction the dinosaurs ran. Let's make this a wide shot so we can see the dinosaurs' tracks in the mud, leading towards us. Turok in the background, his back to us, heading over a rise.

Panel 5: Close on Turok as he turns at the top of the rise, looking back over his shoulder. Dubious look in his eyes. Jaw set. Is he going to go back to help?

1. DINOSAUR (off):   KEEEEEEE!

2. VOICE (off):   Hyaaaa!

3. TUROK'S VOICE: This is *stupid*.

PAGE FIVE

Panel 1: Turok runs after the dinosaurs, following their huge, clawed tracks in the mud. Maybe a wide, high, bird's-eye-view shot, looking down, so we can see him following the tracks.

1. TUROK'S VOICE: Running back towards...

TUROK'S VOICE: ...*people*.

Panel 2: Turok's jaw clenches as he runs and the foot of his injured leg hits the ground.

TUROK'S VOICE: Exactly what I came out here to escape.

TUROK: Nnngh!

TUROK'S VOICE: The *arrow wound* Andar gave me *throbs*.

Panel 3: We look at the scars on Turok's back as he reaches up, grabbing rocks to clamber up the side of a rise.

TUROK'S VOICE: The scars on my *back* catch *fire*.

Panel 4: Turok fits an arrow in his bow as he clears the hill.

TUROK'S VOICE: I've only got *five arrows*.

Panel 5: He raises the bow, staring down the arrow at us with wide, surprised eyes.

TUROK'S VOICE: And whoever was *screaming* is probably already *dead*--

 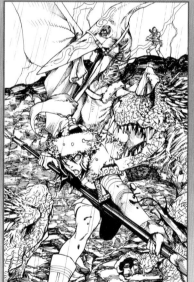 

PAGE SIX

Panel 1: BIG SPLASH. Reveal of our heroine, ALTANI, daugher of Genghis Khan and the leader of his skycorp of pteranodon riders! She's standing before/defending her wounded pteranodon, shouting fiercely as she swings her spear at the snapping cryptosaurs, clipping one of them on the nose, drawing blood! Her pteranodon, who's injured, is cawing, spreading one mighty wing, but its other wing is crumpled, broken. Maybe stick Turok in the far background, peering over the rise at the scene

1. TUROK'S VOICE: --or *not*.

2. ALTANI: HYAAAAA!

3. DINOSAUR: KEEEEEEE!

PAGE SEVEN

Panel 1: Altani stabs a dinosaur in the throat!

1. SFX: SHUNK

2. DINOSAUR: KAAAA--!

Panel 2: It thrashes away, blood spurting, tearing the spear from her hands!

3. DINOSAUR: --aaaaakkk!

Panel 3: Another dinosaur charges at her from the side -- she didn't see this one coming -- she's nimbly dodging, but she's in trouble!

4. DINOSAUR 2:   KRRAAAA!

5. ALTANI: Huup!

Panel 4: Turok runs forward, firing an arrow, yelling to try to get the dinosaur's attention!

6. TUROK: HAAAAA!

Panel 5: The dinosaur that was charging at Altani turns to snarl at Turok -- the arrow in its eye! Altani wide-eyed in the background -- still in fierce battle mode, but also surprised. She's scrambling away from the dinosaur but staring back towards us (and the off panel Turok).

7. SFX: THOKK

8. DINOSAUR: KRRRRAAAA!

PAGE EIGHT

Panel 1: Turok leaps forward, feet first, kicking the back of the arrow, jamming it deep into the dinosaur's eye socket!

1. SFX: SHUUNNK

DINOSAUR: KKKKKAAAAAA!

anel 2: Close on Altani, poised for action, but staring, a bit wide-eyed. She's not omeone who's easily impressed. But she's impressed. (This panel and panel 3 ombined are the big moment when our young heroes first lock eyes. A kind of oody action-adventure meet-cute moment, if that makes sense, Tak. You're onna kill these, I know.)

ALTANI: Whoa.

anel 3: Reverse. Close on Turok, giving her a small smile as the dinosaur tumbles ehind him, thrashing on the ground. He's maybe blushing just a little. He actually oesn't have much experience with women -- and he's never met one as insanely adass as Altani.

TUROK: Hey.

anel 4: But then the Pteranodon rears up over Turok, between him and Altani, ocking him off balance with one great wing, great beak opening! [Note: Let's not rget the Pteranadon has one broken wing. So it's whacking Turok with its good ng.]

PTERANODON: RRREEEEEEEEE!

anel 4: Turok, lying on his back in the mud, struggles to fit an arrow into his ow. Pteranodon looming over him. This could be the end, y'all.

TUROK: Gah!

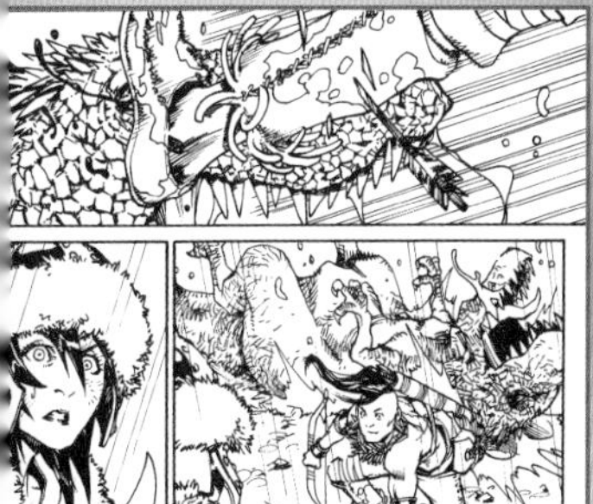

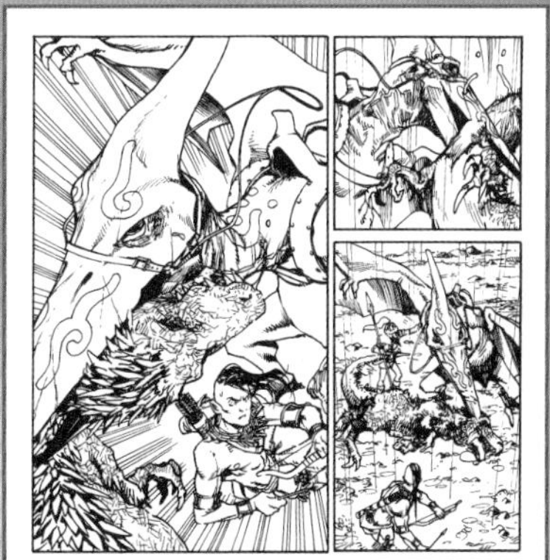

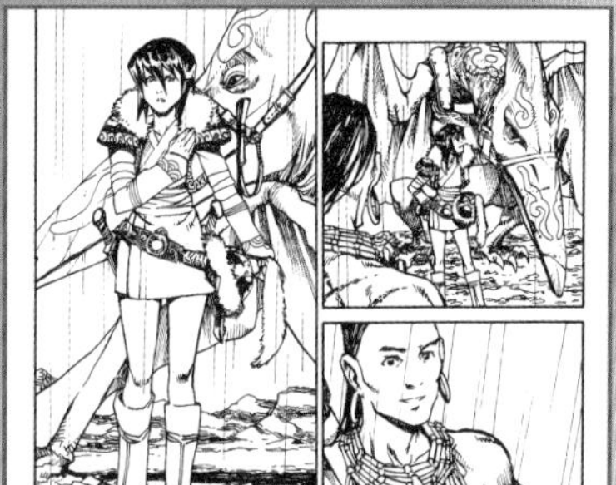

GE NINE

anel 1: BIG PANEL. But instead, the Pteranodon lunges forward -- OVER Turok

-- and grabs the third and last dinosaur by the neck! Turok's on the ground, just a foot or so underneath this insane action! The dinosaur's snarling and thrashing! Mud and blood flying!

1. DINOSAUR: KKKRRRAAAA!

2. PTERANODON: REEEEE!

Panel 2: The Pteranodon twists, snapping the dinosaur's neck!

3. SFX: KKRRAAAK

Panel 3: Turok cautiously slides to the side as the Pteranodon lets the dinosaur' limp body slump down into the mud. Altani, now holding her spear -- and leaning on it a bit, as if tired or stiff, has stepped up to the Pternanodon and is reaching into a saddle bag.

4. ALTANI: <Good girl, Borta.>

5. PTERANODON: rrreeeee.

6. TUROK: Wha...

Panel 4: Altani pulls a dead squirrel out of the saddlebag. Borta is turning, eyein her with an eager eye.

7. ALTANI: <Hup!>

Panel 5: Altani tosses the dead squirrel into the air and Borta gobbles it up. Turo watches, a little amazed.

8. ALTANI: <Good girl.>

9. TUROK: Ha!

PAGE TEN

Panel 1: Altani turns to Turok. Standing straight. Making a formal introduction. B of a military feel with her. She has one hand on her chest -- indicating herself as she says her name.

1. ALTANI: My name is *Altani*...

2. ALTANI: ...daughter of the *Khan* and leader of the *Skyriders*.

Panel 2: Altani turns and pats Borta on the side. Borta's cocking her head, peeri down at Turok.

ALTANI: And this is *Borta*.

BORTA: rrreeeeeee

ALTANI: And we thank you for you help today.

anel 3: Angle on Turok. Small smile on his face. This is pretty amazing. He's uching his chest as he says his name.

TUROK: I'm... *Turok*.

TUROK: You speak my language?

anel 4: Wide two shot. Kind of cute. They just stand, looking at each other. aybe a little shy. It's still raining on them, by the way.

ALTANI: A little.

ALTANI: Where's your tribe?

TUROK: I... don't have a tribe.

0. ALTANI: Hn.

1. ALTANI: Good.

anel 5: Altani sits, a bit heavily, on a rock. Shoulders slumping. And now, for the rst time, we see she has a broken arrow in her calf. We also see that she's etting down a long-bladed knife that she'd been concealing in one hand.

2. ALTANI: Then I won't have to *kill* you.

Panel 1: Wide shot. Later -- sunset. Campfire in the lee of a rock formation. Bort off to one side, pecking at the corpse of one of the dinosaurs. Turok and Altani si on an animal skin by the fire. Small chunk of meat roasting on the fire. Turok's working on Altani's leg, bandaging it.

1. TUROK: Who shot you?

2. ALTANI: The people of the *city*.

3. TUROK: What's... what's a *city*?

4. ALTANI: You don't want to know.

Panel 2: He gives her a look. She's got a small smile on her face, gazing toward the horizon, raising a finger to gesture towards the West.

5. TUROK: Where are you from?

6. ALTANI: Far away. Over the sea.

7. TUROK: There's a *sea*... to the *west*?

8. ALTANI: Ha.

9. TUROK: What are you doing here? Why'd the people of the city try to--

Panel 3: She starts to stand up.

10. ALTANI: All right, that's enough.

11. TUROK: Hey, calm down! You've got a *fever*. You need to *rest*.

12. ALTANI: No. Borta's *wing*...

Panel 4: Turok turns to Borta, who gives him a wary look.

13. TUROK: I'll look at it... if she'll let me.

14. ALTANI: What do you know about dragons?

Panel 5: Turok reaches out, touches Borta's wing.

15. TUROK: I used to keep a few birds.

16. TUROK: Although they were a little *smaller*.

anel 6: Borta nuzzles Turok as he inspects her wing. Altani gazes at them. xpression a little softer than usual. Something almost like wonder in her eyes.

AGE TWELVE

anel 1: Later. Night. It's dark. Turok finishes working on Borta. Splint on her ng.

TUROK: That's it. Good girl.

anel 2: Borta tilts her head back and calls, spreading her good wing. Turok's a tle alarmed, stepping back. But Altani just smiles.

TUROK: Whoa!

ALTANI: Calm down. She just wants a squirrel.

anel 3: Turok opens the bag hanging from Borta's saddle. Wrinkles his nose a t. These squirrels aren't so fresh any longer.

TUROK: Uff!

ALTANI: What's the matter.

anel 4: He pulls out a dead squirrel.

TUROK: Nothing, nothing.

anel 5: He tosses it into the air and Borta gobbles it up.

ALTANI: Good girl!

ALTANI: You have to say "good girl."

TUROK: Good girl!

anel 6: Then he looks over towards an off-panel noise.

DINOSAUR (off, wavy): Kaaaaa...

AGE THIRTEEN

anel 1: We look over Turok's shoulder at the wounded dinosaur with the arrow in s eye. It's hunched a few yards away. Slumped and defeated looking -- one side ore draggy than the other. But gazing at them. Altani's staggering to her feet. urok's a little more calm.

ALTANI: Kill it!

Panel 2: Turok. Thoughtful. Altani behind him, giving him a look.

2. TUROK: Wait a minute...

Panel 3: Turok tosses the dinosaur a squirrel.

Panel 4: It gobbles it up.

Panel 5: Turok and Altani exchange looks.

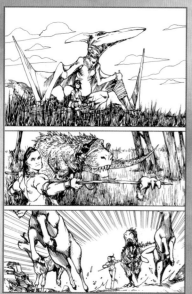

PAGE FOURTEEN

Panel 1: Lovely, sunny day. Altani and Borta sit in the sun on the top of a low hill surrounded by high grass, looking towards us. Both still bandaged. But it's a beautiful day. Altani's actually smiling.

NOTE: I'll probably add Turok V.O. to pages 14 and 15 later -- to help create the sense of a montage over time for these pages.

Panel 2: Reverse on Turok in the high grass with the dinosaur. The dino's injured eye has been bandaged -- there are leather straps around the animal's head, so almost has what looks like a pirate's eyepatch. Turok's holding onto the ends of reins that are connected to the dino's neck -- and he's holding out a stick, from th end of which dangles a dead squirrel. He's leading the dinosaur, which is walking following the squirrel.

Panel 3: Turok and the dinosaur charge, side by side, chasing prehistoric pronghorn antelopes. (ref) Turok's wielding a spear; the dino, wearing the reins, is just roaring.

PAGE FIFTEEN

Panel 1: Sunset. A pronghorn roasts on a spit. Turok sits near the fire, tending th

ast. Altani lies on her blanket on the other side of the fire. The dinosaur and
orta eat another dead pronghorn off in the grass, in the background, like lions at
e kill.

anel 2: Angle on Altani, lying on her blanket, asleep. Looking younger, more
ulnerable in slumber.

anel 3: Detail: But we see she's holding a knife.

anel 4: Close on Turok, small smile.

anel 5: Close on golden grass, brown or red leaves blowing past. Seasons are
rning.

AGE SIXTEEN

anel 1: Nice big, triumphant panel - Turok rides across the range on his
nosaur. He's fashioned a saddle and bridle. The dinosaur has a leather patch
rapped over one eye, but is alert, ready, and obedient, trotting along. Turok is
yeing his dino with a small smile, speaking to it quietly, encouragingly. Let's let it
e nearly autumn now. Grasses of the plains turning golden.

. DINOSAUR: Kaaaaa...

. TUROK: Hey, hey, hey.

. TUROK: That's it.

. TUROK: Good boy.

anel 2: Turok turns to wave at Altani, trotting toward her. She's saddling Borta,
ho's stretching her wings, testing the air. No bandages any longer.

. TUROK: Look at me!

. ALTANI: Ha!

anel 3: Altani expression turns somber.

. ALTANI: Turok. I'm leaving soon.

. TUROK: Oh.

. ALTANI: And when *you* go...

anel 4: Altani points. Turok turns to look, but gestures back the other direction.

0. ALTANI: ...go *East*.

11. TUROK: But... my parents came from the *West*. That's where I was
                 planning to--

12. ALTANI: I know. But--

Panel 5: Turok makes a surprised face, startled and nearly falling out of the saddle as his dino charges towards the West, up a hill. It's smelling something.

13. TUROK: Whoa! Hold on, boy!

Panel 6: Close on Turok, his face falling as he clears the hill and looks toward us

PAGE SEVENTEEN

Panel 1: BIG SPLASH. We look over Turok's shoulder at a group of Native
American warriors on the other side of the hill -- carrying spears and riding on
mastodons! One of them is pointing towards him -- others are letting loose with a
barrage of arrows!

1. WARRIOR: There!

2. WARRIOR: *Dragon rider!*

3. WARRIOR: *FIRE!*

PAGE EIGHTEEN

Panel 1: As arrows rain down around them, Turok spins on his dinosaur, shouting
a warning towards the off-panel Altani.

1. TUROK: ALTANI!

. TUROK: RUN!

anel 2: Borta swoops down overhead, buzzing the warriors. Warriors duck -- one f them is getting clipped by Altani's spear! Turok is staring up in shock/surprise.

. BORTA: SKREEEEEEEEE!

. WARRIOR: GAAH!

anel 3: Close on Altani as she swoops past on Borta's back, shouting down)wards Turok from above.

. ALTANI: *EAST*, TUROK!

anel 4: But a warrior knocks Turok off his dinosaur! Clubbing him upside the ead!

. TUROK: Ukkk!

anel 5: He falls to the ground, cracking his head on a stone.

. TUROK: Haakk!

AGE NINETEEN

anel 1: Turok stares upwards, dazed, blood trickling down his head.

anel 2: Turok's POV. Looking over the heads of the Warriors as they shake their pears and fire arrows. High in the air, Borta wings away into the distance.

anel 3: Black panel. Turok's passed out.

anel 4: Later. Close on Turok opening his eyes. New environment. Dust in the ir.

. TUROK: Nnngh...

. WARRIOR (off): Morning, brother.

Panel 5: Pull back to reveal that Turok's in a caravan of mastodons. He's been :aptured by the Warriors, who are returning home. He's tied up and strapped to he top of his dinosaur, which is docilely walking along, its leash tied to the back of ι mastodon. Turok's blinking, raising his head slightly, looking around. A Warrior's jiving him a wry look.

. TUROK: I'm... I'm not your brother.

. WARRIOR: Yeah. You might want to *reconsider* that *attitude*...

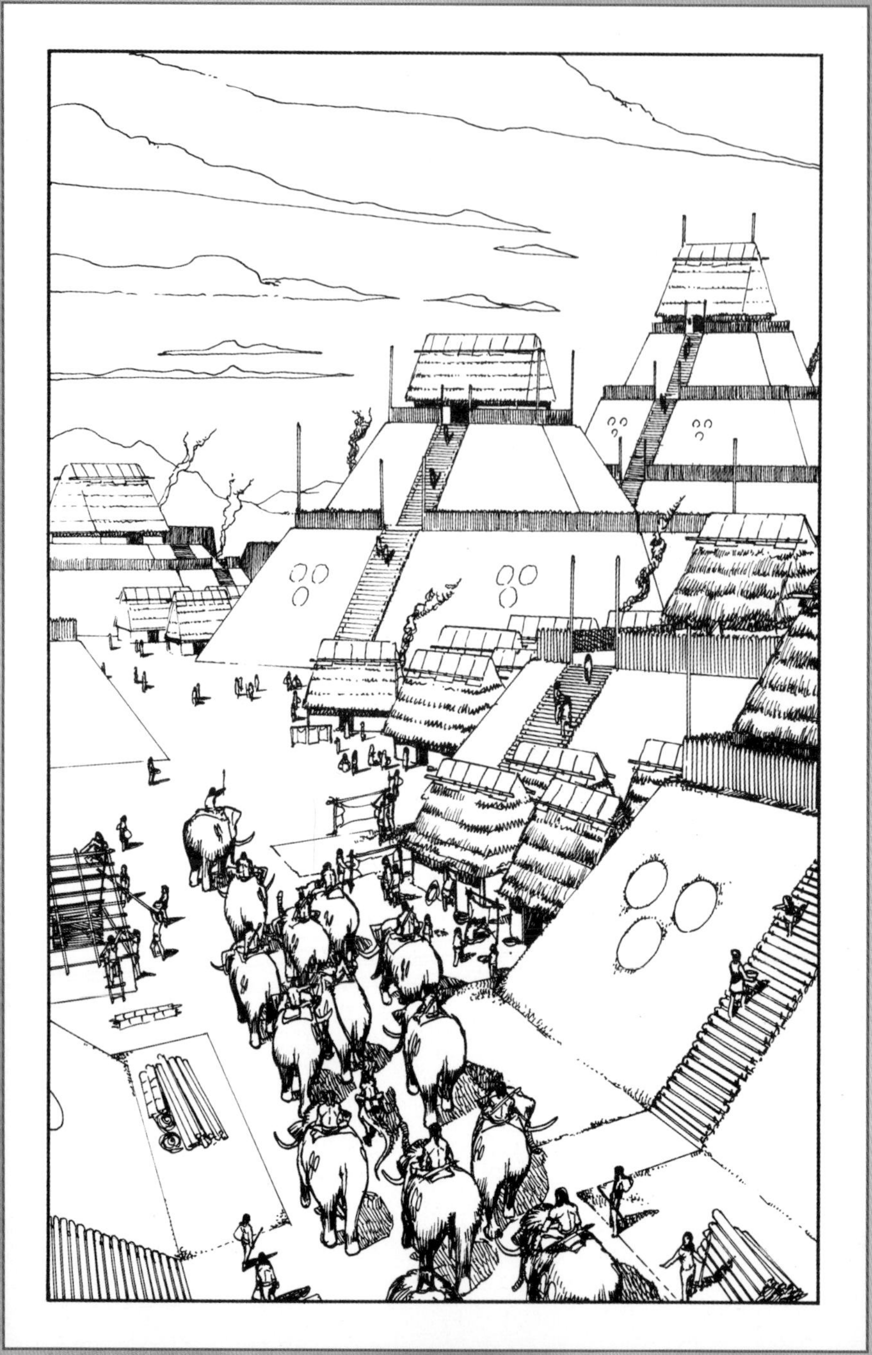

PAGE TWENTY

Panel 1: Reveal of the destination of the caravan: a huge Native American city w
know today as Cahokia. In the middle of the city are huge pyramid like earthen mounds. Thatch buildings all around. A few thousand people live here. Folks are milling around, smoking meat, playing with dogs, threshing grain. (ref ref ref)

1. WARRIOR: ...when you meet the *Chiefs* of *Cahokia.*

2. CAPTION: To be continued!

END.

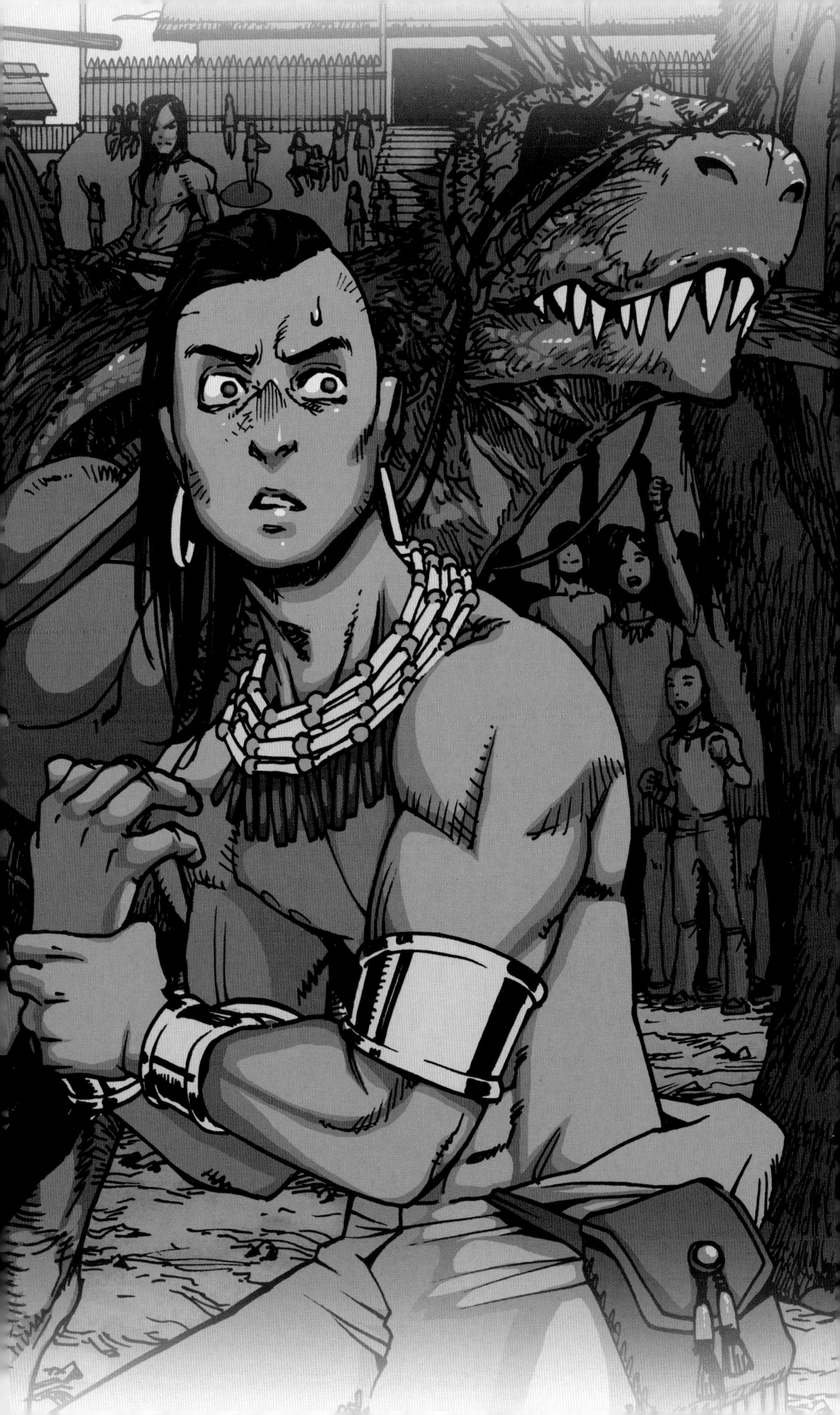

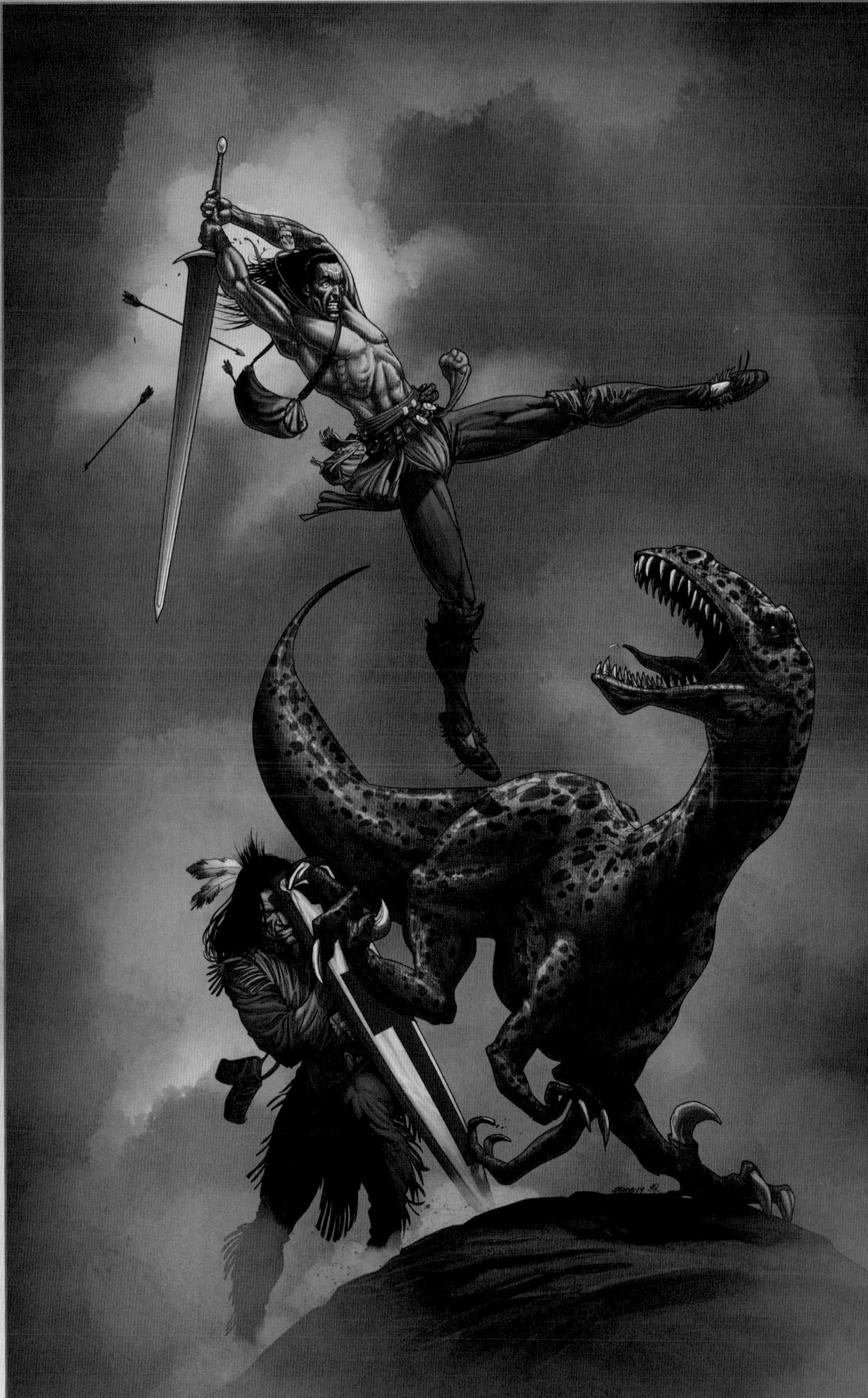

issue #5 cover by BART SEARS
colors by NEERAJ MENON

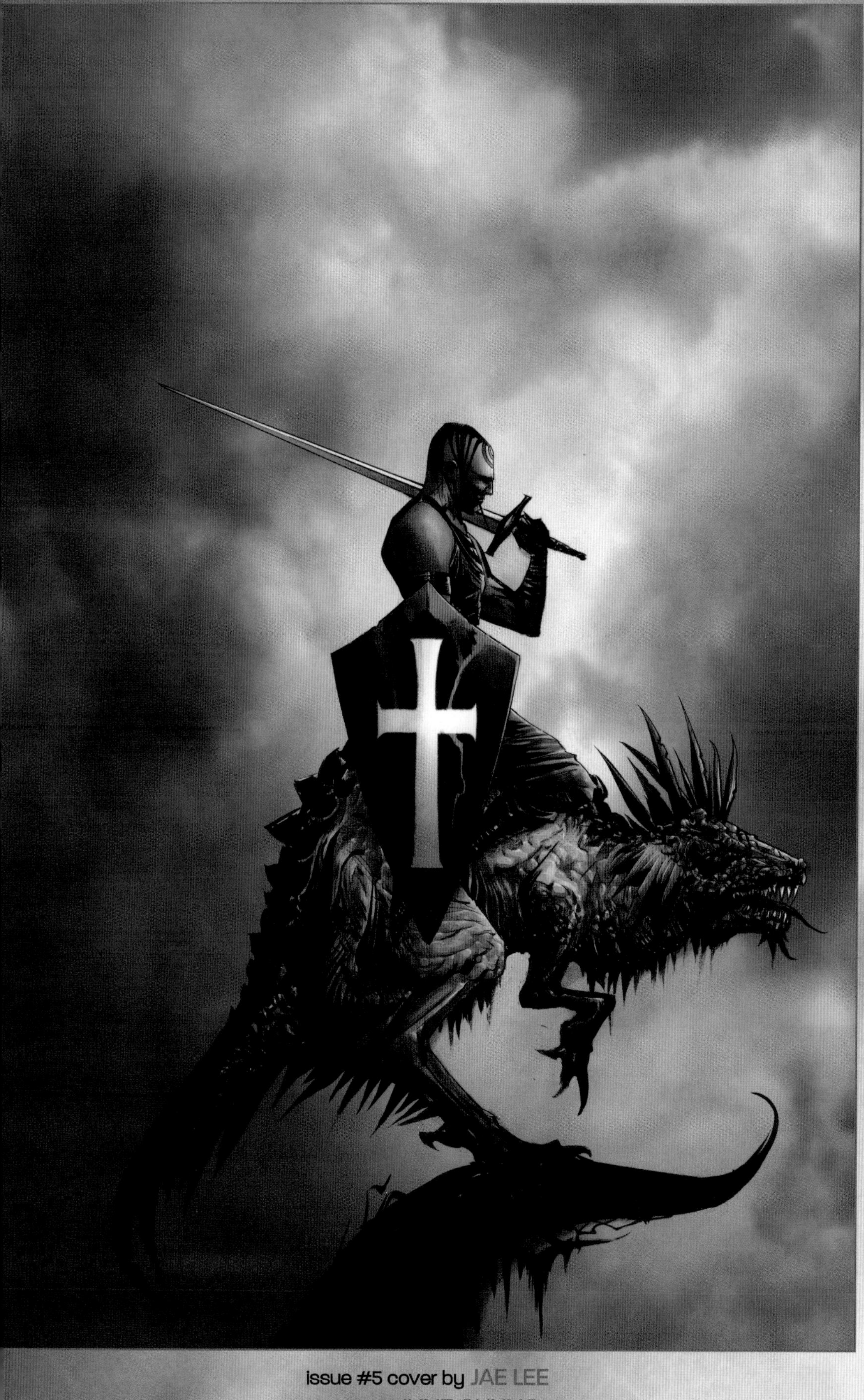

issue #5 cover by JAE LEE
colors by JUNE CHUNG

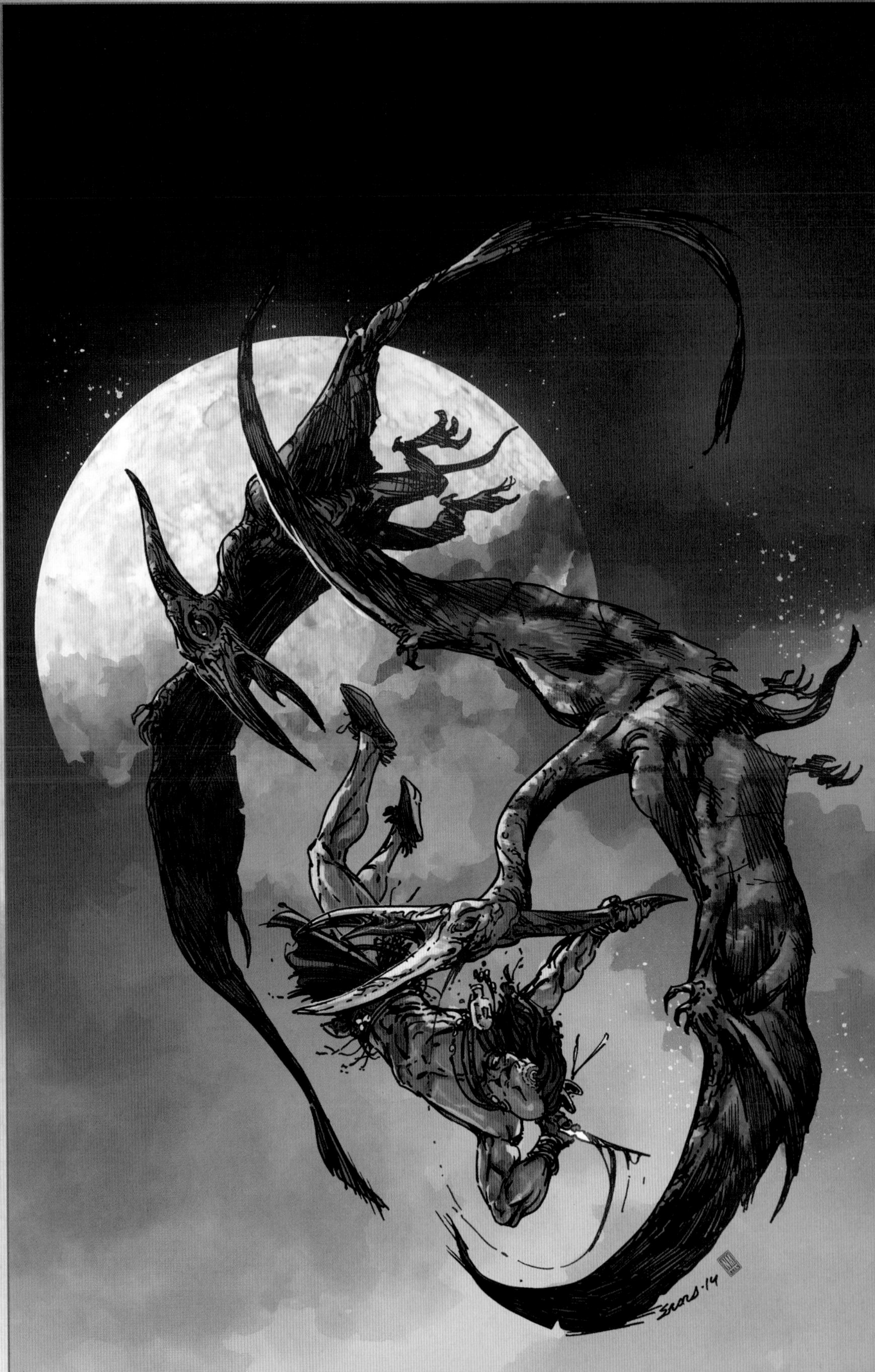
SEARS·14

issue #6 cover by BART SEARS
colors by NEERAJ MENON

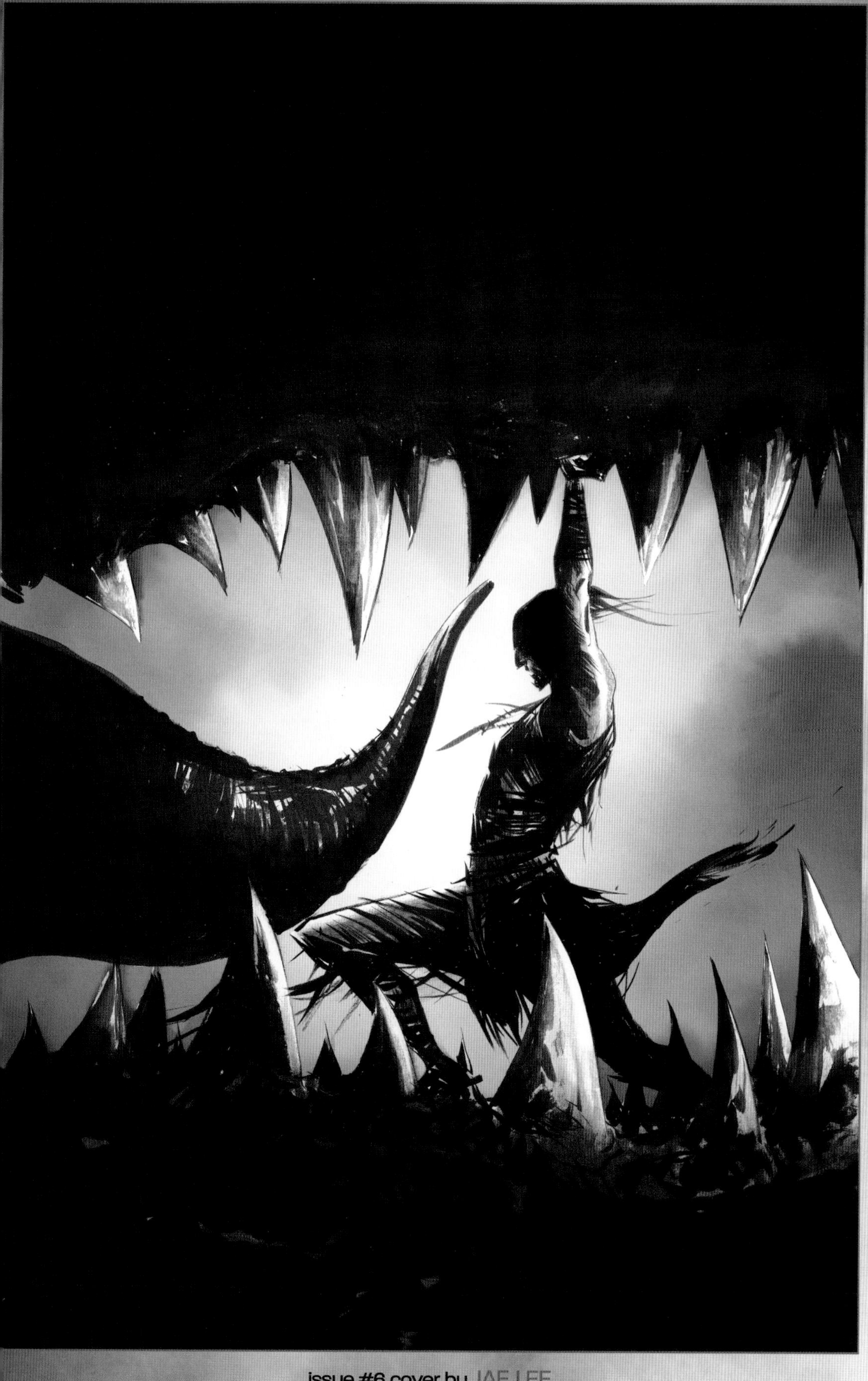

issue #6 cover by JAE LEE
colors by JUNE CHUNG

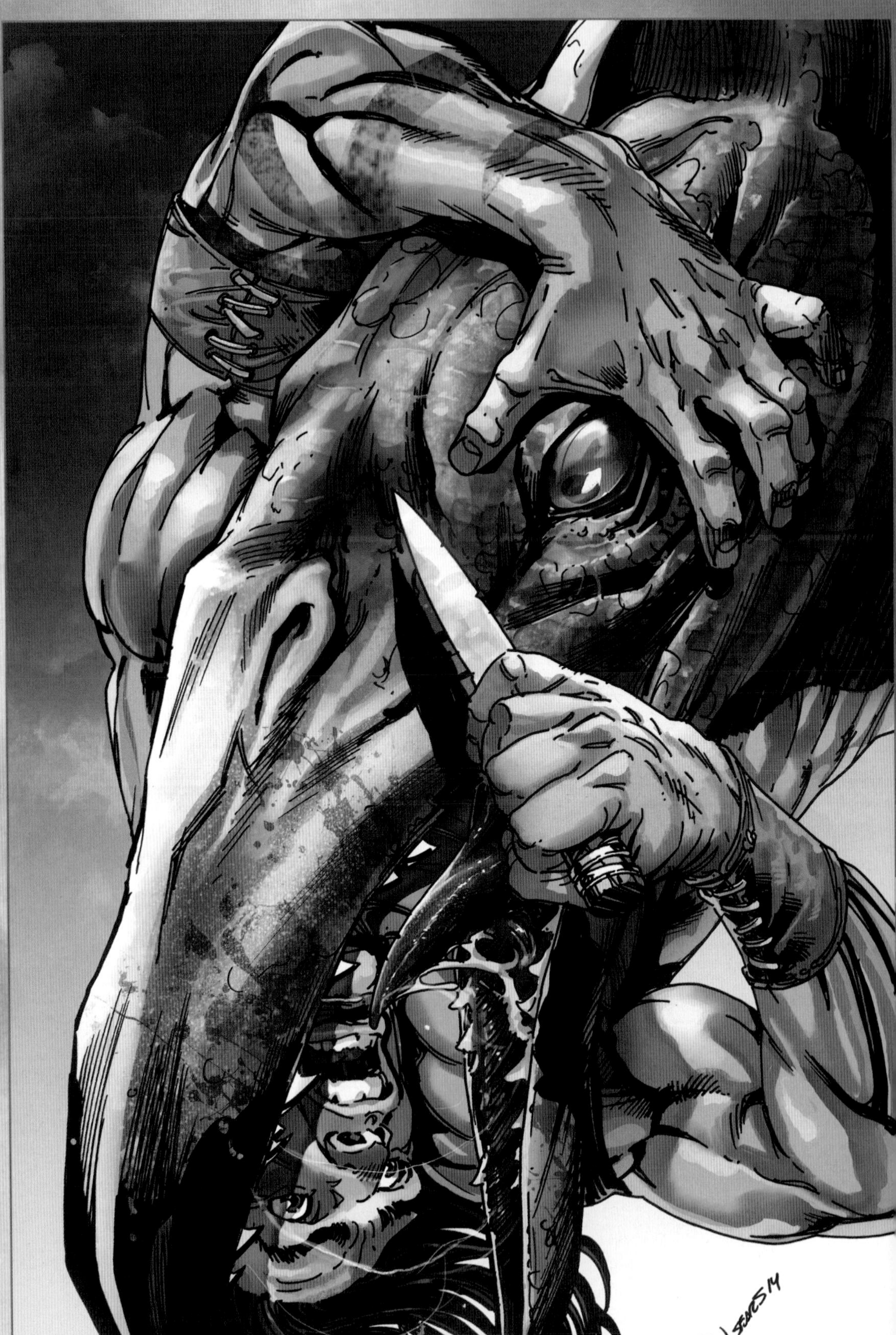
SEARS '14

issue #7 cover by BART SEARS

colors by NEERAJ MENON

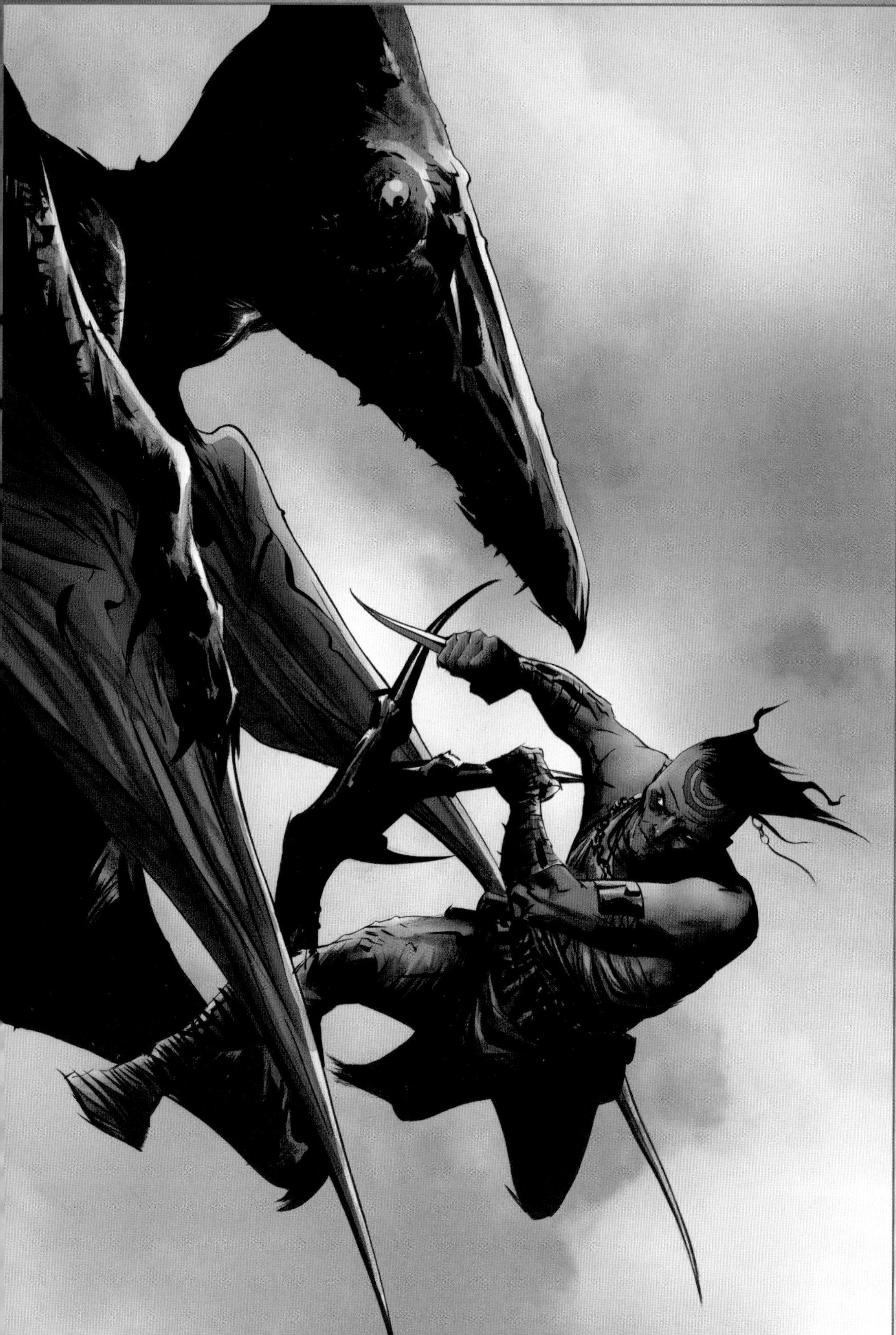

issue #7 cover by JAE LEE
colors by JUNE CHUNG

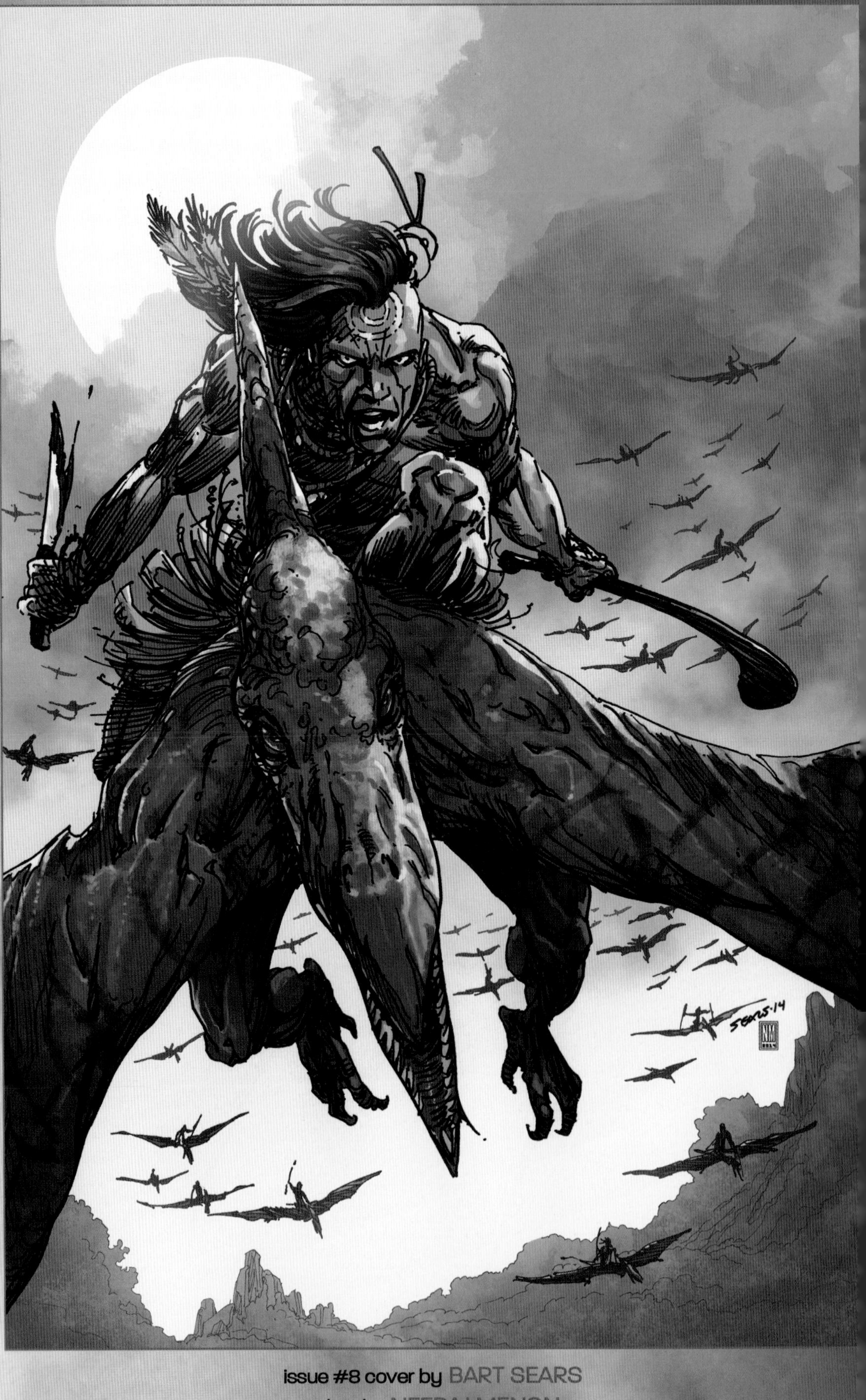

issue #8 cover by BART SEARS
colors by NEERAJ MENON

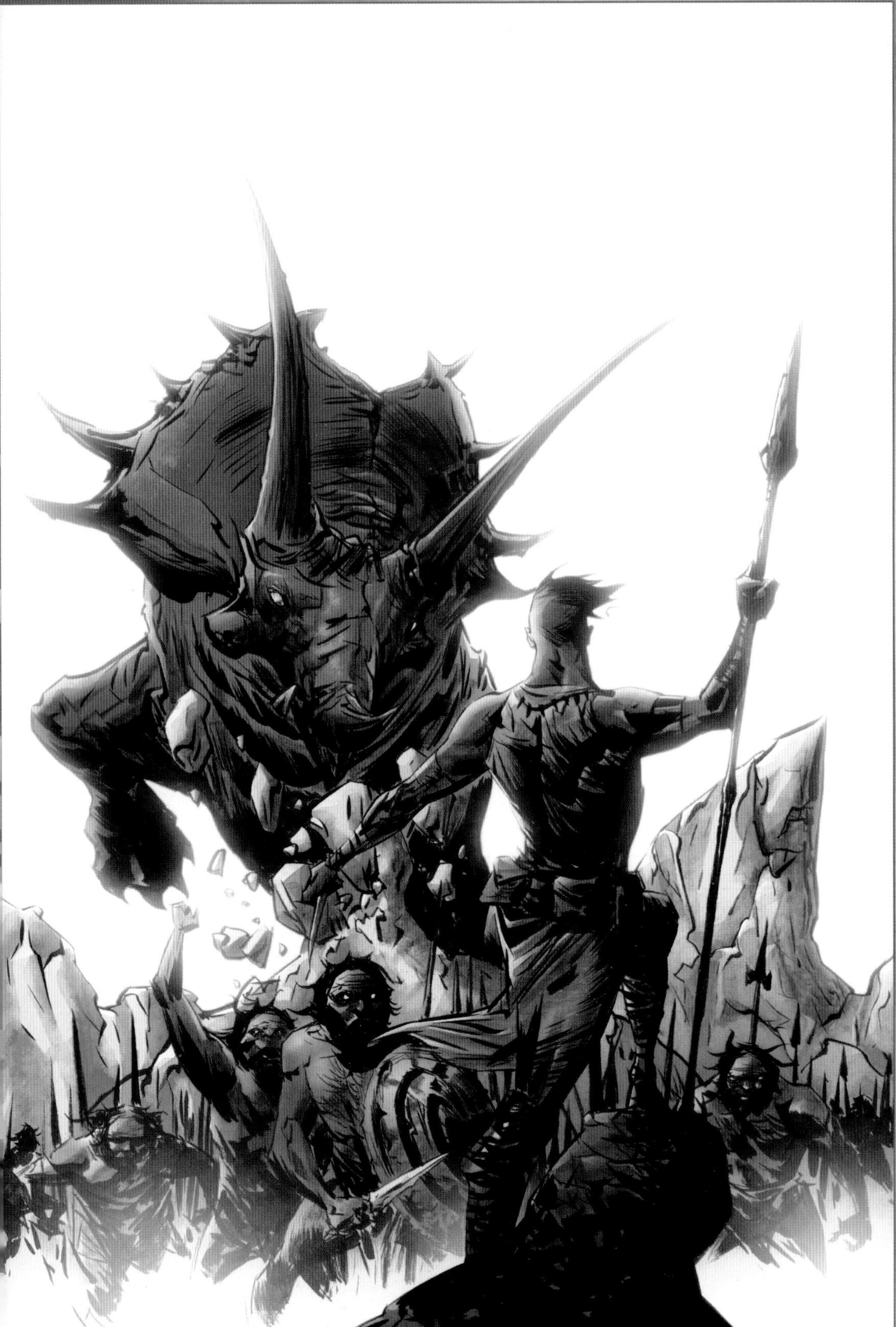

issue #8 cover by JAE LEE
colors by JUNE CHUNG

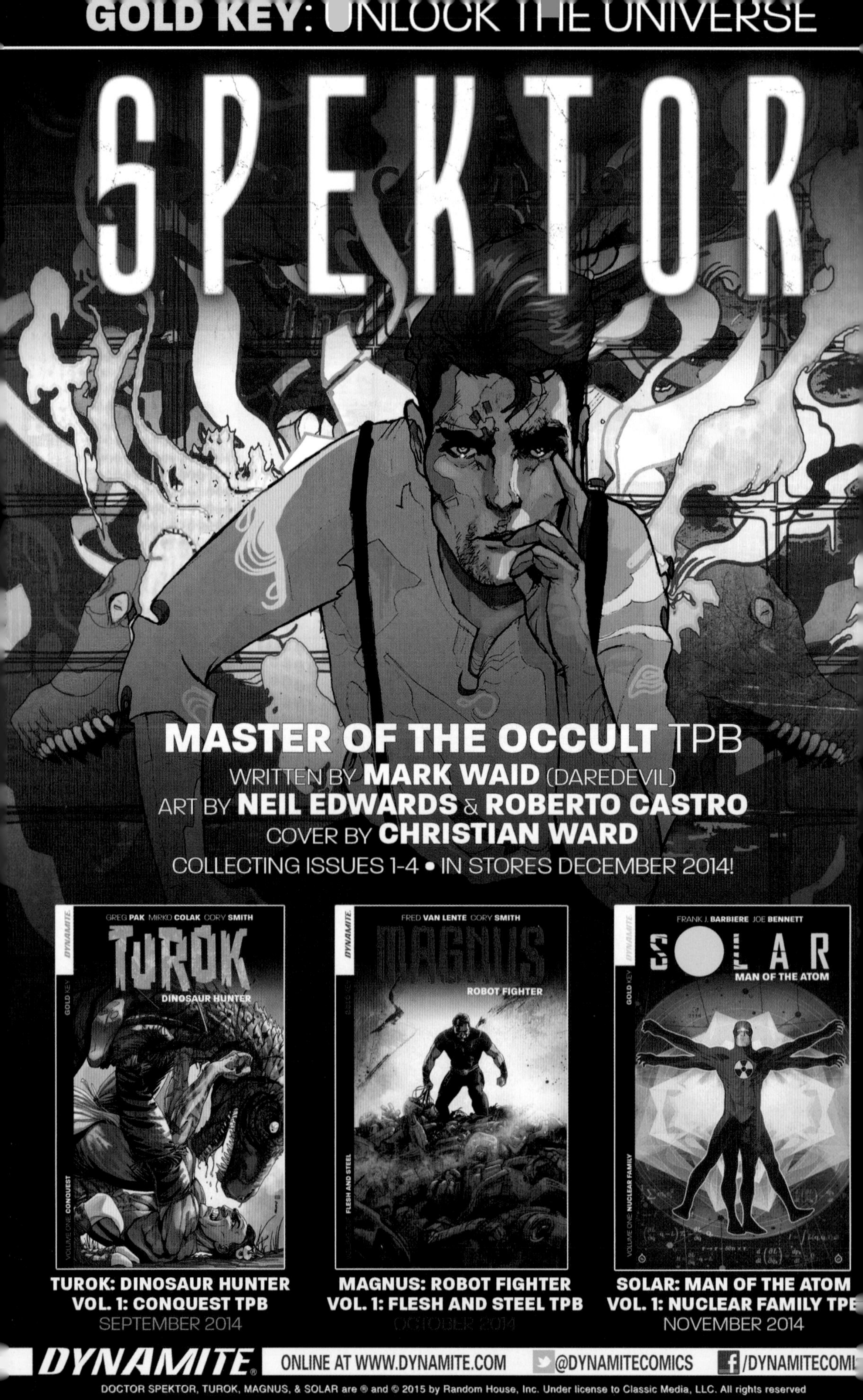

GOLD KEY: UNLOCK THE UNIVERSE
SPEKTOR
MASTER OF THE OCCULT TPB
WRITTEN BY MARK WAID (DAREDEVIL)
ART BY NEIL EDWARDS & ROBERTO CASTRO
COVER BY CHRISTIAN WARD
COLLECTING ISSUES 1-4 • IN STORES DECEMBER 2014!
GREG PAK MIRKO COLAK CORY SMITH
TUROK
DINOSAUR HUNTER
FRED VAN LENTE CORY SMITH
MAGNUS
ROBOT FIGHTER
FRANK J. BARBIERE JOE BENNETT
SOLAR
MAN OF THE ATOM
TUROK: DINOSAUR HUNTER
VOL. 1: CONQUEST TPB
SEPTEMBER 2014
MAGNUS: ROBOT FIGHTER
VOL. 1: FLESH AND STEEL TPB
OCTOBER 2014
SOLAR: MAN OF THE ATOM
VOL. 1: NUCLEAR FAMILY TPB
NOVEMBER 2014
DYNAMITE
ONLINE AT WWW.DYNAMITE.COM
@DYNAMITECOMICS
/DYNAMITECOMICS
DOCTOR SPEKTOR, TUROK, MAGNUS, & SOLAR are ® and © 2015 by Random House, Inc. Under license to Classic Media, LLC. All rights reserved

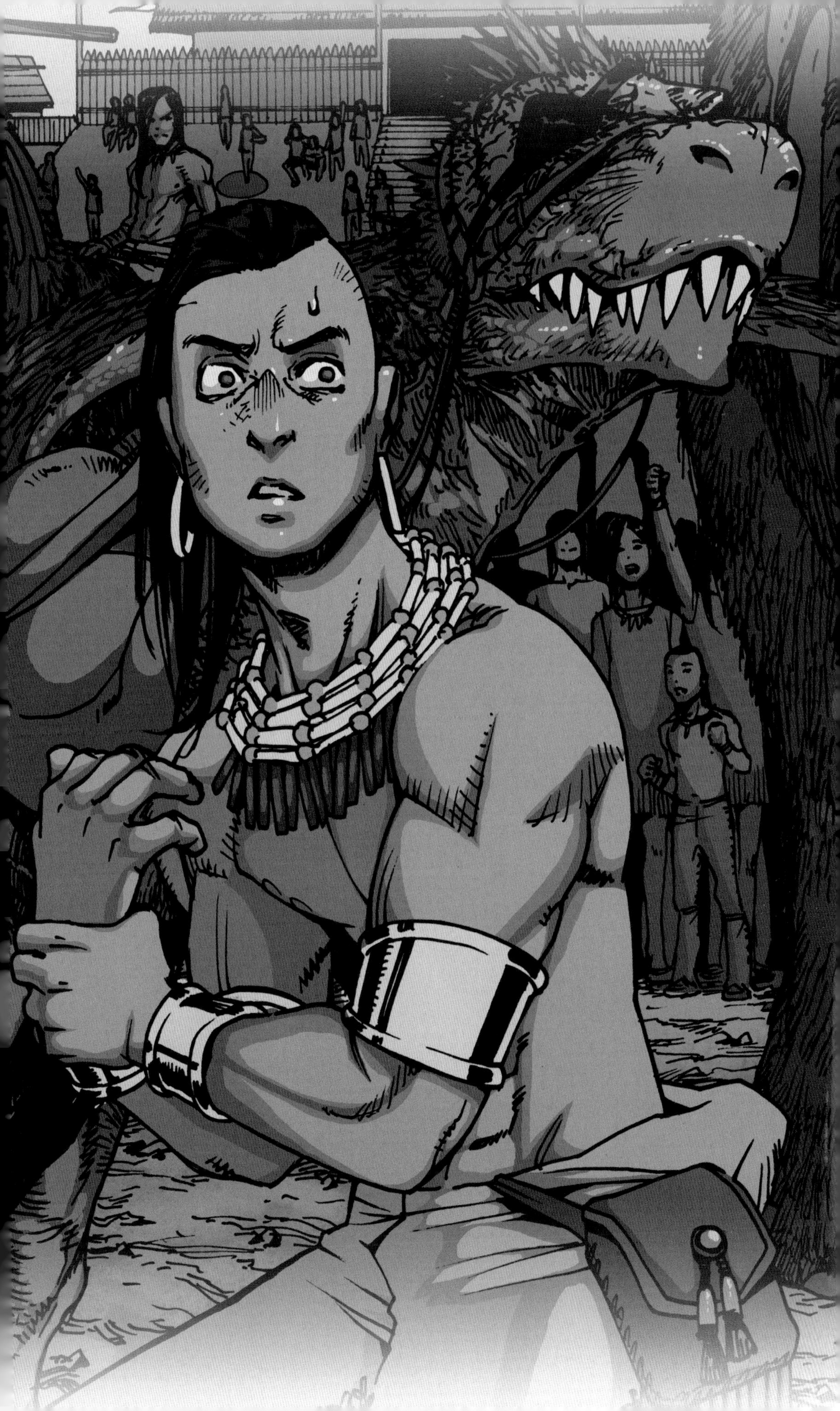

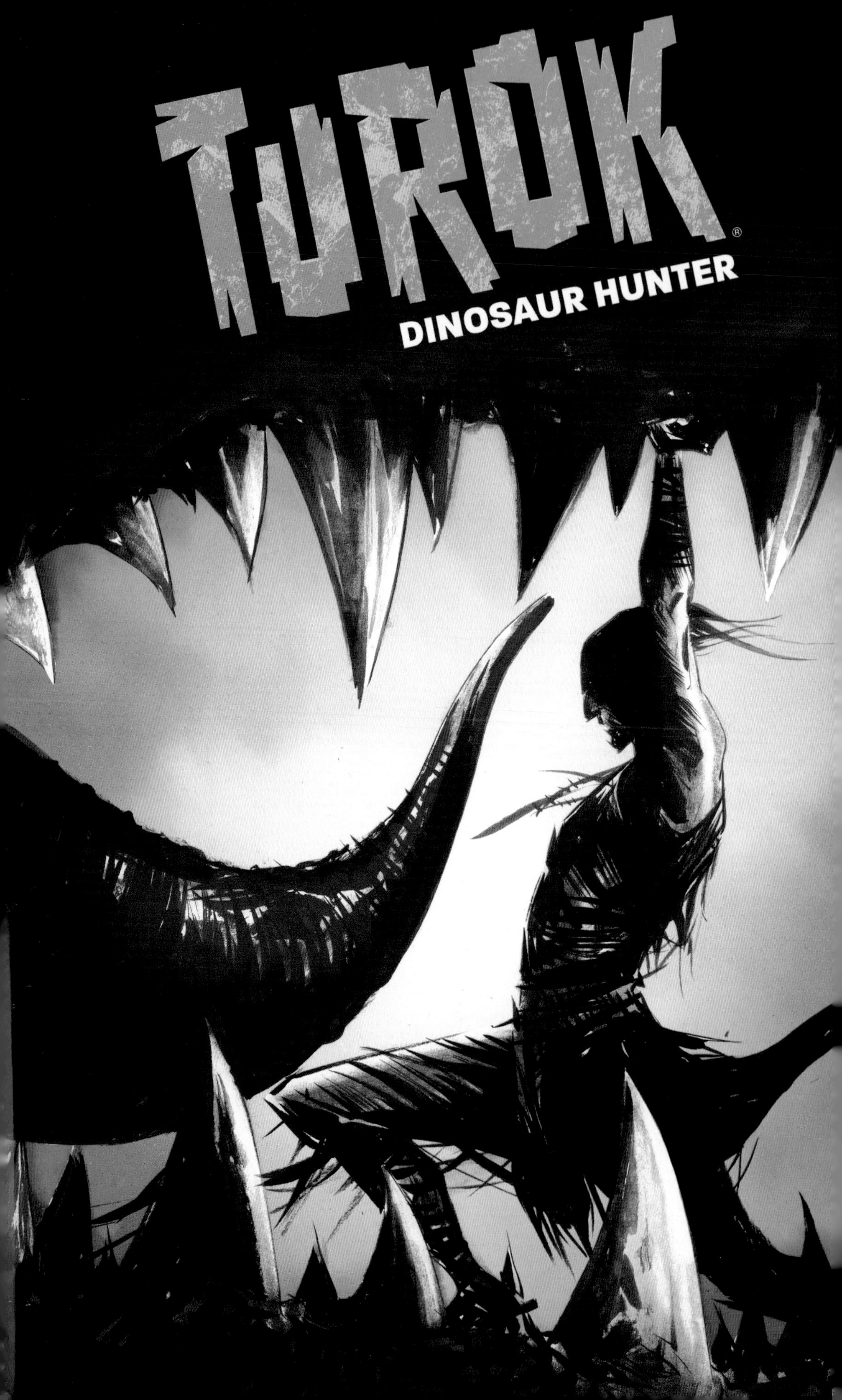
TUROK®
DINOSAUR HUNTER